TIMELESS PASSION

War Cry hesitated and then, as if he'd lost control of his emotions, he bent his head and kissed her, his big hands pulling her hard against him, his mouth claiming hers.

She struggled for a moment in his embrace, but she was no match for his strength . . . or his desires. Last night he had built a fire he hadn't extinguished and now it flared anew. Blossom clung to him, trembling at the heat of his sinewy body as he held her close. If he decided to throw her down on the prairie right here and now and take her, she wasn't sure she could stop him . . . or if she wanted to . . .

TIMELESS WARRIOR

GEORGINA GENTRY

ZEBRA BOOKS
KENSINGTON PUBLISHING CORP.

ZEBRA BOOKS are published by

Kensington Publishing Corp.
850 Third Avenue
New York, NY 10022

First Printing: April, 1996
10 9 8 7 6 5 4 3 2 1

Printed in the United States of America

This story is dedicated to our beloved daughter, Gina, for a most special reason, and of course, to her dear husband, Gene.

And also, for all those readers who have written to me, telling me how they'd love to journey back in time and share in the passion and adventure of the old West!

Every breath you draw, every action you make, affects someone or something, somewhere—for thousands of years and generations to come.

—Hantzis

What we call the beginning is often the end, and to make an end is to make a beginning. The end is where we start from.

—T.S. Eliot
(From "Litte Gidding," *Four Quartets*)

Prologue

There's a ghost in the painting.

Today, visitors come from far and near to see this ordinary painting that hangs above the stair landing in the old Pawnee Bill Ranch house. The ranch, managed by the Oklahoma State Historical Society, is west of the town of Pawnee, Oklahoma, on Blue Hawk Peak and is now a museum.

There are many tales about that painting and much speculation as to what created that shimmering specter in the background. Some docents whisper that eerie things have happened here that cannot be dismissed easily.

Now just suppose that late one night, a lady tourist got sucked into the painting and emerges more than a hundred and twenty-two years ago in the Old West . . . ?

One

Saturday afternoon, June, 1995

"I hear there's a ghost in the painting," Blossom said to the volunteer leading the way into the old Oklahoma ranch house.

The plump lady smiled and nodded. "Well, that's what some folks say. You'll have to make up your own mind. Where you from, anyway?"

"L.A." Blossom brushed her long brown hair back and followed the woman down the hall of the old Pawnee Bill home that was now a museum. "I'm a research librarian on assignment for a story."

"Oh really? Doing a book?"

"Not exactly." Blossom Murdock wasn't proud that she sometimes free-lanced for *Tattletale*, the sleaziest, most sensational of the supermarket tabloids, but jobs were still scarce on the West Coast, and she couldn't be choosey.

The older woman glanced over her shoulder at Blossom's costume. "Well, you're dressed for the part."

Blossom looked down at the long blue cotton dress and high-buttoned shoes she wore. "I feel a little foolish," she admitted, "but the airline lost my luggage and just before I got on the tour bus in Tulsa this morning, I saw this Western shop and thought, 'hey, why not?' "

"Matches your blue eyes," the lady said kindly. "In Oklahoma you can dress like a pioneer girl and no one will laugh.

Now, just take your time and look around downstairs while I take the next group through. Then I'll take you upstairs to see that painting."

"Thanks." Blossom took out a notebook and pen. The old West, and in particular Native Americans, had been an obsession with her as long as she could remember; even when she had been a very young child. She read everything she could get her hands on about those subjects. If the Old West hadn't been her particular passion, she might never have read about this ghost painting.

Maybe she could tie it in with UFOs, Elvis, or something. That would be the only way a slimy creep like Vic Lamarto, the *Tattletale* owner, would buy the story. This detour to a little obscure town in Oklahoma might catch up her bills and pay for Blossom's trip to Nebraska to try to trace her birth parents. She had taken a long time to get up the courage to delve into her own mysterious past.

Absently, Blossom doodled on her pad and looked around at the high ceilings and antique furnishings. A group of tourists brushed past her, laughing and talking.

The plump docent returned, glanced at her scribbling. "Oh, you drive one of those foreign cars?"

"What?" Blossom stared down at her pad. Oh, fudge! She had doodled B.M.W. B.M.W. B.M.W. "No, not hardly!" She laughed, feeling a little foolish because she'd written those same letters many times before. "I guess my subconscious must want one; but I surely can't afford it!"

Or anything else; but at least she had finally gotten the bill paid for her adopted mother's funeral. How would one of those feisty, headstrong beauties in the romance novels survive? Who was she kidding? She wasn't a feisty, headstrong beauty, or she would have created a bigger fuss with that snippy clerk at the airline over the lost luggage. When she got back to L.A., maybe she would enroll in one of those assertiveness classes.

She paused, absently fiddling with one of her silver hoop

earrings while she took inventory. At least the camera had been in her big purse as well as a few toilet articles, her ATM and credit cards. How long could this ghost thing take? By Monday, maybe she'd be on her way to begin her search into the mysteries of her birth . . .

She looked around the antique parlor again and scribbled some notes. The Pawnee Bill ranch had been everything Blossom had hoped it would be; buffalo grazing in the corral, crowds around the arena watching the trick riders and fancy marksmen. She had bought herself some Indian fry bread and paid to take the stagecoach ride. Now if she could just finish up in here and get some photos of that ghost painting.

A few feet away, an elderly volunteer took a camera away from an eager tourist. "I'm sorry, photographs are not to be taken in the house."

Uh oh. Blossom took a deep breath, glad her little camera was safely hidden in her big purse. If she didn't get the photos, Vic Lamarto wouldn't want the story.

"Excuse me," Blossom said politely to the matronly volunteer, "I don't really know who Pawnee Bill was."

The plump docent smiled. "Why, honey," her Oklahoma accent had a decided twang, "Old Bill was a contemporary of Buffalo Bill Cody. In fact, they once were partners in a Wild West Show they advertised as The Two Bills."

"Was Buffalo Bill ever in this house?"

"Oh, yes," the woman assured her. "So was Will Rogers and a lot of the famous people; they all came up here on Blue Hawk Peak to enjoy the scenery and Pawnee Bill's hospitality."

Blossom paused and stared at a large portrait in an ornate frame that hung in the parlor. The subject was a handsome, gray-haired man in a cavalry uniform. He looked pompous, happy, and prosperous. The brass plaque beneath him read: *Col. Lexington B. Radley, Friend of Pawnee Bill's and Patriarch of Prominent Pioneer family, 1848-1945.*

"I—I really came to see the ghost painting," Blossom said, wondering how she could get a photo of it.

"That's really not the most interesting thing about the ranch, you know, it has some tragedies in its past."

The temperature in the room seemed to have dropped and Blossom shivered. "Air-conditioning's awfully high."

"It's not even on, honey. Spooky, isn't it?"

Blossom didn't answer. Already, her mind was at work. Readers would like to hear about the cold, eerie feeling visitors got in this place. She scribbled a few more words in her notebook.

The plump lady smiled. "You said you were a writer?"

"Actually I'm a research librarian." Blossom reached to fiddle with her silver hoop earring; looked around the dining room with its massive oak suite. "What about the ghost?"

The docent leaned closer. "Some say it's a Pawnee brave's spirit who was trapped there long ago because of his love for a white girl."

Blossom smiled. "Really? Sounds like a romance novel."

"What?" the woman said.

A gray-haired docent was just passing and stopped. "Oh, you know, Bertha, those steamy paperback books with the half-naked people on the cover."

"Oh, those! Romances. Such trash!"

Blossom hesitated, feeling disloyal for not rushing to defend the stories she read. She wanted to say that if it weren't for the romance novels, she wouldn't have any love in her life at all, but decided it was not something to admit to. "May I see the painting?"

"Let's give you the whole tour, my dear," the volunteer said. "You know, Pawnee Bill died in this house and his young adopted son was killed in a tragic accident; hanged himself right out there off the windmill."

Adopted. Like herself. Maybe next week, she would solve the mystery that had opened up when she found the faded newspaper clipping.

The two ladies showed her through the house, which for its day must have been luxurious with a wonderful view from the front porch of rolling valleys. Blossom closed her eyes for a long moment and dreamed of running across the prairie in her long blue dress. A handsome warrior would gallop up out of nowhere and throw her across his horse. They would ride away together to live forever wild and free. He would be the epitome of every Indian hero she had ever imagined or fantasized about; a timeless warrior who belonged to her alone. She wouldn't have to worry about *Tattletale* or Vic Lamarto, or all the lonely nights reading romances in her cramped city apartment. "Could you show me the painting now?"

The pair led her up the stairs, talking about the secret door in the upstairs bathroom that led out onto the roof.

A secret door, Blossom thought as she scribbled in her notebook, this gets better and better.

"Here it is," the guide said.

Oh, fudge! Blossom stared with disappointment at the painting hanging on the stair landing. Even if she could get a photo of this Western scene, it wasn't lurid or sensational enough for *Tattletale,* although the confused scene of Indians and a galloping herd of buffalo seemed so real, she could almost hear their snorts and the sound of thousands of running hooves, smell the scent of their bodies, feel the dust wafting up on her own perspiring skin. "It almost looks like reality frozen in time," Blossom said, "but I don't see any ghost."

"You can only see that if you stand at a certain place at the top of the stairs." The volunteer gestured.

Her heart beating with anticipation, Blossom went up the stairs, turned to look. "I still don't see—oh, my God!" Her mouth dropped open as she looked down toward the painting. It was still a big Western action scene—except now in the background, she saw a shimmering blur that seemed almost alive.

A chill went up her back. "What—what is it?"

Her guide shrugged. "No one knows and everyone who looks at it sees something different. The legend is that it's a handsome Indian brave who is trapped there somehow because of a beautiful girl."

A beautiful girl. Well, that let Blossom out. Everyone said she had the most spectacular blue eyes, but no matter what lipstick she bought or what she did to try to improve her looks, she knew she looked like a million other women.

Blossom didn't say anything for a long moment, staring transfixed at the painting. The shimmering blur in the background seemed to breathe and move ever so slightly—or was that her vivid imagination? "A beautiful woman," she repeated, scribbling in her notebook, "that's good, sort of smacks of Snow White or something; does she have to kiss him to get him out of the painting; like a frog being kissed by a princess?"

The older lady laughed. "Nobody knows, although the local Indians say the secret is a circle; but even they can't explain that; it's hearsay handed down by their ancestors." She looked around at the growing crowds. "If you'll excuse us, my dear, we've got others to show through the house before it closes. You just take your time and browse."

"I'll do that," Blossom nodded, still transfixed by the eerie, shimmering presence in the painting. *A circle;* she thought, *can't do anything sensational with that.* She leaned on the banister, imagining that somehow she was here alone late at night. The moonlight would shine through a window, spotlighting the painting in the darkness. She would tell the handsome brave to step down from the painting and suddenly, he would be right here with her.

"You are the one I've been waiting to free me," he would whisper in a deep, sexy voice, "only you, darling Blossom."

He would sweep her into his arms and he would be so strong, she would be giddy as he held her close and kissed her. When Blossom closed her eyes, she could almost taste his warm lips.

Be sensible, Blossom, she scolded herself, what would you do with an Indian brave if he suddenly stepped out of that painting? He wouldn't even have a Social Security number, a job, or be able to drive a car.

So what? Anyway, he'd be riding a spirited paint stallion, not a car. Feeling a bit foolish, she glanced around to see if anyone was watching her, but all the volunteers were busy. She had everything she needed but photos. Blossom paused, trying to decide what to do next. It was against the rules to take photos, yet if she came back without them, that jerk Vic Lamarto would laugh and throw her out of his office. Deep in her heart, Blossom thought that she didn't deserve to be treated any better. If she had been worthy, would her real mother have abandoned her?

The late afternoon sun's rays slanted across the tree tops and valleys surrounding Blue Hawk Peak. Soon it would be closing time and her tour bus would be leaving for Tulsa.

She simply had to get those photos. Nervously, she pulled at her silver hoop earring. What should she do now? She couldn't take the forbidden picture with all these people watching; a guard would probably confiscate her camera and maybe even press charges.

A thought occurred to Blossom; a thought so daring, it almost scared her. Suppose she hid until they locked up the museum, took her photos, went out that secret door upstairs and down a tree or drainpipe? Of course, she would miss her crowded tour bus, but they might not notice she wasn't aboard. The town of Pawnee was only a mile or so down the road. Maybe she could rent a car there.

No, Blossom shook her head, it was just too daring and she winced at the image of being arrested if the caretaker caught her. She went down the stairs and into the parlor,

looking around and trying to make a decision. In her mind,
she saw Vic Lamarto's scowling fat face. The rent on her
tiny furnished apartment was almost due. She needed this
sale badly enough to chance what the caretaker and the local
sheriff would do to her.

Wandering through the ranch house, Blossom paused idly
in the parlor, thumbing through an old book on a sideboard.
Its yellowed pages were full of Western history trivia. Blossom got out her notebook, glanced at the clock on the mantel
as she thumbed through the old book, absently wasting time.
Did she dare try to get the photos? Did she dare not to?
She didn't have long to make up her mind.

Her thoughts were not on the pages before her as her eyes
skimmed a line of print.

. . . *during the Massacre Canyon battle with the Sioux
that August, a warrior named Ter-ra-re-cox was killed in a
vain attempt to rescue an enemy boy* . . .

Laughing tourists brushed past her as she struggled with
her decision. Blossom had never done anything daring in her
whole dull life. She flipped the pages of the book, glanced
at the dim picture of a granite memorial and the caption
under it: . . . *one of many unanswered questions. No one
knows how many pioneers are buried some place other than
their family plots* . . .

Yawning, Blossom started to flip the page, then took a
good look at the name on the stone in the photo. She could
barely make the inscription out: *Blossom May Westfield, born
1851, lost in a stagecoach massacre, body never found.*

So someone else had been stuck with the same old-fashioned
first name. It was weird, though, to see it on a tombstone. She
went back and read the text again, wondering about the pioneer
Blossom and what had happened to her.

Around her, people were moving toward the ranch house
door.

"We'll be closing in a few minutes," one of the guides
said, "everyone hurry and finish your tour."

Oh, fudge She didn't want to have to face this decision. She wanted to run out the door, get on the waiting bus to Tulsa. What would the museum do to her if they caught her? Yet bills would soon be coming due, and this was the only assignment she had right now.

Her heart beating hard with trepidation, Blossom went up the stairs, pausing at the top of the landing to stare at the painting in the pale last rays of sun. The longer she looked at the shimmering presence, the more she felt drawn to it. Even then, she wasn't certain a photo could do it justice.

Glancing around, Blossom noted the docents all seemed to be busy with tourists asking directions back to the freeway. Quickly, Blossom slipped into one of the upstairs bedrooms, the room the docent had said Will Rogers preferred. His picture hung over the bed. She might just hide here until the place closed. From the occasional noises from downstairs and the sound of cars starting their engines in the parking lot, people were leaving. She heard footsteps up the stairs.

"Last call! The museum is closing!" A woman's voice echoed through the upstairs, "We're about to lock up!"

Suppose that volunteer came in here?

"Don't give me away, Will." Quickly, Blossom crawled under the bed, lay there, gasping for air. She heard the docent come into the bedroom, still announcing that the ranch was closing. From here, she could see the woman's black shoes as she paused and looked around.

Blossom's heart pounded so loudly, she wondered if it could be heard. Was she out of her mind to be doing this? This was the sort of thing feisty heroines did in the romance novels she loved.

"Flo, is everyone out?" A man's voice downstairs.

The shoes creaked across the floor and out into the hall. "Yes, Mac," she called. "I checked all the rooms; you can lock up now. My! We are getting a lot of tourists these days, aren't we?"

The conversation faded to a blur as the footsteps clumped

down the stairs. After a few minutes, Blossom heard the outer door close. Her palms felt sweaty as she crawled out from under the bed and looked up at the painting. "Thanks, Will, for not giving me away."

From the windows of this room, she could see the curving highway out front at the bottom of the hill and the cars leaving. She heard the roar of the big tour bus starting its engine. If she ran, she could still catch it.

Blossom almost lost her nerve, knowing there was yet time to run downstairs, pound on the door, shout for help. She could make an excuse about accidentally becoming locked inside. Then she thought again about her rent that was due and facing Vic Lamarto. No, she would get that photo.

Blossom listened to the bus roar away, knowing that it was so crowded, no one might even realize she was missing. The thought occurred to her that if she dropped off the face of the earth tomorrow, no one would realize she was gone. Her adoptive parents were both dead; she had no siblings, no boyfriend. The shy farm girl had never fit in or made close friends in the bustling city of Los Angeles.

The sun was sinking as she went out into the hall and looked around. She must remember to stay away from the windows where someone might spot her. In the gloom of the coming night, the empty house seemed to echo with her footsteps. Being alone in the old ranch gave her an eerie feeling. She could almost believe those stories she'd overheard the docents telling.

Blossom went to a window, cautiously pulled back a lace curtain, and peered out into the twilight. The parking lot at the back of the house was empty now, the windmill where the boy had hanged himself stood starkly silhouetted in the waning light. A fat yellow cat crouched among the old-fashioned roses by the fish pond, staring at the water. Lights came on in the caretaker's house a few hundred yards away. An elderly beagle and an ugly, mixed-breed chow lay on that porch, evidently waiting to be fed. Uh oh. Would those dogs bark when she tried to cross the grounds? Just then, the caretaker opened the door and let the dogs in. Blossom breathed a sigh of relief.

To the west, the sky turned a brilliant scarlet and purple with the setting sun. Oklahoma must have the most beautiful sunsets in the world, Blossom thought with a sigh, although her home state of Nebraska was lovely, too. As she watched the lavender and blue shadows deepen across the valleys around Blue Hawk Peak, she could almost visualize a handsome Indian brave galloping across the rolling prairie to carry her off.

"Don't I wish!" Blossom sighed. Her one sexual experience had been quick and disappointing in the backseat of a high-school football player's car. If he hadn't gotten Blossom drunk, it never would have happened. When it was over, she had felt cheap and used and was only grateful she didn't get AIDS. AIDS had killed her adoptive mother, even as cancer had taken Dad years earlier.

The full moon rose and flooded through the windows, throwing distorted shadows across the worn floors. Outside, the wind picked up and tree branches brushed against the roof and walls of the house, sounding like ghostly whispers. The hair rose up on the back of Blossom's neck, as she heard a coyote wail somewhere off in the distance and the sound echoed and reechoed.

"Stop it, Blossom Ann Murdock!" she scolded herself, "you know there's no such thing as ghosts, even though at night, this place could do for a movie set."

What was it she'd overheard a docent telling a tourist? One time, the cleaning ladies had heard distinct footsteps coming down the stairs. Since there was not supposed to be anyone else in the house, they went to investigate. There was no one there.

Another time, the caretaker had seen smoke coming from the ranch chimney. Alarmed that some vagrant might have broken in and started a fire, he had rushed inside. There was no fire in the fireplace nor anyone in the house.

Locals said the place was haunted because of the freak accident here at the ranch. Long ago, Pawnee Bill's adopted son had been playing with a lasso atop the old windmill and had fallen, the rope around his neck. In her mind, she saw the small body swaying back and forth in the wind. She wondered suddenly which room Pawnee Bill had died in.

"What difference does it make?" she asked aloud, "all you've got to do is get the photo; you can add the eerie stuff later."

She heard a noise and peeked through the window to see the caretaker come out of his house, accompanied by the dogs. The trio strolled across the grass, making their rounds one last time while the beagle heisted his leg on a fence post and the chow chased the cat away from the little fish pond. The caretaker pushed back his cowboy hat and lit his pipe.

She must wait until she was certain they were going to be inside and asleep. If the dogs picked up her scent, they might bark and alert the man. Blossom sat down in a chair so she could watch the director's cottage, wondering if there was a burglar alarm. It seemed like a long time before the trio went in. Outside, a rocker on the porch moved back and forth in the wind. It would be easy to imagine a specter sitting in that chair. She shrugged off the thought. Even though the night was warm, the house was chilled. Blossom decided not to pursue that thought; she was already as scared as a child at a Halloween movie.

Finally, the lights went out at the director's small cottage. At last! Just how she would rent a car when she walked into town, she wasn't sure; especially as late as it was. Maybe she could get herself a motel room for the night and catch a bus out tomorrow. Many of these sleepy little towns still had bus service.

With her big purse hung over her arm, Blossom tiptoed up the stairs and stood looking at the shimmering image in the painting. Strange how it seemed to come alive in the darkness . . . or maybe it was only that the stories that went with it had her imagination running wild.

Her earring was bothering her again. Absently, Blossom took it off and rubbed her ear. They were a pair of antique silver hoops that she had owned so long, she didn't remember how she had come by them.

The moon outside was big and round, throwing a circular shadow across the furniture. Circles, Blossom thought, what was it the docent had said about circles and this painting? There weren't any circles in it that she could see. Abruptly, she remembered from her research that to the Native American the circle was sacred because it was eternal, with no beginning and no end. Blossom had researched the Hopi Indians once and remembered now that when one painted a circle on pottery, he always left a small break in the design to let the energy and the spirit escape.

This place was really beginning to make her uneasy, Blossom thought as she laid the earring on the edge of the wide picture frame. She would need both hands free to deal with the camera. Blossom stared at the image in the moonlight. The longer she looked at it, the more the specter seemed to take shape—come alive. When she had first seen it, the image had been only a shimmering blur. Now as she stared almost hypnotized, the blur in the painting became a man, a bare-chested, handsome Indian brave who looked deep into her eyes and reached out both his hands toward her; his dark, passionate eyes seemed to beg wordlessly.

"Oh, if only it could happen," she said to herself. What would she do if he suddenly came to life, stepped out on the stair landing and took her in his arms? Never mind that he wouldn't fit into modern-day society. Sometimes Blossom felt like she had been born into the wrong place and time. Sometimes she felt as out of place in this modern world as a Victorian lady.

"Mr. Lamarto would say I read too many historical romances," Blossom thought aloud. This ghostly old ranch and the fact that she was here alone were making her imagination run wild. In the distance, she heard the faint rumble of thunder.

Uneasily, Blossom looked toward the window and realized that storm clouds were building on the far horizon and might soon hide the moon, so that she would be in total darkness. Thunder. What was that old, old memory she always associated with the sound; that forgotten fragment from a long time ago?

Maybe she could remember if she would ever confront it, but she was afraid she couldn't deal with it or wouldn't want to know that reality. Anyway, what did it matter? She'd better get her photos and get out before she had to walk to town in the rain. She stared at the confused scene of Indians and running buffalo again. Even more now, the handsome Indian brave seemed to be reaching out to her, as if begging silently for her to take his hands and pull him out of that painting into the real world.

"This is so silly!" she said, and her voice seemed to echo through the deserted house. The thunder rumbled in answer. The specter's dark eyes implored her; it was almost as if she could feel his arms around her and hear him whispering the sweet, passionate things romance heroes said. Almost as if hypnotized, Blossom with her reticule still on her arm, moved closer to the painting. His hands seemed to be reaching out to her, begging her to take them . . .

Blossom reached up and put one hand against his. Strange, it felt almost warm, even though she knew it was only canvas. A wish, she thought, I should make a wish.

"I wish this handsome hunk would come alive," she murmured, without taking her hand from the canvas. In the distance, the thunder rumbled and she held her breath a long moment, then breathed again, feeling silly. Yet the man in the painting looked so very much alive. Strange, she almost felt his big hand clutching hers as the other one reached out to her. As if hypnotized, Blossom slowly reached to touch that hand with her free one, making a circle. Instantly, she felt a surge of power, as if she had closed an electrical circuit. Too late, she remembered the Indian belief. She had unleashed the magic. She had completed that circle.

The sheriff pulled up in the museum yard, slammed on his brakes, and jumped from his squad car, his hand on the pistol in his holster. "Mac?" he yelled. "Is that you?"

The museum director held onto his barking dog as he rounded the corner of the ranch house. "Yep, Buster. The alarm go off down at the station, too?"

"Lightning, I reckon." The sheriff nodded, visibly relaxed, and looked toward the distant flashes splitting the dark sky on the horizon, lighting up the scudding clouds drifting across the full moon. "Most likely a short in the wiring caused by that storm."

"Most likely." Mac let go of the chow that sniffed the sheriff and wagged its curled tail. "I've already checked the doors and windows, looking for any sign of forced entry; nothing."

"Wal, we'll take a look-see anyhow." The sheriff followed Mac to the door as he unlocked it, and they went in. Mac fumbled for the light switch. "Hmm, strange, lights are working."

The dog lay down in the hallway and yawned.

The lean sheriff nodded toward the dog. "Some watchdog! That the new one someone dumped on the highway?"

Mac nodded. "But if there was an intruder, Dog would be barking her head off."

"Helluva name for a pooch!"

"Well, that's the best I could do," Mac said. "You take a quick look around downstairs and I'll look through the upstairs."

"Damn!" Buster drawled, "why is this place always so cold, even in hot weather?"

"It just is," Mac shrugged and started up the stairs.

The distant thunder rolled and the lights flickered.

The officer looked around uneasily and Mac paused on the stairs. "Don't get jumpy. There isn't a living soul here besides us, Buster. Bad night, though; may get a tornado yet."

"Hope not; there's a good old John Wayne movie on the late, late show."

"That is, if the power stays on," the other volunteered. "Rain moving in faster than a New York minute. Let's look quick."

They both hurried from room to room with the lights flickering off and on, then met in the downstairs hall where the red dog now thumped its tail against the oak floor.

"Told you it was nothing," Mac yawned, "now you can return to your movie, and I can go back to bed."

"Just thought we ought to make sure. It ain't Halloween, but you never know what high-school kids is liable to do these days."

The three went outside into the warm night where an occasional raindrop splattered the dusty walk.

Mac paused to lock the door. "Like I told you, Sheriff, there isn't a living soul inside this house; no, not a living soul!"

Two

Was she falling or hurtling through space? Whatever was happening to her was so frightening, Blossom squeezed her eyes shut, willing it to pass. It was just another of her nightmares, she thought in sudden terror; she had had unexplained nightmares all her life, most connected with rumbling thunder.

Stairs. She had been standing on stairs, reaching out to touch a painting. Maybe she was falling down those stairs, or maybe with that storm building outside, she had been struck by lightning. Her hands; someone was holding her hands.

"Mama?" she whispered, then shook her head. Mother was dead; Dad was dead; she had no one—no one.

Timidly, Blossom opened her eyes. She screamed and stumbled backward, realizing the two hands holding hers were a man's, his shadow looming big in the moonlight.

He leaped to his feet, his expression as startled as hers. "Where the hell did you come from?"

She stared at him in bewilderment, jerked her hands away. "How—how did you get in this house?" She saw an Indian; broad-shouldered and bare-chested, a cavalry blue cap at a jaunty angle on his black hair. He wore blue cavalry pants with a yellow stripe down the side and soft, beaded moccasins.

"What house are you talking about?" He gaped at her as if he were seeing a witch or a ghost.

"Why, this ranch . . ." Blossom paused and took a good

look around. They were outdoors in a little clump of trees with a pinto stallion grazing on prairie grass in the background. "What—what happened to the buffalo? They're gone."

He nodded, evidently perplexed. "That's the white hunters' fault. Soon, they'll all be gone."

"The storm . . ." she began again, even more baffled now. The dark sky was calm, stars twinkling, a quarter moon hanging golden in the blackness. "Funny, I would have sworn the moon was full and a storm was coming."

A frown furrowed his handsome dark face. "Are you all right? Where'd you come from?"

"I—I'm not sure. I don't understand how I got outside." She reached up to touch her head. "Maybe I fell; I really don't remember."

He took her arm, led her toward the rock he'd been sitting on. "Take it easy. I must have been dead tired to let you sneak up on me. Last thing I remember, I was warming my hands in front of my fire; I guess I dozed off."

Blossom looked toward the fire. It was nothing but gray, cold ashes. "I haven't told you my name—"

"I know who you are," his brow furrowed, "I've been looking for you."

"For me?" Blossom touched her chest in surprise. Not in her wildest daydream had she ever imagined a warrior this handsome.

"We've all been looking," he breathed a sigh of relief. "It's good I found you; I feared the worst."

She started to point out that she had found him, conjured him up and pulled him out of that painting with all the deepest yearning of her lonely heart; decided that might not be polite. "I'm cold, maybe you could rebuild a big blaze and we'll try to figure this out; that is, if you don't mind. I may lose this job if I don't get my photos and arrive in Tulsa before I miss my morning flight."

He stared at her. "Flight? Flight of what?"

Blossom frowned. She was too weary to think about being shy and reserved. "Look, I'm tired," she begged, "let's not play head games. What about that big fire?"

He relaxed and shrugged. "With the whole country crawling with Lakota war parties? I was taking a chance with a small blaze. Your name fits you."

"You even know my name?" Blossom stared back at him, trying not to notice how darkly handsome he was, the way his white teeth gleamed in his dark face. How had she ended up outside the museum without even realizing it?

"Your disappearance is big news in this area." He stared at her. "You do have such large blue eyes, Miss Blossom."

The way he was looking into her eyes with his dark ones made her pulse quicken. "I was named for the prairie flower."

He nodded and smiled. "I know the flower; perfect name for you."

She felt herself blush. Men never flirted or complimented her, and she really didn't know how to deal with it. A thought crossed her mind. "Did I hear you say 'war party'?"

"Yes. We've been looking for you, Miss, ever since the stage didn't turn up on schedule."

"Why would you be looking for me?" Oh, no, she thought, they know I've been in the house, trying to get those forbidden photos. I wonder what the charge will be?

The warrior rubbed his chin. "Strange question; of course we were expecting you in town. You did ride the stage, didn't you?"

Blossom thought a minute, nodded slowly, remembering a sticky-fingered little boy with the cotton candy. "Yes, I rode the stage, but we never got to town, just around—"

"What happened to the others?"

"The others?" She stared at him. He was a handsome devil with a cocky, arrogant air about him.

"The others on the stage," he said slowly and patiently as

if talking to someone slow-witted. "We've got cavalry patrols and scouts out everywhere."

Blossom tried to remember, thinking it was a strange question. "I—I'm not sure what happened to the others. I didn't look back when I walked away."

"You don't have to talk about it, kid." He frowned and pushed his blue cap back. She noted for the first time that it had crossed brass arrows on the front. "I can only imagine what you've been through; you're probably lucky to be alive."

"The ride wasn't that bad," Blossom said.

"I meant . . . never mind," he made a dismissing gesture. "No farther than you could have walked, I imagine we'll find what's left of them tomorrow."

Blossom cocked her head. "Are you for real? I mean, you're not making very good sense."

He stared back at her. "*I'm* not making sense? You're the one who thinks she can fly." He paused and took another look. "Do you realize you're only wearing one earring?"

Blossom's hands flew to her ears. "Oh, my! I took it off, it's laying on the picture frame."

"A picture frame." It wasn't a question. He was looking at her as if she were insane.

"You should know," Blossom said, "it was your picture."

He sighed and his expression became sympathetic. "I'm sorry, kid, you've probably been through something too terrible to talk about. You're certainly a lot younger than we were expecting."

"I'm going to be twenty-two in August, I'm no kid."

"You are to me."

He was probably in his early or mid-thirties, Blossom decided, and a trifle too cocksure of himself. He's the typical Alpha Male so beloved in historical novels, she thought, this thing gets crazier by the minute.

"Anyway," the Indian said, "the town council will be relieved to find out you're safe."

She wondered why the Pawnee town council would care if she fell down the ranch house stairs? "Oh, I wasn't planning to sue, or anything like that."

He pursed his lips, looking at her. "You talk English, but you don't make much sense."

It was all too confusing. Blossom put her face in her hands. "If you're an Indian, how come you speak English?"

"Don't be afraid; I won't hurt you."

She had been too bewildered to be afraid. Now it occurred to her that she was out in the darkness alone with a stranger who might be a bit stressed out . . . or worse. "Are you a mugger?"

"A what?"

"It was a stupid question. If you were; of course you wouldn't tell me," Blossom sighed. "You're making my head hurt."

He reached out and put his hand on her arm. It felt big, comforting, and warm. "You've had a rough ordeal, Miss. Let's get a couple hours' rest. Before dawn, we'll head for the settlement."

"Can't I make you understand?" Blossom didn't know whether to laugh or cry, "I've got to find my luggage; my flight leaves Tulsa about dawn."

"Where?"

"Are we going to do this again?" Blossom made a helpless gesture. "I told you, I've got a flight."

"Sure you do," he said soothingly. "Now kid, you get some rest. I'll take you in to see Doc tomorrow."

She was weary of people running over her, bullying her. Her parents had been gregarious, out-going people who despaired about Blossom's inability to face up to difficult situations. "Look," she began again, her exasperation overcoming her shyness, "I'd be willing to pay you to drive me to Tulsa, or to some Rent-A-Car. At least get me to where I can make a call."

"Call what?" He was staring at her.

"I'm awfully tired and I don't want to be rude, but I've had a long day. Who are you, anyway?"

"War Cry. The soldiers can't pronounce my Pawnee name; they call me Terry."

Blossom threw back her head and laughed. "Now I understand; it all makes sense!"

"It does? Not to me."

"I wondered why you spoke such good English!" Blossom sighed with relief. "You must be a scout for the army."

He nodded. "Of course. The Pawnee are the best of the Indian scouts. I've ridden with the soldiers since I was a very young boy."

She was asleep; that's what had happened, Blossom relaxed and smiled. She had dropped off to sleep somehow on the stairs or one of the beds at the Pawnee Bill ranch, or maybe at the motel. She might even be in her bed back in her little L.A. apartment. Yes, it all made perfect sense to her now. This wasn't reality; she was asleep and dreaming she was the feisty heroine in an Indian romance novel.

Blossom smiled. "War Cry, of course! Perfect name for the hero of an Indian romance."

"Kid, I don't have any idea what you're talking about, but never mind. Maybe you'll be better if I can get a little food in you."

If this wasn't reality, she could be as spunky as any heroine her favorite authors ever created. "I could go for some pizza," she agreed. "Will they deliver out here in the boonies at this time of night?"

He looked as if he were about to ask a question, shook his head. "All I've got is part of a rabbit I roasted over my fire," he handed her some meat on a stick.

Blossom bit into it. It was crusty and good. "Hmm. You know, this is probably low cholesterol," she said, "did you ever think about opening up a franchise?"

War Cry didn't answer, he only watched her with furrowed brow as she ate. Blossom finished the crisp meat, looked around for a paper napkin, decided against wiping her fingers on the long blue dress, instead, wiped her hands on some dry grass.

If this is a really romantic dream, she thought, I'd like him to make love to me by the fire. Funny, she felt confident; relaxed. Being a romance heroine was fun. "What time period is this taking place in?"

"Time period? It's June."

"I know that; I mean, the year." If it was during the Civil War, she'd need a hoopskirt, if it were the turn of the century—

"You don't have any idea what the year is?" His dark eyes grew troubled.

Blossom shook her head and considered a moment. The dress she wore sported a bustle. It wouldn't do to wear the wrong costume in a historical romance fantasy.

"Don't worry about it." He made a soothing gesture.

"I'm not worried," Blossom said brightly. "If I'm guessing the time right, the dress I have on is about the right style."

He looked incredulous. "You're worried about being fashionable? You poor little thing," he said softly, "after what you've been through, it's no wonder—"

"It has been an ordeal," she admitted. "I'm tired and I'm cold."

The brawny warrior stood, picked up a blanket. When he leaned over to put it around her shoulders, his warm fingers brushed her neck and she felt his breath stir her hair. Now he would kiss the back of her neck and embrace her, she thought with a sigh. "War Cry, did you ever have a pleasant dream that seemed real, even though you were aware it really was a dream?"

"You mean like a medicine vision? Maybe." His big, hard hands were on her shoulders, and she was acutely aware of the warmth and power in them.

She didn't know how long this dream was going to last, but it was something she had always wanted to do; be a beautiful, feisty heroine of a historical romance; no; make that an *Indian* romance. "It's been terrible. I didn't want to come here, but I needed the money. Now I've lost my luggage and can't seem to finish my trip to find out who I really am." She choked back a sob.

He pulled her close and stroked her hair. "It's all right," he whispered, "you're safe now. Poor kid, there's no telling what those Lakota devils did to you, but everything's okay now."

Blossom laid her face against his broad chest and closed her eyes. It felt good to feel him stroking her hair. She wanted to tell him how frustrating and dull her life was and how she dreaded facing Vic Lamarto without the photos for *Tattletale*. His arms were strong around her and she felt safe and secure in his embrace. "I hope this dream just goes on and on; it's even better than the last romance story. But if they catch me before I wake up—"

"Don't worry, little loco girl, they won't catch you." He took her small face between his two big hands and looked down into her eyes. "Trust me, Blossom."

For the moment, she didn't have to face reality. Blossom smiled up at him, thinking he had such strong, chiseled features. How she loved Western romance novels! As a heroine in one, she didn't have to be a shy, awkward librarian for a while. Now was the part of the story where the handsome savage always kissed the girl. She closed her eyes expectantly.

"Go to sleep," he said, "you must be exhausted; I know I am. It's been a long day."

"Go to sleep?" Her eyes flew open even as he moved to his side of the fire. "Is that all? Usually there's a romantic midnight ride at a gallop across the prairie, and then—"

"And then what?" He paused in building a fire, looked over his shoulder at her.

"Oh, fudge! I have to draw you a picture?"

He shrugged and returned to building his tiny fire. She

watched his broad, muscular back as he worked. Maybe this was going to be one of those romantic scenes where they made love by the fire. That would certainly please her. Any minute now, he would turn to her and say something passionate, something sensual, something—

"Want some coffee?"

"Coffee?" She blinked in disbelief as he craned his head to look at her. "No, I don't think so."

"You'll feel better after some rest," he reassured her, then stretched his lean length out by the fire. The blue cavalry pants were tight on his hard, muscular frame, and the tight fabric left no doubt that he was as well-built as any hero she'd ever read about.

Well, of course they were supposed to have some conflict, Blossom thought; there always was in historical romances, along with hot passion and kisses. How could she have verbal conflict with a man who appeared to be dropping off to sleep? Yet it was satisfying just to lay here by the fire and look at his virile, half-naked form. Come to think of it, this was one of the few pleasant dreams she had had. All her life, she had been plagued by strange nightmares of impending tragedy, waking her up breathless and shaking. Neither a doctor nor a therapist had been able to help her. She couldn't really describe the dreams; they centered around thunder and loss; a loss so terrible, she couldn't face it; she refused to endure that reality; she fled from it, running wildly, running . . .

Blossom shook her head to rid herself of the thought. She had developed a habit of fleeing or avoiding things she couldn't deal with. No, this was so much nicer. She watched him lying there. In a romance novel, the heroine would do something quite bold and feisty, maybe go crawl into his blankets. Or he might come over, sweep her up in his arms, take her back to his bed. Blossom envisioned both with a shiver of anticipation. Either way, he would take her dress off and make uninhibited love to her while the coals glowed as fiery as their passion.

"Are you cold, kid? I can see you're shivering."

Here was where the love scene would begin, Blossom thought with a delicious sigh. "Why, yes, now that I think of it, I am a bit chilly."

She waited for him to say something about warming her with his love, come over, sweep her up in his arms. Instead, he raised himself up on one elbow and tossed her an extra blanket.

"Well?" she said, "I'm still cold."

"If I build that fire any bigger, we'll have Sioux swarming all over us," he muttered. "Besides, it's a warm night and you've got both blankets." He closed his eyes.

There had to be more than this. She watched his eyes. Such dark, expressive eyes. She waited. Surely he wasn't going to sleep? If not, he certainly was breathing rhythmically. Blossom lay there, feeling more annoyed and frustrated. Even in her dreams, she couldn't find romance. She was weary, but she was more than a little cross. She might as well have left him in that damned painting.

Wait a minute! Maybe War Cry wasn't supposed to be the hero in this fantasy, although he was certainly the one Blossom would have chosen. Maybe the love interest was going to be a handsome rancher or a dashing cavalry officer back at the town, wherever that was.

Now he was actually snoring. That settled it, romance heroes never snored or passed up a chance to make passionate love to the heroine. War Cry was definitely not scheduled to be the hero. Any moment now, she might wake up and have to deal with the museum guard. At least, if this was her dream, she ought to be able to take charge, be kissed by some handsome man before it ended.

Very slowly, Blossom stood up and grabbed her big purse. War Cry continued to snore. She was more than a little peeved. A sassy heroine would steal his horse and go find the real hero. Quietly, she tiptoed over to the horse. The big paint stallion snorted at her and stamped its hooves.

Blossom glanced over at War Cry. She dare not risk waking him; besides, this horse looked pretty spirited. Blossom hadn't been on a horse since she was a very small girl on the farm, before Daddy lost it to the big conglomerate. Maybe it wasn't far to town and she'd just walk. I'm outta here, she thought.

With that, she crept out of the camp and strode across the prairie. War Cry had gestured vaguely toward the south when he'd spoken of the settlement, so that was the direction she took.

What kind of a fantasy was this anyway? The handsome Indian snored and her feet ached. These little lace-up shoes frontier women wore might be cute, but they hurt almost as much as spike heels. She wished she had her jogging shoes and some sweats.

Abruptly, she stepped in a prairie dog hole and fell. Damn it all anyhow! Blossom lay there a long moment, stretched out in the dirt, shocked at her own profanity. She never swore; she was old-fashioned that way. Maybe a handsome brave or soldier was supposed to happen along and swing her up on his horse.

Nothing happened. By now, if this was an Indian romance novel, the hero would be all over her, kissing her until she was breathless. Puzzled, Blossom stumbled to her feet, brushed herself off.

Somewhere in the darkness, a coyote howled and the sound echoed and reechoed. Undecided, Blossom half turned back toward camp. Suddenly she felt very alone and vulnerable. "Don't be silly, Blossom," she said aloud and started walking again, "if you've lived in L.A., Godzilla shouldn't scare you, you gutless wimp. This is a dream; remember?"

She felt suddenly spunky, independent, and really liberated. It felt good. This experience certainly seemed real; almost like those new virtual reality games. She was puffing a little now from the tight corset, but she'd almost have to undress to get the thing off. Just how far was it to this settlement anyway?

"Dashing romance hero," Blossom muttered, and shifted her purse to her other arm, "if you're out there, I wish you'd come riding up and rescue me. This walking is nowhere."

The quarter moon gave off faint light across the flat prairie as she walked. Now why had War Cry acted as if he recognized her name? *They had been expecting her,* he'd said. Well, most dreams never made very much sense, and they seemed to last a long time when it was only an instant in your brain. "Stop fighting it and enjoy it," Blossom ordered herself.

A thought crossed her mind and she paused. "Oh, dear god, suppose this isn't a dream; suppose I'm dead? Suppose I actually fell down those stairs to my death? Am I having one of those out-of-body experiences?"

She considered a moment. In that case, wasn't she supposed to float above herself and view her own body lying on the stairs, or at least go down a tunnel, see a bright light, and meet an angel or something?

"I don't even care anymore," she wheezed, "if I could just take off my shoes and this corset!"

The coyote howled again. There wasn't anything to do but keep walking and hope she'd see the lights of that town or maybe cross the path of some dashing cavalry officer leading a rescue patrol. Brad Pitt or Kevin Costner would be nice. "Don't you wish!" Blossom grumbled, "On the other hand, this Terry guy was every bit as handsome and sexy. This certainly is the strangest dream I can remember."

She kept walking. Hours seemed to pass, but of course, there was no way to gauge time in a dream. Finally, up ahead, she saw scattered places on the prairie that looked like collapsed mushrooms or big boils. At least, maybe that ground would be softer. "It doesn't seem very romantic to have my feet hurt."

Blossom was walking fast when she started across one of the dark, spongy-looking circles. Funny, it wasn't soft, but sort of crusty. Her momentum had carried her half a dozen yards across the crust when it began to break under her weight. "What the—?"

She was up to her ankles in some sort of gooey muck, almost like sticky gumbo or quicksand, and sinking fast. For a split second, Blossom hesitated, uncertain whether safety lay in running ahead or fleeing backward. Then it was too late. Even as she struggled, she sank up to her knees in the muck, her blue cotton skirt wet and heavy. In her struggles, she dropped her big purse, which promptly broke through the crust of this goo and disappeared. "Oh, fudge! Oh, damn it! The camera! My plane ticket! My ATM card!"

"Think, Blossom; get real!" She tried to calm her own panic. "This is just another of your nightmares, only this time without the thunder. You don't have to deal with this; you'll wake up about the time you start to scream. Yes, that's right! It's just a nightmare like all those others."

Only this time, neither Mama or Dad would be there to comfort her. "Stay calm," she reminded herself as she struggled and slowly sank to her knees in the muck, "you'll wake up just like you always do!"

Yet this seemed so real and it was *different*. The old nightmare that haunted her, the one about the thunder, was always the same.

What was that gleaming in the moonlight on the far edge of this crusty pit? Bones. A cow's skull grinned at her, white against the mire. Some poor cow that had stumbled into this ooze and couldn't get out.

Blossom forgot all her cautions and started fighting to stay above the oozing mud, even as she slowly sank. "Stop it, Blossom!" She reminded herself, "Try to stay calm! You can't die! This is a romance novel you're dreaming, remember? Heroines aren't allowed to die!"

Then why was she slowly sinking as she struggled and fought? "Trouble is," she gasped, "I don't know who's writing this story! Wake me up now, please! Oh, wake me up!"

Three

War Cry awakened gradually next to the cold ashes of his fire. The sliver of moon had disappeared and the night looked dark as the inside of a buffalo. He sat up with a sigh, wondering how many hours until dawn? Yesterday's search had been long and exhausting and he'd slept heavily; unusual for him. He had survived a dangerous life by staying as alert and quick as a bobcat. "You're lucky some Lakota war party didn't find you," he scolded himself.

The girl. He came to his feet, looking around. She was gone, all right . . . or had he only dreamed the missing girl had walked out of the darkness and sat down by his campfire? No, he shook his head, remembering. He recalled only too well the soft warmth of her body as he put a blanket around her delicate shoulders.

No sign of her now. Poor little thing was so addled, she had wandered back into the night. No wonder, with what she had probably witnessed. He should have kept a better watch on her.

Quickly, he saddled up. It would soon be dawn and in that blue dress, she could be seen a long way on the brown prairie. Maybe she'd try to find her way back to the stage. War Cry only hoped he found her before the Lakota war party did; she'd be quite a prize for them. Chewing a strip of dried jerky, he swung up on the big red and white paint. The girl had had such big blue eyes.

"You've been without a woman too long," he scolded himself, "you need to get yourself over to Rusty's Place."

There wasn't any girl at that bordello who was even remotely a prim, respectable lady, so why had he dreamed of one? Because of the missing schoolteacher, Miss Westfield. He was on a patrol, searching for any sign of an ambushed stage; the new teacher from back East was supposed to be aboard. War Cry knew only too well what he could expect to find sometime today along the stage route. With a major Indian war setting the frontier ablaze, no doubt a Sioux or Cheyenne war party had crossed its trail. How many passengers? Poor devils.

He shook his head and after scouting for nonexistent tracks, rode north. He was only too aware that when daylight finally came on this vast prairie, he'd be easy to spot if any hostiles were still around. War Cry pushed his soldier cap at a jaunty angle and shrugged. It was part of his job as an army scout, and he had lived every day of his life with danger.

Just at dawn, he spotted an expanse of blue in the blowing sea of prairie grass in the distance. She'd been wearing a blue dress. He didn't know whether to feel dread or relief as he galloped his horse toward that spot.

With a sigh, he realized as he reined in that it was only a patch of little prairie flowers, blue as a summer sky. Funny, he had always taken them for granted before. War Cry stared down, took a deep breath, enjoying the sweet, faint scent. Blossom. Where could that delicate creature have gone? War Cry urged his paint horse into an easy lope.

He took another breath and his keen nose picked up a different smell; just the faintest scent. It was so slight, no white man could have detected it, but Pawnee warriors' lives depended on their sharp senses. Smoke. It was the barest hint of smoke.

The distant dawn silhouetted the black buzzards taking to the air and circling. War Cry nudged his spirited pinto stallion into a gallop. He topped a hill just as the sun rose fully over the distant horizon, bathing the vast scene in a pink-tinged new day.

"Oh god." He had found the stage—or what was left of it. He reined in again, cautiously searching the prairie for movement before he whipped his horse into a gallop toward the wreckage. The scarlet daybreak was just the color of the blood spilled across the prairie grass. One of the team of horses lay stiff in death, arrows sticking at odd angles from its bay hide. No sign of the other horses; the hostiles had probably stolen them yesterday when they finished.

His horse snorted and stamped uneasily at the stench hanging over the scene like a shroud. "Easy, boy, it's all right."

War Cry dismounted, pulled an arrow from the door of the overturned stage, and inspected it critically. Lakota, all right. The scene reeked of death and violence. He took a deep breath and swallowed hard before he jerked open the door, dreading what he knew he would find there.

Two male passengers lay tumbled inside, eyes frozen wide in death and disbelief. The plump one had a bullet hole in his forehead; the gambler wore a crimson cravat. No, it wasn't red silk; it was blood. The white bones of their skulls gleamed obscenely without their hair. It was something warriors did. War Cry had taken many enemy scalps himself. He scouted for the army, not for the gold it paid, but for revenge. The larger Sioux nation had slaughtered many of his Pawnee people.

War Cry searched the area around the coach. Where was that faint scent of smoke coming from? He investigated and found it. The pair inside the stage had been the lucky ones. A few hundred feet away, he found the driver, spread-eagled and staked down. Old Hank had been a long time dying. War Cry kicked the cold ashes of the small fires away from his friend's hands and feet, and cursed softly. "Sorry I didn't get here in time," he muttered. Hank had been one of the few whites who treated the Indian scouts as equals.

What had happened to the girl? He didn't even want to think about what the Lakota braves would do if they captured her. War Cry did a quick survey of the area, expecting to find her staked out on the prairie, too. The whole war party probably would rape her repeatedly before scalping and torturing her to death.

All he found a few hundred yards away was the small print of a woman's shoe. Poor little thing; she had survived the wreck of the stage and had fled; stumbling into his camp last night. No telling where she was right now. His keen eyes spotted a small object and he leaned over to pick it up. A book. It must have meant a lot to her for the girl to hang onto it when she ran. Idly, War Cry flipped through the pages; romantic poetry, *Sonnets from the Portuguese* by Elizabeth Barrett Browning.

The inside cover was dirty and smudged now, but he could still make out part of the name written in a woman's dainty, flowing hand. Pretty name. His mind went to the blue wildflower again. He wondered if the little teacher had ever gotten to see that flower blanketing the prairie as the coach rolled along?

War Cry winced and closed the book, tucked it in his belt. He had to find her before the Lakota did or thirst and hunger killed her. He pictured her collapsed on the hostile prairie somewhere with vultures feeding off her pale skin, or in some Sioux's lodge being brutally raped or tortured.

He didn't want to think about it. He was abruptly weary of death and violence; it was all he'd ever known. His mother had died in the cholera epidemic of 1849 and his warrior sire had been killed by an enemy Cheyenne dog soldier. War Cry hadn't missed his father; Bear's Eyes had been cruel and brutal to his sons.

He sighed and his own voice sounded loud in the stillness that was broken only by the early morning breeze rustling the dry grass and the cries of the circling vultures. "I've got to find her first, then report back to the fort."

He mounted up and turned south at a gallop. Finding the girl was the most important task at the moment. The army would send a patrol out later to bury the dead and bring in the stage and the passengers' trunks.

He touched the book in his belt as he rode, trying not to picture the ill-fated teacher. She must have been desperate to accept a job out on the frontier with an Indian war going on. She might have been an orphan or a widow, desperate and all alone in the world. The Civil War had left a lot of both. Mostly, he remembered those enormous blue eyes. As he remembered, she hadn't been a great beauty—except when she smiled and her small face lit up.

"Hell, what difference does it make whether she's pretty or not, especially to a Lakota war party?" he chided himself. "If she's lucky, she'll die before they capture her. If she's not lucky . . ."

He broke off and urged his stallion into a lope toward the south, not even wanting to picture her in his mind. War Cry took scalps himself; but rape was something beyond his understanding. Women were eager for his caresses, but so far, he'd never found one he cared enough for to make her his woman.

A man needed sons. Someday soon, he must choose a woman, but he had waited a long time to choose; maybe he would never find one who could satisfy his heart as well as his body. The book pressed into his flesh and he glanced down at it and wondered again about the ill-fated white girl. Captain Radley was in charge at the fort now while Major DuBois was away from the post. The handsome young cavalry officer would have to be the one to write that letter to the girl's family, if she had one, send the book and her trunk back east when the stage was brought in.

Of course, there was always the small possibility that the lady teacher had now been captured and was being held captive. In some cases, the army managed to rescue or ransom a hostage. Too often, the woman had been so brutalized that her mind retreated from the horror she had witnessed or experienced. Sometimes they never recovered from the trauma and spent the remainder of their lives in asylums or in some relative's house staring blankly at the wall. If she were married, often the husband didn't love her enough to want her back after the savages had smeared their seed in her.

The book in his belt lay warm against his flesh, as warm as a woman's skin. The kind of sensitive, innocent girl who read poetry might be better off dead after what she might be enduring at this moment. Gritting his teeth in anger, War Cry kept riding, thinking of the revenge he would extract from the Lakota when the next army expedition caught up with them. He gave no quarter and expected none. The Sioux and Cheyenne were old enemies, and he'd lost many a friend and relative to their warriors.

War Cry rode south toward the fort across the vast, desolate prairie. He knew the old buffalo plains as intimately as he knew the animals who roamed here; every year, there were fewer and fewer buffalo. The giant herds were being systematically wiped out by white hunters, greedy for the gold the meat and hides would bring. He could almost sympathize with his enemies. No wonder the plains tribes had taken the warpath; they depended almost solely on the buffalo for food. The Pawnee hunted the great beasts, too, but they also grew corn and squash.

Up ahead and to the west near the Nebraska-Wyoming border lay that expanse of prairie known by whites as the devil's cattle traps or witches' bogs. Anyone familiar with the terrain avoided those strange, slimy pits. No one knew what caused them, but they were sticky and alkaline and sometimes seemed almost bottomless after a hard rain. Like quicksand, many an unlucky animal had stumbled into one, mistaking the crusty surface of a bog for solid ground. War Cry would veer a little and avoid them. The sight of buffalo or horse bones trapped in the morass bothered him.

A faint sound drifted as the breeze ruffled the prairie grass under his pony's drumming hooves. War Cry tensed and reined in. Had it been only the wind, or was it the triumphant shriek of distant warriors riding hard toward him? He stood up in his stirrups and looked around, every nerve in his hard, bronzed body alert should he have to ride for his life. That sound again. It was almost like a cry; another calf or deer caught in a devil's cattle trap, sinking and dying.

The Pawnee scout rode on. He had to report to the fort and get search parties out for the girl. What was one more small animal slowly smothering in the deadly mud? The cry drifted on the breeze.

"Oh, hell," he muttered, "the least I can do is put it out of its misery." At that, he wheeled his horse and loped toward the strange pools.

A slight movement from the nearest bog. From here, all he could see was mud as the creature struggled. The small animal was so muck-covered from its thrashing that at this distance, War Cry couldn't even decide what it was. He couldn't save it. War Cry realized it was so far from the edge, he'd be risking his own life and that of his horse to ride out onto that crust. He could do it one favor. He reached for his rifle, brought it to his shoulder, and sighted down the barrel. He was a crack shot; his life often depended on his marksmanship.

Even as he made ready to pull the trigger, the mud-covered, shapeless little creature moved again and the morning light reflected off something shiny. What the hell?

"Help!" came the faint plea. "Help me!"

War Cry gave a startled noise of surprise and lowered his weapon. "Hey, out there! Hang on! I'll try to get you out!"

Only as he uncoiled his lasso did it occur to him that the faint voice had been a woman's and she spoke English.

"Oh, please hurry . . ."

Gingerly, War Cry urged his stallion forward. The big paint snorted and hesitated, uncertain of the crusty ooze under its hooves.

"I know, boy," he whispered, "it's dangerous, but we've got to do it."

He urged the stallion forward again and the crust broke under its weight. It sank up to its fetlocks. War Cry dare not go out any farther. To do so would doom both him and his horse and worse yet, end this woman's last chance to live. "Hold on, I'm coming!" he yelled and threw his loop.

It landed near the woman, but not near enough. He saw one muddy arm reaching desperately, but vainly.

"I—I'm sinking," she gasped, "oh, please . . ."

Whoever this fool female was, he couldn't let her die. War Cry urged his stallion in a little deeper, knowing he and his horse could hit a spot at any moment that would suck them both in too deep to escape. Some said the deadly alkaline ooze was bottomless. The gleam of white bones here and there gave mute evidence of the witches' bog's past.

"Hang on!" War Cry urged as he retrieved his muddy rope and made another loop. It was all too evident that this might be the last chance he would have to lasso this victim before she sank out of sight forever. That thought made sweat break out across his powerful shoulders as he concentrated on his throw. For a split second, the rope hung in midair, although it seemed as if time stood still. Then its circle dropped around her. "Hey, I've got you! Just hang on."

She made some slight whimper and nodded. Blue eyes, he thought, she has such large blue eyes. That was all he could see of her; that and the gleam of one silver earring in the morning sun. He began backing his stallion out of this muddy trap, hoping the horse would sink no deeper through the sticky crust.

"Come on, boy, back up," he urged, yanking at the bit. The big paint struggled. War Cry could feel the great horse fighting the pull of the bog. "Come on, boy, do it for me." He patted the stallion's neck and urged it to greater effort. His own hard muscles tensed with the fight, knowing that if the pinto's efforts failed, all three of them could be lost in this bottomless ooze forever.

A mighty lunge and the horse backed toward the safety of the solid ground behind them. "Good boy, keep it up." War Cry's heart hammered now, knowing that they still might not make it. "Hang on!" He commanded the woman as he tightened the rope, "we'll get you out!" The bottomless pit might still make a liar of him, but she needed to be encouraged and maybe he was encouraging himself. There couldn't be a worse way to die than slowly being suffocated and sinking beneath the slimy surface; it was as bad as quicksand.

The stallion's beautiful red and white body was lathered with its efforts as it fought its way backward toward the safety of solid ground under its beloved master's urging. One step, then two. The greedy mud pulled at the stallion's hooves, not willing to give up its victim.

"Come on, boy, come on!" Time seemed to stand still for a long moment, but finally, they were on solid ground. War Cry breathed a deep sigh of relief as he felt it under them. Now he could concentrate on saving the woman. Very slowly, he backed the horse as the lariat tightened around the muddy form. "Hang on! It'll only take a little time!"

The lasso tightened like a bowstring as they pulled. Suppose it broke? He wouldn't get another chance. War Cry didn't want to think about that. If it did break, he'd shoot the poor creature rather than let her suffocate slowly in the muck. "Keep it up, boy, come on," he urged.

For a long moment, the mud refused to give up its victim and War Cry held his breath, certain the rope would snap. He reached for his rifle. At that instant, there was a great sucking sound and the poor bedraggled creature pulled free of the mud. The horse continued to back up and dragged her across the crust and onto solid ground.

War Cry hung his rifle on the saddle ring and grabbed his canteen as he swung from the saddle. He ran to the motionless form, knelt to loosen the rope. Gently, he took her in his arms, put the canteen to her lips.

The woman gulped the water.

"Easy," War Cry cautioned, "just a little at first."

"Thanks," she whispered, "I—I've been there for hours; thought I was a goner."

He poured a little water in his hand and splashed the mud from her face. "You're safe now." Gently, he wiped her cheek. "You're lucky I saw the sun glinting off your earring."

"I lost my purse and my shoes," she wailed, "now what am I supposed to do? Wake up before this nightmare gets any worse?"

"Hey," he grinned down at her. "You're lucky to be alive, lady."

"Oh, fudge! Look at my outfit! My luggage was lost, so I bought this at that Tulsa Western store."

She was hysterical and in shock, War Cry thought. "You'll look fine when you get the mud off. Why, I think you're pretty."

Blossom looked up into his handsome face and blinked. "You really think I'm pretty? Every man I ever met thought I was a plain little mouse."

"They must have been loco. Are you all right, aside from your lost shoes and stuff?"

She nodded. "I don't suppose there's a creek nearby?"

He pushed his blue cavalry cap back and his dark face furrowed. "Are you sure you're all right?"

"I'm alive, if that's what you mean. Just look at this dress!"

"Forget about the dress; you're lucky to be alive."

"Forget about it?" she wailed. "It's ruined! This isn't the way I dreamed this scenario; or maybe I only wished you into existence."

He wiped more mud from her face. "Poor kid, you had walked a long way from that stage, hadn't you?"

"If you say so." It hadn't been but a few hundred yards

from the stagecoach to the Pawnee Bill museum, she thought, but he was right about one thing; she might have suffered a concussion from those stairs. "This mud is beginning to dry and I'm itchy. Is there a stream where I can wash?"

"You're right," he nodded, "once that alkaline gumbo dries, it'll be hell to get off." He stood and swung her up in his arms. "If it hadn't been for that silver earring, I would have shot you for a doomed cow."

"Thanks a heap!" Blossom snorted and lay her face against his massive bare chest as he walked. She had her arms around his neck and she marveled at the sinewy strength of the big man. He carried her with ease toward the stream. It's going to be one of those let's-make-love-in-the-water-scenes, she smiled and closed her eyes, snuggling her face against his brown skin. If I'm dreaming, oh, please don't let me wake up before I get to the good part!

He plopped her down in the water. It was surprisingly cold for such a warm day. She blinked in surprise as he stepped back. "I'm sorry I don't have any soap or a change of clothes for you," he said, "but you can get some of it off, and then I'll take you into the settlement. Maybe when the captain sends out a patrol, they'll find your trunk."

"The captain himself?" Blossom said in confusion. Of course the airline had lost her luggage, but she'd never heard of the pilot taking responsibility for it before.

He stepped back up on the bank and turned to go.

"Is this it?"

"What do you mean?" he asked, shaking his head in puzzlement.

"I mean, what are you going to do now?"

"Why, what you'd expect me to do," he said. "I'll move away so I can't watch you bathe."

"In a sensual Indian romance story? Gimme a break!" She began to splash water on herself with jerky, annoyed gestures. "This is the most pointless, frustrating dream I've ever had. When I get the mud off, I'm outta here; you're history!"

"Take it easy, kid," he made a soothing gesture, "You've had a bad scare and one of us is confused—"

"What gave you the clue?" Blossom snapped. "I thought you'd at least help me get my clothes off!"

He stared at her as if he hadn't understood. "Ma'am?"

It was a good feeling to be a spunky romance heroine for a change. Now if she could just take this new feistiness with her when she awoke, maybe she wouldn't need that assertiveness class when she returned to L.A. after all. "I—I mean, I don't know what I'm going to do; I lost my purse, the camera, and all my ID in that mud hole, and now you're acting like a dork." She began to weep in sheer frustration.

"It's okay," he made a soothing gesture, and squatted by the water, "maybe I've got a shirt in my saddlebags you can put on." He rose and sauntered toward his horse.

She remembered then what she had found so attractive about him; easy grin, good-looking. He'd been so arrogant and virile. Blossom, maybe you are being a bit too feisty, she cautioned herself. Remember, in this time period, even a sassy heroine would be more modest and demure. How could this dream be dragging on for such a long time? Maybe he was right about her being lucky to be alive if she had fallen down those stairs. Perhaps she did have a concussion and was going to wake up with an I.V. in her arm in some hospital; but in the meantime, she was going to enjoy this weird delirium.

The ruined dress was caked with mud, but she couldn't unzip the back by herself. She was still trying when he returned. "If you could just help me with the zipper."

"The what?" He paused on the edge of the water.

"Are you deaf?" She gestured, "You know, catch that metal gizmo back there and pull down on it."

He put his hands on her back and struggled a moment before the zipper came open. "Amazing"

Whether he was talking about the amount of mud inside the dress or on her back, she didn't want to know. Blossom began to splash herself with water. "You could help me a little."

"All right." He waded in behind her. "I've got a buckskin shirt for you."

She felt his hands on her flesh, big and strong and warm. "Hmm, you're doing fine; now if I can just get out of this corset, you can unsnap my bra."

She felt his fingers fumbling with the thing. "What is this, anyway?" He had it open.

"Never mind," she answered, half-standing to get the corset off. She grabbed for it, but the sodden dress slid downward, leaving her half-naked.

He drew in his breath sharply as he stared at her bare breasts, and she saw desire flame in his dark eyes.

Now, she thought, with a smile, now, we finally get to the torrid love scene. Well, it was about time!

Four

Blossom stepped out of the wet dress, folding her arms over her breasts.

"What in god's name are you wearing?"

Blossom glanced downward. "Why, just panty hose. Darn! A new pair and they're in shreds. Did you find me something to put on?"

"You're a naive little thing," he scolded. "Don't you realize most men would take advantage of this situation?"

"Oh?" She blinked her eyelashes demurely. Now came the love scene like the ones in all the novels, Blossom thought breathlessly. He would sweep her up out of the stream in his powerful arms, carry her over and lay her down on the sand, kiss her naked flesh—

"What kind of a rotten bastard do you think I am?" War Cry snorted, "to take advantage of some poor, loco girl who's in such shock, she doesn't know what she's saying!" He turned on his heel and strode over to grab the shirt off the bush where it hung.

Darn, darn, darn! What kind of a love scene is this? Blossom thought in disgust as she freed herself from the shredded panty hose, crouched in the creek to splash water on herself, washing away the last of the mud. Her hair was going to take a more concentrated effort, she decided.

"Here, kid!" He threw her the shirt and turned his back.

"Thanks a bunch!" She caught it and slipped it on as she stood up. She might as well go ahead and wake up now before that museum guard caught her. Was it daylight there, or had she only dreamed that, too?

Gingerly, Blossom waded out onto the bank. "Ouch!" She hopped on one foot, "Stickers! And I lost my shoes in the bog."

"Here, I'll carry you." He swing her up in his arms and she lay her face against his naked chest, smiling up at him. This was more like it, she thought as he walked. She didn't have a stitch on under his big shirt and she was fairly clean now. Probably he would carry her over under some bushes and make passionate love to her, their naked bodies entwined as his hot hands caressed her satin skin, his mouth devouring hers.

Instead, he carried her to his horse, stood her on her feet.

"What are you doing?" Blossom asked.

"What does it look like I'm doing?" He swung up on the spotted horse, reached his hand out to her.

"But I thought . . . never mind, nothing has made sense for hours."

He nodded sympathetically and took her hand. "I know. I'll take you in to see Doc; maybe he can help." His big hand closed over hers and he pulled her up on the stallion before him.

"You are strong," she whispered and leaned back against him, snuggling in as his arms slipped around her.

"Don't do that," he muttered hoarsely against her hair.

She felt his manhood rising against her hips. Was this love scene going to begin on a horse? That would be very awkward. She decided to play innocent and wiggled again. "Don't do what?"

His whole body went tense and he gave a shuddering sigh. "The sooner I get you back to the fort, kid, the better off we'll both be." His breath stirred her damp hair and she settled into his embrace as they rode. His half-naked body felt warm and tense against hers, and she knew he was as acutely aware as she was that she wore nothing under that

big, loose buckskin shirt. A thousand times as she read romance novels, she had lived this scene; the handsome Indian
brave who desired her as no man ever had.

What a fantasy! How often had she wished she could go
back in time and live in the old West when things were
simpler and men were everything a real man was supposed
to be? She wanted to be protected and cherished, secure in
a man's love. Her therapist told her she wanted to retreat
from reality. Maybe that was true; reality could be so painful
and cruel. Blossom thought of the little yellowed newspaper
clipping. She had never gotten over the shock of discovering
that horrible secret. Maybe if she found her birth mother,
she could unravel the details.

She didn't want to think about that, she was enjoying having this man's arms around her too much to ruin her mood.

"This is the longest dream," she sighed. "I'm beginning
to wonder if I'm alive or dead."

He laughed against her ear. "You're alive . . . or I wasted
a lot of effort back there at the bog."

His arms around her felt real enough. Was it possible that
she wasn't dreaming after all? No, of course not. There simply wasn't any other reasonable explanation for how she had
gotten out of the ranch house. "Where are you taking me?"

"Town. Isn't that where you were wanting to go?"

Pawnee, Oklahoma, only a mile or so from the museum.
She was about to wake up, Blossom thought with a sudden
sense of loss; and he still hadn't made love to her. "Get a
grip, Blossom," she whispered to herself, "if you're lucky,
you can get out of the museum before you're found."

"What did you say?" His breath felt warm on her neck.
She wondered how it would feel against her naked skin. His
mouth would cover her nipple and his tongue would . . .

"Nothing." It was all going to end before she could live
the thrill of those love scenes she had only experienced in
the past by reading books. Maybe she had missed her flight,

but maybe the editor could wire her some money and she'd soon be on her way again. Disappointment settled over her.

"Kid, you're awfully quiet; I liked you better spunky."

And of course she wasn't. She was a shy mouse of a girl who let life push her like a rudderless boat, making as few tough decisions as possible. However, it had been fun role-playing while it lasted.

They rode in silence until they came to a small settlement. "Boy, this is really authentic," Blossom said, "no telephone poles or anything."

"Telephone what?"

"Is it like Tombstone, where the town wants to keep it authentic for the tourists? This looks like a perfect place to make a movie; maybe *Tattletale* might do a piece on it."

"*Tattletale?* You know the paper?"

"You might say that." Blossom sank further into gloom. Even out here, they bought the trashy tabloid. So this was the explanation after all; she was back in reality; had probably missed her plane, lost all her ID, and worse yet, didn't get the photos. She'd be lucky if Vic Lamarto didn't blacklist her so she couldn't get research work anywhere.

They rode down the dusty street while people in authentic garb turned to look at them curiously. Horses and a few buggies stood tied to hitching posts. There was not a car or pickup truck in sight. Must be filming today, she thought, maybe I can get a story out of this after all. *Elvis Spotted In Western Movie Town.* No, *Alien UFO Landed In Pawnee, Oklahoma.* "Beam me up, Scotty."

"What?" War Cry asked.

"Never mind," she shook her head. "I'd appreciate it if you'd please take me where I can get a fax or at least a phone."

"I think I'd better take you to Doc's."

He wanted to get her off his hands and get on with his life, Blossom thought with resignation. In a couple of hours, she'd be on a flight to finish searching out the dark secrets in her own mysterious background.

The handsome brave reined up in front of a small, modest frame house at the edge of the settlement. Bright geraniums bloomed scarlet in the window boxes. War Cry slid off the horse, reached up for her. "Here, I'll carry you since you're barefooted."

Blossom slid off into his arms, never wanting to leave that protective embrace. Only when his bare arm slipped under the back of her naked thighs did she remember she wore nothing under the buckskin shirt. "My clothes. What am I going to do about clothes? I can't leave like this."

"Take it easy, kid," he said gently as he carried her up to the door. "We'll find your luggage."

"That's what they told me last time and it ended up in Burbank." Maybe there was at least some small dress shop in this burg, if Vic would wire her some money. She didn't argue with the Indian as he kicked the door with his foot.

"Hey, Doc, let me in! I found the missing girl!"

"Missing? I wasn't missing. I knew where I was all the time."

A curious crowd was beginning to gather, she could hear the excited buzz. "Who is that? Must be that teacher! Terry say what happened to the rest of the passengers?"

She started to tell them she wasn't a teacher, she was a research librarian, but just then an elderly man opened the door, a pleasant, friendly man, judging from his smile. "Why, Terry, what—?"

The Indian brushed past him, "Get rid of the crowd, Doc."

The old man peered at her a moment over his glasses, yelled at the crowd. "Now, you folks just go on about your business, you'll hear all about it later."

War Cry didn't put her down. It was a cozy, old-fashioned room complete with lace tablecloths and flowered wallpaper.

"Young lady," the old man smiled, "you'll be all right now; I'm Doc Maynard."

"You look like old Doc on 'Gunsmoke.' " Blossom smiled with delight.

The old man looked baffled. "Have we met, young lady?"

Before she could answer, War Cry said, "She doesn't always make sense, Doc. I think she probably hit her head."

Blossom decided not to point out that everyone and everything in this dream seemed crazier than she was.

The warrior stood her gently on her feet. The bare floor felt real enough.

"I'll get my wife." The old man went to the kitchen door. "Hazel, come out here, please; I think I may need you."

A plump, pleasant woman came out of the kitchen, wiping her hands on her apron. "Poor thing! I'll make her some tea."

"If you don't mind," Blossom said, "a diet soda would be fine."

The old lady looked baffled. The men shrugged at her.

"I don't mean to be any trouble," Blossom said, "just zap me some tea then in the microwave."

"See what I mean?" War Cry sighed. "She keeps saying loco things like that."

"I'm not loco," Blossom insisted, "at least, I don't think I am; but I am getting a headache. I'd love to have a couple of aspirin, if you don't mind."

"Aspirin?" Doc Maynard scratched his head.

"Surely you have aspirin?"

Doc stared at her over his glasses, shook his head.

"I swear," Blossom sighed, "everyone's into antibiotics now or acupuncture."

The other three looked at each other.

Doc's wrinkled face furrowed. "Young lady, I haven't the foggiest idea what you're talking about."

"My dear," Hazel took her arm gently, "do you realize you're only wearing one earring?"

Blossom nodded. "I left it on the other side of the painting when I tried to pull War Cry out."

"Out?" Doc said. "Out of what?"

"Don't ask, Doc," War Cry cautioned, "it just gets crazier."

"I resent that!" Blossom was so tired, she was forgetting her natural reticence.

Mrs. Maynard looked both alarmed and perplexed. "Maybe some tea would help—"

"Forget the tea, Hazel," Doc Maynard declared. "I think this calls for whiskey. Terry?"

He grinned and nodded, showing white teeth. "Don't mind if I do, Doc; one of the few things that's made sense today."

The old man disappeared into the kitchen, returned with drinks, handed them around. "This should make you feel better, young lady. We'll put you up in our spare room."

"Oh, a bed and breakfast; how quaint! I do appreciate it." Blossom sipped the whiskey. What a crazy twist this was all taking, and yet so real! Why, she would swear she could actually taste the whiskey. She didn't really want to go to sleep, Blossom thought as she drank it. When she woke up, she was going to be back in the real world, either in that museum, in a hospital, or worse yet, her cramped little apartment in L.A.

She realized the men were watching her closely. "I do need to let the paper know where I am."

"Now, just set your mind to rest, Miss," Doc made a soothing gesture. "We'll see that the paper knows."

"I've lost my driver's license and my ATM card, but maybe—"

"To drive what?" Doc Maynard peered at her over his spectacles. "Have they finally passed a law that women actually have to have a license to drive? The way some of them handle a buggy, I can see why."

"Now, dear," his wife scolded him with a gentle smile.

This was more like a situation comedy than a Western romance. Blossom finished her drink. "I've lost all my plastic."

"Plastic?" The old lady blinked at her and wiped her hands on her apron again.

"You know, my ATM card."

War Cry frowned. "What's an ATM card?"

"You know, you put it in the machine and it gives you money."

"Real money?" Doc Maynard said.

She stifled an urge to say, *No, Monopoly money.* "Yes."

Again the other three exchanged glances while Blossom yawned. "You know, I really am awfully tired. Maybe I could rest a little if you wouldn't mind, while you contact *Tattletale* for me." The room looked a little hazy and she swayed, yawned again.

She heard Doc whisper something to the big scout, something about laudanum in her drink. War Cry nodded. "Maybe I'd better carry her. Do you have the spare room ready, Mrs. Maynard?"

The plump woman nodded, gestured. "Right this way."

Laudanum? Wasn't that old-fashioned narcotic? What kind of a quack had stuff like that in his house, but no aspirin?

"I—I think I'd better go." Blossom started for the door, but she had to grab the back of a chair to steady herself.

"Here," War Cry said, "I'll carry you." He swept her up in his arms. "Which way, Mrs. Maynard?"

The lady gestured down the hall and Blossom felt herself being carried. "I—I really need to go," she mumbled.

"Kid, you aren't going anywhere for a while." His voice was soft and gentle as he cradled her, carrying her down the hall. It was so safe, so secure in his embrace; she didn't ever want to leave his arms. She slipped her arms around his neck, holding him close. This was only a muddled dream, she knew, and when she woke up, her handsome hero would be gone forever. "And you never even made love to me."

"What did you say?" He had carried her into a room with little roses on the wallpaper. It smelled of lavender and there were crocheted doilies on the dresser.

At least she wanted one kiss. Before he could react, she reached up, slipped her arms around his neck, and kissed him. For a moment, he stiffened in surprise, then the kiss deepened with heat and urgency. His arms closed around her and she felt his breath quicken and his pulse race. His sinewy muscles tightened beneath her hands and now he was kissing her like he would never get enough of her, forcing his hot tongue between her lips. No man had ever kissed her like this and she writhed in his arms, kissing him with passionate abandon that she had never experienced before, wanting more . . . more . . .

She had never felt so protected and cherished as she did at this moment in the virile savage's embrace. Oh, for a man like this, she would do anything; but they only existed in those wonderful novels.

He managed to pull away from her mouth and looked down into her face, eyes dark with passion, breath coming in gasps. "I must be out of my mind to take advantage of a kid like you—loco or not."

She began weeping softly. "It's—it's not going to happen, is it?"

He laid her on the bed gently, shook his head. "I'm not that big a bastard."

"I'm a dull little mouse, every man thinks so; you don't want me."

He took a deep shuddering breath and pulled away from her. "Kid, you don't know how bad I'd like to . . ."

She was sobbing now, even though the room was beginning to spin. He existed only in her mind, she knew that, and he would be gone when she awakened. "Every woman's fantasy; oh, why can I only find it in books?"

He leaned over and kissed her forehead, pulled the covers up over her. "Speaking of books, that reminds me." He reached into his waistband, held out a small volume.

"I don't understand; I didn't lose a book." She took it anyway, wiping her eyes as she stared at it.

"You must have; I found it near the stagecoach and it's got your first name in it."

Blossom opened the cover, so sleepy now, she could barely see. "Must be a more common name than I thought," she mumbled.

"You don't recognize it?"

She was very tired and the dainty scrawl was blurring before her eyes. She had never seen this book before, yet it was her handwriting. She caught his arm, comforted by the strength and feel of that reality as she took another look at the name. *Blossom.*

It didn't make any sense. The only real thing was this big, protective man whose arm felt so strong and muscular beneath her hand.

She stared past War Cry at the flowered wallpaper behind him. There was a calendar hanging on the wall and she tried to focus her eyes on it, but they were playing tricks on her even as they began to close.

The calendar read: JUNE, 1873.

Five

War Cry stared down at the girl, not answering. She was already asleep, her damp brown hair spread over the pillow. One small hand had a death grip on his arm, the other clutched her book of poetry. Poor little thing; she'd had a terrifying experience. He gritted his teeth with anger as he thought of the Lakota warriors. Even if they hadn't touched her, no doubt she had witnessed the killings and torture from her hiding place in the brush. She might never recover.

Gently, he unclenched her fingers from his arm and covered her up. She stirred restlessly and mumbled something in her sleep. "It's okay," he whispered, "it's okay."

His voice seemed to soothe her. She settled down and smiled ever so slightly in her sleep. Why, she was pretty when she smiled, he thought. Other men might think her plain, but there was something about her; she seemed so vulnerable and defenseless; a real lady.

War Cry turned and went out, thinking she was someone else's problem now. He liked his women wild and passionate; the kind who wouldn't put strings on him. As a scout, he was as free and untamed as a lobo wolf. Besides, the white men would lynch him for even looking at her. With the woman shortage, dozens of white ranchers and soldiers would want to marry her if she regained her senses. If she didn't, what would become of the bewildered girl?

He didn't want to think about it. Among most Indian tribes, a crazy person was considered touched by the Great

Spirit and treated with awe, but he didn't know what the whites would do with such a one. He closed the door and returned to the living room.

Doc shook his head and lit his pipe. "Crazy as a loon, I'm afraid."

His wife wiped her eyes with her apron. "Land's sake, what will become of her?"

War Cry looked from one to the other. "Doc, you think she'll get any better?"

He took the pipe from his mouth and considered. "Maybe, if she's treated gently. There's no way to know how a damaged mind will react."

Mrs. Maynard nodded. "She can stay with us; she was supposed to anyway when she opens the school in late August."

"I'll make my report to Captain Radley," War Cry sighed, unable to forget how light and fragile she had been in his arms, the way the sunlight had picked up the gold in her brown locks.

"And I'd better go tell the mayor and the newspaper what's happened." Doc reached for his hat. "Wonder how she knew about *Tattletale?*"

"Maybe someone sent her a copy so she'd be familiar with the area," Terry shrugged.

Doc regarded him somberly, sucking his pipe. "No chance for any other survivors?"

Terry started to give him details, glanced at the lady. "I'll tell you later."

"I can guess," Hazel Maynard said. "I'm a pioneer woman and I've seen a lot."

"The Sioux have been my people's enemies for generations." Terry pushed his cap back and regarded her. "Yet I can almost sympathize with their plight. When the whites finish killing off all the buffalo, every tribe will be starving; even the Pawnee."

The old lady nodded. "They call it progress, but I've got

mixed feelings about it. Yet when I see victims like this pitiful little teacher . . ." Her voice trailed off.

They said their goodbyes. The two men went out together,
then separated to take care of their own tasks.

War Cry went to the fort. The young private in the outer
office came to his feet, curiosity in his hazel eyes, a shock
of unruly hair slicked back with hair oil. "You find 'em,
Terry?"

"I found them," he nodded. "Is the captain in?"

"You know he is; been waiting for you to get back." The
boy went to the open door, knocked on the wall.

"Come in."

The young man disappeared a moment, returned. "Captain
Radley will see you now."

War Cry went in and closed the door, not wanting to have
the private overhear the conversation.

"Leave the door open," the officer said, laying aside the
book he'd been reading, "you know how I feel about being
closed in."

Both windows were open, too. War Cry obliged and re-
opened the door, knowing the tragedy would be all over the
fort in less than an hour; but gossip had already spread that
the stage was overdue. With an Indian outbreak going on,
that only meant one thing.

"Ah, Terry!" Capt. Lexington Radley leaned back in his
chair behind the big desk and grinned, making a point of
not getting up or saluting. He was handsome in a dandified
sort of way, War Cry noted, dark, wavy hair, hands as soft
and fine as his classic features. Captain Radley offered a
cigar which Terry took, noting it was a cheap one. The back
East dandy wouldn't waste expensive tobacco on an Injun
scout.

"Well, Terry, you found the missing stage?"

"I found it." He struck a Lucifer match with his thumbnail,
let the officer fidget while he took a slow puff.

The young captain gestured the scout to a chair and leaned forward eagerly. "Well?"

"Well what? You should have known what the answer was when the stage didn't make it in. Hank did his best." He smoked and thought about the old man. Someday, maybe the Cheyenne or the Lakota would get him, too; they certainly outnumbered the Pawnee.

The natty officer drummed his well-manicured fingers on his desk. "Ye gods! Are you going to give me the details or am I expected to beg for them?"

"I was just thinking about Hank; good man." War Cry smoked and stared at the officer, who grew uneasy under his gaze.

"Oh, he's dead?" His tone sounded as bored as he looked.

War Cry nodded. "They staked him out and built little fires under his hands and feet. He was a long time dying."

The officer's fine features turned pale and looked queasy. "Good lord! What about the others?"

"Two male passengers dead and scalped; I didn't have time to bury any of them."

"We were expecting a young genteel teacher." The captain half-rose from his chair. "Is she—?"

Terry shook his head and inhaled his smoke. "No, she's alive; I brought her in."

Captain Radley drummed his fingers on his desk impatiently. "Well, why didn't you bring her here? I'll want to question her; did the red devils—?"

"She's asleep at Doc's; his wife's looking after her. She acts a little loco, so there's no telling what's happened to her."

"Is she pretty?"

War Cry shrugged and smoked. "If you like the type; sort of fragile with enormous blue eyes about the color of that prairie flower."

The captain swore under his breath and rubbed his almost baby-smooth skin. "A lady; we finally get an eligible well-bred lady to come out here, and this happens. Damn, I was hoping to take her to the community dance."

"I'm not sure she's up to that; maybe she never will be, according to Doc."

"It'll be a helluva lot of trouble to ship her back East to some asylum and I understand she doesn't have any relatives; that's why she accepted this job. I wonder if that makes her medical expenses the army's problem?"

"You're all heart, Captain."

The other ran a well-manicured finger around his collar. "It's just that I've been so looking forward to meeting a pretty, smart girl of good family background. I plan to buy a big spread here when I leave the service and we get the savages corralled. I'll need a wife to produce sons, and good bloodlines count, you know."

"You sound like you're breeding livestock." In his mind, War Cry saw a sudden image of the shy, fragile girl with the arrogant officer lying on her naked body, pumping his seed into her like a stallion breeding a brood mare. The image annoyed him and he abruptly stood up. "You'll need to send out a patrol to bury what's left of those men and bring in the wrecked stage. The young lady seems very concerned about her lost luggage."

The veins throbbed visibly in the officer's pale neck. "I'm a West Point man; I don't need a redskin scout to tell me my job."

"Believe me, Captain," War Cry tossed the cigar into the spittoon with a contemptuous gesture, "no one around here ever forgets your background or bloodlines. Am I dismissed?"

"You are."

War Cry gave a curt nod and left the office, loathing the arrogant young aristocrat. He wished the North brothers were in charge; the Pawnee scouts idolized those brave officers who shared bread and blanket with their men and never thought of them as redskins.

He stopped to draw a detailed map for the enlisted man outside. "Here's where to find that stage."

The boy looked uneasy as he lowered his voice to a whisper and gestured for the scout to follow him outside, where they could talk without being overheard. "You ain't going, Terry? The captain going to lead this patrol?"

War Cry laughed. "As scared as he is of hostiles? He's only good at leading a cotillion; and maybe dress parades when there's visitors on the post. He'll probably send me."

"I'll be glad when the Major gets back." The boy wiped sweat from his hairless upper lip.

"You and me both." He clapped the boy on the shoulder. "You know where'll I'll be if I'm needed. At least let me get a little grub in my belly before I have to go back out."

"The boys'll feel better if you're doing the scouting."

"I'm Pawnee," War Cry shrugged, "nobody can beat us as scouts, that's why the universal sign for both a scout and a Pawnee is a wolf." He grinned and held two fingers up behind his head as if they were ears. "I'll be at Rusty's Place."

The boy returned his grin. "Captain Radley would have a fit if he knew she lets you come there; he don't like the idea of Injuns mixin' with white women; even if they are whores."

"We can't all be blue-blooded boys from back East," War Cry shrugged as he sauntered away. "Besides, Rusty serves the best steak in town."

War Cry headed down the muddy street and up the back alley. Even a small settlement like this one had a whorehouse. It was off limits to Indians, but Rusty and her girls overlooked that for him.

He went in the back way.

"Terry!" Half-clad girls clustered around him. "Where you been?"

He slapped a couple of them on the bottom. "Looking for that missing stage. Now I could use a drink and a bath."

They clustered even closer, setting up a chorus of squeals. "Let me, Terry, it's my turn."

The argument grew louder as he leaned against the bar and waited.

Rusty came out of her office and he marveled again at how pretty the redhead was. Today, she wore an autumn-colored dress of brown and gold silk that showed off her fine figure. "Go along, girls, I'll take care of this."

"Oh, Rusty." Dolly's painted lips pouted as she pushed dyed black curls out of her eyes. "I was just wantin' to pour him a drink."

"I know what you were wanting," Rusty snapped. "If he needs you later, I'll let you know."

The girls scattered reluctantly.

Rusty spoke with a cultured accent and War Cry wondered again about the mysterious background of the woman with flame-colored hair as she gestured Terry into her office and closed the door. She poured him a drink from her private stock.

He tasted it, sighed. "Good; like always. What's a lady with your class doing in a business like this?"

"You don't want to know and I don't want to tell you," she dismissed the question with a gesture as she sat down behind her desk and surveyed him with green eyes. She might have been in her late twenties or early thirties, he thought, but her eyes were as old and knowing as Delilah's. Yet the mysterious madam never bedded the customers.

A couple of years ago, Terry recalled as he sipped his drink, there'd been a common private, a big handsome guy she'd fallen for; Thompson. He had won a Medal of Honor for bravery, then deserted under mysterious circumstances.

The madam lit a cigarette. "So what's the story on the stage? I had a new dealer coming in."

In his mind, he saw the gambler with the scarlet cravat that wasn't really scarlet. "He won't be dealing any more poker."

"What about Hank?"

"Like the lady said, I don't want to tell you and you don't want to know."

Tears softened the eyes that up until now had looked hard as green glass. "Rough old codger; always hitting me up for a drink between paydays."

War Cry nodded. "He'd share his last crust. The only one alive is the new school marm." He looked down at the mud smearing his big body, remembering the girl. "She seems half loco; no telling what those devils did to her or what she saw."

"Poor kid."

Terry sipped his drink. "Doc says she may get over it; only time will tell. In the meantime, Captain West Point is wondering if her virtue is still intact so she'll be respectable enough to escort to the community ball."

"The bastard."

Terry craned his neck, stretching his powerful shoulder muscles, thinking how unusual it was to see a woman smoking. "I need a bath, a big, rare steak, and some sleep."

She smiled. "For you, anything. I never forget you were a good friend to Thompson."

He finished his drink. "Brave men are few and far between; I could count on him in a fight. Besides, he never called me Injun."

Her pensive expression told him her mind was far away. "I wish I knew where he was."

"He probably had some trouble in his past he didn't want you to know about."

She laughed without mirth. "He wouldn't have been the only one. He could have at least given me a chance." She bit her words off and looked away. In the silence, a woman's laughter echoed from a distant room. "Haven't heard from him; he might be dead."

"Maybe not. He was a crack shot. Besides, it's easy to be swallowed up by the frontier if a man chooses to."

She ground out her cigarette. "Someday, I may do the same thing; make a clean break; start over some place where I'm not known."

"I wish you luck."

She smiled a sad smile. "You're the only man I know who doesn't try to . . . well, you know."

"Would it do me any good?" He pushed his cap back and grinned at her.

"You're arrogant and cocky; you know that?"

"I just know I can handle anything life throws at me; meet it head on."

"Self-confident and independent as hell; that's why women find you irresistible," Rusty smiled. "They all hope to be the one to tame you."

He shrugged wide shoulders. "I'm too wild for that."

She laughed and stood up, reached for a bellpull. "There never was a stallion that couldn't be broken. I'll have a tub of water sent up and a steak ordered. Which girl do you want?"

In his mind, he saw brown hair highlighted with gold and large blue eyes. It seemed almost as if he could feel the warmth of her slight form in his arms riding on the horse before him. She was an educated lady from back East; innocent and fragile; not his type at all. "Let me think about it while I wash up and eat. Our prissy Captain Radley may send me right back out with that patrol—"

"That's not fair. You look dog-tired and the army has other scouts." She paused with her hand on the doorknob.

"I think young West Point is dangling me for bait, knowing how much the Lakota hate me. If he can't get me killed, he at least hopes to get me scalped alive. To the Pawnee, a scalped man might as well be dead; they consider him bad medicine."

"Treat yourself to another drink, and I'll see what's keeping that new hired girl. Poor Myrtle is sweet, but none too bright and awfully plain." Rusty disappeared.

Terry poured himself another whiskey, contemplating a hot, steaming tub of water and a rare steak bigger than a dinner plate. His thoughts went to the girl he'd found on the prairie. Funny, she only wore one earring. He wondered what had happened to the other one? Lost in the devil's cattle trap along with her shoes and other things, he supposed. He tried not to remember seeing her naked in the creek as he helped her wash the mud off that creamy white skin. Blossom; pretty name.

He finished his whiskey, remembering the way she had grabbed and kissed him; so passionate, yet so inexperienced. He'd like to be the one to teach her how. Then he pictured Captain Radley married to her, rutting on her small body while he bred her to raise a passel of kids for his blue-blooded dynasty. Somehow, that thought annoyed the Indian scout. Well, white women were off-limits to Indians. In fact, he and Rusty both would be in trouble if the settlers ever found out Terry took his pleasure here.

The whiskey glow slowly spread through his muscular frame. He wasn't so tired that the thought of a woman's soft body didn't arouse him. He had sampled most of Rusty's girls at one time or another. The woman he wanted tonight wasn't for sale. Still, his groin was throbbing with a man's need as he started up the stairs to his usual room.

Sure enough, a big tub of sudsy water waited for him there. Terry stripped off his moccasins, cap, and blue pants and slid into the warm water with a satisfied sigh. "Oh, that feels good!"

A knock at the door.

"Who is it?"

"Myrtle, sir. Miss Rusty said I was to bring you more hot water." The voice had a decided nasal twang to it.

"Come on in, Myrtle. I hope you have a big steak with you."

She came in, trying not to look at him as she poured the kettle full of steaming water into the tub. She looked a bit

addled, and she wasn't pretty. Her front teeth were too prominent and her eyes were close together. She did have a full-
breasted figure and trim waist, though. "Thanks, Myrtle,
there'll be a coin for you."

Her simple expression lit up. "I don't have to pleasure
you none to get it?"

War Cry smiled. "You don't like to pleasure a man?"

The skin under heavy freckles turned fiery red. "I—I'm
a good girl; never done that. Miss Rusty tells me her customers won't bother me none."

"Just bring me some food, Myrtle; you've got nothing to
fear from me."

The homely girl scurried from the room in slow-witted
confusion.

War Cry smiled and shook his head, began to scrub himself. The hot water felt good on his weary muscles. He closed
his eyes as he scrubbed and remembered the half-naked girl
attempting to wash the mud off in the creek. Blossom might
be a bit strange, but her feistiness appealed to him. In his
mind, he could see her half-naked body and remembered that
even muddy, he had had an almost overpowering urge to
spread her out on the creek bank and mate with her until
he was sated. He was exhausted, but his virile maleness grew
rigid at the thought.

He sudsed himself all over and rinsed off, stood up,
grabbed a towel, and wrapped it around his lean hips. A
knock at the bedroom door. "It's Myrtle again, Mr. Terry. I
done got your dinner."

"Good. Leave it, Myrtle, but you might bring me some more
whiskey." He heard the door close.

With nothing but the towel around him, he sauntered in
and sat down in an overstuffed chair, grabbed the plate. War
Cry inhaled the aroma a long moment before he dug in. He
cut into the steak, thinking he'd been around the whites too
long; their food tasted good to him. The beef was browned
crisp on the outside, pink in the middle, and the potatoes

were swimming in butter. He tore open a light, fluffy biscuit and slathered it with gravy. He was a big man and he could wolf down meat with the best of them.

He was finishing up, wiping his mouth when the knock came again. "Come on in, Myrtle."

Dolly peeked around the corner of the door, grinning and holding up a bottle. "Your brand."

He paused. "What happened to Myrtle?"

"I waylaid her." Dolly came in, closed the door. "I figured after you had a bath and some food, you might have a hunger for something else."

He did have, but somehow tonight Dolly didn't have her usual appeal. "Just leave the whiskey, Dolly; I'm tired."

"I don't believe you." She ran her tongue over her pouty lower lip, shook her black curls loose so they tumbled down her shoulders. She wore only a skimpy silk chemise.

He stood, took the bottle out of her hand, set it on the sideboard. "I'm not up to it."

"Terry, you're always up to it." She slipped her arms around him and kissed him openmouthed, slid her tongue between his lips. She smelled of woman and perfume; an erotic scent.

He drew in his breath sharply and let her do what she would for a long moment. Her tongue was deep in his mouth, her hands running lightly across his bare skin. The towel came loose and he felt it begin to slide down his lean hips toward the floor. Dolly rubbed herself against him, and he could feel her nipples through the thin silk. Her mouth was too wet; too experienced. In spite of himself, he remembered the hesitant kiss of the girl called Blossom. Dolly's hot mouth went to his nipple and her sharp little teeth nipped him there.

His manhood had gone so hard, he was almost throbbing in need. War Cry gasped and glanced down at the smear of her cheap lip rouge on his brawny chest. She began to sink to her knees, kissing his belly as she went, her arms around his waist. "You know what I want to taste," she murmured.

He looked down at her, breathing hard as her lips slid down his belly, her hot kisses leaving smears of lip rouge as she moved lower and lower. No matter how tired he was, when he came into Rusty's place, he'd usually keep a girl on her back for hours, because he was more man than most of them could handle.

Abruptly, he looked at her trail of smeared red kisses on his dark skin and scowled with repulsion. It looked like blood. In his mind, he saw the massacre scene and a girl's frightened face; those large blue eyes.

He stared down at Dolly. He didn't understand it himself, but his desire had left him. Annoyed and confused, War Cry tangled his hand in her dark hair, pulled her lips away. "No."

"What?" She looked up at him from where she rested on her knees, big breasts swelling from the top of the sheer silk. "Why, stud? Ain't I pleasin' ya?"

He didn't know what it was himself. All he could see in his mind was a fragile girl with big blue eyes. "Just get out, Dolly, and don't slam the door behind you." He made a dismissing gesture as he bent to pick up the towel.

Dolly began to hurl obscenities. "What's wrong with you tonight, Injun? You ain't never been too tired before. You can always go all night and you got the biggest and the hardest—"

"Never mind; just get out of here." He hauled her to her feet and pushed her toward the door.

She looked sulky and incredulous. "All right! All right! You know which room's mine if you change your mind; you been there often enough."

He shoved her out the door and closed it, cursing himself for a fool. She had been hot and eager, and he knew from past nights that Dolly could please a man like few women could. Somehow, tonight, he wanted a girl who was inexperienced, one he could teach; a gentle girl that no other man could buy. He must be getting as loco as that blue-eyed girl. Swearing, he dressed hurriedly and slipped out the back door.

The young private caught him as War Cry strode down the alley. "Terry, Captain Radley wants you to take the patrol out to bring in that stagecoach."

War Cry groaned. "I was hoping he'd let me sleep an hour or two."

"I know, but the boys feel safer with you along. They know you won't lead them into an ambush. You know every blade of grass on the prairie and every Lakota trick in the book. Besides, you're a crack shot."

War Cry took off the cavalry cap, ran his hand through his black hair. "All right; I'll pick up a fresh horse. My stallion needs a good rest after all the miles he's covered the last few hours. Give me a few minutes."

He left the private, hurried over to the Maynards. "Is she okay, ma'am?"

The old lady nodded. "Hasn't stirred. I've drawn her curtains so she can sleep the afternoon away."

He had wanted to see her, see if she was as appealing as he remembered. "Well, I guess rest will do her good. Tell her . . ." Tell her what? He stumbled over his words, not looking at the old lady. "Tell her I'll bring in her luggage, she seemed so worried about it."

"All right." She waited. "Is there something else?"

Was there? Why had he come? He felt like a damned fool right now, not an untamed Pawnee scout. "That's all." He wheeled and strode away from the house, headed for the stable. When he got back from this patrol, War Cry vowed, he was going to return to Rusty's and keep Dolly and a couple more of the girls writhing with pleasure all night. Until then, a grueling ride across the plains with danger at every bend and curve would keep his mind too occupied to think about women. No, not women; one woman; her.

Six

When Blossom's eyes opened, for a long moment, she wasn't sure where she was. The last thing she remembered was standing on a staircase reaching to touch a painting and then she'd had all sorts of weird dreams; some of them seemed right out of an Indian romance with beautiful scenery, adventure, and most of all, a handsome, virile hunk she had yearned for in all those romances she had read.

Puzzled, she craned her head, looking around. She was in an old-fashioned bed with an ornate iron headboard. The place smelled slightly of lavender and there were tiny flowers on the wallpaper. "A darling little bed and breakfast," Blossom whispered, "probably right in the town of Pawnee. I must have gotten out of that house, gone to a bar for a drink, had too much, and someone brought me here."

Her vision swept around the room, stopped at the calendar. "What a quaint touch! Someone went to a lot of trouble to make the place look old and authentic."

She turned her head, looking at the bright sunlight streaming through the lace-curtained window. "Oh my god, I'll bet I've missed my plane! What will I do now?"

She sat up in bed, swung her legs over the side, glanced down. What on earth was she wearing? Had she gotten drunk enough to go into some Western store and buy a suede fringed shirt? It was huge on her and she realized abruptly that she wore nothing beneath it. "I can't wear this on a plane!"

The door opened and a sweet little old lady stuck her head in. She looked familiar, somehow. "Are you feeling all right now?" she asked a little too brightly.

"I know why you seem familiar!" Blossom exclaimed, feeling relief. "I've seen you in a television ad; Happy Retirement Village, LTD., or maybe a Golden Agers cruise line."

The motherly woman looked baffled. "Land's sake. I was hoping you'd be feeling better today."

"I—I don't know how I feel." Blossom wiggled her bare toes against the flowered, old-fashioned carpet. "I thought this was some weird dream, but it certainly feels real; at least, I think I'm awake."

"Of course you are." Her tone was soothing as she wiped her plump hands on her apron. "You just forget everything you've been through; think of it as a nightmare."

Part of it had been pretty darned good. Blossom stared at her bare feet, wondering about the arrogant Indian hunk.

"I'm Hazel Maynard." The woman looked at Blossom over her spectacles. "You can put on one of my old dresses, made when I was much thinner. Then you can join me in the kitchen for a cup of coffee."

Maynard. Now she remembered a little of her arrival in this house. "Thank you for your help, I really appreciate it." Blossom watched the old lady digging through a tall walnut wardrobe. "I was hoping they might have found my luggage by now."

"Terry's looking for it. Ah, this might do!" She held up a full calico dress with a design of pink rosebuds. "My shoes may not fit you, but they'll have to do."

"You're so kind." Blossom took the dress. It smelled slightly of lavender. "Now, if you can direct me to a mall, I could buy . . ." She paused, recalling something about losing her purse in a sort of quicksand pit. Her credit cards, ATM, everything. "Maybe I could get an advance from my editor; get him to wire me some money."

"Wire? Oh, I wouldn't count on the telegraph; I imagine the lines are down with all this trouble."

Blossom nodded, remembering the storm on the horizon early last night.

"Now, dear, I'll leave you to dress. Why, it's almost time for dinner." The pleasant lady closed the door.

She didn't see any bra or panty hose, but then, plump Mrs. Maynard's undergarments wouldn't fit Blossom anyhow. She'd been given a pair of lace bloomers, several petticoats, heavy dark stockings with garters, some sort of camisole top. The dress had tiny hook and eye fasteners down the front. "Boy! These reenactors do insist on things being authentic, don't they?"

She got dressed and went into the kitchen. "This is certainly a charming place; so much atmosphere. I'll bet you have a four-star rating."

The old lady cocked her gray head at Blossom for a long moment, hesitated as if she were about to ask something, then shook it. "Do have some coffee, my dear." She poured her a cup. "Now you just sit down and relax."

"This coffee smells so good!" Blossom took a deep whiff. "I'm so used to just nuking some water in the micro, using instant decafe, I forget how good real coffee smells!" She settled herself in a chair and tucked her bare feet up under her. "This is wonderful! I'll recommend your place to my office. Why, the antiques alone must be worth a fortune."

"Antiques?" The old lady looked baffled as Blossom gestured toward the worn oak sideboard and the old quilt thrown across the Victorian settee. "Oh, these old things? We're hoping to throw them all out when we can afford some new furnishings."

"But it's all so authentic." A thought occurred to her. "Has this town been used as a TV or movie set?"

"A what?"

"You know, like 'Gunsmoke'?"

"Yes, we do have plenty of that," the old lady admitted

with a sigh, "especially on Saturday night when the soldiers and the hide hunters have a few too many at the saloons."

"You're all into being reenactors, too?"

The little old lady shrugged. "No, no, my dear, we're Democrats."

Blossom laughed. "Oh, and clever one-liners, too! I'll bet you keep your guests really entertained."

"Speaking of entertainment, if you're up to it, there's a community dance coming up."

"Oh, but I can't stay." Blossom sipped her coffee. "I'd really like to, but I'm only passing through."

Mrs. Maynard's eyes widened behind her spectacles. "We had hoped you were coming to stay permanently, but after what's happened, I can't blame you for changing your mind. Do you have any kin at all?"

Blossom munched her cookie and thought about the secret she had discovered about her past. "I really don't know," Blossom answered, "that's what I was hoping to find out."

Mrs. Maynard clucked sympathetically. "I understand your parents are dead?"

How would she know that? "Yes, Dad died of cancer about the time he lost the farm to the giant conglomerate."

"Oh, you poor dear!" The old lady shook her head. "Well, there's lots of farms being lost; desperate men driven to do anything they can to turn a dollar."

"I was only a child," Blossom sighed. "The local hospital closed down and Mother thought there might be better opportunities in California, so we went there after Dad died."

"Had a relative do the same thing back in the fifties," Mrs. Maynard confided, "everyone thought they'd strike gold out there, but most didn't."

"The fifties, ah yes, everyone says those were great times; I did a nostalgia piece about Rock n' Roll last year." Blossom smiled at the memory. "California was a big scary place for a kid from the country. Mom supported us as a nurse at a big L.A. hospital. She died only a few months ago. AIDS."

"What?"

"She had an accident at the hospital." Blossom remembered that night. If there'd been a doctor in the hospital room at the precise moment Mother had been taking a blood sample from that addict who went berserk, maybe he could have helped subdue the patient, or at least pushed the button to call some orderlies before the needle went through Ann Murdock's rubber glove.

It dawned on her that Mrs. Maynard was staring at her as if she didn't understand English. She was probably shocked, Blossom thought, but it didn't shock her anymore; she'd lost several acquaintances and a coworker to the deadly disease.

"Land's sakes! I'll bet you're hungry." Mrs. Maynard stood up. "Help yourself to the coffee; I'll have some salt pork and potatoes fried up in a moment." She ladled lard generously into the big black skillet.

"With your husband a doctor, don't you worry about cholesterol?" Blossom picked up the pot, poured herself another cup.

"Cholesterol?" The plump lady paused in ladling the lard.

Blossom was a bit weary of this authenticity, it wore thin on those not playing the game. "I don't usually have anything that heavy," she explained shyly as she sat down at the scarred old table. "I usually just nuke something in the microwave or stop at a fast-food. I've taken up jogging trying to keep in shape."

Hazel Maynard paused and stared at her a long moment, looked as if she were about to ask a question, then shrugged, and went back to slicing thick slabs of bacon.

Blossom took a deep whiff of the cooking, closed her eyes, and smiled. She had almost forgotten those tasty, hardy meals she used to have on the farm before Dad died. She had been so young, she couldn't even remember exactly where the farm had been anymore. The Brewster Farms, LTD empire had been swallowing up farms for more than a hundred years, and it had grabbed the Murdock place when Dad couldn't make the mortgage payments because he was too ill to work. The Brewster conglomerate now owned most of the mid-West. "Can I do anything to help?"

"No, you just sit and enjoy your coffee. Terry said he'd come by after he returns from the patrol."

"Terry? The Pawnee scout?"

"Of course."

It dawned on Blossom. "You mean, I didn't imagine him? He's real?"

The old lady paused, eyes widening, her expression troubled. "Did you think he wasn't? Never mind. I imagine the captain will want to talk to you this afternoon."

"The captain?" The police, she thought, oh, fudge! After pretending to be so friendly and hospitable, they're going to charge me with trespassing at the Pawnee Bill ranch after all.

The old lady bustled about the kitchen. "Yes, the captain's a handsome one; several of the girls have set their caps for him, but he's choosey; he inquired about your family before you were offered this opportunity."

Vic Lamarto had sent her here because the town wanted her to write about the ghost in the painting? That didn't make any sense, but then, none of this did.

Blossom decided not to mention that she had come on a search for her roots, that she'd been found as an abandoned newborn and hadn't a clue as to her birth parents. She thought about her job. The ghost painting thing might be something *Tattletale* would want to do a story on, but she still didn't have the photos. "I need to contact Vic Lamarto."

"Oh, you know Mr. Lamarto?"

Blossom blinked. "Do you?"

"Why, of course! Everyone knows Victor, he's the newspaper editor."

Blossom heaved a sigh of relief. "Thank god! I was about to decide I had lost complete touch with reality!"

Mrs. Maynard patted her arm. "There, there, my dear,

you've had a bad shock, but you'll get over it with a little rest."

"I guess I hit my head without realizing it."

"That's exactly what my husband said. Now, we'll have a nice meal and then you can rest some more."

Rest? She had things to do, but she didn't argue with the motherly woman. "If you'll point me toward the refrigerator," Blossom said, "I'll get margarine and things out for you."

"Refrigerator? Margarine?" Mrs. Maynard paused.

"Oh, this place is really that authentic, is it? By the way, where's the bathroom?"

"You want to take a bath?" Mrs. Maynard set the pan down.

"No, I—I need to—"

"Oh, out back." Hazel pointed toward the door.

It was just a little too authentic, Blossom thought as she returned. Funny, they never mentioned the lack of toilets and other modern conveniences in those wonderful historical romances she read.

It was almost noon and Blossom was helping the old lady set the table as the doctor, accompanied by a handsome young man dressed as a cavalry officer, came in. "Look, Hazel, Captain Radley is joining us for dinner."

"Why, what a delightful surprise," Mrs. Maynard wiped her hands on her apron. "Miss Blossom, may I present Capt. Lexington Radley? Captain, this is the new schoolteacher—"

"I'm not a teacher, I'm a research librarian," Blossom corrected, wondering why his name sounded so familiar.

"But you can teach school, can't you?" Dr. Maynard said.

"Well, I suppose I could, but—"

"Never mind," the handsome, black-haired captain almost purred as he took Blossom's hand. "I know what you are; you're an angel, a goddess."

"Are you for real?" Blossom grew flustered and jerked her hand back.

"I beg your pardon?" The officer blinked, then looked at the doctor. They exchanged significant looks.

Blossom was embarrassed. "I—I'm not used to such compliments."

"And modest, too," the captain smiled. "I like that in a woman."

Blossom felt herself flush all the way to her toes. If she wasn't dreaming she was a character in a romance novel, this was the next best thing. Forget the virile Indian scout, this dashing cavalry officer would do nicely as a hero, thank you.

He looked about the room, ran a nervous finger around his collar. "Mrs. Maynard, if you don't mind . . ."

"Oh, yes," Doc said, "the windows." He went to push them up and a nice breeze stirred Blossom's hair.

The officer seemed to breathe a sigh of relief, then stared at her. "Begging pardon, Miss Blossom, but you've lost one of your earrings; I hope it wasn't valuable."

Blossom's hands flew to her ears. "Oh, yes, I'd forgotten to take this one off after I lost the other one." He'd think she was bonkers if she told him about leaving it on the rim of the picture frame.

Doc shook his head ever so slightly at the captain, and in that awkward moment, Mrs. Maynard intervened. "Land's sake, why don't we all sit down and have dinner?"

The captain pulled out Blossom's chair with a sweeping bow. "Allow me."

"Th-thank you." In all her years in L.A., Blossom had never been treated with such politeness and gallantry.

They sat down and Mrs. Maynard began to serve. The food might be loaded with cholesterol, Blossom thought, but it was delicious and made from scratch. She'd been eating fast food and frozen entrees warmed in the micro so long, she'd almost forgotten how to cook.

"So, Miss," the Captain began as they ate, "what do you think of our little town?"

"Just call me Blossom," Blossom said.

"Oh, I wouldn't presume to be so familiar on such short acquaintance, ma'am," the officer said. "I hope you'll like our town, even though you got off to a bad start."

"I—I don't know, but the people are nice." Blossom knew she was hesitant and fumbling with awkwardness before this handsome man. When she'd thought she was a romance novel heroine, she could be spunky and fiery; now grim reality was settling in. She was a plain little mouse and this man must be with the local tourist bureau or the Chamber of Commerce, trying to make her visit memorable so she'd pay it compliments in her story. "I really haven't seen much of it yet."

"Why, I can certainly remedy that," the captain said. "You know, there's a dance coming up; I'd be delighted if you'd let me escort you."

Blossom licked her dry lips. "I'm sorry, but I hadn't planned to stay—"

"Now, don't make any hasty decisions," the captain said.

"He's right," Doc agreed, "even though you've had a bad experience, my dear, I think you'll like this state. Besides, you need some rest."

"Maybe you're right." She hadn't had any time off since her mother's funeral. She was either stressed out or dreaming; otherwise, why would these people all seem so familiar?

Then it dawned on Blossom. Why of course! The virile Indian, the dashing cavalry officer, the kindly doctor, the sweet old lady; characters like these often played roles in historical romances.

"I'd be pleased to show you around this afternoon, Miss." The handsome captain gave her a charming smile. "And of course, I do want you to attend the dance."

Doc wiped his mustache with his napkin. "Now, Lex, do give the other young men a chance to meet her."

"And risk losing this rare gem? Why, I intend to monopolize all the time she'll give me." He smiled across the table at Blossom and she felt her face flush with pleasure. In L.A., with all those model and actress types around, men seldom seemed to look at her twice.

"I'd love to have you show me around, Captain." Maybe Lex Radley was just charming her for good press coverage, but it would be a pleasant afternoon.

"Good!" the captain said as he pushed his plate back. "I'll call for you in an hour." He stood up. "Now, if you'll all excuse me, I have duties to take care of with the Major away from the fort."

When he stood, Doc got up, too. "I'll walk you to the door."

The two left and Blossom sipped her coffee. *These are the most gung-ho reenactors I've ever met, or they've figured out that a lot of curious tourists will flood in here if* Tattle-tale *does a big enough story.*

"He is handsome," Blossom said.

"Well, so is Terry," the old lady said, as she got up and began to clear the table.

Blossom began to clear plates, thinking about the Indian brave. He was too wild and untamed for her. Shy, little mousey girls didn't end up with Alpha males. That had only been a fantasy, like pretending to be a feisty, fiery heroine. Reality was a little tamer; maybe an afternoon drive around town with a handsome actor who was paid by the chamber of commerce to charm ladies of the media, not realizing she was just a researcher. No doubt, the settlement had changed, too. When she stepped outside next time, she'd probably find cute little stands selling fake plastic arrowheads and cotton candy.

Doc returned to the kitchen, fumbled in his coat for his pipe. "Well," he sighed, "I've got to go down to that camp way out on the creek this afternoon; there's been a bad outbreak of yellow fever. They say there's smallpox among the Indians again."

"Smallpox!" the old lady gasped, her face a mask of horror.

Authentic reenactment was one thing, but this had gone far enough, Blossom thought. "Oh, will you please stop? Smallpox has been wiped off the face of the earth; everyone knows that."

Doc frowned. "If that's your idea of a joke, Miss, it isn't funny. Smallpox is killing millions, including the Indian tribes. As I recall, it or cholera killed Terry's mother."

"Okay, if you're determined to do the whole scenario, but it's hokey. As a research librarian, I can tell you the only smallpox virus in the whole world is in test tubes at the Disease Control Center in Atlanta and in Moscow."

"The what?"

She remembered then that authentic reenactors wouldn't admit to anything that hadn't happened by their time period. "What time period is this?" She remembered the calendar. "June, 1873?"

"Of course." Doc took a puff of his pipe and the sweet scent of tobacco drifted to her nostrils. "We always have trouble with yellow fever in warm weather."

Blossom shrugged, decided she might as well join this game. "Those mosquitoes down by the river are what's spreading it. Walter Reed will figure that out while they're digging the Panama Canal."

"There isn't any canal in Panama," Doc protested.

"Well, not in 1873, of course, but that's what will fuel the discovery about yellow fever."

"You know," Doc tapped his pipe against his teeth thoughtfully, "I've always suspected that mosquitoes are involved somehow."

Blossom smiled. "You're quite an actor, Doc."

"Me?" The old man looked baffled. "You don't make any sense, young lady."

The old woman looked from Blossom to her husband. "William, maybe some fresh air will do her good; a buggy ride and all."

A buggy ride? Oh, the tourist bureau had been working overtime to make her stay quaint and charming.

"Perhaps you're right, Hazel. Better get ready, Miss Blossom, Captain Radley will be here to pick you up."

Maybe there was a story in this. Could a mild-mannered research librarian turn into crack lady reporter Lois Lane?

Smiling, Blossom hurried from the room.

Sure enough, the captain did drive up in a fancy buggy pulled by a bay horse. He came to the door, made a sweeping bow. "Your carriage awaits you, Princess."

Blossom laughed as she lifted her dainty skirts and they went out the door. "The surrey with the fringe on top," she smiled with delight as he helped her into the buggy. "I loved the musical."

"What?"

"You know, *Oklahoma*."

"Oklahoma." He said it as if he didn't quite understand what she was talking about. "Well, I'm not much on poetry or novels except for one author. By any chance, are you a reader of Edgar Allan Poe, Miss Blossom?"

"Frankly, I haven't thought about him since my school years. I used to think he was frightening until I read some Anne Rice and Stephen King."

"Who?"

This authenticity among these reenactors could be tiresome, Blossom thought, but she'd be a good sport about it. "I do like *Sonnets from the Portuguese*."

"Oh, love poetry," the captain smiled a bit smugly, "of course, that's fine for gentle ladies." He picked up the reins, "Giddy-up."

The bay horse stepped out smartly down the muddy street. Strange, Blossom thought as they drove along, she had a sense of déjà vu, almost as if she had been here before. Of course, silly, she chided herself, this place must have been used as a movie set, and you've seen almost every Western ever made. You know, like that tourist place in Arizona called Old Tucson. Blossom loved anything about the West.

The captain was making light, charming conversation, mostly about himself and his ambitions, but occasionally, he was polite enough to ask her about herself. "You say you're a librarian, Miss? Genteel position for a lady."

"I never thought about it that way," she smiled back at him. "I was always fascinated by books."

"A sure sign of superior intelligence," he said with a smug nod, "and I'll wager like myself, from a very fine old family, too."

She hesitated. "I'm all alone in the world now."

"I doubt you will be for long." He looked at her as they drove. "At the community dance, men will be clamoring to fill your dance card."

"Dance cards? My! That is an old-fashioned custom."

"This is an old-fashioned town." He smiled at her.

"You can say that again!" Blossom rolled her eyes.

"What?"

"Never mind." She didn't want him to think she didn't like the settlement. There was something quaint and charming about the Victorian qualities of the place.

"Speaking of the dance, I intend to have every one on your card." He gave her his most charming smile. "That is, if you don't think me too forward." His gallantry was refreshing after having fought her way out of too many parked cars, Blossom thought. She didn't have the time to stay several more days in Pawnee, Oklahoma, but she'd just plan on spending less time on her search of court records in Nebraska. "I'll look forward to the occasion, Captain."

"It will be my pleasure, ma'am."

She sat back and enjoyed the ride around the town. They had certainly gone to a lot of trouble to keep the place authentic; not a car or a telephone pole in sight, much less boom boxes blaring away. She searched the horizon, thinking she hadn't seen even a single plane fly overhead. "Tell me, Captain Radley—"

"Excuse me, Miss, but if you won't think I'm too forward, you might call me by my first name, Lex."

"Lex?"

"Actually, it's Lexington." He snapped the little whip over the horse's back. "I come from old aristocracy." He smiled at her. "I'm sure you do, too."

What would he say if he knew she had been adopted as an abandoned baby and didn't know anything about her past? "I'm an orphan."

"So Miss Priddy wrote us. I understand you're a graduate of her school, and she's a good friend of my mother's."

"Of course." Blossom didn't understand any of this, but maybe she had let her mind wander while he was talking about himself. Her thoughts returned to the big virile Indian.

"That's how our town found you," Lex informed her as they drove along. "Miss Priddy recommended you."

She didn't know any Miss Priddy. Maybe they had confused Blossom with someone else.

"How kind of her," Blossom murmured vaguely. She must change the subject and get back on safe ground. "Tell me, Captain, do you love the army life?"

He chuckled. "To tell you the truth, Miss Blossom, I loathe it, except for the fancy uniform, but frankly, my father was impoverished by the war and that hastened his death. The service seemed like a respectable alternative for a young man of good family."

"Forgive me, I had no idea I was delving into personal matters that were not my business."

"Oh, I realize you were only making pleasant conversation as ladies will." He brightened. "I intend to do well. I'm ambitious and making good connections. Plenty of land out here for the taking, and my mother's family still might help me; they're well known and prominent back East."

His mother's people must not have approved of the father, Blossom thought. At least Captain Radley was certain of his parentage.

Actually, for the first time since she could remember, she had begun to forget her shyness and uncertainty over her unknown past. Maybe it was all a state of mind, maybe she could will herself to be like the heroines she admired, instead of an inept mouse.

If she could dream it, maybe she could do it. That sounded like the name of a self-help book; pychobabble. A lot of hucksters with no credentials were writing books these days. That meant simply a matter of role-playing, Blossom told herself. She could pretend she was actually in that time period and behave like a historical heroine; at least until she left this quaint tourist place and returned to L.A.

Blossom kept her mouth shut and smiled, nodding as the captain talked of his ambitions to buy up a lot of land.

"I intend to found an empire for the future generations of my family," he told her proudly.

"Good for you."

"You're delightful! Not many young ladies behave like ladies any more; they're all into Causes."

Blossom was, too, but she didn't say so. She wasn't gutsy enough to march in protests and carry picket signs, but she had signed a few petitions and donated small sums to those groups she believed in. "I presume you're opposed to that?"

"Of course! Why, what man would want to marry a suffragette?"

"I beg your pardon?"

"Oh, I'm sure a genteel lady like you would never be out trying to influence men over the vote."

"Votes for what?"

"Why, allowing women to vote like those crazy men in Wyoming have done."

"Perish the thought that women might someday have a

voice in anything!" Blossom couldn't keep the sarcasm out of her voice, but the captain was oblivious to it.

"My sentiments exactly! You're a lady after my own heart, Miss Blossom, if I do say so." He looked delighted.

"I—I really am tired, Captain, perhaps you'd like to take me back to the house."

"I've overtaxed your strength." He looked anxious. "I hope you're not about to have an attack of the vapors?"

"The what?"

"Perhaps Doc will have some smelling salts at the house."

What she'd really like was a soda or even a beer, but she only nodded as he turned the buggy around and drove her back to the house where Mrs. Maynard insisted that Blossom go to her room to rest.

Lex drove back to the office, his mind on the strange but attractive girl. He found her both charming and refreshingly intelligent. Lex wanted superior offspring, and Miss Blossom just might be able to pass her qualities on to her sons. More than that, she was obviously a person of refinement and good family; just the kind of wife he was looking for. Actually, he'd also like the girl he married to be wealthy, but sometimes one couldn't have everything. Blossom was definitely in the running for the honor. Lucky girl!

Whistling with satisfaction at the momentous decision he had made, he handed the buggy to a lackey. He'd given orders for a patrol, accompanied by that insolent scout, Terry, to go out and bring in the damaged stage. With any luck, one of these days that Injun would get himself killed. The office deserted in the middle of the afternoon, Lex went into the major's office and sat down behind the major's desk. Yes, this was where Lex belonged; a position of authority. He helped himself to a drink of fine old scotch from the bottom desk drawer, opened the door and the windows wide, settled down in the major's chair, and sighed.

One of the few reasons Lex liked the wide open prairie, besides the possibility of cheap land, was the openness. Few people knew why he feared closed-in places. He felt smothered, unable to breathe if he had to stay in a small space. That made it difficult to sit in an office or even ride a train. Coming out here, he'd spent much of his time out on the rear platform.

Lex wiped sweat from his face and sighed. His nightmares were of being buried alive. Maybe he'd been reading too many Edgar Allan Poe stories. No, that wasn't it, and he knew it. He didn't want to think about the secrets of his childhood.

No, he'd think about the lovely Miss Blossom instead. She had all the right qualities to be Mrs. Lexington Radley. Of course, she was going to be honored when he finally proposed—that is, if Doc could assure him the savages hadn't taken her virginity and that her mind was sound despite her ordeal. As the only heir to an aristocratic family, Lex's worst fear was inferior, crazy descendants.

Blossom hadn't realized how tired she was. She lay down for an afternoon nap and dropped off to sleep, thinking she must get to a fax machine and see what she needed to do about replacing all her lost credit cards. She awakened to a tapping at the door.

"Yes?" Blossom sat up; it was dark in the room. How long had she slept?

"Blossom dear," called Mrs. Maynard. "Terry's back and he's brought your trunk."

Trunk? They'd given him someone else's luggage, she thought, she had one small duffle and a garment bag. "I—I'll be right out."

Quickly, she hopped up, felt along the wall for a light switch. If that handsome Indian actor from the Wild West Show was here, she wanted to comb her hair and put on some lipstick. Damn, where was the light switch anyway? "Kerosene lamps and a path out back are just a little too authentic."

Oh, fudge! She kept forgetting she didn't have any lipstick anyway; everything had been lost with her purse. She tried to brush wisps of hair back and smooth wrinkles out of the borrowed pink dress as she went down the hall.

The big Indian was leaning against the fireplace and he smiled when she came into the room. "There you are. Are you feeling better?"

She nodded, thinking he was taller than Captain Radley and more masculine. Had that really been his image in the painting or was she only imagining it? "Much better, thank you. Did you find my luggage?"

He gestured towards a big, old-fashioned camel-back trunk in the middle of the floor. "Hope everything's there, Miss."

"But this isn't mine," Blossom protested.

"Of course it is," he said. "Look, it has your initials on the lid."

Blossom leaned over, stared at the trunk, and blinked. On the top were the initials: B. M. W.

Seven

Blossom stared at the initials, remembering the many times she had doodled the letters.

War Cry caught her arm. "Are you all right? You look pale."

She looked up into his concerned face, feeling the strength of the man's hand on her arm as she swayed. "I—I'm fine."

There had to be a reasonable explanation for this. Maybe if she could find any ID in the trunk, she could return it to the real owner. That still left her without any clothes. Was she in a dream, losing her sanity or mixed up with a bunch of Looney-tunes on some movie set?

Mrs. Maynard must have seen her confusion. "Terry," she said, "why don't you carry the trunk into her room so she could go through it and see if anything's damaged or missing? Land's sake, child," she smiled a little too brightly, "isn't this nice? Now you'll have something to wear to the community dance with Captain Radley."

War Cry scowled, then shrugged. He let go of Blossom's arm and reached for the big trunk. "All right."

"But it's not mine," Blossom protested, "anyway, you can't lift that, it'll take two men to—"

"Just lead the way." He wasn't smiling as he swung the trunk up on his brawny shoulder.

They didn't speak as they went down the hall. She could almost feel his annoyance as she led the way into her room and wondered what he was so upset about.

"Light the lamp," he said, "so I can see what I'm doing."

"I don't know how and I couldn't find the light switch."

In the darkness, she could sense him sliding his burden to the floor.

"I've got a match," he said.

She heard him strike it; then the light flared as he tinkered with the lamp. The kerosene cast a faint glow across the quaint room as he blew out the match. He looked at her a long moment. "So it's true. I heard Captain West Point took you for a buggy ride."

"Captain what?"

He laughed, but his dark eyes didn't laugh. "That's what we call him; he's quite the tin soldier; very ambitious, too."

His tone annoyed her. "So? There's nothing wrong with that." They were standing so close, she almost seemed to feel the warmth of his big body. "I'm thinking of staying over an extra day or two."

"Because of the captain?" He was looking down at her, not smiling.

"Pardon me, but I'm not sure that's your concern."

"You're right." He sounded angry.

Why should he be? She'd been waiting for him to take some initiative, and he hadn't bothered. Still, she hadn't meant to be rude. "He's invited me to the dance. Will you be going?" She wondered how it would feel for War Cry to take her in his arms, dance with her so close that she could feel him all the way down the length of her body.

"Of course not." The Indian made a dismissing gesture.

"I have every right to accept his invitation."

"Every right," he answered, his voice cold.

"You don't like him, do you?"

"Obviously not as much as you do."

"If you had invited me, I might have gone with you," she blurted.

"Me?" His eyebrows went up. "It would create a stir."

"Why?"

"Why?" He was staring down at her, disbelief in his dark eyes. "Indian scouts don't attend balls."

He must not know how to dance, Blossom thought, and felt ashamed that she had embarrassed him. She hadn't attended all that many dances herself. She'd felt so burdened by her own shy uncertainty. "On the other hand, I might go to bed early, leave town tomorrow morning instead."

He shrugged. "I hardly think you'll be going anywhere for a while."

She started to challenge that, then realized that if the phone lines were down as the old lady had suggested, she might be delayed until they were fixed. "We'll see. Now, if you'll excuse me, I've got things to do."

"Excuse me for wasting the lady's valuable time." His voice dripped sarcasm as he pushed his cap back.

"I'm sorry," Blossom said. "I don't mean to appear ungrateful for everything you've done."

"Don't mention it," he shrugged and strode to the door. "I'm only glad I could find your trunk so you'll have something to wear to dazzle the captain and all the other young blades."

"But this isn't—"

He was gone, almost slamming the door behind him. Now what was eating him? War Cry hated the handsome young officer, that's all, she decided, it didn't have anything to do with her.

Blossom stared at the trunk with curiosity. Maybe there'd be some identification in it, so she could return it to its owner. It wasn't locked. She raised the lid and the scent of dried flower petals drifted to her nose. It was a hauntingly sweet smell, as if the trunk had been closed for a very long time.

In the top tray lay a yellowed piece of parchment with ornate writing: *Blossom May Westfield, graduate of Miss Priddy's Female Academy, 1871.* In the flickering lamplight,

Blossom picked it up and stared at it. Now why did that name sound so familiar?

"Because you share the same first name, silly," she reminded herself. On the other hand, wasn't there sometimes a prissy Boston finishing school in romance stories? Maybe Blossom May was a character in a novel she had read.

Blossom laid the diploma aside and dug into the trunk. It was filled with antique dresses, all faintly smelling of dried flowers. "These things would sell for a fortune at a vintage clothing shop; I'll bet some dealer was shipping these back to her store when the trunk was lost."

Curious, Blossom went through them. The colors and fabrics were wonderful, a whole wardrobe, including the shoes. There was even a marvelous blue silk dress with a bustle and a low-cut-neckline; just the thing to wear to a ball. She knew she shouldn't, but Blossom couldn't resist the urge to try it on. It was a perfect fit.

A chill went up her back. "Now what are the chances that another girl named Blossom would lose a trunk of clothes that were just your size?"

Oh, be realistic, Blossom, the first name's caused the mix-up at the airlines; Miss Blossom Westfield no doubt has your duffle and garment bag and is trying to decide what to do next. Blossom whirled and looked at her image in the dresser mirror. "Oh my god, I look like I stepped right out of *Shane*."

She surveyed herself in the mirror, astounded at how well the dress fit and how good she looked in the blue silk. It brought out the color of her eyes and made her almost pretty. With her hair all done up in curls, she could go to this Frontier Days Ball on the cavalry officer's arm and look as authentic as the rest of them. Maybe it wouldn't be too terrible to borrow the dress. She'd have it cleaned before she returned it to its real owner.

As far as that big Indian scout . . . Blossom sighed with uncertain frustration. She didn't know quite what to make of him. "Oh, fudge! What difference does it make? You've lingered as long as you can spare in this picturesque little town. Tomorrow, maybe you'd better plan to be on your way to Nebraska, or you'll never solve that mystery."

Blossom thought about that little yellowed scrap of newspaper she had found in her mother's things, along with that faded old blue-flowered calico dress. Mother had walked in on her and surprised her, otherwise, Blossom would never have confronted her with the newspaper and asked for the truth. Perhaps Ann Murdock had really told her all she knew. Now Mother was dead, and with few clues, Blossom still wondered why a newborn baby girl had been wrapped in an antique Victorian dress and abandoned on a Nebraska hospital lawn?

Her thoughts returned to her present situation. What a bunch of weirdos! Without any money, ID, or transportation, just how was Blossom to get back to Tulsa? Well, she'd at least attend the dance; after that, she'd figure something out.

Mrs. Maynard knocked at the door. "I've got your bath ready and the curling irons hot, dear, do you have a dress?"

"Come in," Blossom smiled, "as a matter of fact, I do."

"What did you say to Terry?" the old lady asked as she came in. "He looked like a thunderstorm when he went out the front door." She paused, peered at Blossom, and gasped with surprise. "Land's sake, you will be the belle of the ball in that dress! Why, the young men are going to be fighting each other for a chance to dance with you! Here, let me help you take it off. I'll press it while you get ready."

"Why, thank you." Blossom began to unbutton the bodice, but her mind was on the scout. What business was it of his if a handsome cavalry officer wanted to escort Blossom to a dance? "I'm afraid I've lost all my makeup with my purse, and my hair dryer's in my missing luggage."

"Makeup?" The old lady's mouth drew into a thin, disapproving line. "Surely you can't be serious, and as for your hair, I've got a curling iron I'll heat over a lamp chimney."

Blossom took off the dress. "Well, at least there's some fragrance in the trunk."

"A light, ladylike scent, I presume?"

Blossom remembered. The scent seemed so familiar, it was haunting. "Well, yes, it smells like wildflowers; you know, that little blue one that grows on the prairie?"

"Fine," Mrs. Maynard nodded approval as she took the dress. "Now, I've got you some bathwater heating on the stove and there's a tin tub. We'll have you ready to surprise the captain."

Mrs. Maynard was as good as her word. By the time they heard the captain's buggy pulling up to the hitching rail in front of the house, Blossom had surveyed herself in the mirror and sighed with disbelief. "I feel like I just stepped out of one of those old John Wayne stories."

"Who?"

The old lady must be a trifle deaf, Blossom thought. "Never mind, it isn't important." She looked at herself in the full-length mirror. The blue silk dress rustled when she walked, and her breasts swelled creamy and curved over the low-cut bodice. Mrs. Maynard had pulled the lacing of the corset so tight, Blossom felt she could hardly breathe. She touched just a trace of the delicate perfume between her breasts and on her pulse points.

Reluctantly, Blossom took off the one silver earring and put it away in the tray of the big camel-back trunk. In that same trunk, she found lace gloves and dainty pearl jewelry. Mrs. Maynard was a marvel with the curling iron. She had helped wash Blossom's hair until it shone, then did it up in a cascade of curls with blue ribbons entwined in it.

"What shall I do about makeup?"

"Why, land's sake, child, what all respectable women do; pinch your cheeks and suck your lips to bring your color out! Now, let's let the captain get a look at you."

"You and the doctor aren't going?"

Hazel shook her head. "He's got cases over at the infirmary to see about, and besides, my rheumatism is bothering me tonight."

They went out to the parlor, Blossom's dress rustling as she walked.

The two men were talking, but the young officer paused mid-word, his mouth dropping open in surprise as he bowed low. "Miss Blossom, you are truly aptly named! Why, your beauty takes my breath away!"

Doc took his pipe from his mouth. "He's right, young lady, you'll be the envy of every woman at the dance."

"You really think so?" Blossom still wasn't confident. Maybe a mouse can change, she thought.

The captain offered her his arm and escorted her out to the buggy. "Every man in town is going to envy me tonight."

He helped her up into the buggy. His fine hands were clammy cold and soft, not like War Cry's big, calloused hands.

"Your accent tells me you're not from this area, Captain Radley."

"Please, Miss Blossom, I know we're newly acquainted, but I do hope you'll call me Lex." He slapped the horse with the reins and the stylish buggy moved down the street at a brisk clip. "No, I'm not; I'm from back East, but there's lots of opportunities out here, so I intend to stay, take full advantage. I hope to be a big landowner and business leader some day."

"How nice," Blossom said, stifling a yawn as he went on in great detail about his ambitions. She studied the little town as they drove down the street. Perhaps she could write an article for *Tattletale*. No, Vic Lamarto might think an authentic dance at a small Western town was mildly interesting, but it wasn't sensational enough unless an alien, a movie star, or Elvis showed up there. Well, she decided, she'd enjoy herself tonight, and tomorrow she'd get to Tulsa and book another flight out if she had to borrow this buggy to do so. It was incredible that there didn't seem to be even a pickup truck or a farm tractor anywhere in sight.

Captain Radley looked over at her again with admiration. "I do hope you'll save every dance for me, Miss Blossom."

She made a noncommittal sound, wondering if War Cry would show up at the dance after all? She was already imagining herself in his strong arms.

They drove to the fort. Buggies and wagons were tied up and down the street, and the sound of music and laughter drifted through the open windows of the big hall.

The officer got down, tied the horse, then came around to her side. "Allow me, Miss Blossom." He put his hands on her waist, helping her alight, his hands lingering there just a moment longer than he needed to assist her. She hoped his lips were warmer than his hands if he kissed her good night when he took her home.

He was actually flirting with her! There were worse things in life than marrying an ambitious, prominent man and living in a small, sleepy town. She thought about her grim, lonely life in L.A.

He offered his arm with a gallant bow and Blossom took it, lifting the edge of her skirt as they proceeded up the wooden sidewalk so the blue silk wouldn't touch the dust. She remembered the feel of his hands on her waist and thought of War Cry's big, strong hands that had almost completely encircled her waist.

What was that movement in the shadows of those buildings? She turned her head, puzzled, wondering if she was correct in recognizing the big frame of the Pawnee? "Of course not," she said aloud.

"I beg your pardon?"

"Nothing," she smiled at the officer, reminding herself again that perhaps she might consider marrying him and staying in Oklahoma. This reenactment hobby of his was fun, and he apparently had assets or he couldn't afford to spend his summers acting in this Western town for the tourists.

The officer hesitated at the door. "I really don't like crowds," he muttered.

"If you don't want to attend—"

"Oh, Miss Blossom, I wouldn't miss this chance to show you off. I'll just stay near an open window."

He seemed to square his shoulders with grim determination and they went into the hall. It was crowded and too warm, good-natured people pushing through crowds to the dance floor or over to the refreshment table. A small cavalry band played from the stage, loudly but not too well. . . . *Oh, Susannah, oh, don't you cry for me, I come from Alabama with my banjo on my knee . . .*

The floor shook under the moving feet as perspiring, happy couples, soldiers, and settlers intermingled as they danced.

This town must be something like that movie, *City Slickers,* she thought. Tourists and city dudes might come here on vacation and pretend to be a cowboy, frontier settler, or cavalry officer for a week. She looked around.

Captain Radley blinked. "Whatever are you looking for?"

"Saloon girls. Aren't there always supposed to be saloon girls for atmosphere?"

The captain turned three shades of red. He choked and ran a finger around his collar. "How—how did you know about Rusty's girls?"

So there were some. Maybe she could interview several of them before she left town. Now that bit of sensationalism would interest Vic. "Uh, never mind." She began to fan herself with her dainty lace fan, cursing herself for making such a social blunder. Of course in an authentic Western town, the sluts wouldn't be invited to a respectable gathering. She noticed then that the young officer's face was pale and his skin glistening with sweat. "Are you all right, Captain?"

He took out his handkerchief and she noted his hand shook

as he wiped his face. "Closed spaces make me nervous," he admitted.

"Oh, claustrophobia," she patted his arm with sympathy.

"Claustro what?"

"A fear of being closed in," Blossom said. "It's nothing to be ashamed of; I get nervous on elevators."

"Elevators?" He was looking at her in confusion, but already, young officers were gathering around Blossom, waiting for the captain to introduce them. He did so, but he didn't seem too happy about it as they asked her to save a place on her dance card for each of them.

"Why, gentlemen, I'd be delighted!" She smiled and flirted, thinking she had never had such a good time. In fact, she was having such a marvelous time, she still wasn't certain she wasn't dreaming. Dream or reality, she wasn't going to question it.

"Miss Blossom," Lex bowed low after he had introduced the last eager officer, "I would love this waltz with you."

It dawned on her with horror that she wouldn't know any of the old-fashioned dances. "Oh, I'm sorry, I don't know how to waltz."

"I can't believe that!" A dark curl had fallen down on his patrician forehead. "All proper young ladies can waltz. You are much too modest, Miss Blossom, but of course, that is to be admired in a woman."

"Really, I don't know—" She was protesting that she'd only make a fool of herself as he whirled her out onto the floor. Any moment now, she thought in abject terror, she would humiliate and embarrass herself by either tripping on the hem of her blue silk ball gown or stomping on one of his shiny black boots.

Instead, her step followed his expertly and they circled the room, dancing so well that others made way for the couple, nodding with approval and murmuring about what a handsome couple they were.

Blossom was astounded at her sudden and unexplained

skill. The captain was an expert at the waltz, she decided, and she was just lucky that he led well enough to make her look good. They finished to polite applause and all the ladies rushed forward to meet her, cooing and smiling as they clustered around.

"So you're the new schoolmarm, Miss Westfield. How lucky that you were saved."

Blossom nodded or curtsied to each person or couple as she was introduced, deciding that it was too complicated to correct their mistaken assumptions. In the first place, she hadn't quite figured it all out herself and anyway, in this small town, maybe they considered a librarian the same as a teacher.

She had never felt so popular and she came out of her shell even more, charming the handsome young officers in smart blue uniforms who begged to be added to her dance card. Also, several handsome, virile-looking ranchers and townsmen came over to meet her.

Good lord, she thought, I've been looking for love in all the wrong places, just like that song. All the hunks are out in the boonies in Oklahoma!

A tall, rangy farmer brought her a cup of punch. "I'm Joe Murdock," he said, "pleased to make your acquaintance, Miss Westfield; this town sure needs a teacher."

"Murdock? Did you say Joe Murdock?" Blossom looked up at him in a state of shock. The suntanned man looked exactly like her dead foster father.

"Yes, ma'am," he nodded politely again, "ain't been out on the Plains long."

She could only gape at him over her punch cup. No, it couldn't be. "Do you—do you like it out here, Mr. Murdock?"

"I haven't quite decided." Concern shone in his honest, weathered face. "There's a girl in Philadelphia wantin' me to come back there, marry her, and clerk in her daddy's store."

"Oh, but then you wouldn't be the Joe Murdock I remember," Blossom blurted without thinking.

He scratched his head in puzzlement. "Excuse me, Miss Westfield, have we met before?"

How could she explain that she'd thought for a moment that she was meeting her beloved adopted father's great-great-grandfather?

"It's just that you remind me of someone," she said. "I do hope you decide to stay out here instead of going back East. There's bound to be some farm girl who'll love the land as much as you do."

"That's just what I've been thinkin', but everyone else has been tellin' me I should go back and clerk in that store." He smiled with genuine warmth. "Thanks, Miss, you've given me something to think about."

Captain Radley claimed her for a dance just then and waltzed her away from the suntanned farmer. "Ye gods, what did that hick want?"

"Just being polite, that's all," Blossom managed to say, her thoughts in turmoil. Reenactors or crazy dreams? Or had she just changed history so that Joe Murdock's descendants would stay out on the Plains, there to find and rear an abandoned baby girl more than a hundred years from now?

Get real, Blossom, or you'll crack up, she admonished herself as she pushed everything else from her mind.

She wanted the evening to never end, she was having so much fun. Although, a time or two, she did look toward the door, hoping that War Cry might have changed his mind and showed up. Then she remembered some of the reenactors comments about "red-skinned devils" and decided that prejudice was alive and well in the Southwest after all.

The dance ended and Captain Radley escorted her back to the sidelines where she fanned herself with her tiny fan. "My, I am hot! I've worked up quite a—" It dawned on her that an authentic Victorian lady would not say "sweat."

"Glow," she corrected herself and batted her eyelashes at the handsome officer.

"Miss Blossom, would you like some lemonade?"

"I'd rather have a Coke or a cold beer," she began, then hesitated when he raised his eyebrows and stared at her. "I mean, lemonade will be fine."

A stout, older man was pushing through the crowd and paused. "Why, Captain, I haven't met the young lady."

"Oh, of course. Miss Westfield, may I present our local newspaper owner, Mr. Lamarto?"

She let the pleasant newcomer take her hand, too stunned to correct her handsome escort that her last name was not Westfield as the captain departed to get her lemonade. "Did you say Lamarto?"

"Why yes." He had gray hair and an honest smile. "You've heard of me?"

First Joe Murdock and now Vic Lamarto. Was she losing her mind or was this wild coincidence? Lamarto might be a more common name than she realized. "Well, I—I'm not sure."

"I've had a reputation as a crusading journalist for many years," the newcomer said. "I know that's not the way to get rich, but principle comes first with me."

She had been mistaken. Obviously this man wasn't any kin to the sleazy Vic Lamarto she knew. And yet . . . ?

"What is the name of your paper, Mr. Lamarto?"

"The *Tattletale*," he said, "I thought it was appropriate for a crusader; always searching out wrong and corruption, being the conscience of the people, so to speak."

Blossom tried to say something, but no words came. This was just too much similarity. Then a light dawned on Blossom. The L.A. tabloid owner had stolen the name and idea from this older man, who was no doubt a relative. Of course, Vic's reason for calling his scandal sheet *Tattletale* made a mockery of what this small-town crusader had intended.

Evidently this nice man had no idea what his ruthless relative had done. She thought about telling him, decided against it. This honest-looking soul didn't appear to have the kind of money it would take to fight an expensive legal battle. Vic Lamarto had the best lawyers in the business and he needed them; he was often sued for slander or libel.

She made small talk, fanned herself, and accepted the cup of lemonade as the captain returned. It was cold and good. Funny, it had been a long time since she'd enjoyed a simple pleasure like lemonade. Even then, it had come frozen in a can. This actually had bits of pulp floating in it, as if the lemons had been freshly squeezed.

Mr. Lamarto drifted on and Blossom danced with a number of cavalry officers. The evening concluded with a wonderful late night buffet and then the captain drove Blossom home.

He sighed with relief. "The crowds bother me, but I'm glad you had a good time."

"You know," Blossom put her hand on his arm sympathetically, "this is really a severe problem for you. A good professional could help you overcome it."

"I have no problem," he said stiffly. "I'll be fine."

"I'm sure you will be." She had erred in commenting on his claustrophobia, Blossom thought, wondering what had caused it. Some men could not bear to admit to what they saw as a weakness.

The Maynards' house was dark; evidently the old couple had gone to bed. Did she see a movement in the shadows?

No, of course not, it was only the hot June breeze blowing across the rosebushes. She could smell the blooms from here.

The captain came around to help her down, lingered with his hands on her waist. "I know I'm being daring, Miss Blossom, but you are so beautiful, and I can't remember when I've enjoyed a dance so much."

Was he going to kiss her good night? Did she want him to? Of course it would be the perfect end to a marvelous evening and he was so handsome and charming. She turned her face up expectantly.

He hesitated, then kissed her hand. She could feel his fingers, cold, yet sweaty and trembling. "Miss Blossom, I—I do hope you will stay over. If I'm not being too bold, I'd like to see you again."

He thought his words were bold? He must be putting her on, but he looked so serious.

"I'll think about it," Blossom said as they walked up to the door, "however, I must get to Nebraska."

He stood there in the moonlight, looking at her again as if she had lost her mind. "Nebraska?"

She nodded, wondering what ailed the man? Hadn't she told everyone from the beginning that she was traveling? She'd never get the luggage mess solved until she filed a complaint with the airline.

"It's very late," the officer said. "Now, Miss Blossom, you get plenty of rest, you hear? Maybe by tomorrow, everything will be back to normal."

It was too much to hope for, Blossom thought. "I'll do that, Captain. Thanks for a lovely evening. I had no idea Pawnee, Oklahoma could be such fun."

She could see his wide-eyed stare in the moonlight. "Oklahoma? You mean, the Indian Territory?"

"I suppose that's an old-fashioned name for it. And to think I'd never even heard of the town of Pawnee."

"Pawnee?" He laughed suddenly. "Oh, I get it! For a moment, you really had me going. Of course you jest!"

Jest? Had she said something funny?

He smiled as he turned to leave the porch. "This is Fort McPherson, Nebraska, a long way from the Indian Territory!"

Eight

"Are you putting me on?" Blossom asked.

"I beg your pardon? My dear Miss Blossom, I assure you I would never do anything that sounds so vulgar—"

"Never mind." She didn't want to sort through this right now; the implications were awesome. "You must have misunderstood, Captain. I was only making a joke."

"Of course I knew that." He took off his hat and wiped the nervous sweat from his forehead. "Such a delightful sense of humor! Well, good night."

"Good night; lovely time!" Blossom kept the smile pasted on her features until she was inside with the door closed, then she leaned against the wall and shook. Was she losing her mind, or was there some diabolical plot to drive her to it? Why would anyone want to?

She considered the possibilities. Maybe the captain was a certifiable nut, although he seemed normal enough except for his extreme claustrophobia. He was egotistical and too ambitious, perhaps, but many men were. A lot of strange things had happened to her in the last twenty-four hours or so, but of one thing she was certain; she might have found her way out of that ranch house and into the little town of Pawnee, Oklahoma; but there was no way she could have traveled hundreds of miles completely across Kansas and ended up in southwestern Nebraska.

She went into her room and took off the blue silk ball gown. Nothing made sense to her anymore. Either this whole town was nuts or trying to drive her there. Maybe this was like that movie, *Deliverance,* where the local folk were isolated from normal society and a bit weird. She had better get out of here.

She couldn't go in the dead of night; she didn't know how far it was, and she had no transportation.

Stay calm, Blossom, she told herself as she dug out a delicate nightdress from the mysterious trunk; tomorrow, you must insist that someone with a buggy drive you to where you can rent a car or find a working phone.

Must insist. She had never been very good at facing up to and dealing with difficult situations. Again, she thought wistfully of the feisty heroines in novels. What woman wouldn't rather be Scarlett than sweet, pliant Melanie?

The sheer nightdress wrapped around and tied with a ribbon; she tied it loosely in this heat. Blossom walked to the open window, stood looking out at the night. Somewhere faraway, a coyote howled and the sound echoed and reechoed. It was a desolate cry, a lonely wail. Too many times, she had felt just as isolated as that coyote, detached and foreign to the world she lived in.

A breeze came up, carrying the scent of wildflowers, warm as a lover's breath. Her whole adventure might be a little crazy, but in retrospect, she had had the most memorable adventures of her life. Funny, in spite of everything that had happened, she realized she felt as comfortable in this place as she ever had in L.A.

A movement outside the window. Too late, Blossom opened her lips to scream, but a big hand reached out, clapped over her mouth, and she was lifted outside.

"Be silent!" War Cry commanded in a whisper, "You'll wake the Maynards!"

She heaved a sigh of relief, relaxed as her bare toes touched the grass when he stood her on her feet.

He took his hand away cautiously. "Are you all right? I didn't mean to scare you."

She realized suddenly that she was all but naked; the ribbon had come open on the sheer lace. He was staring at her body with his lips slightly parted.

In confusion, she grabbed for the two sides, pulling them around herself. "What do you mean, skulking around this house?"

"I wasn't skulking."

"All right, we might call it spying instead," she accused, "you've been following me ever since I arrived at the dance with the captain."

"I was looking after your safety." His tone was angry.

Now what did he have to be angry about?

"Oh, right!" She looked up at him, wrapping her arms protectively around herself, even though she knew he had already gotten an eyeful. "I ought to go back inside." Still she didn't move.

"Yes, you should, kid." He put his big hands on her small shoulders and she felt the power and tension there. "To be caught out here with me, dressed like that, would destroy your reputation."

How old-fashioned to be worrying about a lady's reputation. She looked up at him, thinking how massive he was, how masculine. He was bare-chested, wearing his usual moccasins, blue cavalry pants, and cap set at a jaunty angle. She was all but naked. Warnings began going off in her head because of the way he was looking at her. In fact, he was so close, she seemed to feel the heat from his brawny body.

Blossom clutched her flimsy nightdress even tighter around her. She was too aware of the size and strength and virility of the man; everything else—what state she was in, whether the whole town was eccentric—nothing seemed very important at this moment. "You're upset that the captain took me to the dance?"

"I didn't say that," he snapped, but his fingers tightened on her shoulders. "He's not the kind of man for you to get mixed up with."

"You—You're arrogant enough to decide what kind of man I should date?"

His fingers pulled her ever so slightly toward him. "I didn't save you so he could have you."

"Oh, fudge! I can't believe what I'm hearing. His behavior was totally respectable."

"I watched him take you in his arms, and I didn't like it."

"You could have danced with me."

"We're not talking about dancing and you know it!" He jerked her so close, her almost bare nipples brushed his hard, naked chest.

Was that ragged gasp of breath she heard his or her own? Then she couldn't reason anymore, because he swept her into his arms, his mouth claiming hers. Blossom struggled just an instant, knowing this was lunacy, that she should not be here. Then she felt the heat and strength of him all the way down the length of their bodies, with her lace nightdress sheer as tissue paper between them.

His lips gradually cajoled hers open, caressing the interior with the tip of his tongue.

Oh god, she had never been kissed like this before! She surrendered all sense of reticence and shyness, threw her arms around his neck, molding herself against him so that her breasts felt crushed against his wide chest.

"Blossom," he whispered feverishly against her lips, "Blossom . . ."

She had never wanted a man like this; her pulse pounded like a war drum in her head, feeling his heart pounding against her nipples. She couldn't stop herself from rubbing against the male hardness of him. At that, he made a gasping sound and held her so tightly, she wasn't sure she could breathe as his lips claimed hers ever more deeply. His tongue caressed hers, and her pulse raced. She wanted him inside her, wanted the taste and the heat of him.

He lifted her off the ground as his arms enveloped her,

so that his maleness pressed against her lower belly like an iron bar. He whispered something, or maybe he was asking permission. No, this kind of man didn't ask, he took what he wanted. Was she out of her mind? What was she doing out here in the darkness with this virile savage? She must go back inside, she must . . .

He pressed her up against the side of the house now, one hand going down to stroke her naked thigh as his lips brushed down the column of her throat, paused in the hollow. Surely he could feel the throbbing of her pulse under his tongue.

She couldn't let this continue, Blossom thought in a daze, it was lunacy to have this stranger about to couple with her standing in the dark of the night outside an old house. She must not. Yet her body ached for him, wanting him. She must stop him, she thought again, and bring some sanity to this craziness. She wasn't a virgin, but Blossom had never wanted a man before; even the one who had taken her in the back seat after the football game. Now she had never wanted anything so badly in her whole life as she wanted War Cry to put his hot, pulsating maleness inside her. "Please," she gasped, "please . . ."

His mouth covered hers before she could say more; he pinned her against the wall with his own body. Through the blue fabric of his cavalry pants, she felt his manhood, insistent and swollen with his own need. In her mind, she already saw herself spread out on the grass in the moonlight, this stallion riding her rhythmically while she clawed his back and bit his mouth. Anything, she thought, anything to still this terrible ache inside me.

Not faraway, a dog barked suddenly and then another took up the chorus. In the distance, she heard galloping horses and men shouting to each other.

He seemed to come to his senses first. "Must be a messenger coming in."

Lord, what had she been thinking? Cold reality washed over her. Another minute and . . .

"I—I've got to go." She was so embarrassed by what had happened, she didn't even look at him as she turned and crawled back through the window, closed and locked it. She got into bed, pulled the sheet over her head, lay there trembling, her breath coming in sobs. Was she sorry the disturbance had come a few moments too soon . . . or too late? Good god, what would happen next?

Captain Lexington B. Radley hadn't looked back at the girl in the blue ball gown as he left the Maynards' porch and got in the buggy. His groin was aching so badly, all he could think of was relief. Well, of course he couldn't use a respectable schoolmarm for his pleasure like a common whore. There were girls who were paid to do that.

Lex turned in the horse and buggy to an orderly, strode down the street to Rusty's Place. Just as he had feared, the bordello was crowded, full of randy men, drinking, playing cards and waiting their turn for the whores. Damn. The sweltering room began to close in on him. Lex paused uncertainly. He wanted a woman now and the place was packed, the piano banging away. He'd have to wait.

With enough whiskey in him, maybe the walls wouldn't close him in like a coffin. Lex ordered a double whiskey and then another, leaning on the bar, turning to smile at Rusty as she elbowed her way through. "Can you hurry the girls up some?"

"You guys make me sick," Rusty snapped over the music and laughter. "You go to those prissy socials, act the perfect gentlemen with the respectable ladies, then come over here and rut on my girls like crazed bulls."

"That's what we pay for." Lex drained his glass and motioned the mustachioed bartender for another with a sweaty, shaking hand. "You can't expect respectable girls to let us use them this way." He gulped his drink and gestured for another.

"Watch it, Captain," Rusty warned. "My girls don't have to put up with drunks; you drink much more and the bouncer will put you outside."

Almost in defiance, he drained the glass. "I wouldn't drink so much if I didn't have to wait so long." He looked her over, undressing her with his eyes. "What about you, Rusty, why don't you take on the extras so we can hurry this up? I'd pay more for you."

Her hand cracked loudly across his cheek as she slapped him. "Get out, you uppity swine, and don't come back!"

He rubbed his stinging face as he swayed. "Ye gods! Rusty—"

"You heard me!" She gestured for the ugly bartender, but Lex was already stumbling toward the exit, making soothing gestures. "Okay, okay, I'm going!"

He found himself outside in the street, weaving slightly as he looked back. At least, he was out in the open. Being in that small, crowded place had felt like all those nightmares of his childhood about being buried alive. That new schoolmarm was right, he needed help. Thinking about her made his groin swell. No, what he needed right now was a woman, any woman, and the only women for sale in this little settlement were Rusty's whores. He cursed himself for his drunken stupidity in insulting her. It was an open secret that her heart belonged to the mysterious private who had won a Medal of Honor, then deserted, never to be heard from again. She never slept with the customers.

A maid came out of the rear door, emptying garbage, started back in.

"Hey there!" he called.

She stopped, turned, and looked at him curiously. She was very young, and definitely not pretty, too narrow between those vacant eyes and she was almost bucktoothed. For the moment, he saw only that she had full breasts and a trim waist. Abruptly, he recognized the half-witted girl. "Myrtle?"

"Yes sir?" She paused. "I ain't supposed to linger; I got work to do."

"Aw, Myrtle, don't rush off." She had a ripe, available body; he didn't need intelligence tonight.

"I got to. Miss Rusty promise me an extra dollar if'fen I stay late tonight."

His groin tightened. "How would you like to make a dollar without all that work?"

"What I got to do, Captain?"

"Not much," he staggered over to take her arm. "I've had a bit too much to drink; help me to the stable to get my buggy."

"Is that all?"

He nodded and gestured. "Isn't far."

She hesitated, looking back toward the bordello with music, laughter, and light spilling through its open windows. "I don't know what Miss Rusty would say—"

"Why, she'd want you to look out for her customers." He was pretty drunk, he thought as he fumbled in his pocket, holding up the silver dollar so that the moonlight gleamed on it.

The vacant eyes widened at the coin. "Reckon it couldn't hurt none."

Lex took her arm and together they made their way the few hundred yards to the community boarding stable. As late as it was, there was no one around. Lex took a deep breath of woman scent and the sweet smell of hay. "Myrtle, you ever had a man?"

"Who, me? No, I'm a good girl; Miss Rusty tell me not to do that."

"Why, as pretty as you are, you could be working in one of her upstairs rooms, making plenty of easy money."

"Me? Pretty?" She giggled, but he could see how pleased and flattered the poor dimwit looked.

"Yes, you! Why, from the first time I saw you, I've been wanting to steal a kiss."

"Oh, Captain, go along with you!"

"No, I mean it!" Lex swayed on his feet. "I want to kiss you one time; you ever been kissed?"

She shook her head, blinking at him in the shadowy moonlight of the barn. "I—I never have been."

"Why, I've been wondering if you would be my sweetheart," Lex coaxed. He was having a hard time focusing his eyes. How old was this scullery maid? Fifteen? Maybe sixteen? She'd have to do tonight. He'd rather have one of Rusty's experienced, pretty whores like Dolly, or better yet, that elegant little schoolmarm, Blossom Westfield, but his need was on him and Myrtle was available.

"I—I don't know . . ."

"Just let me kiss you once," Lex wheedled, "and if you don't like it, I'll give you your dollar and you can leave."

She paused. "Am I really your sweetheart? Sweethearts get married."

He managed to hold back his laughter. When he finally married, the chosen lucky mother of his sons would have class, breeding, and intelligence. The name Radley must not be sullied by inferiors. "Let me kiss you, sweetheart," he murmured thickly. He pulled her to him and kissed her.

Myrtle gasped and returned his kiss too wetly and inexpertly.

Lex pulled her over into the shadows. There was a huge pile of hay in the corner. He slipped his arms around her, his manhood swollen and throbbing with his need. "You know what married people do, Myrtle?"

She grew flustered with embarrassment. "I—I ain't for sure."

"But if you're my sweetheart, you'll want to please me," Lex whispered, and he put his hand on her ample breast.

For a moment, she stiffened and he braced himself to clap

his hand over her mouth if she screamed. Instead, she said, "I—I want to please you, Captain."

"We'll just kiss a little," he cajoled and pulled her down into the hay with him, fumbling with the buttons of her dirty dress. God, what a pair of tits this one had; he didn't have to look at her face.

"I—I don't know if'fen I oughta—"

"But we're sweethearts, remember?" Lex crooned to her as he stroked her breast. "And you want to please me."

He could hear her breathing heavily as he stretched out full-length beside her, bent his head so that he could get his mouth on her nipple.

"Oh, Captain, that feels so good, but I don't know if'fen I oughta—"

He didn't intend to let her up now even if she resisted, but she wasn't resisting, letting him put his hands and mouth all over her breasts.

He was swollen so big with his urgency, he feared he might tear the crotch of his pants. "You know what men and women do when they're married, Myrtle?"

"I—I ain't for sure." She sounded uncertain and afraid. Any minute now, she might change her mind. Lex didn't intend to let her do that.

"If we're going to be married, Myrtle, you need to let me do that to you."

"I—we ain't married yet, Captain."

"Well, now how do I know I might want to marry you, if you don't please me?"

"What—what I got to do?"

"Not much, just lie there." He had her on her back now, pulling roughly at her clothes as he positioned her, unbuttoned his pants.

"Captain, you—you're hurting me. I done changed my mind; let me up."

"Oh, now, you want to please your sweetheart, don't you?

It won't hurt," he lied, "this is what Dolly and those others get paid big money to do for men. You can do it, too."

She whimpered and struggled to get up. "Please, Captain, let me go, I don't want to do this!"

Oh god, he wasn't going to stop now if someone put a gun to his head. Lex ignored her pleas as he fumbled to get inside her. She was young and built small all right, but that would only make it more pleasurable.

"Oh lord," she whimpered, "oh don't, please!"

"Shut up, you stupid little slut!" He put all his power into his thrust, clapping his hand over her mouth to stifle her scream as he broke through her virginity and plunged deep inside her. She was warm and wet enveloping his sword, and he smiled with sensual pleasure as she struggled and sobbed.

Lex ignored that as he rode her, using her ripe young body to sate his lust. Ye gods, she felt good! He pictured Blossom in his mind, pretending the sobbing girl spread under him was the respectable schoolteacher.

As aroused as he was, he made only about three deep long thrusts before he came in a rush, filling the girl with his seed. He lay on her with his full weight, crushing her breasts. She was still sobbing as he sat up, looked down at his body in the moonlight and grunted with satisfaction. "So I was your first man; never had a virgin before."

He wiped her blood off himself on Myrtle's dirty skirt, tossed her the coin. "Now, don't you say anything to anyone."

She only sobbed louder.

"If you do," he said, "I'll tell everyone you're a whore and begged to do it to me. Miz Rusty will be mad at you for disobeying her, and you'll lose your job. You understand?"

She nodded, vacant eyes wide with fright. Lex was abruptly tired, sated, and more than a little drunk. Swaying on his feet, he stumbled back to the fort, leaving the trembling girl sprawled in the hay.

* * *

Blossom lay sleepless, staring at the ceiling, her thoughts a jumble. She had come very close to abandoning herself to passion with a darkly virile Pawnee scout that she seemed powerless to resist. It was as if she belonged in his arms; it felt so right.

Her thoughts returned to all the people she had met tonight. No, that was all too confusing. Her mind went to the elegant cavalry captain. He was eligible, too, and seemed attracted to her, but he must be a bit eccentric, or maybe he had battle stress. It had happened to men who'd been assigned to Desert Storm. Yes, that had to be it. Otherwise, why would he insist they were in Fort McPherson, Nebraska instead of Pawnee, Oklahoma?

She shook her head; no, couldn't be. While she might not be dreaming, it wasn't reasonable that she could have crossed hundreds of miles without realizing it. Like Scarlett, maybe she would think about that tomorrow. Maybe in the daylight, everything would make sense, and she wouldn't have to make any tough decisions.

Besides, wouldn't she recognize Nebraska? No, she had left here as a small child. She smiled as she remembered Daddy with his sunburned neck and his faded overalls. Mama said Daddy surrendered the will to live when he lost the farm. He stopped fighting and the cancer had killed him within weeks.

Only then had Ann Murdock taken her adopted child and left, because the small county hospital had closed for lack of funds, leaving the area desperate for medical help for local residents. Ann had to support herself and her little girl. An R.N. could make a good living in L.A.

Mama. Even now as she thought of her, tears welled up in Blossom's eyes, remembering. Oh, if only she could go back and reshape history; save the farm, deflect that infected needle from stabbing through a nurse's rubber glove. Let's face it, Blossom, she scolded herself, you don't have the guts, the initiative to face things head on and deal with them, take action to make changes. You're a wimp.

Mama always said people deal with things in one of two ways, fight or flight. Mama would fight, but you would run. No, you aren't at all like Ann Murdock. Of course not, Blossom thought, she was adopted. As a child, she had begged again and again to hear the story.

Ann would smile and hug her close. "Again, baby? Why, you know it by heart."

"Tell it anyway," Blossom would insist, hoping even as a child that there might be a clue she had missed. She longed to know about her birth parents, even though she adored the outgoing, pretty dark woman who had raised her. They were so different in looks and temperament. Even as a little girl, she had known she was not as pretty, and she was shy, so shy. Sometimes Ann said Blossom behaved as if she belonged in another time.

"Well," Mama would say with a smile as she launched into the familiar story, "I was just coming off my shift at County General. It was thundering, although it hadn't rained. I went out the side door, heading to the parking lot."

"And in your old car, someone had left a baby!" Blossom crowed with delight.

"That's right." She kissed Blossom's cheek. "Here was this darling newborn baby in the front seat of my car."

"Me! Me!" The child laughed with pleasure.

"Well, yes, but I didn't know that yet. I picked the baby up and realized it was only hours old. The night of August 5th, of course. It cooed and opened its eyes that were as blue as the prairie flower she clutched in her little fist."

"And so you named her Blossom!"

"It was the only clue we had, there was no note. However, I knew that the desperate girl who left you there had loved you very much." She ran her fingers absently through Blossom's plain brown hair. "You see, everyone in the area knew the Murdocks had no children. Maybe she chose me, knowing I would love you, too."

"And you and Daddy adopted me!"

"Yes," she agreed, rocking the child gently, "because the police never found out how you got there."

"It doesn't matter." Blossom hugged her and lapsed into silence. Except for the nightmares about thunder, the shy child lived a very average life. Secretly, she wondered why her real mother had given her up? Perhaps, in spite of what Ann said, her real mother hadn't thought Blossom was worth keeping?

Then Dad had died and she was uprooted. Blossom never fitted into the hustle and bustle of L.A., but she grew up, went to college, living a timid and sheltered life.

Her adopted mother didn't tell her about the punctured glove until Ann was diagnosed with full-blown AIDs. With few friends and unable to face the coming tragedy, Blossom retreated into herself. Ann had weakened quickly, so quickly that Blossom took on almost all the shopping and cleaning, doing everything she could to make life easier for her mother. Ann was calm in facing her death; Blossom was not. There were no other Murdock relatives and when her mother died, Blossom would be alone. Strange, Ann used to say, that Blossom was so shy when the Murdocks had both been so outgoing and courageous. Sometimes, she declared with a laugh, Blossom acted like some little Victorian lady.

It was when Blossom was doing the cleaning, that she discovered the yellowed scrap of newspaper and the old-fashioned blue-flowered calico dress carefully hidden away. What was this anyway? She smoothed it out, glanced at the date; August 6, 1973, and read it silently.

BABY GIRL LEFT TO DIE ON PRAIRIE.
Police confirm that last night, a newborn baby girl was found abandoned in the weeds near the county hospital. Nurse Ann Murdock said she was walking to

*her car when she heard the faint whimper and inves-
tigated, thinking it might be a kitten or puppy. It appeared the baby had lain there since late afternoon.
The rumble of thunder from the rainstorm that threat-
ened all day had evidently blotted out the baby's cries.*

*A doctor confirmed that the baby had been left to
die and would have succumbed soon if Nurse Murdock
had not found her. In its desperation, the tiny girl had
dug her fingers into the sod and grasped a prairie
flower, pulling it up with its frantic clawing. The child
was wrapped in an old-fashioned calico dress with no
laundry marks or store tags.*

*Police are still investigating, but with few clues, they
admit the chances of finding out how the child got
there are slim.*

*In an added tragedy, Mrs. Murdock, who was preg-
nant, slipped and fell while rescuing the baby, suffering
serious injury and a miscarriage of a baby girl. Doc-
tors at County General have grave doubts Mrs. Murdock will ever be able to have another child.*

*On a happier note, Nurse Murdock and her husband,
Joe, say they will attempt to adopt . . .*

The scrap of paper fluttered from Blossom's nerveless fingers. Her adoptive mother had lied to her. She had been left
to die. *Blossom.* Abruptly, the name seemed ironic; a cruel
joke. Worse than that was the guilt she felt that Mama had
lost a baby while rescuing her. Everyone knew Joe and Ann
loved children and had wanted a large family.

Blossom had never known such pain. She was wrenched
by sobs that she couldn't stifle. Mama had run into the room,
saw the crumpled note and the ancient dress. "Oh, Blossom,
I never meant for you to find—"

"You—you lied to me," she sobbed, her heart breaking.

"Look, honey." Mama had grasped her shoulders, but

Blossom pulled away. "We—we never meant to. It's just one of those things that's hard to explain—"

"I guess so!" She threw the things down, dissolved in tears. "I was left to die! Thrown away!"

"Blossom, listen to me! Maybe the girl was desperate! Maybe—"

"Then why didn't she have an abortion?" Blossom got up, went to stare out the window at the passing traffic, her mind as blurred as the rushing cars. "Saving me cost you your own child and all those you might have had!"

Ann was weeping, too. "Maybe, like me, she didn't believe in murdering unborn babies!"

"But she left me out there to die—"

"Or be found," Ann said, "maybe she knew someone would find you if she left you near a hospital."

"Then she should have put me on the hospital doorstep." Blossom refused to be comforted. "And look at this rag she wrapped me in!" She held up the faded long dress. "This looks like it came out of someone's attic or a costume shop!"

Ann took it out of her hands, folded it gently. "Oh Blossom, can't you have a little pity? Can't you just imagine her giving birth in her family's basement or attic, looking frantically through boxes or old trunks to find something to wrap you in?"

"I wasn't wanted," Blossom said.

"You are wanted." Ann came up behind her, put her frail arms around her. "You are one of the lucky ones that I don't have to light a candle for."

Ann Murdock was devoutly religious. She kept candles burning at the altar for babies lost to abortion. Blossom didn't feel lucky. Why hadn't her birth mother wanted her? Blossom made peace with her adopted mother, but from that day until Ann died, she had a terrible feeling of inferiority and guilt, and gradually cut herself off from people, losing herself in her job. When Ann Murdock died, Blossom felt all alone.

Now she became obsessed with finding her birth parents and learning her history. Although the hospital was long gone and most of the people moved away, she had planned this trip to clear up as much of the mystery as she could.

Blossom realized suddenly that she was still lying on the bed in the spare room of Doc Maynard's house, staring into the darkness. She would never know peace of mind until she solved the mystery of what had transpired on the afternoon of that fateful August 5th. It almost seemed to her that there was a plot to thwart her. Blossom decided to take some initiative; do something spunky for a change. She got up and began to dress in the darkness. It might be daring, even dangerous, but she intended to get out of this strange town before daylight, even if she had to steal a horse!

Nine

Blossom put on a plain yellow cotton dress from the trunk, wondering again how women ever worked in these fashions? The fashion wasn't nearly as endearing as it had seemed when she read Western romances. In fact, she had never stopped to think what a hassle it would be to wash and iron the many yards of cotton fabric. Of course, women of the old West would probably feel the same way about panty hose and high heels.

She went out the back window of her room into the darkness, silently cursing the long skirt as it caught on a nearby rosebush. If only she had a pair of jeans and some jogging shoes!

Hadn't she seen a stable nearby? Of course she had; every Western movie set had to have a stable. She crept down back alleys to get there, but the town was asleep and she saw no one. Cautiously, she sneaked in a side door of the stable. Moonlight filtered through cracks in the old building to show stalls of horses munching hay contentedly. The sweet scent of alfalfa brought back fond memories of her childhood and her eyes misted as she remembered her father.

Which horse to take? Blossom was an old-fashioned, honest person, her folks had instilled what Vic Lamarto sneeringly called middle-America values in her. The trouble was, with her purse lost, she had no money to pay for the horse. Then she remembered something from her farm days; many horses, if not ridden too far away from their familiar area, would return home when turned loose.

Yes, Blossom decided as she walked up and down, looking over the horses, when she reached a highway or a truck stop where she could catch a ride to Tulsa, she'd turn the horse loose so it could come back to its stable.

Wow! There was a fine-looking horse! Blossom paused before the stall, staring at the big red and white paint. Then she grinned to herself as she realized it was War Cry's stallion. Wouldn't he be mad if she took it and left him afoot?

Blossom hesitated, thinking this might be more horse than she could handle, then shook her head. Riding a horse was a little like riding a bicycle, it was something you didn't forget. She'd been put up on her dad's favorite, old Ned, when she was a toddler, and she'd been an excellent rider before she was old enough to go to school.

She thought about the stallion's owner and what had happened last night. Blossom's face burned red as she remembered how War Cry had reduced her to a helpless, quivering mass with his caresses and kisses. If they hadn't been interrupted, she would have given herself to him and certainly had regrets this morning. The thought both annoyed and embarrassed her. That randy rascal deserved to have her steal his horse. My! The new, more reckless Blossom was doing things she'd never dared dream of before!

"Whoa, boy, nice old boy," she crooned to the stallion as she reached for a bridle. "Scout; I'll bet your name is Scout. Where's Tonto, *kimo sabe?*"

It snorted, flinging its fine head, then settled down as she patted the animal and led it from the stall. In the moonlight, she saddled the paint. Getting on it was something else in the long dress; no wonder girls of that time period rode sidesaddle. Blossom had to hike her dress up to her thighs to mount. Cautiously, she rode out into the night. The small settlement lay quiet and asleep.

Oh, fudge! Which way to go? Milky clouds now swirled

across the sky, hiding the stars. Good! That added darkness would help hide her, but now she had no way to tell which direction to take. Eenie, meanie, minie, moe. . . . She might as well flip a coin because she didn't have the slightest idea where she was. The main thing was to put a lot of miles between her and the town before daylight. When War Cry found his horse missing, he was going to be mad as hell! He'd come after her and the thought was a little scary. Abruptly, she lost her nerve. She didn't feel like a feisty romance heroine, she felt more like a timid Victorian lady. Well, it was done now. Once she found help, she'd turn Scout loose and let him go home.

She rode for hours, searching the dark horizon for anything that looked like civilization. Boy, she hadn't realized Oklahoma was so unpopulated. As far as the eye could see lay rolling, treeless prairie. Funny, she saw no utility poles or giant electric lines. No lights shown on the horizon, nor did any planes fly overhead in the darkness.

In contrast, the night was peaceful and the air smelled fresh and clean. She had lived in a world of noise and pollution so long, she had forgotten how good the country could be. When she crossed a creek, she hesitated to drink from it, but thirst drove her to forego caution. She had forgotten how satisfying cold, clear water tasted, because it had been so long since she'd drunk any that wasn't heavily chlorinated. Kid, you need to get back to your roots.

Kid. That was what he had called her. War Cry was a swaggering, arrogant male chauvinist, all right. On the other hand, she had felt protected around him, something she had never felt around the civilized male wimps she usually met. Well, he was history. Soon she would cross a highway or find a truck stop. Within hours, she'd probably be back in Tulsa and Vic might wire her an advance. It was probably too much to hope for that the airline might have found her luggage.

She might get a *Tattletale* feature story out of this adventure yet. She could already imagine the headline: *The Town That Time Forgot! Old West Movie Town Still Lost In the Days of Custer!*

She loped the horse across the rolling prairie, knowing that it must not be long until dawn. Finally, she paused and looked around for some sign that would give her a clue as to where she was. Boy, this really was an isolated area; she hadn't seen any hint of civilization, not so much as one farm house. Yet there was something vaguely familiar about the landscape. Now why was that? She might have flown over coming into Tulsa, but she wouldn't have seen much from the air. Maybe this terrain had been used in filming one of those Oklahoma land run movies, or a public television special.

She urged the horse forward again, wondering why she hadn't seen any fences. The guy who owned this ranch must have several thousand acres. Come to think of it, up in the Osage country of northeastern Oklahoma, hadn't she heard there were ranches that big? Probably one of those giant conglomerates like Brewster Farms, Ltd, she thought bitterly. She had always wondered how Brewster had begun its empire.

Without a map or compass, she didn't know what to do except keep riding, hoping she'd cross a major road with some highway information signs. After a while, she did come to another creek and decided to follow it. In dry prairie country like this, you could always find people around water. Sooner or later, she'd stumble onto a farm house or an R.V. park, complete with dozens of motor homes.

Strange, she had expected to find some vestige of civilization within an hour or so of leaving that little settlement, yet hadn't seen so much as a telephone pole. The sky was turning from black to gray, and she realized the sun would be coming up soon. She began to picture War Cry going to the stable, finding his horse gone. It didn't seem like such a funny joke now. That Pawnee thought a lot of this stallion, he'd come looking for her with blood in his eye.

In states like Oklahoma, they probably still took horse and cattle rustling seriously. She didn't think they lynched horse thieves anymore . . . did they? Everyone she'd met in that strange little town acted as if they'd just stepped out of a Clint Eastwood movie.

Was that a movement on the horizon? In the grayness of predawn light, she couldn't tell. Blossom reined in and strained her eyes. The terrain looked brown when it should have been green. She blinked, not trusting her eyes because the ground now appeared to move. The wind, Blossom thought, the wind was blowing across dry prairie grass, causing that movement. Then she took another look. Even as the grayness of the sky lightened, she realized what she was seeing. "Oh, my god! Buffalo! There must be thousands of them!"

No, there was more than that.

"It looks like a scene from *Dances with Wolves,*" she whispered in awe. She watched the herd as it grazed, realized that their dark, shaggy coats made it appear the ground was moving.

Was she still on the Pawnee Bill ranch? They had buffalo, all right, but she didn't think there were this many. Oh, now she remembered, she'd heard there was some kind of natural prairie conservatory over near Pawhuska with several thousand wild buffalo. Did that mean she was traveling east or south? When the sun came up, she'd know. She wished she had a map.

The coming dawn gave her a better look at the big creatures grazing across the prairie. No, there was more than a few thousand here; it looked more like millions. In fact, she couldn't see anything else for miles but an undulating sea of brown fur. "Gosh, I hadn't realized there were that many buffalo left in the whole country!"

Now what? She wasn't about to try to ride through that vast herd, if they panicked and a stampede began, her horse might step in a gopher hole and fall, throwing her under the sharp hooves. Maybe she could skirt the herd and keep going. At least with the sun coming up pink over the horizon, she knew which direction she was riding.

She changed direction and kept up a steady pace. In the distance, she saw a wisp of smoke. In a few more moments, the wind carried a scent to her. "A camp fire. That means people and food."

Whether it was an R.V. park or a bunch of Boy Scouts, she didn't much care; either would do. She urged the big paint into a lope, leaving the herd of buffalo hidden in the valley as she rode toward the camp. In the first light of dawn, she could make out the tiny forms of half a dozen people hunkered around a fire.

"Oh, good, it smells like they're frying bacon and making coffee. Tulsa, here I come!"

Just before dawn, War Cry came awake, lay there listening. What was it that had awakened him? It was almost as if he'd sensed impending danger, but there was no danger here in his own cot. His brawny, tense muscles relaxed and he sighed. He'd had a bad night, with troubled, uneasy dreams of the white girl. He needed a woman bad; that must be what was disturbing his sleep. The lustful Dolly came to mind and he smiled. Maybe he'd do that. But then, he knew he would not. It was all that schoolmarm's fault.

Ever since she had appeared out of nowhere in his camp, taken his hands and seemed to awaken him out of a trance, he couldn't think of anything but her. Funny, he guessed he'd dozed off that night, sitting on that log. He remembered feeling so weary, desolate, and lonely, and then in a flash, she had appeared before him, her hands gripping his.

War Cry sighed. She had such small hands. Even now, he could remember the way her fingers had seemed almost lost in his big ones as they completed a circle. He'd felt so protective of this bewildered stagecoach massacre survivor.

He frowned and twisted restlessly, remembering last night,

the taste of her mouth, the warmth of her breasts pressed against his bare chest. He had never wanted a woman as badly as he had wanted Blossom. Maybe it was only because she was so forbidden to him. The white settlers might lynch him if they'd caught her in his arms, and her reputation would be ruined. It was foolhardy for a respectable white woman to love an Indian. The white girl's love could cost him his life.

Yet none of that had meant as much to him last night as the terrible urge to love her, claim her for his own. If he'd had another five minutes, he would have swept her up and carried her off, thinking of nothing but losing himself in her sweet silkiness.

Remembering made his groin ache so that he couldn't sleep. If he could just get her under him once, he was sure he'd lose interest; after all, she wasn't that much different than any other woman . . . was she? If it was white skin and pale eyes that intrigued him, Dolly or some of Rusty's other girls would—

He cursed silently, knowing none of them could fill this aching need. He ought to get up, but for once, he lay there, picturing Blossom making love to him, offering her breasts up to his mouth, pulling him down on her where he could ride her to pleasurable completion. She had surprised him with her passion. Then he frowned. Maybe it was the handsome captain who had aroused her last night and caused her to forget how prim, proper young ladies were supposed to behave. Today, she would hate him for daring to touch her.

He shook his head. Passion and pleasure didn't seem to be in the nature of any of the respectable white women he'd met. On the other hand, Blossom was a strange girl in a lot of ways. That was what made her so intriguing. He lay there thinking about her, not rushing to get up. The stable boy was feeding the horses this morning, and War Cry didn't have to report in for hours. The captain wouldn't be in his office early because he'd been at the dance so late. War Cry closed his eyes and tried to sleep, attempted to get the girl off his mind. He wasn't having much luck.

Blossom rode at a full gallop toward the little camp fire in the first pale light of dawn. Even from here, she could smell the coffee and bacon cooking. Her mouth watered just thinking about it. It might even be one of those dude ranch breakfast trips for tourists, except that she didn't see any chuck wagon. "Hello the camp!"

Even as she rode in, she had a strange sense of warning. The hair seemed to raise up on the back of her neck, but they'd seen her now.

Men. Four or five of the dirtiest, roughest-looking, long-haired men she had ever seen. *Outlaw bikers,* Blossom thought suddenly, except that she didn't see any bikes. Maybe the motorcycles were hidden over in that little grove of trees. Now they were all looking at her with the expression of pit bulls when a small kitten had just been dropped before them. She was keenly aware that her yellow dress was hiked up so she could straddle the horse and the men were staring at her bare thighs, grinning ever so slightly.

Oh my god, what had she blundered into? She hesitated, looked behind her, wondering if she could wheel the stallion and ride out before . . . too late. The biggest, bearded one grabbed the bridle of her horse.

"Well, hello there, Missy, where you headed? A sweet thang like you shouldn't be out riding alone; no tellin' what might happen if you run onto some bad hombres."

"I—" Her mouth suddenly went so dry, Blossom wasn't sure she could speak. She'd had this exact feeling one time when she got lost and ended up in a tough section of L.A. A passing squad car had saved her that time. Desperately, she looked around, but there wasn't even any street, much less a cop or sheriff in sight. Then she realized there were horses grazing in the background. So they weren't outlaw bikers after all. Then why didn't she feel relief?

The bearded one holding onto her bridle grinned up at her. No, he wasn't smiling, he was only showing his teeth; his eyes didn't smile. He wore tanned leather pants and a dirty red shirt so encrusted with filth that she could smell him from here. "Hey, Missy, cat got your tongue?"

The others laughed and moved closer. Five of them: one toothless one; one wearing yellow satin sleeve garters; another with only one eye; another might have been Spanish. Maybe she could bluff her way out of this.

She forced herself to smile. "I—I smelled the smoke of your fire, but I guess I ought to be moving on." Blossom made as if to turn her horse, but the one holding the bridle didn't let go. "You ought to get down and have some coffee, Missy; it ain't sociable not to eat when it's offered."

"Oh, thank you," she gulped, "but I—I don't really think I want any."

Should she try to fight them off, or submit meekly, hoping they wouldn't murder her when they were through? *Fight or flight?* "I—I think I'd better be going now—"

"Grab her, boys!" the big one shouted.

She had waited too late to make her choice. Blossom slashed out at them with her reins as she urged the horse to bolt, but the big man hung onto her bridle. He cursed as the stallion whirled him up off the ground, but he didn't let go. "You little bitch! You're gonna get what's comin' to you!"

Every woman's nightmare. She struggled in spite of her timid nature, surprising even herself, but the toothless one gripped her trim ankle with his dirty hand, pulling her off the horse. "Hey, Buck, I got her!"

"Hang on to her, Gil! You there, Clint, give him a hand!"

"No!" She was terrified, terrified for her life. "Oh, please don't hurt me!"

"Hurt you, honey?" Buck grinned as he came around, took her out of Gil's hands, put one filthy paw on her breast. "We ain't gonna hurt you, we're just gonna give you a little lovin', ain't that right, boys?"

They nodded, grinning like hungry wolves as they crowded closer, while she sobbed and cringed.

The one-eyed one licked his lips in anticipation. "We don't get much chance at women; even whores don't want nothin' to do with our kind."

Outlaw bikers. She'd heard terrible things about them forcing women into white slavery to pay for drugs, yet she still didn't see any bikes. They didn't look like she expected bikers to look, either, no black leather, tattoos, and hobnail boots.

"Please! Please let me go!" she begged, "my editor will pay the ransom; that's what you want, isn't it, money?"

They all laughed at her pleading as the big one carried her over and dumped her on a dirty blanket. "No, sweet thang, that ain't what we want and you know it! We ain't had us any since the last time we cornered an Injun gal, but then, Injun gals don't count."

The others nodded agreement.

The toothless one grinned and spat tobacco juice. "Even whores won't take on hide hunters."

Hide hunters? Only then did she realize that the dark stains that crusted their filthy clothes were dried blood and they all stank like rotten carrion. She was so shocked and incredulous, she exclaimed, "Buffalo hunters? Those haven't existed in more than a hundred years!"

The men paused, looked at each other.

"She's loco," Buck whispered in awe. "Little sweet thang is loco; no wonder she's managed to ride through Indian country without some war party grabbin' her."

"That's right," the one in yellow sleeve garters agreed. "Injuns won't touch a crazy person; think they're protected by the Great Spirit."

Buck? Clint? Gil? One Eye?

"I know you!" she blurted suddenly with relief. "You're

just the usual standard bad guys in most romance novels. Are you reenactors, too?"

"Yep," Gil nodded, a shadow of fear crossing his ugly face. "She's crazy, all right; don't make no sense."

She heard the sound of a galloping horse and they all turned. I'm saved, she thought, just in the nick of time, someone is going to ride into this nightmare and save me! But the man riding into the camp was another stranger, as dirty and mean-looking as the others.

"Hey, Buck, I been watchin' the herd like you told me; it's startin' to move; hear it?"

The rumbling began like low thunder, rolling across the prairie. Yes, it was that old familiar sound from her nightmares, Blossom thought with relief. Thunder. Her reoccurring nightmares always had an element of thunder, along with that helpless feeling of terror. This must really *be* a nightmare, then. The ground seemed to tremble and shake as thousands of the giant beasts started to run.

"Damn!" Buck cursed. "We got to stay with that herd or we won't get the best hides!"

Clint pushed up his yellow satin sleeve garters. "We got no time for her right now; we can enjoy her later."

"You're right!" Buck snarled. "Tie her up and throw her across a packhorse. Money comes first! When we finish our huntin' this afternoon, then we'll enjoy our little crazy sweet thang!"

War Cry took his time getting over to the captain's office. Sure enough, the young private said the officer hadn't come in yet. "I figure he's asleep or in his room reading one of those Edgar Allan Poe stories he favors. Want me to check?"

War Cry shook his head. If the snotty captain was asleep, he'd give the boy hell for disturbing him. Then Terry would have to explain why he'd wanted to know.

War Cry's mind went to the girl. Could the captain pos-

sibly be out socializing or having breakfast with Blossom
this morning? Damn, of course not, she was a respectable
schoolmarm or librarian, whatever that difference was. He
tried to think about other things as he went about his duties,
then decided he had to know. It was almost noon when he
knocked on Dr. Maynard's door.

The old lady wiped her hands on her apron as she opened
it. "Why, no, Terry, she's not here. Matter of fact, she was
gone when we got up, so we figured Captain Radley had
taken her for a dawn ride." She looked up at the sun. "Land's
sake, I'd think they'd be getting back soon." She peered at
War Cry over the metal rims of her glasses. "Shall I give
her a message?"

"No, no message," he answered gruffly. He didn't want
Blossom to know he cared that much. Was it better to let
her think he'd just been lustful last night and she'd been the
most available female? Right now, he didn't give a damn
what the white girl thought.

Turning, he left the porch and strode across the town
square, thinking his horse needed exercising. If he just happened to run across that pair while he was out riding, he'd
pretend it was a coincidence. Somehow, he didn't trust the
captain around a vulnerable girl; the officer was just a little
too civilized and polite—everything War Cry was not.

He walked through the bright sunlight into the dim coolness of the stable, enjoying the sweet smell of hay, horses,
and leather. The stall was empty.

He got an uneasy feeling staring at that empty stall. War
Cry went looking for the young stable boy. "Where's my
horse?"

The runty white boy had hair the color of old hay. "Horse?
I figured you took him out early."

"You don't know where he is?" His gut began to churn.

"Oh, Jesus, Terry, I'm sorry! I just thought you had gone
on a scout—"

War Cry cursed as he checked out the stall. His horse was

more than a possession, it was a comrade. Who would dare take it, knowing it was his horse? It was more than a loss; it was a deliberate insult.

"Saddle me up a spare; some horse thief's going to get killed today!"

He returned to the captain's office. "He ever come in?"

The boy shook his head. "Just now, I saw him at the mess getting a cup of coffee." He looked at War Cry's troubled face, a question in his eyes. "What's happened? Do you want—?"

"No, forget it. Don't even tell him I was here." War Cry hurried to the stable. Was there any chance the white girl's disappearance had anything to do with his missing horse? Of course not. Why, that demure lady couldn't handle his stallion. It had to be some man.

Within minutes, an angry War Cry was galloping out of the fort. Everyone within a hundred miles knew who owned that stallion; so the thief was either drunk, crazy, or issuing a deliberate challenge. War Cry felt for the assurance of his rifle and knife. He'd accept that challenge. Tonight, that thief's scalp would be hanging on the Pawnee warrior's belt!

Ten

War Cry had ridden all afternoon, following the tracks. Because it had rained a few days ago and the ground was still soft, it wasn't difficult. Besides, his big stallion had distinctive hoofprints.

As he rode, he thought about the girl. She was missing. Could she have been kidnapped? Respectable white girls did not go off alone without chaperons or escorts. There was only one set of tracks, so she couldn't be riding along with whoever had taken his stallion. Puzzled, he reined in the sorrel gelding and studied the prints. They weren't deep, like they would have been if his horse was carrying two people or even carrying one man. Could the girl have stolen his horse?

No, of course not. War Cry took a drink of water from his canteen. The water was warm in the summer heat. He urged the horse on, keeping a keen eye on the ground for telltale sign. He was one of the army's best Pawnee scouts; not much missed his keen eyes. If the girl hadn't been kidnapped, where was she? As small as the settlement was, it seemed impossible that someone hadn't seen her this morning.

That brought him back to one inescapable conclusion; as difficult as it might be to believe, that sweet schoolmarm might have stolen his horse. Damn that prissy chit! He should have kept a better watch on her. Just where did the crazy little thing think she was going? He would be the laughingstock of everyone at the post if they found out about it.

Worse than that, there were Sioux and Cheyenne war parties in this country; he'd seen signs even before he'd found that wrecked stage. If the hostiles captured her, they'd use her for their pleasure before finally either killing her or letting the army ransom her. War Cry didn't want to consider either possibility. As angry as he might be with Blossom, the thought of another man putting his hands on her made him grit his teeth with fury. No, he thought suddenly, all Indians feared a crazy person, they were supposed to be touched by the Great Spirit. They might let her pass right through their country without harm.

Hours passed as he rode through the summer heat. He reined in again and studied the tracks as they turned down a creek. Just where did she think she was going? The area she was heading into was isolated and teeming with hostiles. Ahead of him lay the canyon, a favorite grazing area for the big buffalo herds when they migrated. The Pawnee often hunted there, as did the Sioux and other enemies of War Cry's people.

There might not be good hunting much longer. War Cry reined in, scowling at what he saw littering the ground before him. The stench was overpowering and flies rose up in black swarms. Here and there, a buzzard circled, casting a shadow across him. As far as the eye could see lay slaughtered buffalo.

White hide hunters. He knew it immediately, because the Indians used all the animal. These carcasses had only had the hide stripped off and a few had the tongues cut out. The whites sold the tongues as a delicacy, and the hides were cured and sent back east as fashionable coats or lap robes for cold winter sleigh rides. The rest of the meat was left to rot. No Indian would do that; they respected nature too much.

What a waste. The sight made bile rise up in his throat in angry frustration. Millions of buffalo had been slaughtered the last few years and the carnage was growing. There was growing unemployment back East, he'd heard from people coming by the fort. Jobless white men who had learned to shoot in the Civil War bought themselves a Big Fifty and came out to the prairies to earn good money killing the big, stupid beasts.

He urged his horse forward again, riding through and around the dead buffalo because his stallion's tracks led this way. The thought occurred to him that if that huge herd had started to move while the luckless rider was passing through, he would soon find a small crushed mass which would be all that was left of horse and rider.

He came across a campsite. Cautiously, he dismounted, keeping a keen eye out for danger. The ashes of the fire were cold, so the hunters were gone, probably trailing that herd. His stallion's prints led into this camp. Was it possible that his horse had been taken from the fort by some brazen, foolhardy buffalo hunter? Even as he searched the area, he spied a torn bit of yellow cotton.

His heart seemed to stop as he leaned over and picked it up. It still carried the delicate fragrance of that prairie flower, and in his mind, he saw Blossom's big eyes looking up at him. Oh god. Hide hunters were the scum of the earth, so filthy and mean that even ordinary rustlers and outlaws avoided them. Had the naive girl blundered into their camp? Even whores wouldn't socialize with that scum, so Blossom would be a tasty morsel for them. They wouldn't care if she were crazy; that wouldn't protect her at all. And the whites called the Indians "savages."

He didn't want to picture what the hide hunters might do to her. Forgotten was his anger over her stealing his horse. His stallion was fast enough to outrun the hide men, but judging from the torn-up ground, Blossom hadn't had a chance to try.

God damn. The oath came to his mind and he pulled out his knife, checked the blade for sharpness. The sunlight reflected off the steel blade. If they raped her, they'd never rape another woman.

He took off riding again, cautiously following the trail of slaughtered buffalo. Somewhere up ahead, near the canyon, the sound of a big fifty buffalo gun boomed and echoed, then reechoed through the stillness.

War Cry looked up at the sun turning red as blood, hanging low in the faded blue sky. Soon the slaughter would end for the night and the hunters would camp and eat. After that, they would have time to amuse themselves with the girl, if they had her; that is if they hadn't already killed her and tossed her into the canyon.

No, he shook his head as he rode forward cautiously, they wouldn't kill her, they'd keep her to cook their food and warm their blankets. If they finally did tire of her, a fair-skinned girl with blue eyes would be in demand. Farther south there were still Comancheros, mixed blood renegades, who would pay big money or trade whiskey and guns for a white girl. She would end up as an unwilling whore in some Mexican bordello, or sold to some cutthroat in an isolated area who would pay plenty for a white girl where there were no whorehouses or saloons. The thought of Blossom falling into the hands of Comancheros was even worse than her being a captive of hide hunters.

The shooting ceased echoing in the distance and the fireball sun was now touching the far horizon. If he didn't find the girl soon, she was probably going to be gang raped . . . if she hadn't been already.

Blossom lay tied up on a dirty blanket where she had been all day once the motley crew had followed the herd and set up a new camp. The sun was setting and the hunters were returning, one or two at a time. They looked dirtier than ever and there was fresh blood on their clothes and hands. This had gone on too long to be a bad dream.

Buck grinned at her. "Wal now, I see little sweet thang didn't leave while we was gone; that must mean she likes us, boys."

"Kidnapping is a federal offense," she shouted, "but if you'll let me go, I promise I won't tell."

Buck threw back his head and guffawed. "No, you ain't gonna tell anyone, honey, 'cause you ain't gonna get the chance!"

This could not be happening. Was she losing her mind? Had Doc slipped her some mind-altering drug?

She had to accept that all this was real and figure out a way to escape. "My hands and feet have gone to sleep from being tied up and I need to—well; you know."

Gil spat tobacco juice through toothless gums. "Buck, can we have her now?"

"Gil's right," Clint said. "I ain't been thinkin' a nothin' else all day."

Oh lord, she winced at the thought.

"First things first, boys, I'm so hungry, my belly thinks my throat's done been cut. Let's eat first, then enjoy our little sweet thang for dessert." He combed blood-stained fingers through his beard. "Kin you cook, gal?"

She'd do anything to get out of these ropes. "Sure I can, just give me a chance."

He came over, knelt, untied her and when he did, he ran one dirty paw across her breasts. "Just to give you something to think about." He grinned at her and she stared at tiny bugs crawling in his beard. There was no telling what vermin or diseases he carried.

She sat up and rubbed her wrists. It took a minute for the circulation to come back. "Is there a creek? I'll get some water for coffee."

"No, you don't!" Buck snapped, pausing with a bottle of whiskey halfway to his lips. "One Eye'll get the water, just in case you were thinkin' of gettin' away."

"Now where could I go without a horse?" She nodded

toward War Cry's big paint, securely tied and hobbled nearby. "Besides, I need to—you know."

The men laughed.

"Okay, since you put it that way." Buck took a big drink of whiskey and passed the bottle on as he wiped his filthy beard on his red sleeve. "Then you get some food cookin', you hear?"

She nodded, got the coffeepot, walked through the brush out of sight of the hunters. She was afraid they might have followed her as she relieved herself in the weeds, but it sounded as if they were singing and drinking back there. There wasn't any danger of escaping on this vast prairie. Besides, the hunters said the plains were crawling with Indians and they should know. Would she be any better as a captive of hostiles than being the sex slave of this filthy bunch of rascals? She tried to think of something funny so she wouldn't begin to cry. Oh, Vic, what a front page story this would make for you: *Girl Disappears in Movie Town; Becomes Love Slave to Western Reenactors!!*

No, *Tattletale* would prefer: *Dances With Real Wolves! Sex-Starved Actors Pleasure Themselves With Missing Researcher!!*

If she thought very much about this whole thing, she'd lose her mind. It was just like being caught in a movie or Western romance novel. "Except I don't think Buck and the boys have read the script," she muttered wryly as she filled the coffeepot from the creek and returned to the fire.

They were all in a fine humor, she noted, everyone smoking cigars and passing the bottle of cheap rotgut whiskey, while she cut up pieces of fresh buffalo meat and hung it on sticks over the fire to roast. What to do about bread? She searched around and found some flour, a little iron skillet, and other ingredients. It dawned on her that she knew how to make biscuits. Now how would she know something like that? She never used any but the kind that came in a tube. She must have read the recipe somewhere in all her miscellaneous research. She made the biscuits, put the skillet in the glowing coals to bake.

"Why, honey," One Eye took a drink and nodded with approval, "you got lots more talent than I expected."

The Mexican leered at her and pushed his hat back with bloodstained fingers. "There's only one talent of hers I'm interested in, *amigo;* I can cook for myself!"

"You can do the other for yourself, too," Clint chuckled, "but it ain't half as much fun!"

"Amigo, you'd know that better than I would, *si?"*

The others set up a rowdy chorus of laughter.

Six of them, Blossom thought, not looking at them as she cooked. After they were fed, they would spread her out on that blanket and take turns. Should she submit weakly or fight, knowing it was hopeless? They'd beat her senseless and still rape her. She went about her duties as slowly as possible, hoping against hope that the cavalry might be on her trail. Just at the last possible minute, she'd hear the bugle ring out and John Wayne would come charging over that rise and down into the canyon. Strange, in her mind, her rescuer didn't look like John Wayne. Instead, he was big and dark with broad shoulders and a swaggering gait. War Cry.

Get real, Blossom, she thought, even if he weren't furious with you, you stole his horse and left him afoot. She cooked as slowly as she could, yet as darkness fell over the camp, she knew in her heart she was only postponing the inevitable.

"Hey!" Buck shouted at her, "quit messin' around and get that food done; we's hungry!"

What to do? They had given her only a small knife to cut up meat. Maybe she could hide it and use it later. Even as she thought that, One Eye staggered over and took the knife. "I reckon you're finished with this and I wouldn't want you gettin' any ideas."

Her heart sank. Oh, god, what was she going to do?

"Amigo." The Mexican rolled himself a smoke and looked

toward Buck. "The herd's movin' south; we gonna follow it tomorrow?"

" 'Course we are, right on down across Kansas."

Down across Kansas. Didn't he mean north across Kansas? Kansas was above Oklahoma. Either that, or . . . just where in the hell might she be?

Gil spat and frowned. "You ain't aimin' to hunt below the Arkansas River? You know about the Dead Line."

"Wal, we go where the buffalo goes." Buck lit a cheap stogie.

"Gawd," Clint fingered the yellow sleeve garters, "don't you remember how I come by these?"

"Wal, that poor devil didn't need them no more," Buck shrugged and smoked.

"I won't neither," Clint said, "if the Cheyenne or Comanche do to me what they did to him. It's dangerous enough to be huntin' up here on the plains, we get into the Indian Territory, we can kiss our hair goodbye."

"And your life, too," Buck laughed, "they don't call it the Dead Line for nothin'."

"Sí, amigo," the Mexican grinned, "but we have kept our scalps and hunted among Sioux thick as fleas on a mangy coyote all year. The dinero is worth the risk."

"Aw," Buck snorted and took another drink. "It won't be so much of a risk, the army's helpin' the hunters; Washington knows the country won't never be settled until they get them buffalo off the land so's farmers can plow it up."

"Besides," Gil said, "if we kill off all the buffalo, the Injuns will have to go to reservations and eat government grub; that'll solve that problem."

One Eye shook his head. "You loco? There's millions of buffalo and always will be, we won't ever get them all killed."

"They say Billy Dixon's killed millions all by himself out in the Panhandle the last couple of years," Clint reminded him. "At that rate, they won't last forever."

Blossom kept her head down, turning the meat and watching it sizzle and drip grease in the fire. It smelled delicious. She didn't say anything, not wanting to remind them she was around. They were carrying this reenactor thing too far. Surely they knew that by the turn of the century, there would be only about three thousand buffalo in the whole country out of a herd of fifty million. In fact, in 1874, there'd be a major Indian war over the buffalo slaughter.

"Honey," Buck yelled, "if you ain't got that food cooked by now, we're gonna eat it raw!"

"To hell with the food," the Mexican said, and took another drink. "What I'm wantin' is the sweet *senorita*."

A coyote howled in the distance and the men paused, listening.

Buck muttered, "Reckon that's really a coyote or a damned Sioux war party sneakin' up on us?"

War Cry's big paint stallion looked out at the night and snorted. Blossom watched the horse, wondering what it had scented.

"Gawd, you're plumb right, Buck!" Gil said, looking around. "While we're eatin' and enjoyin' the gal, they could sneak right up on us."

"I got my bite." Buck held up a cartridge that hung around his neck on a rawhide string. "I ain't worried."

Clint made a choking sound. "That's supposed to be a comfort; that I can eat poison rather than die slow at the hands of redskins?"

"Aw, you worry too much!" Buck snarled. "We all know we might have to bite the bullet if savages corner us; it's part of the risk. Just don't get caught out without your bite."

The difference between reenacting and fiction was getting more confusing. "In a story I read once, some buffalo hunters were captured by Indians without their bites and died slow and screaming," she said.

They all stopped talking.

"She really is loco, ain't she?" Gil said.

Buck glared at her and spat tobacco juice. "You a Gypsy fortune-teller? You can't save yourself by scarin' us, gal."

The others looked uneasy.

Blossom began to dish up the meat, beans, and biscuits. Being raped by warrior actors couldn't be any worse than what she could expect at the hands of this filthy pack.

The men all dug in like starving animals, using spoons as shovels, wiping their greasy, bloodstained hands on their clothes. She didn't see how Buck's red shirt could get any filthier than it was now. With a shudder, she wondered how long it had been since it had been washed—if ever. Even Buck himself didn't look like he'd had any soap and water applied to his body in months; no, make that years.

Buck sopped his bread around in the gravy and stuffed it in his mouth. "Tell you what," he said with his mouth full. "Someone's gonna have to stand guard while the rest eat their dessert." He grinned at Blossom.

"Or we make the dessert eat us," Clint laughed, and the others set up a rowdy chorus of agreement.

Blossom shuddered at the images that came to her mind.

"Hey, sweet thang," Buck said as he finished gobbling his food, "ain't you gonna eat? You need to keep up your strength with what we got planned for you."

"I—I'm not hungry." She didn't look at them.

"I got something I can feed her," Gil laughed, "but she'd better not bite, just lick it some."

Buck leered at her. "She's got something I'd like to lick; matter of fact, I wouldn't mind bitin' it a little."

"Buck, you been without a woman too long," Clint said.

"I sure as hell have and that's a fact; but that's about to change. I figure I'll have to get some four times a day to catch up with what I been missin.' "

"*Sí*, me, too," chimed in the Mexican.

"Wal, Pedro, you ain't gonna get none tonight." Buck set down his plate with a satisfied sigh. "Somebody's got to stand guard so's the rest of us can give little sweet thang our undivided attention."

Pedro shook his head, anger contorting his dark features. "No, why I got to be the one, *hombre?*"

"Cause you're the last one to join up with us and besides, you're a greaser. We's white men and we don't want to use a woman a greaser's had his rod in."

Blossom lost her temper. "You're all a bunch of dirty animals; I wouldn't give a nickel for the difference of the lot of you!"

"Wal now, lookie here," Buck grinned. "She's got a little fire to her after all. She's been mild and timid as a ewe lamb up to now."

"Some of us have done that, too," One Eye laughed and took another drink. "What about it, Buck, ain't we all through eatin'?"

Slowly, Blossom looked around the circle. In the firelit glow, their faces shone like hungry wolves against the darkness of the night. "You better not touch me," she sputtered, "kidnapping's a federal offense. My employer'll have the FBI looking for me."

"Whatever the hell that is, they ain't agonna find you in the next hour," Buck said, "and that's all we need—for the first round."

"There's six of us," Clint nodded. "I figure by the time I do it once and watch the rest of you, I'll be ready to go again."

"Me, too," One Eye agreed.

Buck grinned and stood up. "See, sweet thang? I told you you shoulda et; you're gonna be workin' hard all night long!"

She backed toward the brush, knowing it was futile.

Buck yawned. "Now, honey, don't make me chase you out into the brush. You know we're gonna do it; make it easy on yourself and just come lie down on that there blanket."

Clint snapped one of his yellow satin sleeve garters. "Hey, honey, I want to slip one of these up your pretty thigh."

"To hell with that," Pedro said. "I got something else I want to slip up her pretty thigh."

"Not you, Pedro," Buck frowned and gestured toward the hilltop. "I tole you, someone got to stand guard. Now you get your rifle and go up there. We'll call you when it's your turn."

Blossom watched the Mexican grab his gun and walk into the darkness, muttering. The other five now turned their attention back to her. Abruptly she turned and ran into the darkness. Behind her, she heard Buck and the others cursing, crashing through the brush. Maybe she could lure them all out and lose them in the night. Then while they were searching for her, she'd circle around, get the stallion and take off at a gallop—

"Gotcha!" Buck's dirty paw clamped over her shoulder, tearing her yellow dress.

She began to fight and scratch, but he only laughed as he swung her up in his arms, carried her kicking and screaming back toward the camp. "Now, you little hellcat, I'll tame you some!"

She wasn't feisty, she was just a timid little mouse, Blossom thought, her heart pounding with terror as they headed back to the fire.

War Cry crept up the rise on his belly, watching the scene below. Only a few minutes ago, he'd thought his stallion was going to give his presence away when it scented him and nickered a welcome. His gut churned as he saw the pack of drunken beasts pawing the girl. He couldn't shoot from here; he might hit her. Worse yet, he knew if they realized he was attempting to save her, they'd use her as a living shield to escape.

He forced himself not to act on his anger, watching the Mexican come up the rise toward him. So they were sending a lookout. War Cry crept into the shadows of the night, reaching for the knife in his belt as he waited. When the man turned to watch the entertainment below, War Cry reached out and clapped a hand over his mouth. The man was strong and he struggled, but he was no match for the big Indian. The man tried to cry out, but instead he made a gurgling protest through the crimson gush as he struggled vainly to hold his life in his body, then collapsed and died with a soft sigh. With one flick of his wrist, War Cry took his scalp.

How to save the girl? Below him, they were tearing at her clothes while she fought them. With them clustered around her like a pack of coyotes, he couldn't get a clear shot. He might outsmart them and run them off. Quick as a shadow, he ran from rock to rock, firing at their feet and shouting in Lakota, "We want the girl and that horse!"

The men froze in place, looking about in a panic. "Do you hear? Sioux war party! They'll torture us to death!"

War Cry shouted again. "There are fifty of us! Walk away now and you can keep your lives!"

"No," the bearded one shouted back in defiance. "You'll sell her and make plenty gold! Let's palaver!"

"Buck, you crazy?" the one in yellow sleeve garters whined. "Let's get the hell out while they'll let us! Let them have the girl!" Without even waiting for an answer, he turned and ran into the night. The others hesitated only briefly, then there was a mad scramble as they fled into the darkness.

War Cry fired a couple more shots and waited. He could hear them stumbling and falling through the brush as they ran, not even realizing in their terror that if there really was a Sioux war party, they'd be out there waiting to ambush them.

The girl in her torn yellow dress looked about wildly. She'd grabbed up a small knife, clutching it as if to defend herself against the whole Sioux nation. Her brave but pitiful defense touched War Cry's heart. Very slowly, he stood up and started down the rise.

* * *

Blossom heard the sound of someone striding out of the shadows. Her hand shook in terror, but still she held onto her knife and tried to pull her torn dress over her breasts. She wasn't a bit better off as a captive of hostile Sioux than she was with the buffalo hunters, and she intended to do her best to fight them off. Her own desperation surprised her. She hadn't thought she had it in her. "Leave me alone, you hear?" She gestured with her small knife, wishing she knew how to handle the rifles the drunken men had dropped as they ran. "The—the army's on its way to save me!"

"I wouldn't count on that." War Cry stepped out of the shadows. "Will an Indian scout do?"

"War Cry!" He was the most welcome sight in the world. Without even realizing she did so, Blossom dropped her little knife, sobbed with relief, and ran into the shelter of his strong arms.

Eleven

Blossom didn't even care that she was pressing her bare breasts against his brawny chest as she threw her arms around his neck, sobbing with relief. "Oh, I'm so glad to see you! You brought the troops?"

He started as if taken off guard by her embrace, or maybe by the touch of her nipples across his bare skin. "Are you all right?"

"I—I think so," she wept. "I was so scared!"

She was so small and vulnerable in his arms, War Cry thought, like a trembling, delicate songbird. "Shh. It's all right, kid; you're safe now." He held her close, folding her in a protective embrace and stroking her hair. He battled the urge to kiss her forehead, murmur even softer things to her.

She looked up at him in the moonlight, her little face smudged and tear-streaked. "I don't understand; were they escaped criminals or survivalists or what?"

The question bewildered him. Maybe two bad scares in as many days had shaken the fragile girl's mind too much. Yet nothing mattered to him except the way she was clinging to him, looking to him for protection. "They were just buffalo hunters, Blossom; they're mean as snakes."

"Oh!" She glanced toward the rise behind them abruptly, the big blue eyes wide with fear. "There's another one up there on guard! He'll—"

"It's okay, Blossom," War Cry murmured, loath to let her

leave his arms. "I took care of him; no one's going to hurt you."

She relaxed against him, shaking, and let him hold her close. He hadn't realized how fragile and feminine she was until he held her. He felt a sudden, white-hot anger at anyone or anything that would harm her.

"We need to get out of here," he murmured, "just in case they return and . . ." He didn't finish, thinking the shots might have attracted enemy war parties if there were any ranging through the area, scouting out the buffalo herd. A Sioux or Cheyenne war party would consider him quite a prize to torture, and what they would do to Blossom was too horrible to contemplate. As a warrior and scout for the army, he was used to risking unexpected death and pain, but the thought that his enemy might hurt this girl was more than he could bear. "We'd better go. Can you walk?"

"I—I think so." She took a breath and squared her slight shoulders, but when she took a step, she wavered.

He swept her up into his arms, marveling at how light she was. "I'll carry you."

Her arms went around his neck and she looked up at him with those wide blue eyes, her soft lips half-open. He blurted without thinking, "Damn, kid, you're a problem for me."

The big eyes teared up. "I don't mean to be, I'm sorry about the horse—"

She had mistaken his meaning, and she looked so vulnerable, so miserable that without realizing it, he bent his head and kissed her lips. It was a gentle kiss, a reassuring kiss and he knew even as he did it that he was on forbidden ground. She was a back East lady, a high-class white schoolteacher. She wasn't for the likes of him.

Yet his heart wasn't listening to his reason. She was so soft and yielding in his arms, her lips moist and slightly open. She tasted so incredibly sweet and tempting that the kiss deepened. Her arms were warm around his sinewy neck and she murmured softly in her throat. He felt his own pulse quicken, desiring her as he had never wanted a woman. He wanted to protect her and cherish her, possess her completely in a way that he was certain no man ever had.

The pinto horse nickered just then, and War Cry came to his senses, cursing himself for his loss of control, for his foolish dreams. "Kid, we—let's get out of here." He stood her on her feet very gently, then reached out to pat the big paint that nickered a welcome. War Cry stroked the velvet nose. "Hey, boy, glad to see you, too."

Blossom watched the man pat the horse, feeling the guilty flush rise to her face. "I—I stole him."

"Well, I didn't think he let himself out of his stall." He was his old self now, cocky, arrogant.

Was he going to hang her or have her thrown in jail? It occurred to her abruptly that he hadn't come looking to rescue her, he'd come because she'd stolen his favorite horse. "We'd better go."

"Look who's giving orders!" he snorted. "You got us into this in the first place." He pushed the jaunty blue cap to the back of his head. "Why did you run away?"

"I—I don't know." And she didn't. She remembered last night, the torrid love scene under the moon. Her blood still pounded in her ears as she remembered the taste of his lips, the swollen maleness of him pressing against her. Just now, her senses had again been dazzled by the touch and heat of the scout, blocking out everything else.

"Was it because of last night?" He looked down into her eyes, but he didn't move. Perhaps he was remembering, too.

"I don't know what you mean." She could sense the electricity crackling between them and had a sudden feeling that he wanted to take her in his arms again, and yet, his eyes showed caution.

"You're not only a horse thief, you're a liar, too. Okay, I'll admit it; I shouldn't have touched you last night or just now, either. Captain Radley would have me whipped if he knew it."

"Why would he?" The fire between them was too strong, like an overloaded circuit, and she looked away.

"Because I forgot my place; forgot who you are, who I am. At the least, he'd have me thrown in the guard house for my boldness."

She looked up at him, feeling the tension growing, the heat building between them just as it had last night. Despite the situation they were in, she wanted to run into his arms, let him sweep her up against his brawny chest. She had felt so safe there.

He must feel it, too. He turned away, reached to unhobble his horse. "Come on, kid, let's get out of here."

She nodded, started to move toward him, hesitated. There was something dark and bloody hanging from his belt. Blossom stared at it in the moonlight. "What—what is that?"

"What?" He had finished unhobbling the horse, straightened, looking back at her.

"That!" She gestured, although in a growing horror, she was certain she knew what it was.

He looked down at it, made a careless shrug of dismissal. "I told you, I took care of the one up in the rocks."

For a moment, she thought she would be sick. "You—you scalped him?"

"It's something warriors do, kid." He made a palms-up gesture, appealing to her.

She backed away in horror as she noticed his hands in the moonlight. They were stained with blood. "Oh, my god! You—you savage!"

His face darkened and went cold. "I'm a savage, all right, but you'd better be glad I got here in time."

"He's dead?" Blossom gulped in disbelief. "He's really dead! Nobody's acting! What kind of place is this, anyhow? Why, it's full of brutal, crazy criminals!"

"Blossom." He made a soothing gesture. "You've had two bad shocks, but maybe with a little rest—"

"Don't you touch me!" She backed away. "I don't know

what's going on here, but even in L.A. people don't take it for granted that you can kill someone and hang his scalp on your belt!"

"Blossom—"

She had to get out of here and find her way back to the real world. It might be violent there, but at least she could understand it. Out here, there wasn't even a phone where she could dial 911. She turned and began to run.

"Blossom, come back here!"

She hiked up her torn yellow dress and ran, stumbled in a prairie dog hole, fell, got up, and began to run again. Behind her, she heard the sounds of him racing after her. Minutes ago, she had run toward him, now she was fleeing. It was like a nightmare that didn't make any sense.

His legs were longer than hers and he ran faster. Despite her best efforts, she glanced back and saw he was gaining on her. His big hand reached out, caught her arm, whirled her around. "You little fool! Why are you running?"

She struggled to break his grip. "Don't you touch me with those bloody hands! I haven't figured out what's going on, but I'm not going anywhere with you."

"Oh, yes, you are. Whatever you think of me, I can't leave you alone out here on the prairie for some Lakota war party to capture."

She fought him and they struggled, but he was so much stronger than she was.

He pulled her up against him, subduing her by sheer strength. Her torn dress was falling off her shoulders. "Stop it, kid!"

"I'm not a kid!" She screamed it at him in sheer frustration, her half-naked breasts pressed against his bare chest as they fought.

"You sure as hell aren't." He hesitated and then, as if he had lost control of his emotions, he bent his head and kissed her, his big hands digging into her body as he pulled her hard against him, his mouth claiming hers.

For only a moment more, she struggled in his embrace, but she was no match for the virile scout's strength. Last night, he had built a fire he hadn't put out and now it flared anew. Blossom clung to him, trembling at the heat of his sinewy body as he held her close, his lips devouring hers. She couldn't stop herself from opening her mouth ever so slightly. That was the only invitation he needed to push his tongue between her lips, searching the warmth of her mouth while she arched herself against him, keenly aware of the touch of his bare skin against her nipples. If he decided to throw her down on the prairie grass right here and now and take her, she wasn't sure she could stop him . . . or if she wanted to. In her mind, she saw them meshed in a hurried, frenzied mating like two wild things, him riding her with all the power in those lean hard hips, her clawing his back bloody as they meshed and bucked in the moonlight.

Instead, War Cry took a deep, shuddering breath and pulled away from her reluctantly. "Oh, how I'd like to . . . Damn you, kid, you make me crazy. When I touch you, I forget everything, even danger. Those hunters just might come back."

Subdued, she didn't fight him as he swung her up in his arms. He didn't look arrogant now. His dark face was set and drawn as he carried her back to the horse.

A thought crossed her mind and even as it did, she dismissed it. No, it was too unreal. "War Cry, what—what month is it?"

"By white man's count?" He thought a second. "June, I think."

She could hardly dare to think it, much less say it. "And the year?"

He looked at her strangely. "You must have had a bad shock if you don't even know what year it is."

She bit her trembling lip to steady it. "Just tell me."

"Okay," he shrugged. "1873."

"No, I mean, really, all jokes aside."

"1873," he repeated slowly. "What year did you think it was?"

Was he playing a trick on her? Why would he? Blossom shook her head. "I could believe that I've hit my head at the ranch and I'm dreaming, or even that I might be back in L.A. having a regular nightmare. I could even believe I had gone to sleep reading an Indian romance, but what you're suggesting is preposterous."

"Kid, I'm not suggesting anything. Here." He gestured toward the horse. "Let's get out of here and continue this discussion in Doc's office."

"Damn you!" Her hand cut across his face, the slap loud in the silence. "Stop treating me like a nut case!"

Slowly, without changing his expression, he reached up and rubbed his hand across the mark she'd left on his face. "If you were a man, I'd kill you for that."

A chill went up Blossom's back. He was big and powerful enough to carry out that threat. "I'm sorry, it's just all so frustrating and I don't understand." She began to cry. "It can't be 1873."

He was looking at her again as if she were a pitiful idiot. "Just what year do you think it is?"

She shook her head, weeping softly. "I was in the museum, trying to get a photo."

"A what?"

"Never mind." She gestured, thinking she was too weary to make sense of it. "There's a painting and it's you."

"Me?" He touched his chest in surprise.

"At least, I think it's you. I had this wild fantasy of pulling you out of that painting and into my time."

"Which is?" He pushed his cap back and scratched his head.

"1995."

He made a sound of dismay. "No wonder the Lakota didn't kill you, if you told them that."

"Hear me out!" Blossom was weeping now in sheer frustration. "I—I think instead of pulling you out of the painting, you pulled me in. That's how we ended up by that camp fire holding hands, completing a circle."

"Are you telling me you've traveled back in time? How can that be?"

She shook her head. "I—I don't know." Quickly, she told him everything that had happened.

He was staring at her as if he'd seen a ghost.

"Do you believe me?" Blossom said.

He didn't answer; he only stared at her.

"You don't believe me," she sighed.

He shrugged. "Either you are loco, and as such, protected by the Great Spirit, or you have big medicine."

That was enough for her at the moment. "I'm so tired," she admitted, "let's get out of here." Her knees began to buckle.

"Kid, can you ride?"

"I—I'm pretty shaky."

Without a word, he swung himself up on the horse and held out his hand to her. She would always marvel at the way her small hand fitted into his big one so perfectly, she thought as he lifted her, light as a flower petal to sit before him. His arms went around her. It felt comforting somehow just as the virile power of the man against her back and his warm breath against her hair was reassuring. She drew courage from his strength and protection.

Had she gone back in time? It seemed like the only reasonable explanation and yet it wasn't reasonable at all. Maybe War Cry was right, maybe she was crazy.

War Cry turned the stallion and they loped out into the night. In the moonlight, she looked down and saw that her almost bare white breasts rested starkly against his tawny brown arm. She reached down and pulled the torn yellow fabric of the bodice together. "My dress is in shreds, what will everyone think?"

"How much like a lady," he snorted, "to worry most about

what others think! Maybe I can sneak you back without any-one seeing you."

She was acutely aware of the heat of that arm under her breasts, and she was certain he was, too.

"I ought to whip your little bottom for stealing my horse."

"You wouldn't dare!"

"Don't push me, kid," his tone was arrogant. "If you were a man, I'd already have killed you for it!"

"I know, they lynch horse thieves in the old West, don't they?" She was talking to keep from thinking, because noth-ing made any sense and she was afraid of the unknown. The only security she had, the only one she could count on, was a bloody-handed savage who would kill to protect her. She settled deeper into his embrace, wanting the reassurance of his strong arms around her as they loped through the night.

Blossom sighed, liking the feel of his body hard and warm against hers. "I know you think me loco, but there's no other explanation; I've come back in time by taking your hands, completing the circle."

"If you aren't Miss Westfield, then where is she?"

Blossom thought a moment in growing horror. "Oh my god! That's the girl whose memorial I saw in the photo. No wonder there's no date of death; they never found her!"

"Blossom," he said patiently against her ear as they rode, "you are that girl, it makes sense."

"No, it doesn't! I tell you, I'm from more than a hundred years into the future. The Sioux killed that poor thing in the stage massacre; I don't suppose they ever found her body. Her bones are probably still out on the prairie somewhere." She paused and lapsed into silence, feeling sadness for the young woman who had come West on the stagecoach to teach school and find a new life for herself, and had found only terror and death instead. She said a silent prayer for the hap-less victim.

"I do not understand this talk of traveling through time,"

War Cry said. "Perhaps you are making a fool of me in more ways than one."

"I don't know what you're talking about."

"Teasing and flirting with me; offering something I can't have—"

"Why," she turned to look up at him, "I never—!"

"I'm not finished," he snapped. "You know what I'm talking about; a prissy white schoolteacher and an Injun scout. If our pompous Captain Radley even had a hint that I'd dared lay a hand on you, he'd be plotting to get me killed or transferred."

"I'm not a schoolteacher and you've jumped to conclusions just because I was so vulnerable."

"Maybe I did," his voice was grim and cold against her hair, "but I thought I knew women pretty well."

"I'm sure you're very experienced with women."

"I shouldn't have dared to touch you."

Blossom didn't answer, remembering his tongue tasting her mouth, the feel of his hard body down the length of hers, his swollen maleness pressing her belly so insistently. Her nipples went turgid with desire at the memory of how his big calloused hand had cupped her breast. "I'll tell the captain how you rescued me from the hide hunters. He'll probably reward you with a medal."

He cursed under his breath. "Is that why you think I did it? You loco little fool!"

Why was he annoyed? "I figure you came after me because I dared steal your favorite horse."

"That's right." His words were clipped, angry. "There's been nothing but conflict between us from the first."

"You're right—that and an animal attraction." Her pulse quickened as she remembered how she reacted when he touched her.

"You shock me, kid, I don't expect talk like that from a refined girl."

"But you weren't too shocked to be all over me with your kisses."

"I—I shouldn't have done that," he sounded as if he weren't used to apologizing.

She didn't answer, not willing to admit that she hadn't wanted to stop him. She glanced down at her almost naked breast against his dark forearm and wondered how it would feel to have his hot mouth on that nipple? In her mind, she didn't picture the captain making love to her, she pictured War Cry.

They rode in silence a moment.

Blossom admitted, "I—I needed to get out of town."

"Bad enough to ride through swarms of Lakota warriors? You got some hidden past like Rusty, or are you as loco as everyone says you are?"

"Who's Rusty?"

"Never mind. She's not someone a high-class lady will ever meet."

A whore, she thought with a surprising flash of jealousy, and had a sudden mental picture of him meshing with a sensual beauty. "Like most men, you've got double standards, you know that?"

"Kid, I don't know what you're talking about. Now hush, enemy braves might hear your voice carried on the wind and a white girl would draw them like flies."

The thought made her shudder and she settled further back down into his embrace as they rode. In her mind, she saw herself at the mercy of cunning warriors more dangerous than the buffalo hunters.

Finally they stopped under a tree to cool the horse. War Cry slid off and held his arms up to her. "Here, get down and I'll get you some water. The captain might have a patrol out looking for you by now, and you wouldn't want to be found like this."

"You're afraid it would mean trouble for you." She tried to pull her torn dress up, but as she slid off the horse, the tattered fabric fell away and her bare breasts were against his naked chest.

She felt his sharp intake of breath and his eyes were intense with banked passion as he looked down into hers. "Kid, you have meant nothing but trouble since the first time I laid eyes on you."

"So you've said." She stood there looking up at him. "Then why don't you stay away from me?"

"Because, god damn it, I want you!" His hands reached out, grasped her bare breasts; his mouth covered hers.

And her body wanted him, too. The moment his thumbs raked across her nipples, she threw her arms around his neck, clinging to him as his tongue went deep into her mouth. He pulled her against him, hard, his mouth taking over the kiss with all the heat and passion Blossom had ever dreamed a kiss could be. Blossom moaned softly in her throat, pressing her breasts against his hands, aching for his touch. In answer, his thumbs stroked her nipples into two aching points and she leaned into him, wanting even more.

That slight encouragement caused his hands to slide to her waist where his long fingers almost spanned it. He lifted her so that he could reach her breast and fasten his lips on her nipple. The sensation caused her to lose what little reason she had left. Blossom pulled his face down even as she arched her back, offering her breasts to his greedy mouth to ravage for his pleasure. She had never felt so wanton and so wild, never known that her body could hunger for a man like this. She held his dark head between her hands, urging him from one breast to the other until her nipples were swollen into two aching peaks.

Then he kissed between them and his wet, warm lips began to work their way down her belly. He turned her so that she was up against the tree. He had one hand on her breast while the other went to cup her bottom as his lips returned to cover hers, teasing hers to open to him.

She couldn't let this continue, Blossom thought in a daze.

The hand on her hip moved to stroke her thigh, then went to touch her most secret place.

She must stop him, Blossom thought, she must not. . . . His fingers reached inside her, stroking and caressing there so that the silky moisture of her spread down her inner thighs, as her body ached for him, wanting him. She must stop him, she thought again, and bring some sanity to this craziness. Yet his big hand touching and teasing felt so good that she didn't want it to end. She was dizzy with the scent and taste of the virile male. A breeze came up and caressed her nipples, still wet from his mouth.

She wasn't a virgin, but Blossom had never wanted a man before; she had acquiesced to please an insistent date because she had been too shy and unsure of herself to say no. Now she had never wanted anything so badly in her whole life as she wanted him to put his hot, pulsating maleness inside her. "War Cry—" she gasped, "please—"

His mouth covered hers before she could say more and he pinned her against the tree with his own body. Through the blue fabric of his cavalry pants, she felt his manhood, insistent and swollen with his own need. In her mind, she already saw herself spread out on the grass in the moonlight, this stallion riding her rhythmically while she clawed his back and bit his mouth. Anything, she thought, anything to still this terrible ache inside me.

Somewhere in the distance, a coyote howled and the Indian started. "What in the hell am I doing with the captain's woman?"

"I—I'm not the captain's woman." She didn't want it to end while this need still raged white hot in her, while her breasts were still wanting him to suckle them to aching.

"The hell you're not. Do something about your dress." He went over and got the canteen off his horse.

She felt like a wanton slut, a bit embarrassed that she had let her own need make her lose control. She took a ribbon from her hair, used it to tie her bodice closed. He returned, his face set, and handed her the canteen.

"Here, use the edge of your skirt, wipe the smudge off your nose."

"War Cry—"

"Don't!" He made a dismissing gesture, strode over to swing up on the horse. Every line of his muscular body was tense and hostile.

She spilled a little water on the edge of her skirt, wiped her face as best she could, shook her hair back. In the darkness, maybe no one could tell how unkempt she was unless they looked closely.

Oh, fudge, now she had to ride back to the fort with him, how awkward. She handed him the canteen. He took it without looking at her, hung it over the saddle horn, held out his hand. He didn't look at her as he lifted her easily to the saddle before him. God, he was strong; his big swollen manhood pressed against her body. He gave a long, shuddering sigh. "When we get back to the fort, do me a favor and stay away from me."

How could she explain that she wasn't a slut, that she had never had a man effect her this way before? She didn't say anything as he nudged the horse and they started off through the darkness. He was right, they were an unlikely pair. The captain was the kind of man she should marry.

Marry? She needed to return to Tulsa. She had a ticket to Nebraska and a job in L.A. Maybe she was crazy, Blossom thought as she leaned against his massive chest and they galloped through the darkness. The thought had just crossed her mind that she wasn't really sure she wanted to go back!

War Cry's groin was aching with need as they rode. He didn't know whether to be angry with her or himself. It was hell having her sitting before him where he could feel her warmth against him. Without thinking, he bent his head and smelled the sweet scent of her hair. All he could think of was how he behaved like a fool every time she got close to him. Last night, he had kissed her passionately and she had run away. Tonight, despite his vow to stay in control, he had been all over her. If it hadn't been for that coyote howling and bringing War Cry back to his senses, realizing what a vulnerable, lonely place they were in, he would have been between her thighs by now, putting his seed in the deepest part of her, marking her as his own.

But she wasn't his and she never could be. A respectable white girl might flirt with an Indian scout when no one else was looking, she might even be bold enough to let him kiss her, but she was only toying with him. She was smart enough to know the aristocratic captain was a sensible choice for an ambitious teacher.

His hated commander had a very good chance of finally bedding the girl, and the night he married her, War Cry would torture himself while lying sleepless, picturing the two in the throes of passion. At this moment, he could pretend she was his woman, warm now in his arms as they loped back through the moonlight toward the fort. He recalled every detail about the silk of her skin, the wet dew of her femininity, the delicious touch of her thighs, and most of all the taste of her mouth and breasts.

It was lust; that's all it was. If he ever got into her depths once, he'd realize she was just like any other woman; in fact, probably not as enticing and skilled as one of Rusty's girls. Rusty's girls. Yes, that's what he would do, he told himself, when he got back to the settlement, he'd go use up all this heat and passion on Dolly. She always reacted like a bitch in heat, and she'd take away this ache in his groin.

"What are you thinking?" Blossom asked.

"Nothing." Hell, couldn't she tell by the swollen throb against her hips? Before the snotty captain gets you, kid, I'd like to show you pleasure, possess you completely. I didn't save your virginity from the buffalo hunters so the captain could enjoy it.

The more he thought about her virginity being wasted on a guy like Captain Radley, the more annoyed War Cry became. *I was a fool not to take her when she was so grateful out there under that tree tonight. Damn that coyote and damn the captain, too.*

He had his arm around her waist and it took all his control not to move his hand up, cover the swell of her breast with it, but he could imagine its softness. He didn't dare let his hand fall on her thigh. She had been so wet and hot that just thinking about her made his manhood ache. Damn her, too, for being so desirable, making him want her so.

"We're probably not much more than an hour from the fort," he said.

"Good. I imagine the Maynards and Captain Radley will be worried."

"It wasn't the captain who came out looking for you," he reminded her.

"It wasn't his horse I stole," she snapped back.

"That's right," he answered, tight-lipped. War Cry wasn't about to look the fool by saying he would have fought off every hide hunter on the prairie to protect her. He swore under his breath. He had saved her so the captain could marry her.

"What's the matter?"

"Nothing."

Her body went rigid against his. "I told you I was sorry about the horse; I would have sent money to pay for him when I could."

"Forget the damned horse. I'm tired of messing with you, kid. Once we get back, I want you to stay as far away from me as possible."

"That suits me just fine. If someone will help me get back to my own time, you won't ever have to see me again."

"Are you going to keep on with that time thing?"

"I knew it! I knew you didn't believe me." She struggled in his arms. "That's it! Let me off, and I'll walk the rest of the way back."

"Stop that before I take you up on it!" He held her even tighter, torn between the instinct to bury his face in the tangle of her hair, kiss the back of her neck, or turn her across his saddle and give her the spanking she so richly deserved.

"Oh, and I just bet you would; desert me out here to find my way back alone."

He gritted his teeth as they loped through the night, his own emotions warring against each other, wanting both to possess her and to be rid of her. Those touched by the Great Spirit in madness were taboo. When War Cry got back to the fort, he would go spend some time in Dolly's bed; that would take care of his yearning and the captain was welcome to this crazy little wench!

Lex turned in his saddle, looked at his sergeant in the darkness. "Troop ready?"

The sergeant saluted. "Ready, sir."

"Then lead out!" Lex gestured smartly and urged his fine chestnut gelding through the fort gates. It had taken a while for word to finally reach him that the new schoolteacher was missing again. Mrs. Maynard had come to him, worried. War Cry had been asking about her, too, the lady said.

Ye gods! Lex hoped the Sioux hadn't gotten her. Why a dim-brained female would go off riding outside the gates after what she'd just experienced with the stage massacre was beyond him. He wondered if that damned Pawnee scout was out looking for her, too?

Lex led the troop out across the prairie landscape. He didn't like getting so far from the fort at night, but everyone would think he was a yellow-bellied coward if he didn't begin a search. That wouldn't look good on his record. The summer wind was warm across his sweating face. At least, out here on the prairie, Lex didn't have to worry about that closed-in, buried alive feeling. What had Miss Blossom called it? Claustrophobia.

She was smart and well educated, proper qualities for the mother of his children. He would insist that she never lock them in closets or chests to punish them as his mother had done to him.

Behind him, bridles jingled as the troop rode. Where was Terry? Lex didn't like the arrogant redskin, but he had the reputation as the best scout in the whole West, and that was saying something, because everyone knew the Pawnee were the best scouts the army had.

If Lex brought the girl back, he would be a hero and it might mean a promotion. Mama would be impressed.

Lex thought about the new schoolmarm again. Bloodlines and family trees were important in a wife. Lex could always keep a slut like Dolly on the side. That decided, the captain picked up the pace and the troop rode through the moonlight, searching for telltale tracks.

Blossom was both weary, annoyed, and confused as they rode toward the fort. His damned horse; that's all War Cry was worried about. Of course, like all men, he would have taken her body if she'd let him. She tried to think about the captain. If Blossom really was trapped back in 1873, and couldn't return to her own time, what was she going to do? Worse yet, suppose her blundering around back there in the past changed history? She'd seen a movie once about a man who went back in time and accidentally changed the course of time. That could happen, Blossom thought, it was like threads in an Indian rug; one thread woven into another and the slightest change might change the future for the better—or the worse. It was too complicated to even consider. Already, she saw the *Tattletale* headline in her mind: *Nazis and*

Communism Triumph as Time Traveler Changes History. She didn't even want to think about it.

Terry reined in, listening.

Her heart thudded faster. "What is it?"

"Horses. I hear horses. Be quiet." She felt his big body tense as he listened and waited. "That's a relief; it's cavalry."

"How do you know that? Suppose it turns out to be a Sioux war party?"

He urged his horse into a lope. "Sioux war parties don't use jingling bridles and the ponies don't wear iron shoes." He rode forward, hailing the patrol.

In minutes, the captain came riding out of the night. "Terry, have you seen Miss—?"

"I'm all right," Blossom called. "The scout found me after I'd lost my horse; he was bringing me back."

Even in the moonlight, she could see the frown on the officer's aristocratic features as he dismounted. It wasn't proper for her to be riding in the Pawnee scout's embrace, at least, not for a respectable lady.

"Miss Blossom, we've been worried to death about you!" He came over, helped her slide down from the pinto horse, ignoring War Cry almost as if he didn't exist. "Here, we brought an extra horse." He signaled a trooper.

Blossom hesitated and then was annoyed with herself. The officer was a very civilized catch, she reminded herself as she slid off and the captain caught her. The image of those clammy hands on her bare skin on their wedding night made her shudder.

"Are you cold?" Without waiting for a reply, he took off his uniform jacket and put it around her shoulders. Then he helped her up on the spare horse while the others watched silently. War Cry's face was as forbidding as a thunder cloud when the captain put his hands on her waist.

"Well," Blossom said to the officer, "it's reassuring to see government troops when there's Indian sign everywhere."

"You didn't see any hostiles?" He sounded nervous.

"No, but I did run into buffalo hunters; War Cry scared them off."

"Isn't he the brave one, though?" The captain's voice was filled with wry irony.

War Cry scowled. "Will that be all, Captain?"

"Yes, fall in with the others. I'll see you get a commendation for helping Miss Westfield." He gave the scout a half-hearted salute and wheeled his horse back toward the fort.

Blossom rode beside the handsome officer, her thoughts in a jumble. Could she have really traveled back in time? It was too mind-boggling to contemplate. War Cry obviously dismissed her as crazy. Would the captain believe her? And just what would she do and where would she go from here?

Twelve

Captain Radley frowned at the Pawnee scout from the other side of the desk and sipped his second cup of morning coffee. He made it a point not to offer any to the Indian. "Ye gods, what a night! So she went riding on your horse and was captured by buffalo hunters?"

"That's about the size of it."

Damn him, Terry was going out of his way to avoid saying sir. The scout had always had a cocky, arrogant manner that annoyed Lex. "It seems strange to me that a young girl who's just narrowly escaped being killed in a Sioux stagecoach raid would go riding alone, and especially on your half-wild stallion."

The Indian pushed his cavalry cap back and grinned with even, white teeth. "Are you calling Miss Westfield a liar?"

"Yes, no, damn it, I don't know what to believe!" Ye gods, he was sick of dealing with this smug savage! He always had a feeling the scout was laughing at him, and here he was, a West Point graduate! Maybe Mama knew someone in Washington she could speak to. Her family were still rich and influential people, even though his late father had lost his fortune investing in Albert Huntington's factories during the Civil War. Huntington had died under mysterious circumstances and there was some sort of scandal over his investments. Ambitious people like the Radleys had lost everything in the collapse of that empire.

Thank god the major would be returning any day now so

Lex could hand this responsibility back to him. "What—what happened out there on the prairie between you and Miss Westfield last night?"

The scout's eyebrows went up. "I don't have any idea what you mean."

The bastard was lying, Lex thought, he could see it in those mocking eyes. He wouldn't put it past this Injun to try to seduce her. Lex sipped his coffee and wondered how to find out.

"Captain, surely you aren't attempting to smear a lady's reputation? Why, if the gentlemen of this settlement thought you would even suggest that Miss Westfield wasn't every inch a respectable lady—"

"No, of course that's not what I meant," Lex clenched his teeth, knowing the settlers could be very rough indeed. An unpopular officer could be ambushed on a lonely trail or exiled to some post worse than this one. He wished devoutly that he could get this scout killed or transferred. Terry was a constant thorn in his side.

"Are you not feeling well, Captain?" The scout grinned. "You look like you've been drug through a brush heap backwards, as the locals would say."

"Damnit, I feel rotten! I was out half the night with that patrol, hunting for Miss Westfield. Where is she this morning?"

Terry shrugged wide shoulders. "Now, why would an Injun scout know that? I imagine after yesterday's adventure, she's still in bed asleep."

The private stuck his head in the door. "Important news on the wire, sir."

"What is it?" Lex growled, "can't you see I'm busy—?"

"Word some Sioux might have been seen West of here, not for sure, though."

"Thank you, Wilson." Lex ran his finger around his collar. Even with the windows open, he felt as if he were sitting in a small box. Last night, he had had another nightmare about being buried alive in a glass coffin. In it, he was screaming for help, but no one answered his frantic cry; they just stared at him as if they didn't hear him. He must stop reading those Edgar Allan Poe stories.

"Captain," the scout said, "are you all right? Your face is pale."

"You overstep yourself," Lex snapped. "I'm fine, except for losing sleep out combing the prairie for you and Miss Westfield."

Damn, he had to get this scout out of the way before he interfered with Lex's plans for Blossom. With any luck, a Sioux arrow would get Terry.

"Terry, I want you to go on a scouting detail for me this morning. Take enough provisions for at least a week."

"For what purpose?" Terry's eyebrows went up.

"Damnit, may I remind you I'm your commanding officer? I ask the questions here!"

"You are the officer in charge," Terry said, "while the commander is away from the fort." His tone made it clear he'd welcome the major back.

"There's plenty of reason to scout the area," the captain said. "I don't want any more stages waylaid and surprised. Now, if you're afraid to face the Sioux—"

"Easy, Captain." The Pawnee's eyes darkened with anger. "Not many men would say that to me; I've risked my life many times for this cavalry."

"The way you were hesitating," the captain blustered, "I thought maybe after finding those passengers tortured to death, you didn't want to ride against the Sioux anymore."

"The Sioux are my enemies," Terry snapped, anger etched on his rugged features. "I'd like to see them all dead."

"Good!" Lex smiled and stood up. "Then you'll scout the terrain and let me know whether there's any big war parties roaming our area."

The Pawnee gave him a halfhearted salute. "If you say so. What about Blossom?"

"Blossom? You, a lowly scout, have the nerve to call Miss Westfield by her first name?" He was outraged.

"I have a hard time thinking of her as anything but a naive kid who needs someone to look after her."

"I believe Dr. and Mrs. Maynard and myself are perfectly capable of looking after the young lady's welfare. You needn't trouble yourself."

He saw the anger flare in the big man's dark eyes, and for a split second, he thought the scout might reach across the desk and grab him by the shirt front. Then the Pawnee seemed to rethink the situation. "You're probably right. I'll get ready to ride."

"Good. Dismissed!" Lex gave him a salute, watched him saunter out of the office. Damn the man, even his walk was arrogant! What could one expect from an Injun? It was unthinkable that any respectable white girl might be attracted to a savage. However, as the scout himself had just pointed out, she was terribly young and naive. That suited Lex just fine.

What was it Miss Blossom had told him lately? That fellow, Colt, would soon be awarded a big army contract for his new .45 revolver. Anyone who invested money was sure to get rich when the contract went through. Could she possibly know what she was talking about?

A chill went up his back. His mother consulted fortune-tellers all the time; his Irish grandmother believed in the Little People. More outlandish things had happened. He reached for a pad and pencil, scribbled a few lines, went to the door. "Wilson, are the telegraph wires back up?"

The skinny young private nodded. "Yes sir. Word along the wire says the Sioux have cleared out, gone back north."

"Good! Here, I want you to send this wire to my business manager." He handed it to the private and watched the boy leave. Lex was risking much of what he had left on this hunch, but there was something unusual about Miss Blossom. A girl who could read the future! Ye gods, he could make a lot of money if it were true! The major would be back any day now. Somehow, Lex was going to get himself a furlough, convince Miss Blossom Westfield that she should marry him, and maybe take her back East to visit his mother. Lex wouldn't marry any girl his mother didn't approve of.

In the meantime, the damned Pawnee scout would be out on a wild-goose chase where he couldn't interfere with Lex's plans. Smiling with satisfaction, Lex decided he would take Miss Westfield out for a buggy ride this afternoon. In the meantime, he wondered if Dolly would give him a quick one? Not this early in the morning, he thought with annoyance. Well, he'd visit Dolly later. The maid, Myrtle, crossed his mind and he shrugged. He'd been drunk or he wouldn't have used that homely, half-witted wench to sate his lust. Myrtle ought to be flattered he'd done her the honor. She'd be too cowed and stupid to tell anyone what had happened in the barn. Humming happily to himself, Lex headed for the barber shop to get himself shaved and ready to woo Miss Westfield.

Blossom was surprised how late it was when she awakened. The morning sun was high in the sky. Last night's happenings came back to her and she ran to the window and stared out. Yes, she was still in the settlement; it wasn't a dream or a reenactment village. She was actually in the year 1873. A million questions came to her mind.

Even as she looked out at the bustling scene, she saw the big Pawnee Indian on his paint stallion riding out of the fort. She almost raised the window and shouted at him, then remembered she was in her nightgown and anyway, proper Victorian ladies did not yell out the window at anyone. He could have at least said goodbye before he left. She felt her face flush as she remembered last night. His hands and mouth had been all over her and she'd come close to letting him complete the act. He was probably laughing at what a push-over she had been.

Blossom was both angry and humiliated as she dressed and went in to join Mrs. Maynard for coffee.

"I'm sorry I slept in," she apologized, "I really meant to get up and help with the housework."

"No need, my dear." Hazel wiped her hands on her apron. "There's a little half-witted girl, Myrtle, who cleans for me when she's not working elsewhere."

Blossom sat down at the table, and accepted a cup of the strong hot brew. "I—I saw War Cry riding out."

Mrs. Maynard frowned. "My dear, I hesitate to say any-thing, because I really like Terry, but . . ."

"But what?"

"Well," the gray-haired matron hesitated again, "I'm afraid many of the locals would frown on your friendship with that brave."

"Isn't that sort of Victorian thinking?"

"Certainly." The old woman appeared baffled. "Anything the British royalty does is newsworthy."

"Some things never change," Blossom murmured.

"What?"

"Nothing. I said the more things change, the more they stay the same."

"Oh," Mrs. Maynard looked puzzled. "By the way, Captain Radley sent word he'd like to take you for a buggy ride this afternoon."

Blossom sipped her coffee. "I suppose that wouldn't raise eyebrows like riding with the scout would?"

"Land's sake! Of course not." She peered at Blossom over the tops of her wire-rimmed spectacles.

"I might as well," Blossom shrugged.

"He's quite eligible and from a fine, back East family."

And dull as dishwater, Blossom thought, but she said noth-ing. What would this old lady say if Blossom told her she was from the future? Blossom couldn't think of any way to make people believe her. More than that, she didn't know if she was here forever, or might be returned suddenly to her own time, or even if she'd be given a choice.

In the meantime, Mrs. Maynard was right; Blossom was asking for trouble and turmoil by getting mixed up with that virile Indian scout. She had never been one to take risks, do daring things. Maybe that was the reason she envied the feisty romance heroines so much. "Tell the captain I'll be delighted to let him take me for a buggy ride."

The captain called for her that afternoon and offered to show her the settlement and the area surrounding the fort. "It wouldn't do to get too far out," he cautioned as he helped her into the buggy. "One never knows when a Sioux war party will venture close."

"I imagine the poor devils are hungry," Blossom said, "with the buffalo being killed off. When barbed wire gets patented next year, the farmers will soon be farming all that land the buffalo used to roam."

"Barbed wire?" He looked at her as he slapped the horse with the reins.

"Someone could make a fortune investing in it," Blossom said absently, "before people realize how it will change the West; there hasn't been a practical way to fence big tracts of land up to now."

"Hmm, I'll remember that." He looked at her, curiosity in his hazel eyes. "By the way, Miss Westfield, I took your advice and invested in that Colt gun deal; I hope you're right."

"Thanks for the vote of confidence," Blossom nodded, annoyed as she thought of the Pawnee scout who thought she was loco. "It's nice that there's someone around here who doesn't have a closed mind; it's been very frustrating."

He smiled at her. "Why, maybe we're a lot alike."

She warmed to him in spite of her earlier misgivings. "Are you following the stock market, Captain?"

"I'm trying," he confessed, "my father's family was hard

hit in the war because they invested in the Huntington Uniform Factory—"

"Oh, I could have warned you that Albert Huntington was going to be murdered. Anyway, he was embezzling funds to spend on women and gambling."

His mouth fell open. "How on earth do you know that?"

Blossom shrugged. "It was in one of—" She hesitated. Oh, fudge! Maybe she had imagined it from a romance novel. If she told him that, he'd laugh. "I—I'm not sure."

"Miss Westfield." He leaned toward her eagerly as they drove along. "You seem to have an uncanny knack for seeing the future."

She started to tell him she was *from* the future, decided he would think her insane. "It—it's just a gift I seem to have."

"Ahh! Second sight! I can understand that. As much as I hate to admit it, I have an Irish grandmother and she believes in the Little People and magic."

"Well, we can't all be aristocrats," Blossom said wryly.

"I knew you'd be understanding, it's quite a humiliation and I don't tell many people; the Irish being what they are."

"I know you won't believe this, Captain, but there will come a time when people aren't prejudiced against the Irish. An Irish Catholic will even be elected president of the United States."

He laughed. "I'm willing to believe that sometimes you might be able to know the future, but I'm not a complete fool. I imagine our chances of electing some Mick are about the same as sending someone to the moon."

She managed to keep her mouth shut on that one. If she told him too much too soon, he wouldn't believe anything she said. In the meantime, she must remember to act like a Victorian lady. She had always thought of herself as timid, but by comparison to the women of this period, she must seem quite bold.

"I don't suppose you get these premonitions about the future very often?" The captain glanced sideways at her.

If she gave him a few accurate predictions, he might finally be prepared to believe she was a time traveler. Until then, she didn't want to end up in an asylum. "Captain, if you've got any investments with Jay Gould, the railroad baron, get them out fast."

"But he's doing so well!" the officer protested.

"In September," Blossom warned, "there's going to be a big scandal around the Credit Mobilier Company, and he'll go broke. Worse yet, it will start a financial panic that will cost many people everything!"

He looked doubtful. "Are you sure about that, Miss Westfield? Gould is a very successful man. I don't think—"

"I'm certain," she said confidently, "and oh, by the way, next year there will be a terrible plague of grasshoppers across the plains. They'll wipe out miles of wheat and corn and many farmers will go bankrupt."

The captain's eyes shone. "So anyone with a little money could pick up farms cheap?"

"I suppose so. I didn't know you were interested in farming, Captain."

"I'm not, but my mother's family still has some wealth left; they might be interested in good land deals." The officer gave her a charming smile. "I think you are one of the prettiest and smartest girls I've ever met."

"Really?" Blossom smiled and couldn't help but feel flattered. Perhaps she had misjudged him. An unsettling thought crossed Blossom's mind. By going back to the past, might she accidentally change the future? Would some tiny thing she said or some action she took change the whole course of future history? After all, she knew that Custer would be killed at the Little Big Horn only three years from now and that President Garfield would be assassinated in 1881. Could she, in good conscience, sit by and not warn the country and the country's leaders about events that would kill millions and create terrible injustice? The thought was so mind-boggling that it took her breath away.

". . . And you'd really like my mother and sisters," the captain said.

"What?" She had been lost in her own thoughts while he prattled on.

"I was saying I would love for you to meet my family, they'd be so interested in hearing your predictions. Mother always has the Gypsy at the tearoom read the tea leaves for her."

"You think I'm a fortune-teller?"

"Why, of course." He blinked at her as they drove along. "Isn't that what you've been telling me?"

Blossom sighed and didn't answer. Like everyone else, he wanted a simple explanation like fortune-tellers and crystal balls. There were a lot of things that would happen in the next few years that Blossom might warn the nation's leaders about. Did she have a moral obligation? Did she have the nerve? They'd all think her crazy, probably lock her up. No, like everyone else in the 1990's, she'd gotten into the habit of not getting involved. Besides, who would believe her?

". . . You'll think me forward, Miss Westfield, but I'd like to see you more often."

Forward? He would never believe that in her time period, couples often ended up in bed after one date. Of course, they didn't have dates in 1873. She studied the passing landscape. "I'm sure we'll see each other around the fort; at least, as long as I'm here."

"Oh?" He flicked the horse with the whip and stared at Blossom. "I'd hope you'd be staying; the children need a teacher so badly when school starts again."

With her knowledge of the future, she could make a big difference, Blossom thought, and she did love children. "Perhaps you're right."

"That is, after all, the reason you came out here, remember?" he smiled at her. "But I know after what you've been through, it would only be natural to want to flee back East."

"I—I'm not sure what might be waiting for me back there," Blossom said truthfully, wondering about the real Blossom Westfield.

"As an orphan and without a husband to protect you, not much, I'm afraid."

"You seem to know a lot about me, Captain." *More than I know about that poor girl*, Blossom thought.

"Well, it was my mother who checked you out when the community decided to hire a teacher. Mother's an old friend of Miss Priddy's." His voice was sympathetic but his tone was smug.

"I keep forgetting how few rights women will have until they get the vote," she thought aloud.

"The vote?" His eyes widened with horror. "You aren't— you aren't predicting, god forbid, that women will be given the vote?"

Maybe she shouldn't spring the future on some of these good ol' boys too fast, Blossom thought as she hesitated, they might keel over dead. "Well," she said, "women are voting in Wyoming now."

"Oh that!" he scoffed, "it's just a sop thrown to them to keep them quiet. You're not predicting we'll have a woman president?"

"No," Blossom said truthfully, her mind on how and when and if she should attempt to tell the country's leaders about what lay in the future? She might save the country from wars and millions of deaths. "By the way, Captain—"

"Lex, if I may be so forward," he grinned at her.

"Lex," she corrected, thinking he really was quite charming. If she *were* stuck back in this time period, she could do a lot worse than an ambitious cavalry officer, especially one she could help by her knowledge. She'd had nothing but conflict with the Indian scout. "By the way, Lex," she said, "if you're looking for a good investment, the telephone will be along in about three or four years. I'd put some money on Alexander Graham Bell."

"You mean the telegraph?"

"No," she shook her head, "this is different; voices can actually be carried on the wire."

"Miss Blossom," he laughed, "I do think you might have a little talent at reading the future, but that seems so far-fetched—"

"Then I'd better not tell you about movies, cars, faxes, and computers," she said.

"What?"

"Never mind." She paused, thinking she could only expect him to absorb so much at a time. By going back to the past, was she going to be able to change the future? And if she could, did she dare? Suppose she messed around back in time and changed the outcome of either World War? On the other hand, she might change some things for the better. No, she dare not do anything but what she had done in her own time period—be a timid observer, not a doer. Don't make waves.

Her adopted father's sunburned face came to her, the tragic look in his eyes as the bulldozer pushed over the house. Maybe somehow she could figure out how to save the Murdock's farm a hundred years in the future. If she could do that by marrying an ambitious officer, helping him rebuild his family fortune, it would be difficult not to consider it.

"Sometime I'd be interested in meeting your family."

"Good, Mother will just love you and you'll love her! The Brewsters are old New England aristocracy."

"Brewster?" Perhaps she had misunderstood him.

"Yes, we've lost most of the Radley fortune, but if half the things you tell me are true, why, I can see that we'll regain it and end up very, very rich indeed!"

Blossom began to laugh. How ironic! All these years she had wondered about the history of the family empire that had swallowed up the Murdock's land and practically everything else in the country, and unwittingly she had just helped Brewster Farms, LTD.

"Is there something funny, Miss Blossom?" He turned the horse around and they headed back to the fort.

"More funny than you know," she wiped her eyes. She had the power to change the future, she thought abruptly, she could marry Lexington Brewster Radley, end up as a very rich woman, and do good things with all that money and power, save the Murdock farm from foreclosure by the captain's family in the next century. The possibilities were mind-boggling and endless. "And Captain, I'd be pleased to see you more often."

He smiled and reached to put his hand on hers. "The only thing, Miss Blossom, there's always the possibility that I might be killed, and that's hardly fair to you—"

"Oh, I wouldn't worry about that," Blossom said without thinking, "you see, I've seen your portrait in a museum. You'll become a colonel, build a rich empire, live to be ninety-seven years old, and sire a family dynasty that will control most of three states."

"A museum? You saw all that in my future? That's a relief!" He took out a handkerchief and wiped his forehead. "Ninety-seven years old?"

Blossom nodded.

"Oh, I do hope you're reading your tea leaves accurately," he said, "and if I may be so bold, do you see you by my side?"

"I don't know," Blossom said honestly. "I don't know who the mother of this dynasty is; I just know you'll have a long line of sons."

He covered her hand with his cold, clammy one. "I dare hope it might be you, dear Miss Blossom. I can hardly wait for you to meet my mother!"

She pulled her hand away discreetly, remembering the passionate heat of War Cry's big hands. She had no clue as to what her role would be in affecting history. Maybe she could do something to stop the buffalo slaughter and the mistreatment of Indians before it was too late. War Cry's handsome face crossed her mind and she sighed. White women did not end up with Indian braves in the old West, unless they were kidnapped. Besides, she must not be selfish, she had a mission; maybe that was why Fate had hurled her backward in time. "I'd be delighted to meet your mother," Blossom said.

"Wonderful! Mother is coming out on the train in several weeks," the captain said, "wanting to look over some investment land. Perhaps we might drive over and meet her train."

Blossom nodded, stunned by her knowledge. Possibly she was going to be the great-great-grandmother of the man who would foreclose on her adopted parents' farm! She might be able to change that tiny part of history without creating chaos in the future. To do so, she would have to give up all thought of the virile Pawnee brave and consider marrying the captain. If that was what it was going to take to save the Murdock's farm, Blossom would make that sacrifice. "Why, yes, Lex," she said again, maybe to convince herself, "I'd be happy to meet your mother."

Despite her words, she thought about War Cry all the way back to the fort.

War Cry couldn't understand Blossom's coolness to him when he returned from his scouting. Then he remembered how he had lost control of his desire, had put his hands and his mouth all over her the night he had saved her from the buffalo hunters. Well, she had forgotten herself while she was feeling grateful, that was the only logical answer. Respectable white schoolteachers did not get mixed up with Pawnee scouts.

Over the next several weeks, he often saw her passing by in the captain's buggy. She nodded politely to him, but otherwise pretended she barely knew him. He tried to stay out of her way as the summer deepened and the days grew lazy and hot. Yet she was never far from his mind. He would wake up in a sweat, dreaming he was making passionate love to her, and curse her and the handsome cavalry officer because War Cry would never have her for his own. The thought of Lex Radley lying between her thighs, putting his mouth on her breasts and his son in her belly was almost more than War Cry could stand.

Yet he stayed away from Rusty's Place, even though Dolly and the others sent messages that they missed seeing him there. What a fool he was, he told himself grimly, to avoid other women because he would never have Blossom Westfield. The captain obviously didn't share his sense of faithfulness. He saw the captain going in the bordello many nights, especially after he had taken Blossom to a dance or for a buggy ride. It occurred to War Cry that he might cause the man some trouble if he told Blossom about those trips to Rusty's, yet he could not bring himself to do so, knowing the knowledge might hurt Blossom.

Damn the white girl anyway! She haunted his nights and days and didn't seem to notice he was alive. War Cry began to think about asking to be transferred out to join Major North's other Pawnee scouts.

With the lazy, warm days, the Sioux had cut back on their attacks, and his frequent scouting turned up little sign of them. His instinct told him they were still somewhere out there on the vast plains, in spite of the humming telegraph wires that said the enemy had moved north. His Pawnee village was a few miles away, he ought to look there for a wife; Cricket was still around and had made it very clear that she wanted to be his woman. Cricket was pretty, dark, and small. He could do a lot worse than marrying a Pawnee girl. Yet when he closed his eyes and envisioned taking a woman, she had brown hair with golden highlights and eyes as pale as the prairie flower.

To escape the sight of the pair together so often, War Cry asked for assignments outside the fort. The less he saw of her, the better, he told himself. It was evident that she would eventually marry the captain. War Cry should forget her. He found to his bitter dismay that he could not.

It was going to be a beautiful morning, Blossom thought as she dressed and combed her hair. She went into the kitchen, humming. "Isn't it a great day?"

Mrs. Maynard nodded, wiped her hands on her apron. She was in the midst of repotting some flowers. "Oh, yes, this is the day you and the captain are going to meet his mother's train, isn't it?"

Blossom nodded, wishing she felt more enthused. "The Brewster family is quite important."

"Hmm." The old lady didn't say anything for a long moment. "It's several miles to the station, no soldiers accompanying you?"

"Oh, no." Blossom poured herself a cup of coffee. "I understand no hostiles have been seen for some weeks now."

"Still, I'd feel a lot better if Terry were going," Hazel said. "I saw him riding out on a scout this morning; certainly haven't seen much of him lately."

"Well," Blossom shrugged, "that's just an impossible situation as you once pointed out. Besides, we don't need War Cry; the captain is perfectly capable of protecting me, and there'll be troops getting off the train to accompany us back."

"I'd say the captain's looking for an excuse to be alone with you," Mrs. Maynard smiled.

"I suppose." Any time now, the handsome cavalry officer might ask her to marry him, and she hadn't decided how she would handle that. Was it her future to marry him? She wished she had finished reading that page in the book. Idiot, how could you be in his future? You came from a different time back to his, remember? Blossom hadn't allowed herself to dwell on that much. She wasn't certain how she could go about returning to her time, and she wasn't sure she wanted to. Like so many historical romance readers, she thought, she had always dreamed of living in this simpler, more romantic time.

"Land's sake, Blossom, you're awfully quiet." Mrs. Maynard broke off a wilted leaf of the plant she was potting.

"I'm just thinking about meeting the captain's mother," Blossom lied. She truly wished she could tell Mrs. Maynard that she came from the future, but she wasn't sure the lady would believe her.

"Well, you'd better hurry." Mrs. Maynard smiled. "He'll be here in a few minutes. I've packed a lovely picnic lunch for you."

Blossom put her arms around the old lady and hugged her. "You and the doctor have been wonderful about taking me in."

"Why, we're pleased to have you! We have no children and I understand you were raised in an orphanage."

Blossom nodded, wondering what had happened to the real Blossom? Probably she was lying dead out there on the prairie somewhere, and Blossom felt guilty that everyone thought she was the missing teacher. She had tried to tell them, but everyone had treated her as if she were insane. It was easier to just go along. "I—I'll finish getting ready," she said, lost in thought as she returned to her room.

She was waiting with her picnic basket when Captain Radley pulled up out front with his buggy. He came to the door and when he entered, he said, "My! What a pretty dress!"

"It was something I had in my trunk." She felt bad about wearing the missing girl's clothes, but they did fit, and it was easier than explaining that they didn't belong to her. People around here were beginning to accept her as normal.

In minutes, they were on their way, moving at a brisk clip.

Captain Radley seemed to be in a wonderfully good humor. "Guess what? I bought into that Colt gun manufacturer as you suggested. My business associates just wired me that the army deal appears to be a sure thing; I'm on my way to being a very rich man!"

"I know," Blossom said, thinking of her adopted parents' farm. She would make any sacrifice to save it for them. "Do take heed of all those other things I told you."

"I most certainly will. Sometime you must read my palm or tell me what you see in the tea leaves." He gave her an admiring glance. "I can hardly wait to get Mother's opinion."

"You mean, if she doesn't like me, you wouldn't consider me seriously?" The thought rankled her.

"Oh, I'm sure she'll like you," Lex assured her, "you're a mild, respectable lady; just perfect to bear the family heirs—if you don't mind me being so bold."

She colored prettily at his comment, but inside, she was thinking he'd have a heart attack if he knew what was going on a hundred years into the future. "Mrs. Maynard was a little concerned that we weren't taking an escort of troops."

"Frankly, my dear, I didn't want a bunch of soldiers along when we had so much to talk about. Besides, there's a new bunch coming in on the train and they can escort us back, if you think I can't protect you."

"Oh, I'm sure it's perfectly safe," Blossom rushed to say, although she admitted only to herself that she'd feel much better if War Cry were riding along with them. War Cry. She must not think about him. A lot to talk about, the captain had said. Oh my! Was he going to ask her to marry him? And if he did, what would her answer be?

She didn't get a chance to decide. Halfway to the station, they ran into a daring Sioux raiding party.

Thirteen

There were wildflowers growing along the dusty road as the buggy clipped along. Blossom took a deep breath of the scent and smiled.

The captain said, "Wonderful day, isn't it?"

She nodded, watching the sun glint on the shiny bars of his blue uniform. Blossom closed her eyes, reveling in the warm scents of summer. Sometimes it almost seemed as if she belonged back here in the old West, and it was getting more and more difficult to remember that she had come from 1995. Funny, she felt much more at home in this era than she ever had in her own time. When she read historical romances, she always felt that she had been born in the wrong period.

As the buggy moved down the road, she wondered if anyone back in L.A. realized she was missing? With her adoptive parents both dead, a shy, lonely research librarian wouldn't be missed in the hustle of a big city. Probably her casual friends and fellow workers wouldn't even notice; they'd think she'd quit and gone to work elsewhere, and she'd been planning to move to another apartment when she returned. With all the more exciting events in L.A., probably even Vic Lamarto hadn't realized she was missing. Too bad he wasn't like his ancestor.

She wondered just a moment about her lost luggage, which might even now still be turning on a carousel at an airport in Singapore or Florida. No one would know the difference

4 BESTSELLING HISTORICAL ROMANCES BY YOUR FAVORITE AUTHORS CAN BE YOURS, FREE!

Kensington Choice, our newest book club now brings you historical romances by your favorite bestselling authors including Janelle Taylor, Shannon Drake, Rosanne Bittner, Jo Beverley, and Georgina Gentry, just to name a few! Each book is filled with passion, adventure and the excitement of bygone times!

To introduce you to this great new club which is part of Zebra Home Subscription Service, we'd like to send you your first 4 bestselling historical romances, absolutely free! And once you get these 4 free books to savor at home, we'll rush you the next 4 brand-new books at the lowest prices available, as soon as they are published.

The way the club works is that after your initial FREE shipment, you will get our 4 newest bestselling historical romances delivered to your

doorstep each month at the preferred subscriber's rate of only $4.20 per book, a savings of up to $7.16 per month (since these titles sell in bookstores for $4.99-$5.99)! All books are sent on a 10-day free examination basis and there is no minimum number of books to buy. (A postage and handling charge of $1.50 is added to each shipment.) Plus as a regular subscriber, you'll receive our FREE monthly newsletter, *Zebra/Pinnacle Romance News*, which features author profiles, contests, subscriber benefits, book previews and more!

So start today by returning the FREE BOOK CERTIFICATE provided. We'll send you 4 FREE BOOKS with no further obligation: A FREE gift offering you hours of reading pleasure with no obligation...how can you lose?

We have 4 FREE BOOKS for you as your introduction to KENSINGTON CHOICE! To get your FREE BOOKS, worth up to $23.96, mail the card below.

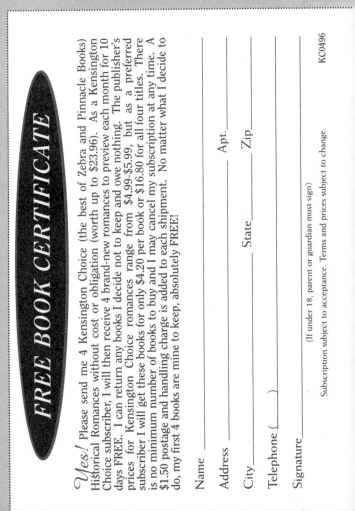

FREE BOOK CERTIFICATE

Yes! Please send me 4 Kensington Choice (the best of Zebra and Pinnacle Books) Historical Romances without cost or obligation (worth up to $23.96). As a Kensington Choice subscriber, I will then receive 4 brand-new romances to preview each month for 10 days FREE. I can return any books I decide not to keep and owe nothing. The publisher's prices for Kensington Choice romances range from $4.99-$5.99, but as a preferred subscriber I will get these books for only $4.20 per book or $16.80 for all four titles. There is no minimum number of books to buy and I may cancel my subscription at any time. A $1.50 postage and handling charge is added to each shipment. No matter what I decide to do, my first 4 books are mine to keep, absolutely FREE!

Name _____

Address _____ Apt._____

City_____ State _____ Zip_____

Telephone (_____) _____

Signature _____
(If under 18, parent or guardian must sign)

Subscription subject to acceptance. Terms and prices subject to change.

KC0496

4 FREE
Historical
Romances
*are waiting
for you to
claim them!*

(worth up to
$23.96)

*See details
inside....*

KENSINGTON CHOICE
Zebra Home Subscription Service, Inc.
120 Brighton Road
P.O. Box 5214
Clifton, NJ 07015-5214

or even care if she never came back. Would she even get to make a choice as to whether to go or stay?

The captain hummed a tune, a Stephen Foster number, Blossom thought, "Beautiful Dreamer." That was certainly appropriate.

Beautiful dreamer, wake unto me, starlight and dewdrops are waiting for thee; sounds of the rude world heard in the day, lull'd by the moonlight have all passed away . . .

Blossom wondered again about the fate of the real Blossom May Westfield? "Did the troops do a thorough search when they went out to the scene of the stagecoach raid?"

The captain nodded, "It was horrible, Miss Blossom, something you don't want to hear about."

"You—you didn't find any trace of missing people?"

His handsome face furrowed. "I can't imagine who you're thinking of, Miss Blossom, everyone's accounted for."

Except poor Blossom May Westfield, she thought. If I ask him to lead a search for her body, how will I explain myself? His fancy family won't want him marrying some crazy person, and the little teacher is most assuredly dead. She remembered the memorial pictured in the museum book. They never did find her body, she thought, poor thing!

"The train will probably be late; it often is," Lex said.

"That's because they haven't standardized time yet," Blossom said without thinking. "In 1883, America will adopt four standardized time zones so trains can make all their connections."

"That's one of your predictions?" He was staring at her.

How could she tell him she was from the future? "I—well, at least, I feel that is what will happen."

"You are an uncanny jewel," he said, admiration in his tone. "So far, your predictions have been right. If you keep this up, the Brewsters will be very, very rich!"

"Oh, I can assure you of that," Blossom tried to keep the irony out of her voice.

"Good!" He nodded with satisfaction. "There'll be a

bunch of new troops coming in on the train to escort us back. Just before we reach the station, there's a lovely little grove of trees. I thought we'd enjoy a picnic with that basket of homemade cake and fried chicken Mrs. Maynard sent."

"Haven't eaten fried chicken since I picked up a bucket last week from the Colonel."

"You've had supper with a colonel? Which one? Custer?" Lex was staring at her.

"No, Sanders."

"Sanders?" His forehead furrowed. "I don't think I know—"

"Never mind!" She hastened to say, "Fried chicken sounds wonderful." Blossom was having second thoughts about meeting Mrs. Radley. From everything Lex had said, she sounded overbearing and pompous.

War Cry came to her mind and she shook her head. No, she must forget about him. If she married Lex, it might change the future, and ultimately, she might save her adopted parents' farm. She would make that sacrifice for their happiness.

She looked to one side and saw a wisp of gray floating on the horizon against a pale blue sky. "Captain," she pointed, "is that smoke?"

"Oh, it's probably a cloud," he dismissed her.

As they watched, another puff drifted and then another. She felt the blood run cold in her veins. "If it's a cloud, why is it coming in little puffs like a signal fire?"

In answer, Captain Radley slapped the horse with the reins and hurried it to a trot. "I was assured that there aren't any Sioux raiding parties in this area."

"I think someone forgot to tell the Sioux," Blossom whispered, almost hypnotized by the tiny figures topping the crest of the distant rise. The figures became a dozen or so riders. The riders started down the hill at a gallop.

"Ye gods!" The officer's eyes grew round with fright. "Hang on! Maybe we can outrun them!"

He whipped up the horse and Blossom grabbed the seat

as the buggy rattled over the uneven road, dust and small rocks flying under the red wheels.

Terrified, she clung to the bouncing seat while the captain struggled to keep the galloping horse on the road. She looked back over her shoulder at the riders coming down the hill and onto the road behind them. Sioux warriors. Scarlet and ochre paint distorted their dark features and their mounts were painted, too. Sunlight glittered on the metal lance heads, necklaces, and bracelets they wore. As they took up the chase, they set up a chorus of shrieks as if they had scented blood.

Blossom hung onto the seat and stared at the dark, half-naked men galloping toward them. We aren't going to make it, she thought, because there's no one to help us. It's too far to the train station and too far back to the fort. "Hurry!" She whispered, "Oh, can't you go any faster?"

"I'm doing the best I can!" The officer was almost whimpering as he applied the whip to the lathered, galloping horse. "A buggy against mounted men doesn't have a chance!"

She took a deep breath to steady her nerves and smelled fear on the handsome captain, and the hot sweat of the horse mixed with the fragrance of crushed wildflowers. The dust clung to her skin in the summer heat.

Lex looked almost paralyzed as he urged the horse. His face had gone pale and sweat ran down his handsome features and into the collar of his snappy blue uniform. It almost seemed to her that she could hear his heart beating with panic, and the shouts and shrieks of the galloping war party drifted on the summer breeze.

Lex whipped the horse to go even faster, but out on this bare prairie, there was no place to run and no place to hide. The buggy rattled as it hit a rock, righted itself, and kept going. Blossom hung on so tightly, her fingers ached. She didn't have any confidence in the captain's ability, she realized, she wished devoutly that War Cry were here, he'd do something to save her.

Oh, fudge! This is ridiculous, she thought, I can't die in an old West Indian raid, I belong in another time. If they kill me, will I return to my own time or will I be lost forever in a limbo between centuries?

The war party was gaining on them now. Looking back, she saw their features clearly, the dark faces, the scarlet paint and feathers, the decorated Indian ponies. She didn't want to die, she wanted to live, yet there was no way to outrun them. The buggy hit a rock in the road.

"Look out!" she screamed. Abruptly, she felt that split second sensation of flying as the buggy overturned, then the pain and taste of dust as she hit the road.

She looked up as the Captain staggered to his feet, pulled out his pistol, his face distorted with terror. "Can't let those red devils take you alive!" he shouted and pointed the pistol at her, hand trembling.

"No, Lex! No!" She held up her hand as if to block the bullet. She'd seen those old Westerns, knew it was supposed to be better to die than to be taken alive, but she wanted to live; oh god, how she wanted to live!

The officer hesitated, stuck the pistol in its holster, ran to the weary buggy horse, pulled out his knife. In a couple of lightning strokes, he cut it loose from its harness and swung up on its bare back. "I'll go for help!"

"Don't leave me!" she screamed, staggering to her feet.

He hesitated, and she almost seemed to see the thought cross his mind, *the weary horse might carry one person, but not two.* "I'll go for help!" he shouted again and took off down the road toward the fort.

"Lex! No! Don't leave me!" Blossom stumbled after him, but he didn't even look back as he disappeared toward the fort. She stood there, watching the cloud of dust from the retreating horse while the war party galloped toward her. The coward had deserted her; left her to her fate!

What to do? Turning, she lifted her skirts and ran away

from the oncoming riders. Maybe there was a hollow or some tall grass ahead. Maybe . . .

The shrieking riders surrounded her, blocking her with their sweating mounts, poking her with the butt of their lances. With a white girl captive, they seemed to lose interest in the escaping cavalry officer.

They had her trapped in a circle of their horses. She tried to run between them and they blocked her. A big, ugly brave, his face distorted by scarlet paint, grinned at her but there was no humor in the dark eyes. "I claim her!" he shouted in broken English, swinging down off his black pony.

Blossom was certain they could see her heart hammering in her breast as she backed away from him. "Don't you touch me!"

The warrior looked over his shoulder at the others and seemed to be translating. They set up a chorus of laughter like coyotes yelping.

The big, half-naked brave advanced on her. "Soldiers killed Scarlet Arrow's woman," he said in broken English, "you soldier's woman; you take her place."

"No!" Blossom tried to run, but she was blocked by the circle of ponies.

The brave chased her down amid hoots and jeers from his friends. He grabbed her, laughing as she fought him. "Spirit! She has spirit, this one! She will raise my son, give me many more!"

"No!" Blossom fought and bit as he slapped her into submission. "No!"

Scarlet Arrow struck her until she went to her knees, attempting to protect her face. She tasted blood from her cut lip, and fear made her forget her caution. "The soldiers will come! Let me go, or you'll be sorry!"

"Soldiers!" He sneered and looked toward the road. "That one too cowardly to sire sons. He make gift of you to Scarlet Arrow."

He grabbed her shoulder and Blossom turned her head and

bit his hand. Even a timid mouse could fight back if pushed hard enough.

Scarlet Arrow jerked his hand back, nodded approval. "You bite like wolf bitch! Much good in my blankets."

She fought him, but he picked her up and threw her across his broad shoulder. Her skirt had worked its way up so that she felt the heat of his arm across the back of her bare legs. Blossom began to pound him on the back, but he paid no more attention than if she were a child. He carried her to his horse, dumped her in a heap while he reached for a bit of rawhide to bind her. Even as she struggled, he twisted her hand behind her back while she cried out in pain. He paid no attention to her whimpering as he tied her hands behind her.

"No, I won't do this!"

He threw her across his horse. "You my woman now! I try to take one from stagecoach, she get away; you not escape!"

Blossom May Westfield, she thought with a sudden cold chill; she was going to take the missing schoolteacher's place in this Sioux raider's blankets. Was it justice or irony?

There was no more time to think as the warrior mounted behind her, his hands on her body. "Tonight, you give me much pleasure."

The war party turned and galloped in the direction from which they had come, while Blossom, hanging over the black pony's side, craned her head to look frantically down the road where the cowardly captain had disappeared. Damn him anyway! The chances that he would get a patrol together and be able to track these raiders were slight. When darkness fell, it would be hopeless.

She wished now that she had let Lex put a bullet in her brain. Ironic, she thought as the horses galloped over the hill, she had been willing to marry the captain in her attempt to change history, now it was going to be for naught. She thought of the Pawnee warrior who had saved her life before. How she wished he were here to help her now!

As it was, the big Sioux ran his hands over her familiarly. "Tonight, you pleasure me, white girl."

She was not going to go to her doom like some meek little Victorian schoolteacher, Blossom vowed. All her life, she had behaved like some mild, unassuming lady, and what had it gotten her? She didn't know how, but perhaps under cover of darkness, she might be able to slip away. In her terror, she looked toward the sun now low on the western horizon. Right now, she must concentrate on staying alive; she'd worry about everything else when the time came.

Seated on a box in the stables, War Cry had been cleaning his rifle when he heard guards' shouts and the sound of a galloping horse. He ran out as a lathered, exhausted horse stumbled to a halt, Captain Radley sliding off as people came running from all directions.

War Cry felt a sudden chill of apprehension. Without thinking of what the cavalry might do to him, he grabbed the officer, spun him around. "Where's the girl? What happened?"

"Sioux war party," the captain gasped and looked as if his knees might buckle under him. "I—I came for help . . . buggy wrecked."

"You left her out there?" War Cry's voice rose to an angry shout. "You deserted her?"

"I—I tried to shoot her, but she begged for her life. So many of them, couldn't do anything."

"You cowardly—!" War Cry brought his fist back to strike the man, his fury boiling over inside, but Doc Maynard ran up, caught his hand.

"Easy, Terry, you'll only make trouble for yourself!"

"Doc, you hear him? He left her to the Lakota! You know what they'll do—"

"I—I'll lead a rescue party," the captain said and then his knees buckled and he fell into Doc's arms.

All around them, people were murmuring. "Brave fellow! Probably couldn't do anything else! Where were they going?"

"To meet his mother at the railroad," someone else whispered.

War Cry stepped away from the officer and the lathered, gasping horse. Cold anger and fear for Blossom's safety washed over him. He shook his head, trying to clear away images of the Lakotas grabbing her while she screamed and fought. By now she might have been raped by all of them, or be enduring slow torture. Or they might already have her on her way to sell to the Comancheros for service as a white slave in Mexico. He turned and strode toward the stable.

"Terry," Doc called, "where are you going? We'll organize a rescue—"

"If you have to wait for the captain to lead it, it'll be too late," Terry yelled back over his shoulder as he kept walking. He could ride faster alone.

Even as he saddled up, he knew he was taking a terrible chance. His name was on all Lakota warriors' death lists because he had killed so many of their braves. To his enemies a bullet in the heart was too easy a way to go. If they caught him, they would delight in keeping him alive while they killed him by inches.

His mind was on old Hank as he grabbed his weapons and led the paint from the stable. God, what a horrible way to die, and even worse to know his hair would hang from some enemy warrior's belt. The girl was not his to protect. In fact, the last several weeks, she had been cool, hardly speaking to War Cry. He should let her wait for her fancy white officer to rescue her; then she'd know what kind of coward she had chosen to be her mate.

Even as he thought it, War Cry knew he couldn't shrug it off as not his responsibility. In his mind, he saw her as he had seen her that very first time, suddenly appearing in his camp, holding onto his hands, her eyes as big and blue as prairie flowers. He couldn't ignore her plight. War Cry swung up into the saddle and rode out.

Across the parade grounds, they were carrying the captain into Doc's office and soldiers were running from every direction. By the time the white men got organized, it would be almost dark, so they would probably wait until morning. Morning would be too late.

War Cry rode past the sentries and away from the fort at a gallop. He didn't want to be stopped.

The railroad. They had been on their way to the train to meet the captain's mother. War Cry turned his stallion in that direction and took off. Probably someone would wire the train to halt because of the new outbreak, and Mrs. Radley would go back East and await instructions.

He gritted his teeth, angry with the captain for taking Blossom away from the fort with no escort along. Why had he done that? Because he wanted to be alone with her, War Cry realized. Well, now the Sioux had her, and they'd make her pay for the dashing officer's cowardice.

The sun was low on the horizon as War Cry rode, following the recent buggy wheel tracks in the dust of the road. He wasn't sure what he would find in the wreckage of the buggy; he didn't even want to think about it. Warfare among the tribes was bitter and merciless, and the Lakota had nothing to lose by killing white women and children. Their own were slowly starving for want of buffalo.

An accomplished tracker, he read sign; an unshod pony track here where the Sioux must have picked up the track of the buggy, a broken blade of grass there where they had veered off to disappear behind a low rise. No doubt the warriors had been watching that buggy for a long time before they ambushed it. They had wanted to make sure the buggy was far enough from the fort that the noise of gunfire wouldn't drift on the wind and alert the soldiers. One inexperienced officer and a girl would be easy prey.

She had flaunted her charms before War Cry, let him kiss

and touch her, then she had transferred her affections to the captain. Yet in spite of his bitterness, he kept following the buggy tracks. In the beginning, he had found the white girl. Her life belonged to him until he handed that responsibility to someone else. To do less might anger the Great Spirit.

It was not yet dark when he found the wrecked buggy. He got down, hardly daring to breathe as he looked over the scene, afraid he would find her small broken body somewhere near. The wind made the overturned buggy wheels turn in the air. He smelled the scent of food, found the basket. A picnic; they had been planning a picnic. The sheer stupidity of the captain and the white man's total disregard for Blossom's safety amazed and angered War Cry. No doubt Radley had planned to find a shady place under a tree and seduce her along the way.

The girl was too stupid and addle-headed for belief. Up to now, he had thought of her as only slightly loco, now he was angry with her for her complete naivete and trust in the elegant officer. Captain Radley had little character, and the white girl was either incredibly stupid or naive not to see past that fine blue uniform with the shiny brass buttons.

War Cry gathered up some of the food and tucked it into his saddlebags. It would beat jerky and hard tack if he were out here long enough to get hungry.

That was questionable, he thought as he studied the trampled grass. There were at least a dozen riders, maybe more. In his mind, he saw her surrounded by the savage Sioux as she tried to run. Judging from the way the ground was torn up, she had attempted to escape and had been recaptured. No doubt she been thrown across a horse and taken to the Lakota camp to be raped or tortured at their leisure.

For a moment, he pushed his cap back, pondered returning to the fort for help, or at least riding to meet the patrol which would be coming eventually, then shook his head. It was late afternoon and soon dusk would turn the sky to pale pink and lavender. Certainly by the time help came from the fort, it would be too late to help Blossom. Hell, what did he care what happened to her? She wasn't his responsibility. Blossom had depended on the wrong man. War Cry would have died to protect her, not fled as the captain had.

He mounted up and followed the tracks away from the wrecked buggy, remembering the way she had looked only hours before. Blossom. Pale skin and eyes that were overly large and just the color of the prairie flower. When she moved, her brown hair caught the sun and it reflected golden highlights. The shameless chit had teased him with her charms, but she would never give her body willingly to an Indian brave.

She had meant to make a sharp bargain—trade herself in marriage to a wealthy white officer. War Cry sneered at the thought of Captain Radley. What kind of man would not protect his woman? If Blossom had belonged to War Cry, he would have fought to the death for her. Now, like a fool, he was risking his life when he meant nothing to her.

He frowned as he paused and checked the ground for sign again. Yes, they were still headed north toward Sioux country. Sioux. They didn't like that name; it meant enemy, but it was an accurate description. Those braves might not be too worried about being trailed, thinking the cowardly captain would ride all the way to the fort for help. By the time the soldiers came, the Lakota would have broken camp and scattered across endless miles of prairie, difficult to track as a leaf on the wind. Nevertheless, he kept on the trail as time passed and the sun sank toward the horizon.

War Cry paused on a ridge in the twilight, thinking about the consequences of his actions. She wasn't his woman; why should he risk his life? Yet when he thought of another man touching her, he gritted his teeth in possessive fury. Forget her, he told himself, a beautiful white girl can never be the woman of a Pawnee scout.

A sound came to him in the distance, a rhythmic sound carried by the wind. At first, he thought he had imagined it, and he tensed, listening. When it came again, he recognized it—the sound of ceremonial drums. War Cry pushed his blue cap back and considered. Yes, somewhere in the distance, the renegades were celebrating. War Cry didn't even want to guess the reason. As darkness fell like a pale gray blanket across the prairie, he nudged his horse into a gallop, his heart beating hard with apprehension.

Again he paused to listen. His horse was lathered and blowing as War Cry waited. The drumming was louder now, drifting on the wind in the darkness. Occasional faint shouts and singing drifted to his ears. The Sioux were celebrating. He tried not to picture what might be happening in that camp as he mounted up and followed the sound across the prairie.

Soon his keen nostrils picked up the scent of smoke and cooking meat. He listened, ears as alert as a wolf, and heard the faint neighing of horses, the sounds of voices. He moved forward more cautiously now, reined in among the shadows of darkness near the camp, and hid his stallion in a grove of low brush. He tied a piece of soft rawhide around his stallion's muzzle so it would not nicker and give him away if it scented another horse. Quiet as a shadow, War Cry checked his weapons and crept through the darkness toward the tipis. Brule Sioux, possibly a war party of Spotted Tail's people, and maybe some Oglalas; all bitter enemies of the Pawnee. Over the last half-dozen years, the Pawnee had scouted against them for the soldiers.

A herd of horses grazed in the distance and a huge fire roared in the center of the camp. Around that fire, drunken warriors danced and chanted to the beat of drums. He spoke enough Lakota to understand their victory songs. They had stolen a white soldier's woman and she was to be the property of Scarlet Arrow.

Scarlet Arrow. Yes, War Cry knew that cruel warrior. How many times had that Sioux killer left his red-painted arrow stuck in a burning Pawnee lodge or a dead Pawnee elder?

War Cry looked over the group, knew the numbers were

too many. If Blossom was the captive of Scarlet Arrow, she was in no immediate danger of being killed. He must plan to enjoy her tonight, maybe keep her permanently if she pleased him. That certainly gave War Cry time to go for the cavalry. Sometime tomorrow, he could lead Captain Radley and a big force to the rescue.

Yes, that's what he should do, if he wanted to live. Yet, if he did so, that left Blossom to the mercy of her captor for tonight. War Cry shuddered, knowing that at the least, her small, fragile body would be used to please the brave. At the worst, Scarlet Arrow would share her with his friends.

War Cry shook his head. No, he could not let that happen, even though he was vastly outnumbered and had no chance against this whole war party. He would be risking his life against great odds, but he had done that many times. He did not fear death anymore, for he was a courageous warrior with many coup marks against the enemies of his people, the Sioux and Cheyenne. Yet, why should he die to save a woman who had spurned him?

In his mind, he remembered those pale blue eyes looking up at him, her small face between his two big hands, the taste of her mouth, the way she had clung to him, and how he had felt, gathering her fragile body into his protective embrace.

War Cry checked his weapons one last time. It might cost him his life, but he couldn't abandon her to the Sioux warrior's lust!

Fourteen

Inside a tipi, Blossom hung by her wrists from a framework of crossed poles. Through the opening, she could see the big central camp fire and the warriors dancing around it. She didn't want to think what her fate might be. In her mind, she saw the cowardly officer fleeing, with no thought to her safety. War Cry's strong features came to her mind. He would never have let the Sioux take her without killing him first.

This can't be happening, she thought wearily. How can I have gone back more than a hundred years in time only to be raped and tortured to death? If she disappeared without a whimper, no one in the real world would even know she was gone. God, if she were going to die anyway, why hadn't she given herself to the virile Pawnee warrior and enjoyed those precious hours of ecstasy in his strong arms?

The glow of the roaring fire illuminated the tipi interior. She looked down at her half-naked breasts, visible in the torn dress, and tried not to think what Scarlet Arrow had planned for her. Maybe if she were lucky, they would just kill her, not torture her, although judging from the chanting and dancing outside, they didn't plan to cut short their entertainment. She wouldn't think about that, she would think about War Cry.

In her memory, he kissed her slowly, thoroughly, dominating her mouth as he swung her up in his arms, light as a flower. She closed her eyes and remembered the feel of his lips on her nipples, his rough hands moving across her skin. In her mind, he made love to her, slowly and satisfyingly, touching and teasing her until she was breathless with desire, then filling her as he gave of himself while her body locked onto his and tried to take even more from him. She would arch against him, her nails digging into his lean, hard hips, urging him to ride her harder while his mouth sucked her breasts until she moaned with pleasure. When she had touched that peak of passion, the virile savage would begin anew to bring her to ecstasy.

A sudden sound and Blossom started back to reality. Scarlet Arrow stood in the tipi opening, swaying a little as he grinned at her. "Now I use you, soldier's woman. You please me, maybe I not share you with my friends."

"No, you can't do this! I don't even belong in this time." She tried to pull free of her bounds, but she was helpless. "I will not be your woman; kill me instead."

He laughed and crossed over to her, ran his hand familiarly across her bare breasts. "I could make you beg for death out there by that fire, woman." He jerked his head toward the roaring blaze outside. "Instead, you will live. Tonight, I put my seed in your belly. It will please me to see these swollen with milk to feed the many sons you will give me."

She tried to pull away from his groping hand, and when his hand went to her face, she turned her head suddenly and bit his fingers.

He slapped her. "I will teach you to obey me, woman, and you will soon be glad to do anything I demand!"

She spat at him. "I will die first."

He shrugged. "You were the bluecoat's woman, you cannot be much choosey."

"I am not the bluecoat's woman."

"You were with him."

She said then what was in her heart without even thinking. "I am proud to be War Cry's woman."

His face distorted with anger. "The Pawnee scout to the bluecoats?"

"Yes!" She flung it at him with disdain, "And he is twice the man you are."

She saw the fury on his ugly face as he struck her. "So you are the woman of the Lakota's worst enemy! Hearing that, I would rather mate with a rattlesnake; knowing you could never be trusted not to kill me when I slept."

"You're right," she gasped through bloody lips. "I will kill you when I get the chance, and if you get me with child, I would strangle it with its own birth cord rather than give it life."

He shook his head. "Your defiance seals your fate, white girl. You will be an evening's pleasure for this war party before we kill you slowly."

She fought him as he cut her down, dragged her outside. He was shouting in Lakota. She couldn't understand his words, but his meaning was all too clear as he dumped her by the fire.

Blossom struggled, but she had no chance as other warriors hurried to help Scarlet Arrow. They spread her out and staked her down so that she was helpless. Then the big Sioux reached out and tore her calico dress so that she lay there almost naked in the firelight. A murmur of appreciation ran through the watching braves and she saw desire flare in their dark eyes. She called out to the women in the camp for help, but they shrugged and disappeared into their tipis.

Scarlet Arrow laughed. "You waste your time! Our women feel no mercy for the whites; many of them have been used for the pleasure of bluecoats and buffalo hunters. Now we will take revenge. Later, we will kill you very slowly so that when your Pawnee scout finally comes, he will know what we think of his people."

"But I am already here!"

"War Cry!" As Blossom stared in disbelief, War Cry stepped out of the shadows and strode toward the fire. Straining her neck to see, she thought she imagined the Pawnee scout, but there was no mistake. It was War Cry striding across the circle, the firelight playing on his bare chest, the sinewy muscles rippling under his dark skin, the tight blue cavalry pants, the jaunty cap on his black hair.

For a long moment, the Sioux seemed almost frozen into silence by the sight of the lone enemy walking boldly into their midst, and they turned toward Scarlet Arrow. "Grab him!"

The warriors obeyed his command and War Cry did not fight them. Instead, he sneered arrogantly, as if commoners had put their dirty hands on a prince. "You fear me so much then, Sioux dog?"

Scarlet Arrow pulled his big knife and the sharp steel of its blade gleamed in the firelight. "If the soldiers are about to attack this camp, you will die before the first Lakota does."

War Cry spat at his feet. "A lone Pawnee can whip a few cowardly Sioux! I bring no one; I come alone." He shook the men's hands off him.

"You are a fool!" Scarlet Arrow sneered. "Tell me why you take such a risk?"

War Cry looked down at Blossom and his look said everything. "I come for the girl."

There was a long silence, broken only by the crackle of the fire, the faraway whinny of a horse in the big herd, a dog barking somewhere. Around them, curious women came out of their lodges, murmuring to each other, looking with admiration toward this brave enemy.

Scarlet Arrow grinned, but there was no mirth in his dark eyes. "She means so much to you then, that you would die for her?"

"She is in my heart," he said in English and touched his chest. "I will trade my life for hers. Let her go and keep me. Would you not rather torture me to death?"

Blossom cried out and struggled to break free. "War Cry, no!"

Scarlet Arrow threw back his head and laughed. "Why should I choose? I have you both!"

"You are a coward!" the Pawnee sneered. "Brave only when surrounded by your own warriors."

"I am braver than any Pawnee dog!" the Lakota snarled and brandished the knife. "I already have one young son, but your woman will give me more after I geld you and cut your throat!"

"Again I say you are brave only because there are many. You would fear to meet me alone in hand-to-hand combat."

Blossom protested, "War Cry, no!"

The men ignored her.

War Cry said, "The woman is a worthy prize for a victor. I will fight you for her."

Scarlet Arrow glanced over his shoulder at Blossom. "Why should I fight you for her; she is already mine."

"Not as long as I live," War Cry said, and he pulled his own knife.

"Then make ready to die!" The Sioux crouched.

A murmur drifted through the crowd as word spread and people came running, surrounding the big, fire-lit circle.

Oh god, what could she do? Blossom tried to pull free, but the stakes held her half-naked body pinned against the ground.

War Cry shook his head. "It does me no good to fight if it changes nothing."

"What is it you bargain?" The Sioux glared at him.

"Do battle with me," War Cry challenged, gripping his flashing blade. "If you kill me, all will know you are truly a brave man with my scalp hanging from your lodge pole. Then you may keep the girl; use her for your pleasure and to bear you sons."

"No!" Blossom shrieked, "I will not—"

"Shut up, woman," the Sioux commanded, "you are only

a prize, you have no say in this." He looked at the Pawnee, a slow smile spreading across his dark features. "And if you win?"

"I will take my woman and ride out with safety."

"No, War Cry," Blossom protested, "he's taller and bigger than you are, you can't—"

"Is it a bargain?" he asked, ignoring her outburst.

The Sioux looked around the circle, seeming to consider his chances. His warriors were gathered around him, and to defeat this well-known enemy before them would do much for his war record and his pride. He turned to look at Blossom. "You will watch your man die," he announced, "and know which is the better stallion. While his blood still soaks into the earth, I will take you before all my people to fulfill this bargain!"

There wasn't anything she could do to stop them, Blossom thought as she struggled against her bonds. She knew War Cry was a brave and fearless warrior, but the other man was bigger, maybe stronger. "Let my man leave unharmed," she shouted, "and I will submit to you without a fight."

"Blossom, no!" War Cry protested.

The Sioux threw back his head and laughed. "You hear, Pawnee dog? She cares about you enough to bear my sons without a whimper if I will spare your life; it is almost tempting!"

War Cry crouched into a fighting stance. "I will kill the man who touches her."

"Big words for a lone warrior."

"And you are all words and no fight, you cowardly coyote of a Sioux!"

With that insult, the hulking enemy seemed to lose his temper, rushing in, knife blade flashing. "I will feed you your own manhood as you die, Pawnee dog, but I will keep you alive long enough to see me put my seed in your woman!"

War Cry gripped his knife tighter, feeling the sweat run

down his bare chest as he faced Scarlet Arrow. The other man was bigger with longer arms, which gave him the advantage. "You will let me take her and ride out if I win?" War Cry demanded.

"It is so spoken," the other said.

War Cry glanced around the big circle of silent enemy. Yes, they would honor Scarlet Arrow's word, it would be dishonorable to do less, but the look in all the silent, solemn faces told him they did not expect their warrior to lose.

In the flickering firelight, Blossom's pale, naked body gleamed, and he thought she had never looked so beautiful and desirable. If he lost this fight, all these enemy warriors were going to take their vengeance on the girl. He knew it and they knew he knew it; that made this fight even more important. Some of the men had even turned to look at the writhing beauty, hot desire in their dark eyes. They were already picturing taking their pleasure with the enemy's woman.

He would not lose; he must not lose, War Cry thought as he crouched. With a roar, the big Sioux charged at him like a maddened bull. Gracefully, War Cry stepped aside, realizing his adversary was a little drunk; that might help even the odds. It almost seemed to him in that split second that he could hear the intake of breath of a hundred people, smell the camp fire and Scarlet Arrow's sweat as he turned and faced War Cry.

Past the warrior's shoulder, War Cry saw a handsome young boy, not more than eight or ten winter counts old. Scarlet Arrow's son, he thought, and then there was no more time for thought because the Sioux rushed him again, knife hand flashing downward in the firelight.

War Cry tasted the salty taste of tension as he reached out, caught that down flashing hand, brought his own knife up. God, the enemy was strong!

Scarlet Arrow caught War Cry's knife hand by the wrist. His fingers were like bands of steel as they meshed and strained, each trying to use his body to unbalance the other. The Sioux's sweating face was right up in his own, War Cry recoiled from his sour whiskey breath as they struggled. "Pawnee, make ready to die!"

He had no energy to waste shouting insults, War Cry thought as they strained and struggled, each trying to jerk his knife hand free. Then War Cry reached out, quick as a heartbeat, tripped the other man and they went down, struggling in the dirt, rolling over and over as they fought. The dust clung to their sweating skins as they struggled, but the Sioux was bigger. He managed to tear the knife out of War Cry's fingers, send it flying.

His white teeth gleamed in triumph as he brought his own blade up, but War Cry was quicker. The Pawnee rolled out from under the other, staggered to his feet, breathing heavily. His knife lay too far away for him to reach, he started in that direction, but was blocked by the grinning Sioux. "So now your life will run out and make mud of this dust, Pawnee," he snarled, "and then I will mate your woman!"

War Cry looked toward the knife laying across the circle, dodged, trying to pass the Sioux warrior, but Scarlet Arrow moved into his path, still grinning. Around him, War Cry heard the murmurs of satisfaction and whispers of disappointment in Lakota.

"It is over so soon then?"

"What did you expect? Scarlet Arrow is a better fighter!"

"Our warrior will bed the enemy's woman tonight."

Not while he still had strength to fight, War Cry thought as he charged the Sioux bare-handed. The thought of that animal lying between Blossom's silken thighs was more than he could stand.

They grappled together, War Cry knowing he was at a disadvantage as they struggled, because of the other's weight and long arms. Somewhere in the background, he thought he heard Blossom's soft weeping. He wondered for a split second if she cared enough to weep for him or if she only wept for her own fate, knowing his death made a gift of her body to Scarlet Arrow?

Every muscle and tendon in his body seemed to ache and protest as the combatants rolled over and over in the dirt. The big Sioux grunted like a buffalo bull with his effort as they fought their way around the fire-lit circle.

The Sioux were all yelling now, encouraging Scarlet Arrow to strike the fatal blow. "Kill him! Kill the Pawnee dog!"

"No, leave enough life in him so that he can watch us take his woman, then we kill him!"

He did not intend to die easily, War Cry thought, as they fought and rolled. Every nerve in his weary body was screaming in protest. He was exhausted and growing more tired by the minute, but he could not quit. Even as he weakened, he looked toward the captive, naked girl and that renewed his spirit. Her fate was in his hands and he would not let them have her; she belonged to him! He was fighting for the chance to possess her, make her his woman. If he fought to the death for her, surely she would love him for it, give herself to him.

Scarlet Arrow made a swing with his knife. War Cry dodged away, but not quite quick enough because his body was so weary. The sharp blade slashed. He felt the pain as the blade cut into the flesh, felt the hot blood run down his arm even as the enemy braves set up a chorus of encouragement for their champion. Blossom cried out. He glanced to see her small face, saw that she cared for him, cared that he was hurt.

She cared. It was enough to give him renewed strength. He charged into the big Sioux warrior once more and as the man fell, he landed on the blade of his own knife.

Scarlet Arrow screamed out in agony as the blade went deep into his chest. War Cry staggered back, breathing hard. "It is ended!"

"Not yet!" The other man's young son ran in, grabbing

for the knife in Scarlet Arrow's chest, "I will take revenge, Pawnee!"

"I fight no children!" War Cry gasped and shook his head, even as one of the other warriors caught the struggling boy.

"No, Fire Arrow!" The warrior who held the boy commanded, "our honor is at stake here; we gave our word!"

The young boy looked up at War Cry, fury in his handsome face. "Know then that I will hunt you down! Watch your back, for always, Fire Arrow will be your enemy!"

War Cry took a deep breath. "You are a brave boy, you speak only what I would do myself. Someday, we'll meet again."

Now he staggered across the silent circle, picked up his own knife, leaned down to cut Blossom free. "I will take my woman."

He cut her loose and she was in his arms, half-naked and sobbing. "Kid, it's all right; you're safe now; don't be afraid."

She was still trembling as he swung her up in his arms, held her small body against his big chest protectively as he strode out of the camp toward his horse tied in the brush.

She looked up at him as he paused in swinging her up on his stallion. "Will—will they come after us?"

He shook his head. "Not this time, their honor is at stake. The next time we meet, it will be a different story."

He put her up on the horse, swung up behind her, held her in the protection of his embrace. "Let's get out of here."

"I—I was so afraid he'd kill you," she wept against his bare chest as he turned the stallion, and they rode out into the darkness back toward the fort. He felt her hot tears on his skin and her nipples warm as silk against him.

"His son will come after me someday," he said with regret. "Scarlet Arrow's son is very brave. His honor will not be satisfied until he collects that debt. Until his death, I will always know I have a bitter enemy waiting for revenge."

She clung to him as they loped through the night and he

held the trembling, half-naked girl tightly against him. He
had protected her with his life and he would do so again,
but it was a bitter victory. He had saved her so that the
captain could have her. Well, she was alive; that would have
to be enough for War Cry; he loved her so.

Blossom snuggled against him as they rode. She had never
felt as safe as she did at this moment, held against his
brawny chest in the protective embrace of his strong arms.
"You seem to be continually saving my life."

He shrugged and stared straight ahead. "So it seems.
Maybe Captain Radley will appreciate me saving his
woman's virginity enough to give me a medal, or at least
a reward."

"Is that why you did it?" Somehow, she was terribly disappointed. Anyway, in this innocent time, how could she explain to the warrior that she was not a virgin? That
innocence was out of style in the time she came from? Too
bad, Blossom thought, because she saw the significance of
saving her virginity as a great prize that could be given only
once to a most loved man. Why in the twentieth century
were women giving their virginity away as if it were worthless?

She realized that he had not answered her question. His
mouth was a grim line as he rode, not looking down at her,
yet she could feel the swell of his big manhood against her
body. Like a stallion, he had fought to the death for her, yet
now he was taking her back to the fort to the captain who
had fled in panic to save his own life. It wasn't fair; it wasn't
fair at all.

Blossom made her decision then. War Cry had earned the
pleasure of lying between her thighs. She pressed her naked
breasts against his chest, feeling the swelling of his desire.
She could already picture his dark face against her white
breasts, his big hands holding her small waist. She could

feel the tension and the power of the man, knew how much he wanted her, knew he had earned her love. Tonight, somewhere along the trail, she was going to give him that reward.

Fifteen

Blossom was exhausted but they were still riding through the darkness toward the fort. "Can't we stop?" she pleaded, "and ride on at daylight?"

War Cry nodded. "There's a little grove of trees and a spring not far up ahead; we'll stop there."

She remembered then that she was almost naked as he looked down at her with smoldering eyes in the moonlight. Neither of them said anything more as they rode, until he reined the horse into the shadow of some trees. "We can rest here a couple of hours."

He dismounted, held up his hands to her. Blossom slid off into his arms and he held her very close a long moment. She thought she could detect a slight tremble in his strong body.

It seemed to take some effort for him to step away. "Cover yourself; a man can only take so much."

Self-consciously, Blossom pulled the edges of her frayed dress together.

He didn't look at her as he tossed her his blanket roll, dug in his saddlebags. "I've got a little of your left-over picnic and there's a spring here."

She spread the blanket on the grass. In the moonlight, she saw the dried blood on his arm. "You're hurt."

"It's a small cut; nothing much." He busied himself getting the food and tied the horse out to graze.

Wearily, Blossom sank down on the blanket and took a

deep breath. The faint scent of crushed wildflowers permeated the warm summer air. In the moonlight, she saw the refuge where they stopped was covered with the little blue prairie flowers.

War Cry sat down on the blanket, tossed her some fried chicken and bread. "I wonder what else the young tenderfoot had in mind besides food?"

Blossom felt her face burn as she ate. "Nothing happened."

"That's probably because the Sioux interrupted the captain's plans."

The chicken was crisp and delicious and when she dug into the lunch, she found oatmeal cookies. "Thank you for saving my life back there."

"Part of my job," he said, eating and not looking at her.

"I think not!" Blossom retorted. "The wimpy captain fled without a backward glance; evidently saving women isn't in his job description."

"Kid, I don't know what to make of you," the warrior grinned and paused. "You talk strange; I've never met anyone like you before."

"War Cry, I—I know you don't believe me; but I swear I'm not from your time; I come from the future."

She waited for him to laugh. Instead, he cocked his head, studying her gravely. "Is it possible or are you loco? I sense there is something unusual about you; I've known it from the first time you appeared out of the mist, holding onto my hands."

She leaned closer. "Do you remember anything about a painting of a running herd of buffalo?"

He seemed to consider, shook his head. "I only recall a sadness, a deep sense of loss for what seemed like an eternity."

"You were a spirit trapped in a painting in my time. I tried to pull you into my existence, but instead I was transported back to yours. Can you understand that?"

His handsome face furrowed and he shook his head slowly. "A spirit should be on its way to walk the Hanging Road to the Sky. It would be a terrible fate to be trapped in between."

"Maybe, given the choice, you were trying to come forward in time; but why, I don't know." She was frustrated with confusion about what it all meant.

He laughed easily and once again, he was his arrogant, cocky self. "But you see, I am very much alive, so none of this makes sense."

"You think I'm certifiable, don't you?"

"What?"

"Loco. You think I'm talking crazy."

He studied her, brow furrowed. "Kid, I don't know what to think about you. Perhaps you are a shaman with big medicine; or maybe you are only a girl who had a terrible shock in a Lakota stagecoach attack."

Blossom sighed. If the army ever found poor Blossom Westfield's body, maybe War Cry would believe her. Then she remembered the memorial pictured in the book. The missing girl had never been found. Well, if she were in War Cry's place, she'd have doubts, too. "I don't suppose it matters whether you believe me or not."

"Blossom, I'm trying. You'd better not tell this to anyone else, they'll lock you in a madhouse." He shrugged and finished his meat, wiped his mouth.

She had never felt such frustration. "But I can tell everyone what is going to happen for the next century, maybe change history."

"If you could change history, would you dare?" He looked deadly serious.

"I don't know." Blossom thought about it. "Some things, some injustices *should* be changed, but suppose I do something to change the outcome of good things? When I have to make that decision, I may not have the courage. The implications are awesome!"

He shook his head. "It would take courage, all right."

"I can only wonder why you were attempting to pass through that painting and into my time," Blossom said.

"Can you read the future?" he asked.

"A little," she confessed. "I can tell you that unless something changes, Captain Radley will live to be ninety-seven years old and become the patriarch of a very rich and powerful family with many children and much land."

"Many children?" War Cry raised one eyebrow. "And are you to be the mother of those children?"

She shook her head. "I don't see everything. I know that Captain Radley's mother's family will end up taking my adopted parents' farm away from them. If I marry him, I might be able to change that, don't you see?"

"What about me? Have I saved you for him?" War Cry leaned back on his elbows, studying her.

Blossom put her head in her hands. "I suppose you have; I don't know. It's all so confusing"

"More important, if you're from the future, are you going to stay?"

"Again, I—I don't know if I get a choice in that or the consequences if I do." It was a reality she didn't want to face or think about at the moment. She had spent her whole life running from hard choices and responsibilities. Blossom had never really taken charge of her own life.

He didn't comment as he lay down on the blanket.

She looked at him in the moonlight. "Does it matter to you if I go or stay?"

He shrugged. "That doesn't seem to be my choice to make."

"If you had a choice of going more than a hundred years into the future; would you?"

He looked up at her, and for once, sincerity replaced the jaunty arrogance. "I would follow you into the future or into hell if the Great Spirit would allow it."

She was touched. "I had no idea—"

"It is a weakness I should not have admitted." War Cry frowned. "White girls do not end up with Indian braves; it's hopeless. Tomorrow, I'll return you to your captain."

She leaned over him and she knew the dress gaped open so that he could see her breasts. "I owe you for rescuing me."

"I don't want you to owe me." He sounded angry.

"Obligation is not what I feel at this moment," she whispered, leaning even closer.

She saw the dark intensity of his eyes and he took a deep breath. "I said, I don't want—"

She leaned over and brushed her lips across his half-opened ones.

"Don't play with me, white girl." He sounded tense as a coiled spring.

"Or you'll do what?" she challenged in a whisper against his lips.

He came up off the blanket suddenly, took her in his arms, rolled her over on her back, kissing her with passionate abandon.

She had never been kissed with such heat and intensity before, and her senses were giddy with the power and taste of this man. The sensation of his mouth on hers overwhelmed her and she slipped her arms around his neck, pulling him down to her.

She was acutely aware of the scent of crushed blue wild-flowers around them, the feel of his muscular body against her bare breasts.

He was shaking as he paused and pulled away, breathing hard. "A man can only stand so much."

"Then don't stop," she whispered and arched her back, offering her breasts to him. "Oh, please don't stop!"

He made a soft noise in his throat, half curse and half prayer as he bent his head. She felt the warmth of his breath against her skin and then his mouth, wet and hot on her nipple, sucking there until it sent a whorl of desire through her belly and on down to the vee of her silky thighs.

She couldn't get enough of the feel of his greedy mouth, she thought, gasping as she held his dark head there until he had sucked that nipple into a peaked rosebud of desire. Then she offered him her other one as his big, rough hand surrounded it, pushed it up into a creamy mound of pleasure for his lips.

She couldn't stop herself from writhing at the sensation as his tongue moved in swirls around the circle of her nipple and his rough hands massaged her breasts. "Oh, I want you!"

His hand moved to her belly, stroking there while his lips teased both her breasts, moving up her throat to her mouth. She opened her lips, sucking his tongue deep even as she felt his fingers tease and invade her body. When she hesitated, he nudged her thighs until she let them fall apart, opening herself up to his stroking fingers.

"Blossom, you're wet, so wet . . ." he whispered against her ear. The warmth of his breath thrilled its inner depths, sending goose bumps down her skin as he put his fingers deep inside her. "You want me?"

She nodded, tilting herself so that his fingers could tease even deeper.

"Then say it," he commanded. "Say you don't belong to the captain, that you won't regret this . . ."

"I—I'm your woman," she murmured. "I've wanted you, wanted you to mate me ever since the first time I saw you."

He tangled his fingers in her hair, bringing her mouth up to his nipple. "If you want me, show me," he ordered.

She had never thought desire could feel so hot. Almost in a daze, she put her sharp little teeth into tasting and nibbling his chest while he writhed and groaned at the sensation. Blossom tried to remember not to dig her nails into the rippling muscles of his back, and she ran the tip of her tongue down the corded muscles of his chest.

Would he be disappointed that she wasn't a virgin? She

couldn't think about that now, all she could think about was how badly she desired him. She pulled him on top of her, glorying in the hardness of his small hips, the power of him as she touched his virile, throbbing manhood.

He hesitated a moment. "Blossom, tomorrow, you'll regret—"

"Never," she whispered. "Never!"

He needed no further urging. She saw the need in his dark eyes as she spread her thighs and he came up on his knees. Very slowly, he came down against the outer petals of her femininity.

He was big; god, he was big. She felt the wet, hot head of his manhood against her as she wrapped her legs around his lean, muscular form. Then she dug her nails into the corded muscles of his back and brought him down into her. She couldn't stop the sudden cry she made at the flash of pain as his hard manhood went deep.

"Blossom, have I hurt you? I didn't—"

"Don't stop," she begged and held him to her. "Oh, please don't stop!" It was incredible that it should have hurt, Blossom thought, she was not a virgin, and yet she felt as if she had been impaled on a hot steel rod. As he slid deep into her, she seemed to feel the glowing heat of him pulsating all the way down to the very center of her being. So this was what it was like to be loved, she thought with sudden wonder.

The male dagger of him deep in her velvet place made desire build and she began to move under him, wanting more.

He put his arms around her, his tongue deep in her mouth as he began to ride her, giving her his full length and all the power behind those hard-driving hips. For a moment, she was not certain she could take all of him, but her body responded by wanting still more.

If he were like modern men, he would be gone in a rush before she even had a moment to let her desire build, Blossom thought, remembering her past experience. Yet it was almost as if that had never happened, as if this was her very first time.

"More!" she urged, tilting up so that he could ram deep within her. "I want everything you have to give!"

"I—I'm afraid I'll hurt you," he gasped, as he rode her harder and more intensely. "I don't want to hurt you!"

He was hurting her, all right, he was more man than she could take, but it was a good hurt that was gradually building into something else. Her whole body felt as if it were afire with desire and she rose up on the blanket to meet him with each stroke, wanting him to thrust even deeper. By now, she thought in confusion, any other man would have lost it, leaving her unfulfilled, but he was riding her hard and rhythmically, his hands and his mouth all over her, tasting and teasing.

She felt as if she were about to experience something she had never known before, as if she stood on the edge of a deep, dark valley and an uncontrollable urge was pulling her toward the cliff's edge. "I can't . . . I don't know how . . ."

"Trust me," he whispered gently against her ear, "trust me; I love you."

Blossom relaxed, letting him pleasure her, trusting him to guide her, take care of her, building her ecstasy until he made one deep final stroke. Then she let him carry her over the edge of the precipice, until she began to fall at a dizzying speed, clutching him to her, gripping his body with hers deep inside so that he could not escape until she finished this wild, breathless fall into blackness. She was attempting to squeeze the seed she craved into her womb, and then for a heartbeat, or eternity, she was aware of nothing at all except hurtling through that blackness in the most exhilarating sensation she had ever known. Only vaguely was she aware of his sudden gasp and then he, too, stiffened. It almost seemed to her that she could feel him throbbing deep inside her as he gave up his seed. For a heartbeat or eternity, they meshed and clung together.

She lay there, feeling him convulsing, emptying his life force into her womb, shuddering with the effort of giving what her body demanded from him.

For a long moment, he lay there with her in his embrace, breathing hard. "I never had anyone like you before. You take everything I've got to give."

"You didn't like it?" Now she was shy, wondering if she'd done it right, shocked at her own boldness.

"Like it?" He took her face between his two big hands without uncoupling from her, kissed her lips, her eyes, and cheeks. "No one else will ever live up to you!"

She felt the same way as she relaxed, feeling his damp, naked skin against hers. This wasn't like the movies or groping around in the backseat of a car with some drunken boy who was trying to prove his manhood; this was mating in the oldest sense of the word; like Man and Woman had been doing for millions of years.

He hadn't disengaged, but was leaning on his elbows looking down into her face, stroking the hair from her forehead. "You're mine now in every sense of the word. I can only hope you don't regret it."

"I don't. I wanted this."

He moved just enough so that he could kiss her throat and the curve of her breast. "I meant to return you to the captain."

"The captain wasn't willing to fight for me or protect me," she murmured. "He doesn't deserve to lie with me."

"Is that all it is? I deserve it; you're obligated because I saved you from the Sioux?" She caught the warning edge in his voice as he pulled away from her.

"I—I didn't mean that."

"I understand what you meant, kid. You've given me your virginity out of obligation. I didn't want it that way."

She started to tell him she wasn't a virgin, then saw the scarlet stain on his body. How could this be? Sometime in the future, she had given herself with haste and regret to a callow boy who meant nothing to her. Had she undone her own future? It was too confusing to contemplate. Blossom stared in confusion at the scarlet smear on her thighs. It was as if this were the very first time, and she was glad he had been the one.

Blossom, are you losing your mind? she thought, he can't be your first man. And yet, there was the telltale sign on her thighs. She got up and went over to the little spring to wash herself off, taking off the torn dress, aware that he smoked and watched her in the moonlight.

Blossom didn't try to hide herself, in fact, she gloried in her body as she crossed back to the blanket, walking naked and proud, saw the desire in his eyes again. She came over, threw the dress down, sat next to him, leaned against his shoulder.

He stiffened, then seemed to surrender to her touch, put his arm around her, hugged her naked body against his big, dark one while he smoked. "It was my fault, kid, I've wanted you from the first moment I saw you."

She leaned against his broad chest, liking the feeling of secure protection his muscular arm created. She lay her face against his chest, listening to the strong, steady beat of his heart. "I don't have any regrets."

"You will tomorrow." His voice sounded bitter, but he didn't take his arm from around her. He ground out his smoke, then bent his head, kissed her hair. "White school-teachers don't let Injun scouts make love to them."

"I said I didn't have any regrets."

He stroked her. "You're such a naive, innocent little fool! You think the town would let you teach or that the captain would want to marry you, if he thought you'd given yourself to an Injun brave?"

She was silent, thinking. But what she thought about was how she had traveled back in time to him, and if she would be able to stay, or even if she would get a choice? Even then, she wasn't sure what her choice would be. She would not face that reality tonight. "I am just so tired," she admitted, closing her eyes, "very tired, so much has happened."

He kissed her eyes. "I know. Go to sleep, Blossom."

"Suppose the Sioux come back?"

"I didn't say *I'd* sleep, kid." He reached out and picked one of the small blue blossoms, put it in her hand. "Here's my promise that I'll always be there for you."

Always. She took the fragile flower, inhaled its perfume. True love is like a blossom, fragile, yet beautiful. This one would remind her of tonight and this man forever. *Forever, my timeless warrior.* She closed her hand over it gently, thinking she would press it in her book of love poems when she got back to the fort. *How do I love thee? Let me count the ways . . .*

She had never felt this protected with the men of her own time; they all seemed like such wimps compared to this Indian scout. "I like it in your arms," she whispered as she snuggled deeper into his embrace and her eyelids fluttered closed. "I feel I belong here. Funny, it seems like I've been searching for you for so very, very long; even during the nightmares—"

"No more nightmares," he promised and kissed her forehead, "not as long as you're here with me."

She believed that suddenly; that as long as she was with him, she would not be in the middle of that rolling, terrifying thunder, screaming with an overpowering sense of loss and fear.

"Blossom, are you all right? You were trembling." He pulled her against his broad chest.

She tried to sort through the memory in her mind. "A terrible sense of dread, something that's happening that I can't face; won't face; a horrible sense of loss. I—I'm running from it, fleeing and refusing to accept it . . ."

He put his finger under her chin, turned her face up to his, dark eyes puzzled. "No man or animal can hurt you when you're with me."

She shook her head, attempting to clarify her thoughts. "I don't know what it means; I wish I could explain." She held the small flower up to her nose, sniffed its wild fragrance and smiled. "Somehow, the scent and the sight of this little prairie blossom brought the memory back; it's part of it all somehow."

"The flower?"

She nodded. "Maybe someday, the puzzle pieces will suddenly fall into place and I'll see the whole picture clearly."

"If you really *want* to see it. Maybe it's some reality you refuse to face." He stroked her hair.

"If I have a character flaw, that's it; running from reality; letting life push me like a leaf in the wind." Blossom shrugged and closed her eyes. "This blurred nightmare is one of my earliest memories. Maybe it's something that happened to me in my mother's womb or as I was being born."

"Whatever it is, I'll protect you as long as I have life. Now rest, Blossom, and after while, we'll ride on."

She settled into the safe refuge of his arms and slept.

She awakened with a start, still cradled against his chest. "Have I been asleep long?"

"Not long." He seemed troubled and preoccupied. "We ought to ride on before dawn."

Her spirits sank. "Somehow, I don't want to go back to the fort just yet; face that." She didn't say what she was thinking; what he was probably thinking; that in the white world, they could not be together.

He paused in wrapping the blanket around her. "I've been wondering how I was going to explain your nakedness to the captain; he won't like me riding in with you this way."

"He ought to be glad I'm alive, after what he did."

"He'll be upset about what other white men will think about you being naked with me."

"That's right; these are Victorian times, aren't they? A

woman who dares show an ankle is daring. They all would faint if they could see how much some women are showing in my time period."

He shook his head. "You're such a strange one with this talk of the future. Would I like it there?"

Blossom considered a moment. "I don't know. Perhaps your people are no better off than they are now."

"In that case, I don't want to hear about it." He stood up, pulling her to her feet. "I could take you to my Pawnee village; maybe one of the women there might have a white woman's dress."

Blossom smiled and slipped her arms around his neck.

For just a moment, he stood rigid, then held her against him so tightly, for a moment, she couldn't breathe. "What heartache have I let myself in for by loving you, kid?" He said it so softly, she had to strain to hear him.

She clutched the little flower he had given her, thinking she would keep it forever as a symbol of tonight and a love that could transcend time and space. She began to put on the frayed dress. "Let us not go back to the fort. We'll pretend reality doesn't exist for a while."

"You must finally learn to face life head on instead of fleeing from it," he said, as he pulled away from her; untied the horse.

"I wish I were courageous like you," Blossom said, clutching her precious flower. "I run instead."

"That doesn't change things," he said softly, "you're only fooling yourself." He swung up on the big paint, lifted her lightly to sit before him.

"My adopted mother was a strong, brave person; I always wanted to be like her and never was."

"It's never too late to start," War Cry suggested as he nudged the horse forward.

Blossom thought about her adoptive parents, feeling a great sense of loss. If only she could go back and change things. No, that was impossible; weren't history and the past frozen in stone? Or were they? The past was like a great woven blanket; pulling one thread could unravel the whole thing. Yet she must try to save her family's farm, even if it meant marrying the captain when she loved the Indian brave. War Cry would never understand.

His strong arms went around her as they rode. "Thank you for last night," he whispered against her hair. "I will never, never forget that for one brief moment in time, you belonged to me."

And you will be my forever love. She was overcome with a sense of loss and sadness. We can't end up together, she thought, it isn't in the pages of history. Had they both been lost somehow or were they not important enough to be mentioned?

They rode through the night in pensive silence. In the distance, a village of rounded Pawnee earthen lodges rose up darkly against the first gray light of the coming dawn. As they approached, dogs barked and horses whinnied. They rode in as people came out of their lodges, yawning. Women carried water, men built camp fires. Small toddlers scampered about and old ones stared at the pair as they rode through the village.

A pretty dark girl came running from a lodge. "War Cry! I'd know that horse anywhere! I've missed you . . ." Her voice trailed off and she stopped as she seemed to see Blossom for the first time.

"Hello, Cricket," War Cry called. "I've brought someone with me."

"So I see." Her voice went cold and her pretty face turned stoney.

Blossom knew jealousy when she saw it. "Hello."

"Who is this, War Cry?" The girl stared at her with sultry eyes. "I don't think we've met."

He dismounted, held up his arms for Blossom to slide

down. "Cricket, see if you can find Blossom something more suitable than this torn dress, and then rustle up some food."

Cricket looked as if she might protest or argue, then tossed her black hair and snapped, "All right, white girl, come with me. We'll leave the men to talk and smoke."

Blossom rearranged her bodice to cover herself and followed her, noting that every line of Cricket's back was hostile. The pretty Pawnee girl was in love with War Cry, whether he knew it or not. No doubt Cricket would do everything in her power to hang onto the big, virile warrior. Now Blossom wished they had ridden on to the fort, but it was too late. Just how far would the jealous Cricket go to protect her turf?

Sixteen

The Pawnee girl led Blossom inside her earthen lodge. "What happened to your clothes anyway?"

"I was captured by a Sioux war party, but War Cry rescued me."

"Humph," Cricket sneered, digging in a small leather box. "It was foolish to be where the enemy could get you." She found a faded, rumpled dress and tossed it to Blossom. "Here's a castoff one of the women at the fort sent in a charity basket. I didn't like it, but it will do for you."

"Thank you." Blossom took it, forcing herself to smile. She always avoided unpleasant confrontations. I'd love to be Scarlett O'Hara, she thought, instead, I'm Melanie.

"How do you know War Cry anyway?" The girl's face was as hostile as her tone.

She wanted to tell Cricket that she was being rude and asking questions that were none of her business; Blossom hesitated. "That's a very long story."

Cricket folded her arms across her ample breasts. "I've got time."

Blossom took a deep breath and began to put the dress on. There was really no point in explaining to the Indian girl about going through the painting and back in time. "I—I was lost and he found me; took me to the fort."

"How lucky for you." Cricket did not smile.

"Isn't it though?" Blossom smiled too sweetly as she buttoned the dress. "He's been wonderful in helping me."

"White girl, I hope you aren't taken in by his charms; women always like War Cry."

"Including you?" Blossom kept the smile frozen on her lips, surprised at her own spunk.

"Well, yes, I've known him a long time; everyone says he will finally ask me to be his woman."

Blossom turned to leave the lodge. "I wouldn't hold my breath."

"What's that supposed to mean?" The girl bristled as she blocked the doorway.

"Never mind." Blossom tried to step around the girl, but again Cricket blocked her path, smiling as if she realized the white girl was too timid for confrontation.

"White girl, I think maybe you should learn to keep your hands off another's man."

"That might be news to War Cry," Blossom said, but inside, she wondered just what there was about the big scout that Blossom didn't know? She didn't doubt that most women found the virile Pawnee attractive. "Besides, this is not a civilized way to settle anything."

Cricket threw back her head and laughed. "What makes you think he likes his women civilized, white girl? He likes them passionate and hot!"

"I presume you're speaking from personal experience?" She was amazed at her own retort.

"Why, you white—!"

"Blossom, where are you?" War Cry's voice echoed suddenly outside.

Cricket half-turned toward the sound and Blossom took advantage of the distraction. She pushed past the girl and out into the light. "Here I am."

He grinned at the sight of her. "Good, Cricket found you something to wear."

"Why, yes, and we've been having a nice conversation."

"Hah!" The Pawnee girl brushed past her and stood glaring at her.

War Cry's eyebrows went up, and for a moment, Blossom thought he would comment or ask a question. Before he could, Blossom asked, "Shouldn't we be going on to the fort?"

"Scouts just reported that there's Sioux and Cheyenne war parties out in the area," War Cry said. "I think we'll wait until dark to move on."

Cricket looked as if she could barely control her anger. "Won't the white soldiers be looking for this white girl? It would be a scandal if she were to stay out too long with a Pawnee brave."

Blossom smiled sweetly. "Thank you for your concern over my reputation."

"It's just that the soldiers at the fort know War Cry," Cricket smiled back, but there was no laughter or warmth in her dark eyes.

The warrior frowned. "What's that supposed to mean?"

Both women glared at each other and shrugged. Curious women and small children had gathered around Blossom to gawk. Blossom smiled and nodded to them and a few smiled back shyly. I could win these people over, she thought, and wondered if there was the tiniest chance that she and War Cry could make any kind of a life for themselves.

Are you crazy? she asked herself, you must marry Lex Radley and try to change history, if possible, to save the Murdock's farm. Besides, Cricket is probably right; War Cry has an easy, confident manner among women; maybe you're only another conquest to him. She looked at the virile brave again, remembering last night. She still had the tiny flower he had given her, and no one could ever take away the memory of those precious hours they had spent in each other's arms.

War Cry interrupted her thoughts as he gestured toward an earthen lodge. "Blossom, this is my lodge, although I'm not here much. You can rest while I meet with the council; we'll ride on in the safety of darkness."

"All right."

He turned and strode away, his whole manner as arrogant and cocky as it had always been. Blossom's heart lurched, remembering his virile strength, his tender kisses. If only . . . no, she must forget him. At least she had had one night of ecstasy in the warrior's arms. Most women never had an experience like that to cherish.

It seemed to Blossom that she could almost feel the jealous Pawnee girl's glare stabbing into her back as Blossom went into War Cry's lodge. It was pleasantly cool inside the thick walls, Blossom thought as she lay down on a blanket. Outside, the summer heat shimmered, but in here, it was comfortable. Just what did she think she was doing, anyway? She had no business getting mixed up with a Pawnee brave who might belong to a jealous girl ready to cut Blossom's throat to keep him. She wondered just how many women around the fort had also enjoyed the cocky brave's kisses?

War Cry joined the warriors at the big camp fire and the pipe was lit and passed around the circle with much ceremony. Leaders of all four of the Pawnee bands were here, he noted, so important things were being discussed. Some of the old ones still wore the distinct roached hairstyle of long ago times, when the Pawnee still practiced the grisly Morning Star sacrifice of enemy virgins.

Old Sun Chief, *Sakuru lashar,* looked toward War Cry. "What is the news from the fort?"

War Cry shook his head. "Not much with Major DuBois away. The whites worry about money; many of the scouts have been let go."

Koruksa tapuk, Fighting Bear, nodded. "Yes, it works a hardship on our families now that we were used to the money the *lachikuts* (the long-knife soldiers) paid. There are not enough buffalo now because the white hunters kill the big beasts only for the hides or tongues."

War Cry stared into the fire. "The Cheyenne, the Arapaho, and the Sioux need meat as much as we do."

"Teradeda!" Enemies. A wrinkled old warrior sneered in the Pawnee language as he took the pipe. "They outnumber us and sooner or later, will overwhelm us, drive us from this land."

War Cry accepted the pipe, took a deep, sweet puff before passing it on. "The army says it will protect us."

The great leader, known to the Pawnee as *Tirawahut lashar* and to the whites as Sky Chief, studied him gravely. "You know the white men's hearts, *Ter-ra-re-cox,* do you believe them?"

War Cry thought about it. "Some of them are good; some of them think of all Indians as enemies and would be happy to see us all gone." He thought of the captain.

An old warrior wearing a scalp shirt frowned. "Already, I see the way they covet our land."

"We will never give it up!" Sky Chief snapped. "All these generations, we have fought the Plains tribes to hold onto what is ours. All these lands along what the whites call the Republican River and the Platte belong to us."

"That is true," War Cry agreed with a nod. "Right now, it is in the white man's best interests to help us—as long as they fear the Cheyenne and Sioux."

Another brave took the pipe, smoked, and passed it on. "Those two tribes have been our enemies for many, many winter counts. The Cheyenne will never forget that we stole their Sacred Medicine Arrows in battle. They have had bad luck ever since."

"They got two of them back," Fighting Bear reminded the speaker. "We were foolish to trade them to the Sioux so they could return them to their allies. Better we should have kept the arrows so the Cheyenne bad medicine would last."

War Cry stared into the fire. "Even now, they tell me, Long Hair Custer is up in the north country, exploring for the Great White Father. If his soldiers find gold, the Sioux and Cheyenne will soon be under attack up there."

"Good!" Sun Chief grunted. "That will keep them busy. They will not be attacking our villages, slaughtering yet more of our women and children."

"Hah!" a warrior snorted. "Our enemies will always find time to murder us with no mercy."

A chorus of agreement went up around the circle.

The ancient shaman, Beaver Robe, looked at War Cry with interest. "Who is this white girl who accompanies you? I sense somehow that she has big medicine."

"She is mine," War Cry said solemnly. "Already, I have put my seed in her so that she will give me sons."

Sky Chief frowned. "This is not good. The white men do not even like us to look at their women, even though they use ours for their pleasure. It will cause much trouble."

War Cry could feel all their eyes upon him and he stared down at the ground. "I know in my heart you are right. Already, a bluecoat captain is angry because she smiles at me. Sooner or later, he will find a way to take revenge."

"She is just a woman, after all, even though she has eyes the color of the prairie flower," a shriveled warrior said. "And one woman is pretty much like another after the lodge is dark at night. Better you should give her back to the soldier captain so he won't make trouble for you or your people."

The old shaman, Beaver Robe, took the pipe, blew smoke toward the sky while the others waited respectfully. "I would like to talk to this white girl."

War Cry nodded, "Yes, respected elder." Deep in his heart, he knew that the chiefs were right. A white girl like Blossom was forbidden to him, even though he had saved her life, even though she had given herself freely to him. That would make no difference to the soldiers. "Let us talk about the annual hunt," he said, wanting to change the subject. He didn't want to think about giving Blossom up.

The others shook their heads and their faces grew grave as the pipe passed from one to another. "There are very few buffalo this summer," one said, and the others grunted agreement. "We have lookouts posted for many miles watching for the shaggy beasts to cross our territory again. When that happens, we will hunt and hope there is enough meat to last the winter."

"The whole countryside is crawling with Sioux," War Cry protested. "They will be watching for the buffalo, too."

Sky Chief looked at him a long moment, shrugged. "What else can we do? This is the way it has always been. We have sided with the whites for their help and the guns they supply us, because our enemies are as many as leaves of trees."

Another cleared his throat. "Our friends, the Poncas and the Omahas, talk of moving down to the Indian Territory. We could do that, too."

War Cry snorted with disdain. "We would let the Sioux chase us from our own country like whipped cur dogs?"

"Bravery against superior numbers will only stretch so far," an old man sighed. "It is not like it was when *Pani Le-shar* led us and the army needed us badly."

That was true, War Cry thought. Maj. Frank North—the white officer so admired by his Pawnee scouts that they called him *Pani Le-shar,* Pawnee Chief—was doing little or nothing, stationed at another fort. War Cry's younger brother, *Asataka*—the one the soldiers called Johnny Ace—had ridden against the Cheyenne Dog Soldiers at Summit Springs back in 1869 with *Pani Le-shar.* However, the army had let most of its Pawnee scouts go, and many were hungry now that the buffalo were fewer.

War Cry said, "Perhaps the buffalo will yet drift through our country again in time for the late summer hunt. I will see if the army will ride with us for protection."

A weathered brave curled his lip with disdain. "There was a time when Pawnee warriors were feared and did not need the protection of the white man."

"That was long ago," Sky Chief reminded the other gently,

"before the white men's diseases killed so many of our people, and our enemies took advantage of our small numbers to attack us again and again."

War Cry said nothing, remembering. His own mother had been one of those to die in the great smallpox epidemic the wagon trains had brought through this country back in 1849. The Pawnee had always been friendly to the whites, and as a reward, their numbers were only about one-third what they had once been.

Sky Chief looked at War Cry. "In the meantime, do not keep this woman, no matter what your heart tells you. It will mean much trouble with the soldiers."

War Cry frowned and stared into the fire. "My heart tells me you are right, but I think of nothing except her embrace."

Sky Chief shrugged. "Use her a few times; your lust will pass. Then take one of our own women for a wife. Think of the good of your people before you anger the white men."

This was not what he wanted to hear, but War Cry nodded. "I will think on this. Keep a lookout for the buffalo herd and send word to the fort. I, too, will want to take part in this hunt."

Sky Chief stood up slowly, signifying the meeting was at an end. War Cry stood, too, and the circle began to break up. He walked back toward his lodge, deep in thought. They were right, he knew. Nothing good could come of his hunger for this white girl. After he had enjoyed her body a few times, perhaps she would seem like just another woman after all. He would do as the old ones demanded, take a Pawnee wife when he finally had to choose. What about Cricket? She was one of the people and she had never made any secret of the way she felt about him.

Blossom looked up as War Cry joined her in the lodge. He looked different, she thought, troubled and unhappy. "What's happened?"

"Just as I feared," he said, "there have been many Sioux spotted in this area over the past weeks. Our elders are wanting to arrange our annual summer buffalo hunt, yet they fear the large numbers of Sioux warriors lurking in this area. They outnumber us."

Something tugged at Blossom's memory, something troubling. She frowned.

He looked at her. "What is it?"

"I don't know." Blossom shook her head. "Some memory attached to summer and a buffalo hunt . . ." She didn't say anymore; she couldn't remember what it was she knew. Or was it only that she chose not to remember? She didn't have the answer to that and she brushed the thought aside.

"It's not something we have a choice about." He sat down next to her on the blanket. "The tribe has to have meat and so when the buffalo are seen again, we'll have to begin our hunt, whether we have to run a gauntlet of enemy warriors or not."

"This is a dangerous time we're living in." Blossom frowned.

He shrugged and reached out to touch her. "When in history has it not been a dangerous time to live?"

Blossom thought about the time she had come from; drugs, gangs, terrorists. "I suppose you're right." She wondered if he would want to accompany her back to her time; or if he could?

"Old Beaver Robe, the shaman, wants to meet you," War Cry said. "It is indeed an honor for you. I will take you to his lodge just before sunset."

"Sunset? We need to get back to the fort."

He shook his head. "We dare not offend the old man; he will be making medicine and studying signs for the next few hours. Besides, he is somewhat of a mystic. I think you will be intrigued by him."

* * *

Just before sunset, Blossom and War Cry walked to the old man's lodge. The ancient shaman was as brown and weathered as old leather. He was staring at the pink and purple sunset in the distance and barely acknowledged their presence with a nod. "I would speak with the girl alone."

War Cry looked as if he wanted to protest, then nodded. "Yes, Old One. I will wait in my lodge."

A bit hesitant, Blossom followed the shaman inside. He sat where he could see outside, staring at the lavender sunset as if he drew strength from it.

He sat down by the small fire with his legs crossed and gestured her to sit. The place smelled of smoke and magic herbs, Blossom thought as she looked around the dim interior. Only then did she notice the big hide with the paintings on it hanging behind him on the lodge wall. "That's the star chart!" she exclaimed. "I know about it!"

Beaver Robe turned his dark eyes toward her, studying her gravely. "Tell me how you know this thing."

"Well," Blossom leaned forward eagerly, "it's a map of the sky with the stars' track put in so well, it is accurate back to the time of Columbus."

The old shaman nodded. "It is a star map, but I do not know this Columbus."

"Someday," Blossom said, staring at the thing in awe, "someday, this piece of history will belong to the Chicago Natural History Museum."

The old man reached out, took both her hands in his, and stared into her eyes. "I feel the energy, the magic of the circle in you," he said so softly she had to strain to hear him. "There is something unusual about you; what is it?"

Blossom hesitated. Should she tell the ancient brave the truth? Would he think she was insane? She decided to trust him. "Great elder," she said in a most respectful tone, "I come from the future; more than one hundred years after your time."

"Ahhh." Then there was a deep silence, broken only by

the low rhythm of village drums in the background. She waited for him to either laugh or comment on her sanity. After what seemed like an eternity, he turned dark eyes toward her that seemed to burn into her soul. "How came you here?"

"I completed a circle. I—"

"Yes, I believe that. The circle is a forever symbol of magic, of power." He let go of her hands and sighed. "Sometimes I see into the future myself, but it makes me sad because I seem powerless to change anything."

Emboldened by his belief in her, Blossom spoke before she thought. "Oh, Great One, if you knew the future and could change it, would you dare?"

He looked at her gravely. "All of us have the power to change the future, if only in the smallest way. All mankind is tied together with nature and the universe, and our decisions, our choices create that which is yet to come. We do not inherit the earth from our ancestors, we borrow it from our descendants."

"In the time I come from," Blossom said, "many no longer believe we have that responsibility of choosing which path to walk. They believe we are all helpless victims of circumstances."

Beaver Robe's wrinkled brown face reflected disdain. "We all make choices every day that affect the rest of us, selfish, shortsighted choices."

Blossom leaned forward. "Old One, I do not understand why I have been sent to this time."

"Tell me your story."

Briefly, she told him what had happened. "Even War Cry hesitates to believe me, though I think he tries. Everyone thinks me loco."

Beaver Robe shrugged. "Has it not always been like this? No one believes a person of vision."

"But why have I been chosen for this magic?"

He shook his head. "I do not know; it is the power of

the circle and of love. If your love be great enough, I sense it is within you to change the future greatly, but beware! Every breath you draw, every action you make, affects someone or something, somewhere—for thousands of years and generations to come."

The old man stared out the door at the horizon. Around them, the sun had set and the coming dusk had turned pale lavender and blue, almost the color of the prairie flower. In the silence, Blossom stared into the small fire. She had come back to change history; was the old shaman warning her she must not try to do that?

"Great One," she said. "Was my coming only an accident?"

The old man looked up at the sky, his weathered face calm and peaceful in the twilight. "The Great Spirit does nothing by accident; you have been returned here for a reason."

"Returned?" Blossom shook her head, "No, you do not understand; I am not of this time period, I come from the future."

"No, *you* do not understand," he said stubbornly. "You are sent to correct the history that will be."

"Should I stay here or return to my own time?"

"Do you know your time?" He stared at her solemnly.

"You are talking in riddles," Blossom blurted, a little annoyed with the ancient shaman.

"All life is a riddle." He surveyed her solemnly. "You must not tell what I have revealed to you. To do so will be to destroy the magic."

He had revealed nothing, only confused her further. "But what—?"

"None is so blind as he who looks but will not see. I will clarify: You may be given a chance to choose so that things might be as they should have been."

She was not certain she would get any clearer explanation from him. Perhaps he had told her almost all he knew. "How do you know these things?"

"I have seen you in medicine visions, my child." He looked at her with quiet confidence. "I have been waiting and wondering what it all meant."

"And what *does* it mean?" Blossom persisted.

He shook his head. "I do not understand all the Great Mysteries, but this I know: love is more important than life," the old man whispered. "This will be your final chance; do not make the wrong choice again."

Again?

"I don't understand. Are you saying I just have this one tiny window of opportunity, and if I don't take it, I create havoc?"

"You already create havoc, do you not?" the shaman said softly. "The key is the day of your birth and the circle . . . there is no more to tell. You must not discuss my sacred visions with anyone. I have spoken." His voice trailed off and he seemed to go into some kind of trance.

Blossom waited, but Beaver Robe stared at the horizon. In the background as darkness fell, the drums beat steadily. The hot summer wind picked up, bringing the scent of the familiar wild blue prairie flower to her nostrils.

"I must know more," she pleaded.

Beaver Robe did not answer or even acknowledge her presence as he stared into the growing darkness.

The meeting was ended. Mystified even more, Blossom stood up, nodded with respect to the old man, and walked out of the lodge. *The day of her birth and the circle.* Did he know something about her real mother or how Blossom had come to be abandoned on a hospital lawn? It was only a lot of hocus-pocus and mumbo jumbo, she thought, and yet, something about him had made a chill run up her back.

War Cry came out of the lodge as she walked up. "Well?"

"Nothing he said made any sense," Blossom complained.

"You whites are not patient as Indians are patient. Wait. Perhaps the pieces will fall into place at the precise moment you need them, and you will understand," War Cry said.

She wished she could discuss it all with him, but she had been sworn to silence. Perhaps the shaman did not want anyone else to influence her decision when the time came. Or maybe the old man was a con artist and she should forget the whole thing.

They began to walk toward the horse, past curious crowds of Indians. In the crowd, Blossom saw Cricket's jealous face.

War Cry said, "Can you talk about it?"

Blossom shook her head. "To do so is to destroy the magic."

He nodded solemnly. "Beaver Robe is a man of great vision, Blossom. Listen and believe what he tells you."

How could she when she didn't understand? *You will be given a choice so that all might be as it should have been. We all have the power to change the future, if only in some small way.*

The power of the circle. What had he meant by that? Sacrifice, he had said. Yes, she had meant to make a sacrifice, stay in this time period and marry the captain, even though her heart belonged to War Cry. Did old Beaver Robe mean she must return to her own time instead? She, who hated making decisions, might be faced with some of the toughest ones of her life. "I feel like I'm on borrowed time," she murmured.

He put his hand on her shoulder, stood looking down at her. "Blossom, we are all on borrowed time, each and every one of us. Life is fleeting and fragile and we should not take it for granted."

Sometime soon, she might have to choose whether to leave this place and the man she loved forever. Maybe the old man had meant she was going to die. Blossom was very much afraid of death. She blinked rapidly.

"Kid, you're crying, why—?"

She shook her head and turned away. She didn't want him to say anything that would weaken her resolve. When that mysterious time came, that window of opportunity, would she have the courage to make the right choice? "I—I only wish I knew the answer to that."

"The answer to what?" He pulled her to him and held her close.

She shook her head and wiped her eyes. She knew now why she must not share the secret with him; he'd try to stop her. "We need to get back to the fort."

He caught her arms. "What is this sudden change in you? You aren't regretting what happened last night?"

Did she? She had given her heart to a handsome, swaggering Indian brave who belonged more than a hundred years in the past. There could be no happy ending to this, and she was angry at the injustice of it, angry with him. "How many other women have you said you loved; whispering sweet things in their ears about how much you cared?"

"None, except you," he answered. "I don't suppose you'll believe that."

"You've made love to Cricket?" Blossom demanded. In her mind, she saw him between the dark, pretty girl's thighs, holding her, kissing her.

"I never lied to you about that. Cricket is free with her favors—"

"She's in love with you."

He shrugged. "I can't help that."

"Women like you too much," Blossom said.

"I'm a man, Blossom." He sounded angry with her. "Men have needs that some women are eager to fill."

"And that's what I was to you?"

He caught her shoulders. "Yes!" He almost shouted at her, "I never wanted or needed a woman like I needed you last night. I don't know or care what time period you are from; I don't intend to ever let you go!"

Before she could answer, he pulled her to him, kissing her with passionate abandon. Blossom struggled in his arms, but he was much bigger and stronger than she was. His tongue slipped between her lips and caressed the inside of her mouth, while he flattened her breasts against him as he crushed her to his hard chest.

It was going to be her choice to make, she thought as desire flamed in her heart, and when it came, she would do the right thing, no matter how much it hurt, what sacrifice she had to make . . . or would she? A woman could be so weak when she was being asked to give up such a great love.

Oh, why had the old shaman warned her? She didn't like making decisions, taking chances. Blossom preferred everything safe, planned out, and methodical, not wild and spontaneous as had been the case ever since she had gone through that painting and back in time. Reluctantly, she pulled away from him. "I—I think I regret last night."

He sighed. "Regret acting like a woman?"

Blossom didn't answer.

"Very well!" His voice was cold. "I'll return you to the fort and your white captain."

It was better this way, Blossom thought, blinking back tears. If she fell any more in love with War Cry than she already was, she might not have the inner strength to do what had to be done. "That will be fine."

He snorted and checked the cinch of his saddle. "You've been nothing but trouble since that first night I found you on the prairie. The old chiefs are right!"

He cupped his hands so that she might put her foot in them, mount up. He untied the horse and swung up behind her as she reached down into her bodice to take out the little blue prairie flower he had given her.

How do I love thee? Let me count the ways . . .

She might never again experience anything like those moments in War Cry's arms again, so she would save the flower forever. Or maybe it would be the only evidence that this hadn't been some strange hallucination. She kept her body rigid, not settling back against him as they rode out.

She felt him sigh as he urged the horse into a canter. "It

was a mistake," he whispered, and she didn't know if that was regret in his tone. "I never should have touched you."

Her heart and her body would never forget. She must start letting go of him now; get used to living without him. "You're right," she agreed, "it was a big mistake and tomorrow, we'll pretend it never happened!"

Seventeen

They met Captain Radley at the head of a patrol riding along the road as Blossom and War Cry rode to the fort.

The officer held up his hand to halt his troop. "Thank god you're alive! Where have you been?"

"I might ask you the same thing," Blossom answered cooly. "War Cry found me out on the prairie after you ran away and left me."

She heard a faint snicker run through the patrol. The officer's pale face reddened, and he ran his finger around his collar as if it were choking him. "Well, I—I—when I saw how many savages there were, I decided I'd have to return to the fort for reinforcements."

She felt War Cry's body tighten with tension against her. "You abandoned a girl out on the prairie and saved yourself?"

The smothered laughter grew louder while the captain's face turned an angry red. "I told you, I was going for help."

Blossom sniffed in disdain. "I don't need your help now, Captain, thanks to this Pawnee scout." She nudged the horse forward and they rode on toward the fort.

Behind them, the captain yelled, "War Cry, I want to see you in my office later!"

"Yes sir." He didn't look back.

Immediately, Blossom regretted her rash words. "Oh my, I've embarrassed that coward and he'll take it out on you."

"I can take care of myself, kid; don't worry about me."

Yet she couldn't help but worry as he turned the horse toward Doc's office. "I think the captain could become a dangerous enemy. According to history, he lives to be ninety-seven and rises to the rank of colonel."

He stopped in front of Doc's office, dismounted, looked up at her thoughtfully. "The old shaman is right; you have big medicine. I should have known it from the moment you appeared out of nowhere. Perhaps that is why you survived the Sioux attack on the stage."

He still didn't quite understand, Blossom thought, but it was just as well. She sensed that sooner or later, she would probably be returning to her own time for eternity. She slid off the paint stallion and marveled at how strong War Cry's hands were when he helped her down. "There are things I can't tell you; just know that I may only have a little time here."

He nodded somberly. "We all have only a little time, a moment in the vast scheme of things like a comet flashing across the blackness. Instead, we all act as if we will last forever, like the mountains."

He had misunderstood her meaning; he thought she spoke of death. Whatever the decision might be that she faced, she must make it alone. They walked toward Doc's office.

War Cry said, "If you really have seen the future, can you tell me what happens to my people?"

She paused and looked up at him. "I—I don't remember much detail. If I could tell you your fate, would you really want to know?"

He seemed to think about it a long time. "I'm not sure. If anyone could *really* know what lay in store for them, would they choose to?"

Blossom shrugged. "I'm a research librarian, but I depend on computers, Internet, and millions of research volumes, I don't carry all my knowledge in my head."

He looked mystified and she made a gesture of dismissal. "Believe me, I can't explain all that." She tried to recall what she knew of the Pawnee or if she'd ever read anything specific about a warrior named War Cry. Some hazy memory floated just out of her reach, something she couldn't quite or didn't want to remember. "I know your people end up in northern Oklahoma, Indian Territory. None of the tribes came out well against the whites."

War Cry made a derisive sound. "It doesn't take big medicine to guess that."

She paused at the door, wavering. "I think I'm going to tell Doc everything; but I'm afraid he'll think I'm crazy."

"Doc's pretty smart. Remember, Blossom, your medicine is powerful; the old shaman said so."

"If I come back and change even the slightest thing, suppose that detail causes a ripple effect that creates some terrible evil in the future?"

"Or changes that evil to something good?"

She wasn't one to take chances. "War Cry—"

"Yes?"

How could she tell this man she loved that sooner or later, she would leave him forever? The shaman had told her to keep that secret. "Never mind. Are you coming?"

He shook his head and pushed the jaunty blue cap back. "Soon the captain will be back in his office, and madder than a bee-stung bull, but I'll be expected to report."

She watched him stride away, loving his big-shouldered masculine gait. He swaggers when he walks, she thought, a real Alpha male.

Doc sat at his desk, looking over some files. As she came in, he stood up. "Ah, Miss Blossom, we were so worried about you—"

"We were waylaid by a Sioux war party, but War Cry found me."

Doc hurried to pull up a chair for her. "That's what Lex said. He said he barely escaped, came back to get a patrol—"

"He ran like a scared rabbit," Blossom laughed, taking the seat. "War Cry was the one who saved me."

"I figured as much." Doc grinned and ran his finger over his mustache. "Hazel will be so relieved. Are you hurt?"

Blossom shook her head. "That's not why I came, Doc. I have some things I want to tell you."

Doc's weathered face grew somber. "All right, I've heard a lot over my long career; I don't think much of anything would surprise me now."

"This may." Blossom took a deep breath. "I know you'll think I'm loco and ought to be locked up, but hear me out."

He sat down and leaned back in his chair. "I'm listening."

"I'm from the future; I've come back in time from the year 1995."

He stared at her a long moment. "Would you repeat that?"

She said it again.

"Hmm." He got up from the desk.

Oh fudge! she thought, he's going to call someone and have me locked up.

Instead, he went over to a cabinet, poured them each a small glass of sherry, brought it back. "I've had a feeling you were different somehow since the first time I saw you, but I've got an open mind. You talk and I'll listen." He handed her the sherry.

Blossom took it gratefully and sipped it. The taste was bracing. Quickly, she told him how she had touched the painting, unknowingly completed the circle, and was suddenly in the year of 1873.

Doc drank his sherry and stared at her. "You're serious about this? You're really not Blossom May Westfield, the missing schoolteacher?"

Blossom shook her head. "I don't know what happened to that poor thing, dead in the stagecoach massacre, I guess. History says they never found her body."

"Isn't it sort of unusual that her clothes fit you and you both have the same first name?" Doc scratched his head.

"It can only be sheer coincidence," she dismissed it as she set the glass on his cluttered desk. "Lots of women wear that size dress and the name's become very common. In my time, there's even a television show by that name."

"A what?"

"Some day, I'll try to explain about all the new inventions, Doc. I'm not a teacher; I'm a research librarian for *Tattletale.*"

"Our little country paper?" His shaggy eyebrows went up.

"Well, in 1995, it'll be a big sleazy tabloid and Victor Lamarto won't be proud of either his descendant or what he's done with his crusading little paper."

"I don't even know what a tabloid is, I'm afraid."

"You don't believe me, do you?" Blossom sighed.

"I'm trying really hard to," Doc admitted. "Just think what it would be like to talk to someone who really is from more than a hundred years in the future, mind-boggling." He clasped his sherry in both hands, leaned toward her eagerly. "Suppose what you say is true? Tell me, have there been a great many changes in medicine?"

"Doc, you wouldn't believe what medicine is doing now, transplanting body parts."

"You are joking me, aren't you? Why, I'd be thrilled to hear they've discovered a cure for yellow fever."

Blossom shook her head. "I'm not joking, Doc. Smallpox has been wiped off the face of the earth and exciting things are happening in medicine. And, like I told you, yellow fever is carried by mosquitoes, and they'll discover that while digging the Panama Canal."

His eyes grew big behind his glasses. "They'll really dig a canal across Panama?"

She nodded. "It would take forever to tell you everything that's happened."

"Well then," he smiled, "people must be healthy and happy."

"No, there's still cancer and a terrible disease called AIDS that's going to kill millions if no one finds a cure."

"But at least," he leaned forward eagerly, "in the future,

the country is civilized, and they don't have to fear outlaws and violence anymore?"

Blossom bit her lip to keep from laughing at the sheer irony of his words. "Not hardly! In some ways, neither the country nor the world has changed much; sometimes it seems people look out for themselves and no one else."

"That's discouraging." He frowned. "I've tried so hard to make a difference, but I'm just a small-town sawbones after all." He leaned back in his chair. "Hazel and I don't have much, very little money and no children to carry on for us. Sometimes I feel like a drop of water in the ocean of Time. I wanted my life to matter; do great things for mankind."

"You'll make a difference, Doc; even though you may not realize it. We all can; no matter how small, no life is worthless."

"Then that's why you've been sent back here," Doc said. It was a statement, not a question.

Blossom laughed. "I wasn't sent, Doc. I stumbled into this thing, but I can't stay."

His face turned somber. "How do you know that?"

She knew she could not tell everything; old Beaver Robe had warned her. "If I'm in a time that isn't my own, it upsets history."

"I see." He stood up, went to stare out the window at the passing cowboys and buggies. "What about Terry? Does he know?"

She felt the tears rise in her throat and she shook her head while she swallowed hard. "I'm not sure I can make the right choice, if and when it ever comes. I alone have to make that choice; War Cry might try to interfere."

He stood up and went to the window, looking out. "I had such high hopes for the future of this country. What's happened?"

Blossom sighed and admitted, "In some cases, nothing's improved over the civilization you've got. There will be two terrible world wars in the future."

"Over what?" He stared at her over his eye glasses.

"I don't remember," she admitted. "In the second one, m'
mother said the Nazis rounded up millions of Jews and sen
them to camps to be gassed and cremated."

"Good lord! And we call the Indians savages!"

"I know; 'Ask not for whom the bell tolls; it tolls fo
thee.' Humanity is poorer for the loss."

Doc sighed thoughtfully. "So much sometimes turns on
some small thing. What history has been changed because
some immigrant ship sank on its way to America, or perhaps
the child who might have written the next great symphony
or made the next great medical discovery died as an infant?"

Blossom stood up. "That's what scares me. History is like
a piece of fabric; all these little threads. If I pull one, I migh'
change the future—for better or worse. Suppose I cause the
Nazis to win World War II or the Berlin Wall to never be
torn down?"

"My dear," Doc said kindly, "I haven't the foggiest idea
what you're talking about."

"That's okay." She smiled at him. "It's mind-boggling. I'm
almost afraid to think what I can do with this knowledge—if
anyone will believe me. I may not have the courage to try;
courage was never one of my stronger qualities."

Doc paced his office, lost in thought. "If you've been de-
liberately sent back in time to change history, you need to
talk to President Grant or the congress."

"Then you believe me?" Her heart leaped.

He grinned at her over his spectacles. "I may be crazy,"
he said, "but I do. Sometimes even scientists have to go on
blind faith without a shred of evidence to back them up."

"You know," Blossom admitted, "I never told anyone this,
but I wanted to be a doctor or a medical researcher. You
make a difference in a world when nothing else seems to."

He pulled at his mustache. "Can't women in the future do
things like that?"

Blossom nodded. "Part of the reason I became a librarian,

I guess, was that I lacked the money for all that additional schooling and there weren't enough scholarships. Oh, who am I kidding?" She shrugged in defeat. "I also lacked the self-confidence and the initiative to go for the whole enchilada; I wasn't willing to go for broke."

"Young lady, some of what you say doesn't make much sense," Doc smiled.

"I know; it's slang. What am I going to do, Doc? People will either laugh or lock me up if I start telling them all this," Blossom said.

Doc paused and studied her. "You might avert disasters, save lives. President Grant should hear this."

Blossom shook her head. "Now how would I get an audience with the president? And even if I could, I don't have the money to travel to Washington."

Doc went over to his desk. "I knew Ulysses in the Civil War and I've got a little money set aside."

"I couldn't take your money," Blossom protested.

"Well, I can't go," Doc said. "I'm the only doctor on the post. Besides, no one would believe me anyway."

"Oh, fudge!" she exclaimed. "You think they'll believe me?"

"Your insights are very convincing, young lady." Doc chewed the tip of his mustache. "Think of the good you could do by changing the course of history."

"Think of the chaos I might cause, too," Blossom reminded him. "I'd just soon not stick my neck out, thank you very kindly."

"You disappoint me, Blossom."

"That's not fair! They probably won't listen anyway," Blossom argued. "In my time period, they've been warned about everything from pollution to the national debt, but nobody cares; all they do is shrug and go on."

Doc stopped his pacing. "If I give you a letter to the president and some money for a train ticket, will you at least try?"

"One person can't make a difference!"

"You just got through telling me one could. Besides, how do you know if you don't try?" Doc confronted her.

"I—I'm afraid," Blossom said as tears welled up and she choked them back. "I'm just an ordinary person who wants to mind her own business, not take any chances, and not get involved."

"A perfect recipe for the decline of civilization," Doc said.

"That's exactly what's happened," she admitted with a guilty flush.

"Then you'll do it?"

Blossom hesitated. "My mother would have done it; she was a heroine."

"It's never too late to start."

A long moment of struggle within herself. The office was so quiet, she heard the old building creak in the prairie wind. "All right, Doc, I'll give it my best shot."

Doc wiped the June heat from his face. "I'll make the arrangements and let's keep this secret. Young lady, in a few days, you are going to meet with President Ulysses S. Grant!"

This time as Captain Radley's buggy took her to the train, they were accompanied by a troop of soldiers. Blossom was cool to him, but he seemed to be on his very best behavior. "You know, Miss Blossom, I wish you'd let me make amends. I really was going for help when I left you."

Blossom didn't answer, staring straight ahead at the bay horse pulling the buggy. She didn't believe for an instant that he'd done anything but flee in terror. Yet someday, this handsome blackguard's family would own a giant agro-corporation powerful enough to take over her family's farm and most of three states.

"Miss Blossom, I got a wire from my mother yesterday when the telegraph wires were repaired. She returned to Philadelphia after the train was stopped in the Indian scare.

Her side of the family is quite powerful, so if you'd call on her and I gave you a letter explaining—"

"Dr. Maynard has already given me letters of introduction," she said coolly. "I don't think I'll need your help, thank you."

"When you return," he looked around, lowered his tone as if to make sure the troopers didn't hear, "I'd like a chance to make amends."

Blossom frowned. "I don't think so." There was no point in telling him that she expected to return to her own time, nor had she told him why she was going east. She'd said something vague about visiting old friends.

"This isn't the time or place to discuss this," he said, "but I have feelings for you. Perhaps when you get to know me better, you might give me serious consideration."

"Are you asking me to marry you?" She was incredulous, and it must have shown both in her expression and her tone, because his handsome face turned brick red.

"Well, yes, if you want to be blunt about it."

"Well, I—"

"Don't give me your answer now, Miss Blossom, but do study on it," he said smoothly. "After all, by your own admission, didn't you say I'd live to be ninety-seven years old and found a great family dynasty?"

She nodded, reluctant to admit his future success.

He gave her his most charming smile. "Like I said, dear Miss Blossom, don't make any decisions yet, think on it. However, I must admit I think my heart will break if you don't marry me."

She didn't answer, lost in thought. She wondered now if this was what she had been returned to set right? If she and the captain married and produced a child, would that event keep the Murdocks from losing their farm over a hundred years from now? "I'll think on it."

"You'll never know how happy you've made me." He tried to take her hand, but she kept them in her lap and resisted.

"I swear, when you get back, I'm going to shower you with such devotion, you'll have to accept my proposal."

"I said I'd think on it," Blossom snapped, looking across the prairie as the buggy rolled down the dusty road, the summer heat stirring up butterflies as they passed. Her mind was on War Cry, and she was angry with herself that she couldn't forget the brief time she had spent in his arms. That had been a mistake; she must think of the bigger picture and the consequences of history.

They said little the rest of the trip to the station, but when Captain Radley put her on the train, he was still vowing his faithful devotion until she returned. Then he stood on the wooden platform with his troops and waved while the train headed east across the dusty Nebraska landscape.

Blossom watched him waving until he was only a tiny dot on the horizon behind her, but her thoughts were on the Pawnee brave. She couldn't take War Cry with her when she returned to her own time, but if he knew, he would try to thwart whatever was scheduled to happen, keep her from leaving him forever.

"I'm not brave enough to do this, take any risks, do anything daring," Blossom whispered. Safe, she always played it safe. If she'd had any courage and confidence, she would have tried to get into medical school. No, hiding back in the stacks of dusty books and computer files was a good place for a shy mouse like herself.

"Oh fudge! Stop thinking like that," she scolded herself. "You're now on your way to meet the president of the United States to try to change history. That takes a little guts, after all." She smiled, thinking a Victorian lady wouldn't say guts, she'd say intestinal fortitude.

Blossom got out her book of poetry to entertain herself as the train swayed and clattered over the tracks heading east. When she opened the little volume, the pressed flower fell from between its pages. She picked it up, smiling gently. The faint fragrance still lingered, and she remembered making love to War Cry in the grass at night and how he had given her the blossom.

How do I love thee? Let me count the ways. I love thee to the depth and breadth and height my soul can reach . . . I love thee to the level of every day's most quiet need, by sun and candle-light . . .

Oh lord, she must not, *could* not love him at all! There was no future in it. Yet she didn't throw away the dried flower, she tucked it carefully between the pages and put the book away. Ahead of her lay a long trip and a formidable task. She, who always avoided confrontation, was going to try to convince the president of the United States that he should believe she had journeyed back in time more than a hundred years. Grant had been a tough, hard-bitten general in the Civil War; how could she expect him to believe her? The rhythm of the rails finally lulled Blossom to sleep and she dreamed of War Cry and his warm embrace.

Captain Radley scowled as he watched the train pull out, even though he continued to wave until it was only a small dot on the eastern horizon. Damn that uppity girl! Miss Westfield ought to be thrilled to accept his proposal, instead, she was turning him down. He had always gotten what he wanted, his mother had seen to that because he was her adored only son, even though she sometimes punished him severely. Lex thought about being locked in the toy box again and shuddered. Ye gods! Would he ever get over this fear of closed-in places? When preachers talked of hell as punishment for sins, Lex always pictured being buried alive forever, with no one answering his cries for help.

Sweat beaded on his forehead and he took out a handkerchief and wiped it away as he returned to the buggy. He must stop thinking like that or he would never get over this fear. Maybe he should talk to Dr. Maynard about it. No, of course he couldn't do that. Lex looked straight ahead at the plodding horse as he turned the buggy around. To ask for help would be to admit a weakness that might slow his rise in the army. Hadn't Miss Blossom predicted he'd end up a colonel, rich, respected, and live a long, long time?

He breathed a sigh of relief at the thought. He must stop reading those haunting stories. He'd think about the girl instead. However strange she might be, it appeared Blossom could read the future, and in doing so, could make him a very rich man. His mother was always consulting with astrologers and Gypsy palm readers, so he could believe a girl might be able to see the future. Blossom's prediction about the Colt revolver had come true, and he'd made some profit on that. Blossom Westfield was just the wife he needed and he'd do whatever it took to get her.

Thinking about women made his groin ache. For the briefest instant, he wondered if that half-witted wench, Myrtle, had told anyone what he'd done, then decided she'd be afraid to. Besides, it wasn't as if she was anyone of importance.

Tonight, he wanted a classier female and he wasn't drunk this time. With his intended bride out of town, he could go to Rusty's Place without fear of Blossom finding out. After all, a man had needs. There was one more thing he wanted to take care of. He had to get that damned scout off the post permanently.

It was dusk by the time he returned to the fort, washed up, and wrote the note. Humming to himself after he'd left the letter, he headed for the bordello, his mind on women. He saw Terry riding in from his scouting mission, grinned to himself. The captain was about to remove that thorn from his side forever.

Music and laughter drifted on the hot summer night as Captain Radley entered Rusty's. The troops had just been paid and the saloon was full of soldiers. Buffalo hunters and settlers competed for a place at the bar. Smoke swirled across the big room and the scent of stale beer and cheap perfume drifted to his nostrils.

The walls seemed to close in on him. He elbowed a cowboy aside and pushed up to the bar. "Gimme a whiskey."

He saw Myrtle sweeping up some broken glass over by a table. When she saw him, her face paled and she scurried away. The captain took his drink and smiled at himself in the bar mirror with satisfaction. No, the little half-wit wouldn't tell. He must have been very drunk to feel any lust for that ugly slut.

Dolly sidled up to the bar beside him. "Hey, handsome, buy me a drink."

He turned, smiling at her as she pressed her breast against his arm. "Let's skip the preliminaries, Dolly."

She laughed and he noted that her lip rouge was smeared and her breasts were swelling out of the top of her crimson dress. "Okay, since you want to be crude; let's go."

He nodded and followed her as she led him in threading her way through the raucous crowd and up the stairs. He watched the way her hips moved in the tight red satin and felt his manhood swell with need. Below him, a chorus of drunks around the piano were singing an off-key version of an old song: *". . . Buffalo gals, won't you come out tonight, come out tonight, come out tonight? Buffalo gals, won't you come out tonight and dance in the light of the moon?"*

They went into her room and she closed the door, but still, the faint sound of music and dancing, the click of the roulette wheel drifted up the stairs and into the room. "A quick one?" she asked. "Or you wanta stay awhile?"

"Open the windows; it's close in here." He'd forgotten how small this room was, like a box. Lex flopped down in a comfortable chair, thinking about Blossom and how she'd spurned him. Snotty bitch! He'd have her yet. "I got me a real need, Dolly. I plan on being here all night."

Her greedy, painted eyes lit up as she turned from pushing up the window. "Okay, handsome, can I pour you another drink?"

"Please." He drained his glass and held it out to her. "I like to see the merchandise."

She smiled archly as she took the glass, reaching down to unbutton her low-cut bodice so that her breasts were bare. She swung her hips as she went over to a cupboard, filled the glass, brought it back to him.

He reached out with one hand, grabbed her breast and squeezed it, took the drink. "I like you, Dolly. We understand each other."

"You ain't been around lately." She put her hands on her hips, looking annoyed. "I hear you been chasin' after that prissy little schoolteacher."

He sipped his drink. "Now, that's got nothing to do with us, Dolly. A man picks out a particular kind of girl to marry, but that doesn't mean he has to give up having fun."

"Then if you marry her, you wouldn't quit coming in here to spend money?" She appeared mollified.

"Of course not." He wondered how many men had already mounted Dolly tonight, and the thought aroused him. He held out his drink. "Put a little sugar in it for me."

She smiled, sauntered over, took the drink. As he watched in anticipation, she dipped her bare nipple in the glass.

"More."

She grinned at him, dipped her other nipple in the liquor, returned to his chair. He took the drink, set it on the chair-side table, reached out to pull her down on his lap. Very slowly, he began to lick the whiskey off her breasts while she writhed in his lap making soft noises in her throat. No, he wasn't about to give up hot little bitches like Dolly. If he married Blossom and she really could read the future, he'd have plenty of money so he could have all the whores he wanted, while Blossom provided him with intelligent, well-bred heirs. "The best of both worlds," he muttered.

"What'd you say, sport?"

He reached down to unbutton his pants as he slid Dolly off onto the carpet at his feet. "Never mind. I got a nice candy stick. You gave me some sugar, now I got something sweet for your little mouth."

Dolly giggled. "Turn about's fair play and we got all night, honey!"

War Cry had seen the captain going into Rusty's Place and wondered if the officer had seen him. He had a need for a woman himself tonight, but only one woman could put out this fire in his groin. Blossom. He imagined her pale blue eyes and creamy breasts; he needed her as he had never needed another woman. Damn her, she had ruined him for other women. He couldn't think of anyone but her.

So instead of heading into Rusty's, he went back to his quarters to clean up. Maybe if he went to Doc's, he could see Blossom. Then he shook his head. Give it up, he told himself, she doesn't want to see you anymore. Yet War Cry couldn't imagine life without her. He wanted her sleeping in his arms every night, he wanted to give her his child. More than anything, he wanted her to love him as he loved her.

Small chance of that, he thought bitterly. Something had changed once she had talked with the old shaman, Beaver Robe. Maybe Blossom was now as aware as he was that a romance between an Indian and a white girl had no future unless she had the nerve and courage to turn her back on everything and everyone, dare to love him anyway. Unfortunately, Blossom seemed to lack the brave spunk to confront anyone. She was too shy and uncertain—or maybe she just didn't care enough about him to go through what it would take to be his woman.

There was a note on his bunk he hadn't noticed before. His heart leaped with anticipation. Maybe it was from Blossom. He grabbed it up and read it in the flickering lamplight.

Only then did he realize what it was. He was being discharged from his service as a scout. War Cry was ordered to leave the post and the army's employment effective immediately. It was signed with a flourish by Capt. Lexington Brewster Radley.

Damn the man! War Cry crumpled the paper and tossed it away. He'd figured the captain would go to any length to keep him away from Blossom, but he hadn't counted on the rash officer firing him. War Cry was the best scout on the post. Did Blossom have any knowledge of this?

War Cry strode through the darkness, crept back to Blossom's room, knocked on the window. No answer. The light was still on in the front part of the house. He went around, knocked politely on the door.

Doc answered, peering out into the darkness. "Terry! Glad to see you! You've been gone?"

War Cry nodded. "Just got back from a scout. Can I—can I see Miss Westfield?"

Doc's face furrowed. "She's not here, Terry; she's gone back East on a trip."

"A trip? When did she leave? Is she coming back?"

"I told her I wouldn't tell you."

War Cry grabbed him by the coat front. "Doc, we're friends, but if you don't tell me—"

"You really care that much about her, do you?" Doc disentangled himself from the other's strong hands. He looked behind him as if he wanted to make sure his wife wasn't in the room. "Blossom told me that long story about coming from the future."

"Did you believe her?"

"It's hard not to; she's so convincing."

War Cry remembered the way she had made love to him. Yes, she could be very convincing, all right; she could even make a man think she cared about him. "Where has she gone, Doc?"

The old man looked almost shamefaced; hesitated. "She

doesn't think she's got much time here; that she's got to go back."

"Back?" He felt a sinking in his gut. "Back where?"

"Whatever time she belongs in; I wasn't supposed to tell you that."

War Cry leaned against the wall. So that was it. Somewhere in the depths of his mind, in his distant memory was another loss; a loss so terrible that he'd have done anything to stop it. It was only a fragment, like a crazy dream that he couldn't make sense of. No, that couldn't be. He couldn't have suffered such pain before; Blossom was a once-in-a-lifetime love. He could never love again as he loved this blue-eyed girl. Yes, she was so special, she had to have come from another time; even old Beaver Robe had sensed that. "Doc, tell me the rest."

"Well, I suppose I might as well. In whatever time she's got left, she's trying to do something worthwhile. I gave her money and letters of introduction. She's going to see the president and tell him what she knows of the future."

War Cry felt a chill of apprehension. "She isn't very brave. You let her make that trip alone?"

"The captain escorted her to the station, got her safely on the train. I couldn't go because I'm the only doctor this area has. She asked me not to tell you."

She hadn't wanted him to know and the captain had sent him out on patrol until she was safely gone. He felt a sinking feeling. "Is she—is she coming back?"

"I don't know." Doc looked sympathetic. "No telling what will happen when she gets to Washington."

"I should have gone with her," War Cry muttered half to himself. "She's liable to run into trouble."

"But you're busy here at the fort—"

"The captain just fired me," War Cry said wryly. "I've got plenty of time."

"Oh? I'm sorry to hear that, Terry."

"I should have gone with her," he muttered again.

The old man looked at him over his spectacles. "You're not thinking of going to Washington? You could get into a whole lot of trouble up north—"

"So could Blossom," War Cry snapped as he turned to leave the porch. "I'll see you when I get back—if I get back."

"But, Terry—"

"You can't stop me; she needs me. I told her I would always be there for her; that's a promise I intend to keep!" He turned and strode into the night with Doc Maynard protesting behind him. No wonder the captain was in Rusty's Place! Blossom was gone and he figured she'd never know the difference.

He didn't give a damn about what Lex Radley did; all War Cry worried about was Blossom. He'd never been more than a couple of hundred miles in any direction from the fort or his Pawnee village, and the thought of a long journey deep into the white man's bustling city gave him pause. In his mind, he saw Blossom's small face, her vulnerable eyes. Yes, she could get into serious trouble if she began to tell a bunch of white people she came from the future. There was no help for it, War Cry had to follow her, whether to Washington or straight into hell!

Eighteen

It is sweltering hot, Blossom thought as she stared out the train window. The July wind blowing through the opening felt like a blast furnace with the cinders and smoke drifting into the car. Too bad there were no air-conditioners and jet planes. She'd forgone the corset, yet the heavy dress and stockings still made her skin damp with heat.

The sensation made her think of the frenzied loving she had experienced with War Cry, and she sighed wistfully in spite of herself. There were some things in this time that were superior to the twentieth century.

She watched an old man sway down the aisle toward the water cooler, grabbing at the back of the horsehair seats to keep from falling. He paused next to her to cough into his handkerchief and Blossom found herself pulling away, wondering if he had tuberculosis, a prevalent disease of that period that was making a comeback in modern times. Even as she wondered, he finished his journey to the water cooler at the end of the swaying, creaking car. There was a tin dipper attached by a chain to the water keg. The old man poured himself a dipperful of water, drank it down.

Right behind the old man came a young girl who started to drink out of the same dipper.

"Don't do that!" Blossom half-rose from her seat to protest.

The freckled-faced girl stared at her. "What?"

"It might be full of germs," Blossom said, "get a paper cup."

The whole car seemed to be staring at her and mumbling.

"Excuse me, ma'am," the girl said, "but I don't know what you're talking about." She drank out of the dipper.

Well, at least she had tried. Blossom sank back down in her seat, marveling that she had had the nerve to say anything.

In this day and time, no one thought much about a whole train sharing a dipper. In small towns everywhere, there were similar dippers hanging by a chain next to the town well with the entire populace stopping to use it. Behind her, she heard a man hacking and coughing, spitting on the floor, and shuddered. Who in the twentieth century realized those rustic-looking "Don't Spit on the Sidewalk" bricks that were sold in antique shops were once part of an effort to stop the spread of disease?

Blossom returned to staring out the open window. Strange, so much of the landscape along the track looked vaguely familiar to her. Why was that? She'd never traveled by train before, leastways, not that she could remember. Sometimes she imagined other scenes of places and people she was certain she'd never met . . . well, maybe she might have read them in a historical romance novel, she admitted to herself.

She checked her reticule to make sure she still had her letter of introduction from Doc Maynard. Was she doing the right thing in trying to see the president? Before, she had always been a shy and docile observer, not an active participant in events. She held the letter up to the sunlight and reread it. Yes, this letter would clear the way for her. Abruptly, a gust of wind took it from her fingers and blew the paper out the window.

"Oh, my god!" She stuck her head out the window, staring after the blowing paper that took off across the prairie as if it had wings. Cinders and dust blew in her eyes as she stared in horror.

Blossom jumped to her feet, ran down the swaying aisle

and grabbed the conductor by the arm. "You've got to stop this train! My letter has blown away; it's very important!"

The old man blinked. "Hey, what's that you say, Miss?"

"You've got to stop this train so I can retrieve my letter!" She was shrieking now, not caring that people were staring.

He pulled out his big gold watch and peered at it. "We're behind schedule now. Surely you don't expect me to stop a train over a scrap of paper?"

In vain, Blossom tried to explain, but to no avail. What to do? She returned to her seat. Well, now what? She wasn't sure what to do next. She'd always avoided dealing with tough decisions, and yet, back here in time, she kept running into them.

"I know!" She brightened. "At the next station, I'll wire Doc to send me another!"

The best laid plans . . . At the next stop, she was told the wires to Fort McPherson were down again. The train blew a warning blast that it was preparing to leave the station.

"Oh, fudge! No, dammit, dammit, dammit!" People turned to stare, evidently aghast at hearing a lady swear, but Blossom was too desperate to care. Hiking up her full skirts, she ran for the train.

Once aboard, she tried to think things out. There was no way to get another letter of introduction, she was on her own. She'd just tell the president the truth about losing it, or maybe the wires would be back up by the time she got there and Doc could telegraph Grant a message explaining everything.

Unfortunately, when she arrived in Washington, D. C., she discovered that the president and his family were at some vacation home in Long Branch, New Jersey, rather than in the city. It seemed, because of the mosquitoes and the unhealthy atmosphere, everyone who could had left town for the summer.

"What else can happen?" Blossom grumbled to herself as she took a carriage back to the station. Carefully, she opened her purse and counted her money. Doc had given her a little for emergencies, but not much. "Oh, for my credit cards or my Frequent Flyer program! In those historical romances, they never tell you how slow and boring those old trains are."

What to do? What she felt like doing was wringing her hands helplessly and giving up, but this money of Doc's was hard-earned. She couldn't let him down. She tried the telegraph again, but there'd been a storm somewhere on the plains and it wasn't working.

Maybe she could contact Lex Radley's mother. In her mind, she imagined sending the Philadelphia society matron a telegram. That wouldn't help, she realized, they didn't wire money in those days. Besides, from everything Lex had said about his stern parent, Blossom didn't feel she could expect any sympathy anyway.

She recounted her money and checked the price of a ticket to New Jersey. She might have just enough if she ate nothing but bread and crackers all the way. Once there, she'd just have to rely on Grant's help.

It took some trouble to end up on the ornate gingerbread front porch of the president's summer home, and she was hungry, but that didn't matter.

Blossom wasn't sure she had the right house; there didn't seem to be any secret service or official-looking, grim-faced men around. She walked right up on the doorstep and rang the bell. A little Irish maid answered the door. "Yes, Miss?"

"Is—is this the Grant home?"

"Mum, Wednesday is Mrs. Grant's day to be at home to callers, but if you'd like to have me give her your card . . ."

"A card?" Oh, those damned Victorian calling cards that had seemed so charming in romance novels. "I—I seemed to have arrived without any," Blossom gulped, "but I've come a long way and it's very important."

The girl looked at her uncertainly while Blossom stood there in the heat, perspiration plastering her long dress to her body. Air-conditioning, Blossom thought, I'd give my soul for a little air-conditioning. "Oh, please," she said to the maid, "I've come a long way to see the president."

The maid's expression seemed to soften. "He's not in, Mum, but I'll see if Mrs. Grant will see you."

Blossom leaned against the ornate gingerbread porch column and waited, wondering what to do next?

However, in a few minutes, the little maid returned. "This is most unusual, miss, but I told Mrs. Grant you seemed so desperate—"

"Bless you," Blossom said as she entered. "May John Kennedy offer your descendant a fat government job!"

"Who?"

"Never mind, just thank you." Blossom followed the girl inside. The comfortable, Victorian home was filled to over-flowing with bric-a-brac and overstuffed furniture, lace curtains and flowered wallpaper. No wonder Mark Twain called this the Gilded Age and the name had stuck.

The Irish maid led Blossom out onto a screened-in porch where a plain-faced, plump lady sat in a wicker rocker. "Hello, my dear."

"Mrs. Grant? My name is Blossom Murdock. I had a letter of introduction from Dr. Maynard, but I lost it." She tried not to stare, having forgotten that Mrs. Grant was cross-eyed. In fact, if she remembered correctly, when Julia had wanted to have corrective surgery attempted, the President had assured her that he liked her eyes just fine and she remained cross-eyed.

"Do come in, my dear. Would you like some lemonade and tea cakes?"

"I certainly would; it's terribly hot outside." Blossom accepted the cold glass with a smile and gulped it. She tried to be dainty about the tea cakes, but she hadn't had anything to eat except crackers for several days. Despite herself, she found herself gobbling the food. "I had really hoped to meet with your husband."

"Ulys will be back later; he's meeting voters down at city hall this morning." She leaned back in her wicker chair and it creaked.

"Don't you people worry about security?" Blossom drained the cold lemonade and reached for another cookie.

"Security?"

"I mean, after Lincoln's assassination, I'd think you'd worry about such things."

Julia's plain face saddened. "That was dreadful, wasn't it? But surely we've seen the last of presidential assassinations."

"No, there'll be three more," Blossom blurted without thinking, "the next one will be President Garfield in 1881."

"What did you say?" With Julia Grant's crossed brown eyes, it was difficult to know if she was looking at Blossom, but there was no one else in the room.

"Mrs. Grant, I've come because I have information of upmost importance to the president."

The First Lady nodded. "Oh?"

How much should she tell Julia Grant? Should she wait for the president? She stared longingly at the last cookie. The First Lady promptly offered her the plate. "Are you hungry, my dear?"

Blossom felt her face redden, but she took the cookie anyway. "A little," she admitted. "I didn't have enough money for the extra ticket and food, too."

About that time, she heard the maid answering the front door and the sound of a man's voice. The Irish voice said something about the porch and within minutes, she heard a man's footsteps. Blossom turned. He was stocky and bearded, a cigar clenched between his teeth. Ulysses S. Grant came out onto the porch.

She was seeing an actual historical figure. For a moment,

all Blossom could do was gape at him, thinking what a moment in time this was for her and what an interview it would make. Then she shook her head. All *Tattletale* would be interested in was not the Civil War or his presidency, but the seamy stuff such as his drinking and the corruption in his administration. A full minute must have passed while she stared up at him, even though Julia Grant was in the midst of making introductions.

"Charmed," the president bowed and took a seat. He looked just like he did in the books, Blossom thought, gray-streaked beard, dark eyes.

"Ulys, dear," his wife fanned herself, "must you smoke those terrible things around ladies?"

"Oh, I'm sorry, I do forget sometimes." The man ground out the cigar. "I forget how ladies are wont to faint at the scent of tobacco smoke."

Blossom decided this wasn't the time to tell him that many modern women had taken up that questionable habit.

He looked at his plump, plain wife with genuine fondness. "So, Mrs. G., is this an old friend of yours?"

Mrs. Grant shook her head. "Ulys, dear, Miss Murdock seems a little, well, desperate, and said something about a letter of introduction from a Dr. Maynard."

The president grinned. "Doc? How is the old rascal? Haven't seen him since the war."

"Fine, he sends his best." How to begin?

"Ulys, she says she has a message of upmost importance."

"Oh? From Doc Maynard?"

"No, from the future," Blossom blurted, then realized from the way they both looked at her that she should have used a different approach. Oh, fudge, she had made a mess of it!

Grant combed his fingers through his beard. "The future? Are you a Gypsy fortune-teller then?"

"Not exactly," Blossom said. "Please believe me; I know it sounds crazy, but I come from the future, and I'm here to warn you about what it holds."

They were both staring at her.

Mrs. Grant seemed to whisper to her husband, "She said something about assassinating someone named Garfield."

"No, that's not what I said!" Blossom protested, "I said Garfield would become president and he would be killed."

"What?" Grant leaned closer.

She had their undivided attention now. How much should she tell? How much would she be able to get the president to believe?

"I know you're going to have a hard time believing this, but I come from more than a hundred years into the future; 1995, to be exact," Blossom said. "I had a letter of introduction from Dr. Maynard, but it blew out the window."

"I see." Grant raised one eyebrow skeptically.

"If you'll hear me out, I could stop you from making many mistakes and save the country itself a lot of grief."

The president and his wife were exchanging glances. Blossom rushed on. "I'll prove to you that I know what's going to happen next. Your brother, Orville, is going to be under suspicion for corruption. In fact, General Custer will comment on it and lose your favor."

"Custer? You know George?" Grant frowned and Blossom remembered that the showy officer wasn't Grant's favorite.

"Not really," Blossom said, "but you are going to send him up to the Dakotas next year to search for gold and it will start a new Indian war."

President Grant made a dismissing gesture. "Oh, it doesn't take a fortune-teller to know that, we've always got an Indian war about to break."

"But suppose I tell you that there will be three more Presidents assassinated?" Blossom asked. "The next one will be Garfield."

"Garfield? Never heard of him!" Grant looked bored and annoyed.

"And three years from now, someone is going to attempt

to steal Lincoln's body from his tomb on Election Night to hold it for ransom."

Julia looked at her. "Who would do something terrible like that?"

"I—I've forgotten," Blossom admitted, "but believe me, it will happen. However, there's a lot more things on the horizon, flying machines, horseless carriages, world wars, if you'll just listen to me, maybe we can change history."

"Flying machines? You mean like balloons?" The President asked.

"No, these are big machines and they show movies as hundreds of people fly across the ocean to Europe," Blossom said.

"Movies?" Julia Grant looked at her cross-eyed.

"Flying to Europe? Ridiculous!" the president grumbled.

"I know it sounds crazy," Blossom hurried on, "but if you'll listen, I got so much to tell you about how to stop yellow fever. It's the heat and the mosquitoes—"

"Yes, my dear," Julia Grant leaned over and patted Blossom's arm, "it has been a very hot day outside, and I notice you didn't have a parasol."

"I'm all right," Blossom said, shrugged her hand off, "please don't treat me like a child; I just have so much to tell you of upmost importance!"

The other two exchanged glances.

Mrs. Grant said, "Of course you do! Now, you just tell Ulys, and I'll go get us another pitcher of lemonade." She picked up the pitcher and went into the house.

Blossom leaned closer. "Mister President, I don't have much time; I think I may be whisked back to the future any day or any moment."

He made a soothing gesture. "Now, young lady, you take all the time you want. Just how do you know Doc Maynard? Are you one of his patients?"

"Not exactly." Blossom thought it was a strange question, but the bearded man was smiling at her with a guarded, yet encouraging expression. "I realize we're really taking a chance in changing history, but I still think it's something that should be done."

"Miss Murdock," he eyed her thoughtfully, "you just take all the time you need and sit quietly; I'll be happy to listen."

So he might believe her after all. Blossom heaved a sigh of relief. "Well, I touched a painting, and in doing so, completed a magic circle and got yanked back in time."

"I see." The stocky man pulled at his beard. "You're a time traveler like those novels that Jules Verne fellow writes?"

"Oh, you've heard of him? It was sort of like that. By the way, you might be interested to know in my time we have been to the moon."

"And is it made of green cheese?"

"Mister President, please don't joke! I'm trying to tell you some of the most important things you'll ever hear! There's a terrible panic going to sweep across the country this September, because of a scandal that hits Wall Street about the railroad."

The president looked uneasy and made a soothing gesture. "Now, don't get excited, Miss."

Blossom had a sinking feeling. "You don't believe me, do you?"

"Oh, but of course I do!" President Grant reached out and patted her hand. "You say you're a patient of Doc Maynard's?"

"Well, more of a friend, although he did look at the bump on my head when I fell."

"I see, a bump on your head," the President repeated. "And how did that effect you?"

This wasn't going very well, Blossom thought as she shifted in her chair and wondered what had happened to Mrs. Grant who had never returned? The only thing she could do was start talking, do her best to warn President Grant about as many details as she could, and hope he believed her and acted on some of it. Blossom began to talk about some of the events of the future while the man's eyes got bigger and bigger.

"You say Custer will be killed in three years?"

Blossom nodded, "The Seventh Cavalry will be wiped out up on the Little Big Horn—"

"Ridiculous!" Grant made a dismissing gesture. "A handful of savages won't be able to do that—"

"Believe me, it will happen," Blossom assured him.

She heard the front door bell ring and low voices in the background. Then Mrs. Grant came into the room, accompanied by two burly policemen with handlebar mustaches.

The police captain touched the brim of his cap respectfully. "Mister President, you have a problem here?"

"Now, wait," Blossom protested. "I came on a perfectly reasonable mission—"

"I'm afraid," Mrs. Grant said, "the poor thing's got brain fever."

"Aye," the cop nodded, "delicate lady out in the sun without a bonnet or a parasol; ought to know better."

"Now, see here," Blossom protested, rising to her feet, "if you'll just contact Doc Maynard, he'll explain—"

"She's evidently one of his patients," the President muttered, "I guess we are going to have to start having some security so lunatics can't wander in off the street."

"I am not a lunatic!" Blossom's voice rose.

"Of course not, my dear." Mrs. Grant smiled sympathetically. "And I'm sure that with a little rest, you'll be just fine."

Blossom began to protest, but one big policeman took each arm. "You'll regret this!" Blossom shouted, trying to break free. "I could tell you everything that's going to happen for the next one hundred and twenty-two years!"

"Sure you can," the cop said and they began to lead Blossom away. "Now we've got a nice hospital for you to rest in."

Blossom did the only thing she could do, she slugged him with her reticule and ran toward the front door, but she tripped over a cast iron doorstop and they caught up with her, dragged her out the front door, kicking and struggling. "Will you listen to me? I'm not crazy! I've got important things to tell the president!"

"Aye, and I'm little Bo Peep," the big Irish cop said, "now you just come along to the hospital like a nice young lady."

"I've got civil rights and I vote," Blossom protested. "You can't do this to me."

"You vote?" the cop asked as they carried her toward the paddy wagon. "Are you from Wyoming then?"

"Don't be silly, all women can vote in the time I come from." Blossom struggled as they loaded her inside.

"Ah, saints preserve us, ain't that a horrible thought?" one of the cops said with a laugh as he slammed the door.

They weren't going to believe her, she might as well save her breath, but at least, she could do something to worry the cop. "Another thing," she yelled out through the barred door, "they'll pass prohibition in about fifty years, and you can kiss all that good Irish whiskey goodbye."

"American men would never vote against good Irish whiskey," the cop answered.

"No, the ladies get rid of it after they get the vote!"

"Which is the best reason I can think of for not letting the lasses near a ballot box," said the other. "Come on, Mike, let's get this one to the hospital and get on with it."

Blossom froze in silence, listening as the pair went around, climbed up on the seat of the paddy wagon, and snapped the little whip at the horse. An asylum, she was being sent to some asylum. Her civil rights were being violated, but no one seemed to care. Oh, fudge! What was she going to do?

Even though she protested at the top of her lungs and kept asking for someone to call Doc Maynard, stern-faced nuns came out of the grim, red brick Victorian building to help the police get Blossom out of the wagon.

The thought that she might disappear into some hospital or insane asylum without a trace panicked her and caused her to put up an even more spirited fight, but it wasn't bravery, she thought, just sheer desperation and fear. Soon she found herself locked in a small, sparse room that smelled of soap. At least the place was clean.

As the day lengthened, she was brought a bowl of thin soup and some bread by a tall, thin nun who promised to pray for Blossom.

"Look," she gave the nun her most winning smile, "there's been some mistake. If you'll just call Nebraska and get Dr. Maynard on the phone—"

"The what?" The elderly nun stared at her with suspicion.

"Never mind!" She winced with distaste at the thin soup and stale bread. "They don't serve stuff this bad in modern prisons," Blossom grumbled.

"You've been in prison?" The old nun began backing toward the door.

"No, I didn't mean that," Blossom said, "look, if you'd just send a wire to Doc Maynard—"

"Aha! Just as the president said, you've been under a doctor's care?"

"Look, there's a lot you don't understand here," Blossom argued desperately. "I've returned to this time to try to change history, but I've got to get out of here first!"

"I'll pray for you, poor dear." The tall nun turned and fled, locking the door behind her.

Blossom ran to the iron door, gripped the bars of the tiny opening, looking down the deserted hallway after the fleeing nun. "Help me, please!"

"I'll pray for you!" the nun called back as she left, and after a moment there was nothing to see although the click of the woman's shoes still echoed through the building.

What a mess! What to do? Doc Maynard might never track her down. She could be lost without a trace in an 1870s hospital for years *and* not have accomplished anything! Well, first things first. Blossom returned to sit on her cot, ate the soup, thinking it was the worst thing she had ever tasted. No, not quite as bad as some of those instant or frozen things they advertised on television.

War Cry. His handsome face came to her mind as she flopped down on her cot, stared at the small window that threw shadows of iron bars across her narrow cot. Blossom watched the shadows lengthen, wishing War Cry were here; he'd do something to help. It might be months before word filtered back to Doc about what had happened.

With the coming darkness, the occasional screams of the insane drifted through the building and she shuddered. If you weren't already crazy, this place could make you so. She wasn't sure she could get through one night in this horrible place, much less weeks or months or even years. Sleep was impossible. On the hard little cot, Blossom wrapped her arms around her knees, wondering if she could get through the iron bars of the window?

She went over and looked out at the hospital grounds through the bars. The place seemed asleep and deserted, but even if she could crawl between the bars, which she couldn't, it appeared to be a three- or four-story drop to the ground below. She checked the door. It was locked from the outside. By pressing her ear against the small barred area, she could hear the elderly nun going down the hall, her footsteps and the echo of the keys rattled like ghostly bones.

Blossom frowned. The small room was sultry hot. She wished she had a book or a television or a radio for entertainment. She had no light to read by anyway, even though she still had her book.

Blossom went to the outside window and tried to read by moonlight. Good thing she knew many of the poems by heart. Elizabeth Barrett Browning, what a short life, but a true love story! She and the famous poet, Robert Browning, had eloped against her father's wishes and she had written these poems to her love. *How do I love thee? Let me count*

*the ways . . . I love thee to the level of every day's most
quiet need, by sun and candle-light. I love thee freely, as
men strive for Right; I love thee purely, as men turn from
Praise . . .*

She thought of the Pawnee scout and felt lonelier than
ever. Maybe if the elderly nun did a bed-check in the middle
of the night, Blossom could talk her into a game of cards—or
at least some conversation. If she didn't make a friend in
here, she might not survive, and she had to get a message
to Doc Maynard. Maybe all this wasn't happening to her;
maybe she had dreamed it. If she closed her eyes and dis-
avowed it, maybe it would all go away.

Hours passed as she sat on her cot and watched the moon
make shadows through the barred window. Somewhere, a patient wailed and screamed in a way that made her shudder.
There wasn't much hope for the mentally ill in this time
period.

"Now Blossom," she muttered, "aspirin won't even exist
for a quarter of a century, you certainly can't do anything
about tranquilizers and all those other mood-altering drugs."

It was going to be a very long night, she sighed and
thought about War Cry. If nothing else, she could pretend
that he was here with her; it made it less lonely somehow.

The sound came down the hall of the tall nun with the
rattling keys. "Blossom? Blossom?"

Now why would the old lady forget? She put her face
against the small grill of the door. "I'm here."

The figure paused, holding up the lamp. "Where?"

That was no woman's voice.

"Who are you?" Blossom asked.

"Be quiet!" The figure hurried toward her. "Or you'll alert
the Mother Superior."

"War Cry! What on earth—!"

"Be quiet, kid." He unlocked the door, slipped inside. "I
tied up and gagged the nun, took her uniform and her keys."

Blossom leaned against the wall and laughed as he held the lamp high. "If you only knew how silly you look!"

"Hush! You'll feel more than silly if we get caught!" He tossed her a black and white habit. "Here, I stole this one off the clothesline."

"How on earth did you find me?"

"It took some doing! Are we gonna get out of here, or are we going to discuss the weather and the president's vacation home?"

Quickly, Blossom slipped on the outfit. "I feel like a counterfeit, I'm not even Catholic."

"You think I am? Come on!" He took her hand, tiptoed out into the hall, closed the door behind them. "With any luck, we'll make it to the train station and be on our way before they find the nun."

"And without luck?"

"You don't want to know!"

Blossom had a sudden, chilling image of War Cry thrown in some prison and herself in this mental hospital forever. "How on earth do you think two unlikely-looking nuns are going to move through crowds and get aboard a train?"

"Kid, you need to learn to take some chances." He grabbed her arm. "All we can do is try. Now come on, Sister Blossom, let's go!"

Nineteen

Somehow, the two of them walked out of the hospital and along the darkened streets without any trouble. They passed one cop standing on a street corner who yelled at them, "Good sisters, where are you two bound for in the middle of the night?"

War Cry glanced at her, his eyes stricken. Blossom would have to handle this now. "Aye, and we're on our way to someone's deathbed to join the good father there."

"Ah, poor devil, I'll pray for 'em, Sister." The cop crossed himself and the pair kept walking.

Blossom didn't look back. "I feel rotten, lying like this."

"Would you rather be saying your prayers in your cell?"

"Oh fudge! I suppose you're right. Stop swaggering; nuns don't swagger."

"How would I know?" War Cry grumbled. "It wasn't my idea to go see the president, yet here I am. I'm beginning to think I'm as loco as you are."

"I didn't ask you to come."

"You could at least be grateful!" He grabbed her arm and propelled her along the road. "Kid—"

"I know, I've been nothing but trouble since the first time you laid eyes on me."

She heard him swallow hard. "Sometimes things seem dull without a little trouble around."

"What's that supposed to mean?"

"Never mind." He stared straight ahead as they walked.

Blossom got a lump in her own throat just thinking abou
returning to her own time without him. "Just what are yo
doing here and how'd you find me?"

"Doc was worried about you going alone, so I took i
upon myself to come after you."

"I can take care of myself." They were walking along a
deserted street, heading out of town.

"May I remind you, kid, that all you managed to accom-
plish was getting thrown in the looney bin? If I hadn't askec
about the president's whereabouts when I got to Washington
and then heard about the disturbance at the president's summer home at that corner store in New Jersey where I stopped
you might be making rag rugs and stringing beads for years
before Doc figured out where you were."

Blossom was exhausted and her feet hurt. "I tried; I really
tried to warn them and no one would listen."

"Why are you surprised?" War Cry asked, "Is anyone listening to the prophets making predictions in your time period, whatever that is?"

Blossom thought about it as they walked down the dusty
road in the moonlight. "Well, no, I suppose not. People only
hear what they want to hear."

He gestured. "Doesn't sound like people change much."

She paused, looking up at him. "Do you know what a
ridiculous-looking nun you make?"

"Oh, shut up!" He kept walking.

"It isn't polite to say that to a lady."

"Kid, you are the damndest lady it has ever been my mis-
fortune to meet."

She hurried to catch up with his long legs. "You ought
to be ashamed, swearing when you're dressed like that."

"I'll apologize to *Tirawahut,* the Great Spirit, but not to
you. I'm beginning to think I should have left you there."

She was tired and her feet hurt. It also was sprinkling
rain. "I thought we were going to get on a train?"

"Maybe farther out," he said. "They might have soldiers around the station who would spot us."

"You're right," Blossom sighed. "We don't exactly look like we stepped right out of *The Bells of Saint Mary's.*"

"What?" He stared at her, bewildered.

"Never mind, it's a movie. Anyway, maybe my attempt to change history isn't such a good idea. Events and people, everything weaves together like a handmade Indian blanket. Something I might change in this time might change something for the worse in the future."

"Or for the better," War Cry suggested.

"Well, we'll never know, will we?" Blossom shrugged. "So far, I haven't managed to change a single thing." Maybe I wasn't meant to, she thought morosely, it was just a terrible mistake, me ending up in the wrong time. Will I have the courage to correct that if and when that moment comes?

She looked over at War Cry, caught his hand, and squeezed it as they walked. *Oh, how can I leave you?*

"What are you thinking?" he asked gently.

She could not tell him. When the moment came, it would be her decision to make, hers alone. "I was just thinking what a timid mouse I've always been. I've watched life happen rather than participating."

He shrugged. "Most Victorian women might be classified as timid mice."

Probably the other Blossom was like that, she thought, *fleeing from a miserable existence back East, hoping for happiness and romance out West.* Blossom wished she knew more about her. She reached up to touch her earlobe absently. "I guess that one earring is still lying by the picture frame," she whispered to herself. The other one was in the big camelback trunk at the Maynards' home.

"What are you muttering about?" War Cry asked.

"Nothing. It's starting to rain. Do you suppose we could find a place to rest awhile?"

He paused and looked around. "There's a farm in the dis-

tance, maybe we could crawl up in the barn for a few hours
get rid of these clothes. With any luck, we'll come to some
little town with a train station sometime soon and catch a
train back to Nebraska."

Blossom made a slight sound of dismay. "Oh, fudge!"

"What's the matter?"

"You—you don't want to hear this."

He rolled his eyes. "Try me."

"I ran out of that hospital room without my reticule and
my ticket. All I've got is my book."

"Well, now, that'll be a big help, won't it?"

Blossom tried to think. "Maybe we can get Doc to wire
us some money," Blossom suggested as they turned off the
road and walked through the darkness toward the farmhouse

"Send money over a telegraph wire?" War Cry laughed
"I don't think so. Besides, we may be miles from a telegraph
office."

"Then I guess we'll have to hop freight trains," Blossom
said. "I remember in an Indian romance I read once, the
couple caught a ride in a boxcar."

"I've still got *my* ticket," he said. "I don't know how far
you can get on a book of poetry."

She paused and glared at him in disbelief. "You'd ride and
let me catch a cattle car?"

"Riding with cows in the summertime wouldn't be too
pleasant. Look, there's some clothes hanging out on the line
in that yard."

"We're going to steal clothes?" The thought horrified her

"I'll leave a couple of dollars pinned to the line to pay
for them," he said.

"I don't know . . ."

"Otherwise, you'll have people stopping you to ask for
blessings all the way back to Nebraska."

"Lead the way, Sister War Cry."

Lifting their long black skirts, they tiptoed across the grass toward the lighted house. As they approached the clothesline, a dog began to bark inside. It sounded like a big dog.

Blossom hesitated, imagining that huge dog, an irate farmer with a gun. War Cry was already ahead of her, pinning money to the line with a clothespin, taking work clothes for himself.

"Hurry up!" he commanded. "That mutt is barking louder!"

She had never done anything this daring in her whole, timid life. Blossom looked over the clothes. "I—I can't decide what to take."

"We're not going to a fashion show, Missy; grab something!"

The barking was even more frenzied and she heard a man's voice through the open window, "What is it, Bowser? We got a fox out there? Wait 'til I get my shotgun!"

Blossom grabbed a boy's shirt and pants off the line, hiked up the black habit, and began to run for the road, War Cry right behind her. The ground was uneven and she fell once, got up, kept running. She heard the dog come bounding out of the house, barking.

Oh, lord, she was going to die from a shotgun blast in the back! And she was sullying a nun's habit; her mother must be spinning in her grave!

Behind her, she heard the yowl of a cat and frenzied barking, then a disgusted farmer. "Damn, Bowser, just a cat? Leave the thing up that tree and come back in, you hear?"

She turned and looked at War Cry, so completely out of breath, she couldn't speak for a moment. "You should have seen yourself with your skirt hiked up, running across the grass."

"Oh, hush," he gasped, "let's head for that barn down the road, get some sleep."

They staggered toward the barn.

"You think the police will be looking for us?" Blossom asked.

"I don't know," he admitted as they went in and he peeled

off the black habit. "I don't know what the charges would be, but I guess it's not as bad as murder or robbery."

Blossom took off her habit, hung it over a stall door. "I feel really bad about stealing the nuns' clothes."

"I left some money to pay for them."

She flopped down on a pile of straw and sighed. "Gosh, this feels good."

He sat down next to her. The moonlight filtered through the cracks in the barn walls, throwing shadows across the straw. "I'm sorry I don't have any food."

"We'll figure out something tomorrow," Blossom said. "I do appreciate what you went through to get me out. Going to see the president was a stupid idea."

"Not so much," he said, "you were trying to do something worthwhile; it isn't your fault no one would listen."

"Just as well," Blossom said, "if I changed one little thing, it might create major havoc in the future. Funny," Blossom mused, "I do feel at home in this time period, almost as if I belong back here."

"Maybe because you belong with me." He lay back on the hay and looked at her, the occasional moonlight filtering intermittently through the boards of the barn.

She closed her eyes so he couldn't see her tears. She loved him as she had never loved a man, but they were from two different worlds. She reached over and patted his arm absently, trembling with grief.

"Are you cold?" Without waiting for an answer, he pulled her close and put his arms around her.

She lay her head on his broad shoulder. "I'll always remember how you held my hands, made the magic circle that brought me into your world."

He reached down, took her small hands in his two big ones. "I've never quite understood you, kid, but I've loved you on blind faith that somehow, my world could become your world, too."

She must not cry or succumb to telling him what the old

shaman had said. "It has meant a lot to me to know there really can be such a love."

"There still can be." He stroked her hair away from her face, kissed her forehead.

"No." She didn't want to face this. "Let's not talk about the future right now, okay? I do appreciate that you cared enough to come get me."

She looked up at him as they lay there in the straw, thinking that if she could, she'd sacrifice everything, even her life for this man, she loved him so.

War Cry leaned over and kissed her. For a long moment, she kept herself stiff, reminding herself that it wouldn't do to get any more emotionally involved, that it couldn't work out. The kiss deepened as he took her in his arms and she lost the battle with herself not to yield, let him pull her body against his so that they blended together. She was soft as lace and velvet, he was hard as steel and granite.

His tongue touched between her lips and traced along the soft line of her mouth. She meant to pull away, but his hand slipped inside her camisole and stroked her breast, outlining her nipple with his thumb. Her lace strap fell down her shoulder and he kissed her neck and the hollow of her throat. "I need you, Blossom," he whispered and his breath was warm against her naked skin. "I love you . . ."

How do I love thee? Let me count the ways, I love you to the height and breadth my soul can reach . . .

No, she must not love this man, there were too many things against it and soon she would be returning to 1995. Yet tonight, she was in his arms and he was holding her close, caressing her, kissing her as if he would never let her go. She didn't discourage him as he kissed and explored her skin, making goose bumps at the heightened reaction to his rough, big hands moving ever so slowly and gently down her body until she shivered with delight.

"Make me a baby," he whispered in her ear as his tongue touched there.

She smiled in spite of herself. "Now, that really would complicate things, wouldn't it?"

"You don't want my baby?"

More than anything, she thought, but it cannot be. "Make love to me anyway."

"I was planning to."

Outside, the rain beat a soft pattern on the roof. Inside, on the sweet-smelling hay, there seemed to be no one else in the world but the two of them.

Slowly, he untied the lace of her camisole and kissed between her breasts.

Blossom sighed and closed her eyes, enjoying the feel of his lips caressing her skin as he tasted and teased each breast. "Don't stop, it feels good."

"I didn't intend to." His mouth was wet and hot as he sucked each breast into a sensitive peak, while his hands massaged them thoroughly.

She felt her body go dewy wet with the wanting of him as he kissed his way down her belly and put his tongue in her navel, making her tighten her muscles with anticipation. His finger reached to tease the bud of her femininity while he stroked her hair and kissed her deeply, expertly.

Blossom couldn't stop herself from arching against him as she reached out and gripped his maleness. He was as big as a stallion, hard and throbbing with the life he had to give. She wanted his child, but they would share only the pleasure of the mating.

She desired nothing more than to be in his embrace, his body hard and deep within hers here in the sweet-scented hay of this darkened barn. Then he kissed her again and she forgot all reservations and returned his kiss with equal fire, arching herself against him as his hand went down to stroke her thighs.

"Come to me, Blossom," he whispered, "come to me; give yourself and your love."

"This love can't last," she choked back tears.

"No one is guaranteed a tomorrow, Blossom. Take my love tonight and if there's no tomorrow for us, we won't regret it."

"I don't want to talk about tomorrow, I—I don't deal with decisions; I run from them." Even as she said that, his fingers were roaming up and down her body, stroking her breasts as his warm, moist lips teased her flesh.

"Then you don't want me to do this? Or this?" His lips returned to her belly as his fingers teased the soft petals of her womanhood.

"Stop . . . stop that." She was struggling for control.

"You mean don't stop, don't you?" He murmured against her ear.

"When you do that, I don't remember what I mean," she admitted even as he pulled her to him to kiss her again. She wanted him, her body was actually aching with her need. She couldn't think straight. It occurred to her that by always avoiding reality and tough decisions, she had never really experienced life . . . except what she had experienced with the Pawnee warrior.

War Cry was slowly spreading her thighs. "You want me, Blossom, you know you do."

"I—I didn't say I didn't want you," she was weeping softly now.

He kissed her eyes, kissed the tears off her cheeks. "What is it?"

She knew she dare not tell him. "Nothing, I'm just tired and cold, that's all."

He lay down on her body between her thighs ever so gently. "I'll warm you, kid." He gathered her into his arms and she had never felt so safe and protected as she did now with his two strong hands brushing her hair away from her face.

In answer, she wrapped her legs around his lean hips so he couldn't escape as she arched her body toward him.

He came up on his knees, slowly slid his throbbing length deep inside her, lay on her a long moment. "Don't think;

don't do anything but feel me deep inside you where I belong."

Oh, he was big, all right. She could feel his hot length throbbing all the way into her depths. She shuddered with her need and sighed loudly.

"Now, come with me," he said and began to ride her.

She couldn't have disobeyed him even if she wanted to. Her body seemed to have a rhythm of its own, moving with him as he rode her, slowly at first, deeply. She found herself digging her nails into his brawny back as she rose up to meet him, wanting him to thrust even harder and deeper, although she could feel him down to her very core of her being. He kissed her face, her eyes, his tongue exploring the depths of her mouth.

The rhythm was building harder and faster, harder and faster . . .

She couldn't stop herself from arching up under him, trying to take his maximum length deep into her depths.

"Now I'm going to give you my baby," he whispered and began his climax.

It could never be, Blossom knew, but the thought excited her body to a frenzy as she felt him shudder and go tense, knew he was spilling his virile seed deep within her waiting vessel. She wanted more; wanted all he had to give; wanted to drain him dry. She dug her nails into his back, holding him to her with her long, slim legs even as she lost control and seemed to be swept away into a technicolor whirlpool of mutual desire and pleasure.

When she came to, he was stroking her damp hair away from her face and looking down at her with tenderness. "I don't know what you're withholding from me, but—"

"Let's not talk about it," Blossom snuggled down into his arms. "We've got tonight; that'll have to be enough."

"The hell it is!" He held her against him possessively, "If you've promised yourself to the captain—"

"It isn't that; it's something the old shaman told me."

A long pause while he held her against his wide chest so protectively, so possessively. "It isn't good, is it?"

She had told him more than she should. She couldn't speak, she only shook her head. "I don't want to face or think about it."

"Then that will have to be enough for me," he said solemnly, and kissed the tip of her nose. "I'll love you for whatever time we have left, whether it's one day or one lifetime."

She buried her face against his chest and snuggled into his strong arms. "That's all anyone can ask," she whispered. The way War Cry held her close, she couldn't think of anything more wonderful than to sleep in his arms every night. She dropped off to sleep with her head on his wide shoulder.

The next morning, she put on the boy's clothes they had taken from the line. The pair picked some apples off a tree for breakfast and kept walking. Finally, they came to a small town that had a train station and traded War Cry's ticket in so they'd have a little money for food. He sent a telegram to Doc Maynard that they were on their way back to Nebraska and would get there when they could.

They bought some bread and cheese at a small country store and got curious looks from the locals.

Blossom finished off her bread as they walked. "What do we do now?"

"Trains have to stop and take on water every once in a while," War Cry said. "We'll walk along the tracks until we see a water tower and then we'll wait and hop any westbound train than stops."

"That could take a long time," she complained.

"Do you have any better suggestions?" he asked wryly.

"May I remind you that I had a ticket? I could be traveling comfortably back to the fort at this very minute—"

"All right! How will we know where the trains are going?"

"I haven't the least idea," War Cry shrugged, "except hop one that's going west. Sooner or later, we'll figure out where it's bound."

"We might not even end up in the right state," Blossom complained.

"That's the best I can do," War Cry said with infinite patience. "Do you have any better ideas?"

"Oh fudge, no!" Blossom wiped the perspiration from her face and kept walking. "Maybe I could work as a barmaid in one of the saloons along the way, buy us tickets."

"You want to end up under some randy cowboy or in some hurdy gurdy dancehall with some drunk railroad worker pawing you?"

"It always seemed pretty exciting in novels."

"Believe me, I don't think you'd find it exciting," he said, walking straight ahead. "Besides, I'd kill any man I caught putting his hands on you."

"You're definitely a primitive Alpha male!"

He glanced over at her. "Is that good or bad?"

"Women in the twentieth century are being taught they're supposed to prefer Beta males."

"Which are?"

"I don't know; sort of like the captain, I think, sensitive men who read poetry."

He snorted with derision. "Men like that could never survive in the West."

Should she tell him that the captain would not only survive, but prosper? The Pawnee's fate seemed less promising. She paused and wiped her face. "It's terribly hot and I'm used to air-conditioning," Blossom complained. "What day is it, anyhow?"

"How should I know? Middle of July, I think; now keep walking."

They finally came to a water tower and sat down in the shade of a bush. A train that was headed east stopped to fill up, then with a hiss and puffing, pulled slowly away.

"I don't want to spend days sitting here waiting for a train," Blossom said.

"The other alternative is to start to walk again until we find another water tower, or steal some horses and ride."

"Ride all the way back to Nebraska?"

"Blossom, there are only a couple of ways to cross distance after all."

"Oh, for my Frequent Flyer card!"

"What?" He looked over at her.

"Never mind, there's no airport to land at if there was a plane."

He laughed. "No wonder the president had you locked up. I have a hard time remembering that you're not a lunatic. Everyone else would say you are Blossom May Westfield, who's under some kind of delusion that she's been to the future and back."

"Thanks a lot!" She whacked him on the shoulder. "That's called reincarnation; or are you saying I'm crazy?"

"No, I'm the crazy, for turning in my ticket," he grumbled. "I can see this is going to be a long, long trip. Now hush and get some rest."

She was annoyed with him and miserable in the July heat. Blossom crawled into the shade of a bush to sleep.

It was after dark when a train headed west stopped to take on water. Making sure the crew didn't see them, the pair sneaked into a boxcar filled with hay and settled down for a long night. And though she didn't intend to let him, they ended up making love again as the train hurtled through the darkness.

Before dawn, they pulled into a good-sized city, but Blossom couldn't tell where they were. Next thing she realized was that the boxcar they were in had been put on a side track and unhooked from the train. "Great! Now what do we do?"

He reached out and pulled her to him. "Wait to see if our car gets picked up again and if it doesn't, we'll find another train."

She snuggled down on his shoulder. "This is a crazy way to travel; we could end up in California."

"We'll watch for town signs. Besides, we know what the terrain looks like on the plains, we'll get off when it begins to look like Nebraska."

"Lots of places look like Nebraska," she said. "We wouldn't know if the train was in Kansas or Iowa."

"I'll figure something out." He sat up and yawned. "You hungry? We've still got some cheese and crackers left."

She took a hunk of the cheddar. "Suppose we run out of food before we make it to the fort?"

"I'll steal something."

"I'm no thief!"

"Well, you may go hungry and stay honest then."

About that time, an engine backed a string of cars onto the track, banged into their boxcar as it made the connection.

"Oh fudge!" Blossom said, "I wish I knew where we're going."

The sun was coming up behind them. War Cry put his face against the slats and looked out. "At least we're not headed east. This'll work out."

"I wish I could be that sure." She settled down in the hay.

"We could make love." He picked up a straw, ran it across her cheek.

Blossom brushed it away. "We just made love, you rascal. Besides, it's too hot."

"Then we'll stare out at the landscape and try to figure out where we are, and *then* we'll make love."

"You know," Blossom smiled in spite of herself, "I had forgotten what people did with their time before television and movies."

"What—?"

"Don't ask," she gestured, "you don't want to know."

They traveled a couple of days. Sometimes they hid out; twice, they changed trains. Blossom put her hair on top of her head and pulled a cap down over her eyes, thinking she'd attract less attention as a boy. They bought cheese and crackers in small country stores and picked apples and peaches off trees near the tracks, filled War Cry's canteen at passing streams. Finally, Blossom noticed that one small station they passed said *Doakville; Iowa.*

"Iowa? Did you see that?" she asked, "we don't want to go to Iowa, we want to go to Nebraska."

He shrugged. "At least we're in the same vicinity. We'll figure out soon how to change trains and maybe end up in Nebraska."

The prairie was whizzing past their boxcar as the day progressed. They had reached a long stretch of prairie where the heat shimmered around the train.

"This is so boring," Blossom said. "Even a train robbery would break up the monotony."

"A what?"

"You know," Blossom gestured, "a train robbery."

"Never heard of such a thing," War Cry looked skeptical.

"Why, of course you have. You know, Jesse James and the Daltons and all that."

"I've never heard of a train being robbed, and I don't know any of those people you mentioned."

"Believe me, you will," Blossom said. What did she remember about train robberies from all those years of reading data banks and research books? There was just too much to remember about what she had read of the old West.

The train stopped briefly at a small town. From behind her hay bale, Blossom saw the sign: *Adair, Iowa.* Now, why did that sound familiar?

Within minutes, the train pulled out again.

"What's the matter?" War Cry stared at her.

"I don't know; something tugging at my memory; a date, maybe."

"Your birthday?"

"No, that's August fifth."

"Only a few days from now. We'll have a giveaway."

"What's that?"

"An Indian birthday party. You have to give gifts to those who come."

Blossom smiled. "At a white birthday party, we expect people to give us things, not the other way around."

"Now why does that not surprise me, kid?" he asked wryly.

"Oh, hush, and let me think. I can't decide why that town's name, Adair, would stick in my memory."

"It must not be very important," he yawned and leaned back against the hay.

"Let's hope not." She dismissed the thought from her mind and tried not to concentrate on the sinewy muscles of the half-naked Indian brave. The heat put a silken sheen on his rippling muscles that made her remember how strong and powerful he was when he took her in his embrace and made love to her.

The train swayed and clattered over the tracks in a rhythm that made her sleepy.

Abruptly, the whistle blew hard, and the engine hit its brakes with a squealing scream.

War Cry came up with a jerk. "What the—?"

She heard the distant gunfire and the faint sound of galloping horses even as the train began to slow. She put her face against the slats of the railcar and looked out. "Riders coming!"

The train shuddered as it rolled along the steel rails, the brakes still screaming. Galloping riders rode alongside. They were a tough-looking bunch, Blossom thought. Why did they look so familiar?

"Oh my God!" She recognized a couple of them suddenly from all the old West books she had read. "Now I know why that town seemed so familiar! What day is it?"

"What kind of fool question is that?" War Cry asked.

"What day is it?" Blossom demanded again.

"I don't know, 20th or 21st of July, I think, why?"

Blossom began to laugh. "You aren't going to believe this, but I think we just happen to be in time to witness Jesse James's very first train robbery!"

Twenty

The train whistled long and loud as the locked wheels slid along the steel rails.

"Hang on!" Blossom shouted. "They've piled rocks on the track and we're going to derail!"

War Cry grabbed Blossom, bracing her against him protectively as he held onto the side of the boxcar. "How do you—?"

The screaming brakes drowned out his voice even as the engine shuddered, slammed into something, and derailed with a crashing rumble, taking some of the cars with it. The muscles of War Cry's big frame went rigid as he hung onto her, daring gravity to tear her from his arms. Abruptly, the boxcar came to a halt, leaning at an odd angle.

She pressed her face against the side of the car, watching the riders thunder past, galloping toward the engine. "We're seeing history being made!" Blossom yelled with excitement. "What a story for *Tattletale!* Imagine actually seeing the real Jesse James! I want to see this!"

"Blossom, are you loco? You can't—"

She paid him no heed, forgetting caution, forgetting everything in the thrill of witnessing history in the making. Blossom pulled her cap down over her ears and clambered out of the boxcar, running toward the express car with War Cry shouting behind her.

Ahead of her, the disabled engine lay on its side, spitting steam like a dying dragon. The bandits' lathered horses stood tied to a nearby bush. Screams and shouts drifted on the warm air from the passenger coach's open windows. Breathlessly, she forgot caution and ran inside.

Scattered among the ornate scarlet velvet seats and brass lamps were carpetbags and box lunches. In the smoke and confusion, women screamed and children cried, while half a dozen masked men roamed up and down the aisles, pointing their guns at white-faced businessmen in derby hats and shouting orders.

In her own excitement, Blossom forgot danger. "You've got your nerve, Jesse James! How dare you derail this train and scare little kids like this?"

A dark-haired, masked bandit whirled on her, holding his pistol to her head. All she could see were his intense eyes. "Who in the hell are you, boy?"

Oh fudge! What had she done? It took her three tries to get the words out. "You—you wouldn't believe me if I told you!"

"Try!" He cocked the weapon.

"Hey!" another masked man yelled over the noise. "We haven't got time for this!"

They couldn't kill her, Blossom thought suddenly; she didn't remember that anyone was killed in Jesse's first train robbery. That knowledge made her bold. "I certainly know you, you cheap robber! How dare Jesse James think of himself as some kind of Robin Hood when he's taking little old ladies' pocketbooks!"

"God, the kid's recognized Jesse!" one of the bandits shouted. "Now, what do we do? Kill him?"

"Bring him along!" Jesse thundered, gesturing with his pistol. "I don't know how he knows me, but I aim to find out!"

Uh oh. Maybe there was some little footnote in history that she had overlooked. Had Jesse taken a hostage in that robbery? She couldn't remember, and she was too scared to be cautious. If some innocent, unimportant passenger had been gunned down that day, maybe history hadn't recorded or had overlooked it. Or suppose, just suppose she was about to change history with her meddling? There was nothing to do but plow straight ahead; she'd blundered big time! "Now," she sputtered, "now see here, I'm on my way to Nebraska, and I'll not go with you slimy, cheap thieves!"

"Oh, yes you will!" Jesse snarled. Even as Blossom protested, one of the others grabbed her by the arm and dragged her down the aisle. The gang exited the coach.

"You can't do this!" Blossom shrieked. "I don't even belong in this period of history!"

"Then what are you doing here?" Jesse yelled as the three outlaws mounted up and threw Blossom up on a horse.

Her hat fell off and her brown hair tumbled to her shoulders.

"Hey!" the meanest one yelled. "Lookie here! We got us a girl!"

Two more masked bandits came running from the express car. "We got the gold!"

"I hope it was worth our while," Jesse grumbled, waving his pistol.

"There's three thousand dollars in the bag," Blossom said before she thought as she struggled to get off the horse.

"Now Missy, just how would you know that?" Jesse didn't wait for an answer. "Let's get the hell out of here!"

Even as she protested that the gang was changing history by kidnapping her, one of the bandits whacked her horse on the rump.

Blossom hung on for dear life as she galloped away with the gang. When she looked back over her shoulder, she saw War Cry's grim face as he ran from the boxcar as if to stop the men from fleeing, but he had no weapon and no horse.

So this is what really happens to feisty, sassy heroines, Blossom thought as the bunch galloped away from the wrecked train. Maybe I'm one of those little footnotes in history books that I overlooked. It's only a few days until ny birthday. I'd like to live long enough to have a cake and everyone sing happy birthday to me. Oh fudge! The happy birthday song doesn't exist in this century. It occurred to her that facing death as she might be, her thoughts were pretty silly. Once a librarian, always a librarian, she thought. Now that I've gotten myself into this mess, what am I supposed to do?

It didn't appear she was going to have any choice. The bandits kept the hard pace for a few minutes, then stopped in a grove of trees to change to fresh horses that were tethered there. Again they set off at a gallop, Blossom hanging on for dear life. At least, since she'd been raised on a farm, she knew how to ride.

It seemed like forever before the men stopped to walk the horses and cool them out. The bandits had pulled their red bandannas from their faces now. Blossom thought Jesse was handsome in a hard sort of way.

"Now, gal," he snapped as he fell in besides her, "tell me how you knew me and how come you're dressed like a boy?"

"I've read about this robbery," Blossom said, "and you ought to be ashamed of yourself! The engineer is dead back there and the fireman's hurt."

"How could you have read about it when it just happened?"

"Because I'm from the future," Blossom said recklessly, "and you're going to be shot in the back by one of your own men in the year 1882."

Jesse laughed and rubbed his unshaven jaw. "Now just who is going to shoot me in the back?"

"Bob Ford."

Jesse laughed and the others joined in. "Hear that, Bob? You're going to shoot me in the back, my good friend!"

"That's rich!" Bob turned and looked at Blossom, laughing. "Now, why would I do that, girlie?"

"Because of the reward," Blossom said, "and they'll write a song about you." She began to sing; *". . . that dirty little coward that shot poor Mister Howard, and laid poor Jesse in his grave!"*

The men stared at her and one of the others shook his head. "Well, Jesse, now you've gone and done it! You've stolen a crazy girl off the train. What are we going to do with her?"

Jesse paused, took off his hat, and wiped the sweat from his forehead in the broiling July sun. "Damned if I know. Any of you men want her?"

"You can't just give me away like I was a prize in a box of Crackerjack!"

"A what?" They all stared at her.

"Never mind, it doesn't exist yet; at least, I don't think so."

"Aw, she chatters like a blue jay," Bob Ford grumbled and wiped his sweating neck with his bandanna. "She's not all that pretty, either. I pass."

"I beg your pardon!" Blossom fumed. "When I'm cleaned up, I might not be Miss America, but my face wouldn't cause a horse to bolt and run away."

"Bob's right," another shrugged. "I wouldn't put up with all that palaver if she looked like Lola Montez, that dancin' beauty."

"She's too noisy for my taste," said a third.

"Girlie, can you cook?" Jesse asked.

"I'm pretty good with a frozen dinner, but I wouldn't win any bake-offs," Blossom admitted.

"See, Jesse?" Bob said. "She don't make no sense."

"That ain't my biggest worry at the moment," Jesse snapped. "Frank, how long do you think before they're on our trail?"

Frank James combed his fingers through his mustache. "We cut the telegraph lines, Jesse, but when the train's overdue, they'll come lookin'."

"Then mount up again, boys," Jesse ordered. "Let's put

ome more space between us and the posse that's sure to be
n our trail."

"I'm no threat." Blossom's courage was deserting her now
hat the excitement was dying down. "Why don't you let me
o?"

"I don't think so!" Jesse snapped. "Mount up!"

There was nothing to do but get back on the horse. Blos-
om asked, "Just how far are we from Nebraska?"

"Not far," Jesse said, "but that's not where you're going,
irlie, we're heading back to Missouri."

"Hell, Jesse!" Frank grumbled. "Why just don't you give
er a map to the hideout while you're at it?"

"Frank, I wasn't doing no such thing," Jesse said. "Mis-
ouri is a big place."

Blossom almost blurted out she already knew where the
ideout was, she'd read all those Westerns about the James'
ang. No, she was in enough trouble already.

Frank fell in beside her as they rode. He wasn't as hand-
ome as his brother and didn't have as much charisma, she
hought. "So, girl, did I hear you say something about read-
ng the future? What are you, some sort of Gypsy fortune-
eller?"

If she told him the truth, he'd think she was loco. "Sort
f," Blossom murmured.

His eyes lit up with curiosity. "I heard you tell Jesse his
ate; what's mine?"

"You'll do time in jail and then live to a ripe old age,
harging tourists money to see you in a Wild West show."

"Aw, that's hogwash!" he scoffed. "Reckon you don't
know nothin'; reckon you're just guessin'."

"I think your gang will ride some with the Daltons and
Youngers if I remember correctly," Blossom volunteered.
"That bunch'll be almost wiped out trying to rob two banks
at once in Coffeyville, Kansas."

"That's silly!" Frank scoffed. "Nobody ever tried to rob
two banks at once."

Blossom shrugged, "I told you they got wiped out doin' it."

Bob Ford was watching her. "You give me the spooks, you know it, girl? There's something strange about you, dressed like a boy."

"You should have seen me as a nun; Whoopi Goldberg never looked so good!"

They all stared at each other.

"She speaks, but she don't say nothin' I understand," Jesse muttered. "I think she's bad luck."

"Me, too," snapped one of the others. "Either that or she's loco."

Oh god, now what? If she was supposed to return to her own time, maybe this was the moment she exited 1873, before Jesse James could shoot her.

War Cry. She didn't want to leave him wondering what had happened to her. He'd spend eternity searching for her somehow, she knew he cared that much.

Jesse looked back over his shoulder. "Gal, I don't reckon you got any rich relatives that would want to ransom you?"

Frank snorted, "Now, Jesse, does this little ragamuffin look like she's got any rich relatives?"

Bob Ford guffawed. "And she's not purty enough that any sweetheart would pay to get her back."

"I resent that!" Blossom said, and then was shocked at her own defiance. She had always been one to color within the lines, do as she was told, follow the rules. She was beginning to think just like a historical romance heroine. Yet what could she really do?

Jesse waved his arm in a forward motion. "Let's get a move on now that the horses are rested. There's bound to be a posse on our trail soon."

The gang took off at a gallop and Blossom had no choice but ride along. Why hadn't she kept her mouth shut? She didn't have any business mixing into this historic event; she might change history for the better or worse. More than that, he gang might decide to shoot her. She shuddered at the thought. Being killed back in the pages of time where no one even knew what happened to her didn't sound like the way she wanted to go. It would be sort of like being run down on the L.A. freeway; she wouldn't even merit a couple of sentences in the news. "Oh, War Cry, where are you?"

War Cry had stood staring in disbelief as the train robbers abducted Blossom, then swore in frustration. He had no weapon and no horse; he couldn't go after them. There was no telling what the gang was liable to do with Blossom. A girl would slow them down. War Cry could track them if he only had a horse.

He looked up at the sun, low in the blazing July sky. When the train didn't arrive on time, they would send out a search party, but that would probably be several hours. Maybe if War Cry searched the area, he could find a horse and take off after Blossom and her kidnappers. "And what'll you do if you catch up with them?" he grumbled to himself, "you don't have a weapon."

He'd worry about that when he got to it. In the distance, he saw a barn. Maybe they'd have a horse he could borrow. He started off at a run, leaving the disabled train, disgruntled passengers, and angry crew behind him. Why'd this have to happen now? They had only been a few hundred miles from the fort.

There wasn't anyone around the barn and War Cry hesitated to go to the weather-beaten house in the distance. The only horse in the barn was an old black nag. Maybe there was something going on in town so that everyone was gone for the day. At least, he wasn't going to be shot as a horse thief, at least, not yet. He found a worn bridle and saddle, led the old horse from the barn. "Come on, Dobbin, we've got to track those train robbers." He patted the old nag's

head. "Once I find her, I'll turn you loose to find your wa
home."

He mounted up and returned to where he'd seen the rob
bers disappear over the ridge. As one of the army's bes
scouts, he'd have no trouble picking up their trail. He'd follow
them until dark caught him, although he couldn't push thi
old horse too hard, he might kill it. On the other hand, when
it got dark, he wouldn't be able to follow their tracks any
more. War Cry nudged the old horse and took off at a slow
trot, following the occasional broken twig and crushed gras
blade.

"Oh, Blossom, you're a strange one," he muttered. "My
life's never been the same since you appeared out of the
darkness."

He hadn't realized how much she meant to him until he
saw her being kidnapped by the robbers. Why had the Grea
Spirit sent her to War Cry? Strange, it was almost as if he
had loved like this before. No, he shook his head as he rode
all he could remember was an overwhelming sense of loss
when he tried to recall that past love.

As he rode, War Cry prayed that Blossom would be safe
until he could find the robbers. He would follow, no matter
where the trail led; he loved her so.

He didn't have any plan, although he tried to think of one
as he followed the trail. Without a weapon, he couldn't take
the offensive or even follow and pick them off one at a time
until the odds were more in his favor. There were possibly
a half dozen of them, and without a pistol or even a bow,
those numbers were overwhelming. There'd be a posse coming, but the trail would be cold by then, the wind swirling
dust over faint tracks.

He stayed on their trail, deciding that after dark, when the
gang bedded down, he might be able to sneak into the camp,
get Blossom out. Of course they would post a guard. War
Cry would deal with that when he got there. He considered

waiting for the posse, shook his head. It would take hours
to get a posse together.

He kept riding, stopping now and then to check for tracks.
At least he hadn't found Blossom's body . . . so far. Every
time he topped a rise, he expected to see a small bundle of
rags lying along the trail where the robbers had decided she
was more trouble than she was worth and put a bullet in her
head. The thought made him grit his teeth with desperation
and fury, not wanting to admit even to himself how much
he cared about the strange, endearing girl.

The sun sank slowly in the west as War Cry rode. If there
was going to be a full moon tonight, he still might be able
to follow the trail. On the other hand, if he could see, the
robbers could see him, too. He'd have to be careful about
letting himself be silhouetted against the moon.

As darkness fell, War Cry stopped now and then to rest
the old horse, drink from the streams they crossed. His belly
rumbled and he wished he had some food. He thought about
roasted buffalo hump, its fat dripping into the flames as it
turned on a spit over a camp fire. Even now, his tribe might
have begun its annual hunt and there would once again be
meat in the lodges. Of course their old enemies, the Sioux,
might also be tracking that same herd, if they were in the
area, but then, the Pawnee had lived with that hard reality
for many years.

That was an added danger. Without weapons and alone,
War Cry wouldn't stand a chance if he happened across any
Lakota war parties. On this horse, he couldn't even hope to
outrun them. As hated enemies of the Pawnee, those Lakota
braves would delight in slowly torturing him to death. He
was a fool riding out here alone through country that might
easily hide roaming enemies.

If the robbers realized they were being followed, it would
be easier for them to kill the girl. Or they might gag her
and lay in ambush for him somewhere along this trail in a
ravine or behind some straggly bushes. He cared more for

her than his own life, he realized that now. He wished she cared so much for him. Blossom was hiding something from him, some secret; he could feel it in his heart. Maybe she had never loved him as he loved her and thought only of returning to her own time. No matter. He loved enough for both.

War Cry kept riding, even though he was bone-tired and hungry. Every slight noise or crackle of a twig brought the hair up on the back of his neck, and the moon in the darkness threw giant shadows across the ground ahead of him.

Bacon, he smelled bacon. He reined in and stood up in his stirrups, sniffed the wind. Yes, it was the scent of food. It couldn't be Lakota, not with the scent of coffee and bacon. Maybe the gang had finally camped for the night. He rode toward the scent, then stopped to tie a scrap of leather around the old gelding's muzzle so it wouldn't nicker at the sound of other horses and give him away. He tethered the horse to a tree and crept closer.

He sighed with relief when he saw the gang sitting around a camp fire. Blossom was handling a skillet and pouring tin cups of coffee.

One of the men spat the coffee out, wiped his mouth. "You call this coffee, girl? Worst I ever tasted!"

"I'm used to instant," Blossom shrugged, "I didn't know how much to put in. I thought I'd know how since I could make those biscuits before, but I guess I was wrong."

One of the other men took a bite of the food, made a face. "What damn biscuits? No wonder you ain't married, girlie, you don't cook worth a damn!"

"I'm a research librarian," Blossom snapped, "not Julia Child."

"Who?" An unshaven one stared at her.

"She's a fancy chef on television."

"This gal don't speak English," grumbled another, "least-wise, I can't understand what she's talkin' about."

"A librarian," the mustached one wiped his mouth on his dirty sleeve. "Does that mean you can read?"

"Yes."

The man unrolled a tattered poster. "What do this say?"

Blossom took it. "It's a reward poster for this bunch; says they'll give $100 for information."

"One hundred?" the unshaven one complained, "I'd think we'd be worth more than that."

Blossom handed the poster back. "Don't worry, it'll go up in time for Bob to shoot Jesse in the back."

"I wouldn't do that," the dark one protested.

"Yes, you will," Blossom said, "unless by kidnapping me, this gang has changed history."

"She's loco," one of the men muttered, "we pass up all the pretty and rich gals on that train and take a plain, poor crazy one."

"I resent that!" Blossom said as she poured more coffee.

"Stop all that yammerin'!" Jesse yelled. "I get tired of listenin.' Let's get some rest and ride on before dawn."

Bob gestured toward Blossom. "So what do we do with her?"

Jesse said, "I ain't gonna be kept up all night by her cryin' and you all fightin' over her; let her be."

Behind the bush, War Cry heaved a sigh of relief. If any of the men had decided to rape Blossom, War Cry wouldn't be able to stop himself from charging into the fray, but it would be suicide without a weapon.

Jesse said, "Bob, you take first watch. Tie up the gal and everyone settle down."

Grumbling, Bob did as he was told. Taking his rifle, he went out to stand watch over the horses. Within minutes, the camp settled down for the night.

War Cry hunkered down to wait and watch, wishing he had a piece of that bread and bacon. Even if Blossom couldn't cook, anything would be good right now.

Hours passed. War Cry watched and listened, wondering

how far the posse was behind him or even if there was a posse. He could use a little help right now. If he waited until dawn to take action, he'd be at a disadvantage again. Whatever he was going to do, he had to put his plan into action before first light.

With stealth, War Cry crawled through the grass to where Bob sat leaning against a tree with his rifle cradled in his arms. War Cry looked at the rifle with longing. If he had that, he could even the odds fast.

He'd better see about Blossom's safety first, he thought with reluctance. He crawled through the grass back toward the camp fire. Blossom lay tied up near the edge of the woods. He'd have to move quick before she had a chance to scream and wake the sleeping bandits. Quiet as a snake, War Cry slipped through the grass to her, his hand darting out to cover her mouth.

Blossom came awake with a start, fighting against this shadow that had appeared suddenly out of the darkness. She was going to be raped by one of the robbers now that everyone was asleep. Well, it would be after the fight! She bit the fingers that covered her mouth.

The man cursed softly under his breath, but he didn't take his hand off her mouth. "Damnit, Blossom, it's me!"

Her eyes widened as she looked up at him. Of course it was War Cry, she recognized his voice. Oh fudge! She hoped she hadn't bitten him too badly. She lay still as she felt him untying the ropes that bound her. Then he gestured for her to follow him. Heart beating loudly, she crawled after him. He was headed out toward where Bob stood guard, she realized. "Can I do something to help?"

"Shh! You'd wake the dead!" he whispered, "you've been nothing but—"

"I know, I know." This was not the time to point out that he was the one who had yanked her into the painting and if it hadn't been for him, no doubt she'd be finished with her research assignment and back in L.A. in time for her birthday. As it was, she might not live that long, even if it wasn't in the history books. "I'll distract him, you grab him."

He reached out as if to stop her, but Blossom was already on her feet and walking through the shadows toward the man sitting guard. "Hello, Bob."

"Damn, girl, you startled me!" He had grabbed up his rifle. "What are you doing free?"

"Oh, the ropes were loose and I thought you might like some company." Blossom gave him her most disarming smile.

"You know, honey, you're really not a bad-lookin' piece of calico." Bob Ford relaxed and grinned at her.

"Boy, would the National Organization of Women have a field day with a male chauvinist pig like you."

"What?" the outlaw scratched his head.

"Never mind." Blossom forced herself to smile at him as she knelt down. In the shadows behind him, she could see War Cry crouching. She had to keep Bob's attention. Slowly, she began to unbutton her shirt. "I've got ideas on what we can do to pass the time."

He grinned and rubbed his dirty hand across his mouth. "Seems like we got the same idea, girlie. Hurry up and get them clothes off."

Slowly, she unbuttoned her shirt while Bob's eyes grew larger with anticipation. About that time, War Cry reached out of the darkness and slugged the sentry. Bob slumped to the ground.

"You sure took your sweet time," she complained.

"Me? Looks like you were giving him quite a show there." He grabbed the rifle, then turned, and crept through the darkness toward the tied horses.

How dare he be indignant when she was trying to help! Blossom trailed after him. War Cry untied a bay horse. "Here, take this one and I'll catch another—"

About that time, all hell broke loose across the camp, noise, galloping horses, gunshots, shouting men.

"Must be a posse!" Blossom yelled as she mounted up. The other horses were rearing and breaking free as gunshots rang out.

"Oh, damn, why couldn't they have waited another five minutes?" War Cry snarled as the loose horses scattered. "Here, take the rifle while I catch a horse! Let's go!"

She took the rifle, but then her horse bolted, and it was all she could do to stay in the saddle, hanging on with both hands as it galloped through the night.

Somewhere ahead, she saw War Cry swing up on a horse and gallop away. "Let's get the hell out of here before the posse mistakes us for the gang!"

In the confusion, men were shouting and firing wildly. Shots flashed in the darkness and she smelt the burnt powder when she took a breath. Horses neighed and reared, thundering through the camp. She followed War Cry and galloped away, expecting to feel a bullet tear into her flesh at any moment!

Twenty-one

Blossom and War Cry galloped away from the outlaw's camp, gunfire echoing behind them in the darkness as the posse attacked.

They rode a long way in the night before they reined in and dismounted to cool the horses.

"Well," Blossom said, "at least you didn't kill Jesse James. I don't know what sort of tidal wave of events that would have brought about in the future."

"Maybe I misunderstood what this trip to Washington was all about," he said wryly. "I thought you were *trying* to change future events."

"Perhaps I shouldn't be trying," she shrugged, "after all, so far I don't seem to be having much luck."

"You don't know how lucky you were, kid, that I showed up. No telling what they would have done with you tomorrow." He pushed the jaunty cap back.

"I'm sorry, I just forgot myself in the excitement of the robbery."

He rolled his eyes. "So now, instead of taking the train, we've got to cover a couple of hundred miles through hostile country on horseback and with almost no ammunition?"

Blossom swallowed hard. "Uh, there's a little more than that."

He sighed audibly. "Why do I think I don't want to know this?"

"Well, I couldn't help it," she rushed to defend herself. "I had a skitterish horse and . . ."

"And what?"

"I—I dropped the rifle."

He rolled his eyes heavenward. "Why me, god?"

"Look at the bright side." Blossom shrugged. "Now you don't have to worry about ammunition."

"Blossom," he seemed to be speaking with great forbearance, "we're hundreds of miles from the fort with nothing but my knife and enough rawhide string to make a few snares."

"I trust you." Blossom sat down on a log. "Whatever happens, I want you to know I wouldn't have missed this adventure for the world; it's been just like I always knew it would be all those lonely nights when I was curled up with a book, dreaming of the old West."

He appeared mollified, staring at her. "Why are you saying that? You sound so final."

"N-no reason," she lied.

He reached out and put his hand on her shoulder. "Kid, in spite of the trouble you've caused me, I have to tell you, I wouldn't have missed this for the world either, I hope it never ends."

She couldn't bear to look into his dark eyes, afraid he would see the truth there, so she didn't answer. It was a long, awkward moment.

"Well," War Cry cleared his throat, all business now. "We've got to be moving on. It's going to be quite a challenge."

"I've got implicit faith in you." She swung up on her horse.

He laughed. "What I wish you had was an extra pistol or a rifle."

"Don't be sarcastic."

"Kid, I don't even know what the word means." He

grinned at her and mounted up. "Let's go to Nebraska; there's a buffalo hunt starting that I need to be in on."

Buffalo hunt. Why did that pull at her memory, making her uneasy? "How far are we from the fort, anyway?"

"A l-o-n-n-g way. How do you expect me to know?"

"In romance novels, the Indian scout always knows exactly where he is."

"Sorry to disappoint you; in this darkness with no moon, I'm as lost as you are. Maybe when we get a clear sky, I can at least head in the right direction." He nudged his horse into a walk. "Right now, I'm just trying to put as much distance between us and those outlaws as possible."

She thought about her failed mission as the horse clopped along. "Oh, fudge! I hate having to tell Doc I couldn't get anyone to listen to me."

"Who knows what would have happened in the future if they had and history had been changed?"

"You believe me, then?"

He nodded. "I guess I always did. There's something about you that jogs my memory. Anyway, you're too strange and talk too crazy to be a regular girl."

"Thanks. I think. Suppose I've already changed history by coming back and it can't be undone?" The thought was chilling. What future chaos had she created? For the good of the world and mankind, when that window of eternity opened, she was going to have to take it; no matter that it would mean being separated from her lover forever.

They rode a long time. Finally, he said, "You're awfully quiet, kid. What are you thinking?"

If she told him; he'd try to stop her. "Not much; just how much these few weeks have meant to me."

"Me, too," his voice was soft. "Blossom, I know a white girl and a Pawnee brave would have a tough time in this world as we know it, but a lot of our tribe is moving to the Indian Territory."

"So?" She stared straight ahead as they rode.

"There's tall grass and good water, I hear. A man migh farm a little, raise a few cattle. It might not be as fancy life as you're used to, but I thought maybe . . . well, yo know." He sounded awkward, embarrassed. "Hell, I neve asked a woman before; I don't quite know what to say. You customs are different than the Pawnee."

All her lonely years, she had dreamed of a man like this the kind of life he was offering; yet she could not put he personal happiness ahead of her conscience and her duty Ann Murdock had raised her better than she knew. "I—I jus don't think it would work out."

"I see; or maybe I don't." His voice went cold, hostile. "Yo just let me make a fool of myself, grovel, and now you say no.'

"It isn't what you think!" She couldn't bear the hurt ir his tone.

"I don't know what I think. Aren't you even going to give me a reason?"

Tears gathered in her eyes and she was glad it was dark so he couldn't see them. "We aren't a likely pair; you've known that from the first. And anyway, I don't think I belong on a little ranch, I'm used to a big city."

She thought of her monotonous job and her cramped little apartment in L.A. after the freedom of the open plains. More than that, she envisioned life without War Cry and that was too painful to bear.

"I suppose I was loco to think you'd even consider . . . never mind." His powerful body looked stiff and hostile ir the light as the moon peeked from around scudding clouds. "I won't bother you again."

Blossom swallowed hard but didn't answer as they kept riding. All she would take with her when she returned to the twentieth century was the memory of this man and his love. If she closed her eyes, she could remember his kisses, the gentle touch of his hands, the protection of his powerful embrace, his breath warm on her ear.

It was a good thing it was dark, she thought, because he

couldn't see the tears running down her face from the anguish in her heart. No one could make this choice but her, and when that moment came, whenever and whatever it was, she wasn't at all certain she'd have the courage to do what she must.

Back at the fort, it was night, and Doc was working late in his office when he heard a soft knock at the door. Now what?

"Come in."

Rusty peeked around the door. "You alone?"

He nodded, stood up, wondering what the madam wanted? He knew her only slightly as he knew everyone in town. "Come on in."

She entered, closed the door, hesitated.

"Sit down and I'll get you some sherry."

"I came to settle up any bills my girls might have run up over the past few weeks."

"I wasn't worried about the money," he said gently and poured two glasses.

She dug in her reticule, laid some bills on the desk.

"Rusty, if you need to talk; I've got plenty of time."

"You're a good guy, Doc; one of the few good guys in town besides War Cry."

He sat down on the edge of his desk and handed her the sherry, watched her sip it, her delicate fingers nervous. "Can I do anything?"

"No, nobody can do anything," Rusty shook her head. "I'm going to pull up stakes. I reckon I've stayed in this town long enough."

Doc sipped his drink. "What do you mean?"

"I'm leaving, Doc." Rusty finished her drink, set the glass on his desk. "There's too many memories here."

"I hate to hear that, Rusty," Doc said. "You going looking for him?" He thought about the big handsome soldier who had won a Medal of Honor for bravery.

"I don't know. Would it do any good?" Rusty went to the

window, stood looking out into the darkness as if lost in thought. "I thought I could get over him, but I can't; everything in this town reminds me of him. I'm turning the place over to Dolly."

"What about Myrtle?"

Rusty turned toward him, her eyes softening. "Dolly promised she'd look after her, give her a job, keep her around."

"Rusty," Doc said softly, "you don't know where Thompson is; he might even be dead."

"He could have at least written," she said bitterly.

"A lot of these soldiers have bad pasts. Maybe he figured he was such a hardcase, so unredeemable, you couldn't really love him."

"He should have known better than that." Tears came to the lovely green eyes.

"Or maybe he didn't want to involve you in his trouble, after all, a court martial for desertion—"

"I got old trouble of my own, Doc, that make his look minor." She hesitated.

"I know, Russet; I know."

"What did you call me?"

Russet; a color of autumn, yes, she was aptly named. Her green eyes met his and he thought she was as beautiful as she had been that night he had seen her at a physicians' banquet in New York City years ago. Who could forget the beautiful, elegant Russet Dorchester, wife of society's most prominent surgeon? He remembered the newspaper headlines, too. "I meant Rusty," he said.

"All this time, you knew. There's a reward. Why didn't you—?"

"I saw the bruises on your neck the night your husband won that award, even under all those diamonds. When he was found stabbed with one of his own scalpels, I had a feeling he deserved it."

She began to cry softly. "Oh, Doc, you don't know the half of it! I ran out of the house that night with nothing but the dress and the diamonds I wore."

He shrugged. "I recognized you the day you arrived here; but sometimes, justice takes care of itself."

"You're a good guy, Doc, thank you."

He handed her his handkerchief. "If things had been different, I might have had a daughter like you, Rusty."

She wiped her eyes and shook her head. "Not like me, I'm ashamed of what I've become. I never expect to see Tommie again, but the memories of him are too much; I've got to get away."

"It's never too late to make a fresh start, Rusty."

"No," she shook her head in despair and the lamplight reflected off the auburn hair, "there's no hope. You know what happens to whores and madams as they get old, lose their looks. I'll die in some gutter."

She sounded so heartbroken, he winced. "Rusty, there's never a time when there's no hope; remember that. You might find Thompson out west somewhere; marry him and raise a passel of kids on a ranch."

"Who are we fooling? You know what the chances of that are—little and none. My future's already been written; set in stone."

There was nothing else to say. She seemed resigned to the fate of all saloon girls. "You're leaving soon?"

Rusty nodded. "I'd just as soon no notice was taken of it. My bags are packed; I'm taking the next stage out."

Doc cleared his throat. "I wish you well, and I hope you find your soldier."

She came over, kissed his cheek. "Doc Maynard, you are one of life's genuinely good people." She turned and hurried out the door, leaving him staring after her.

As Blossom and War Cry traveled across the Plains, the days were tense, the pair barely speaking as they traveled toward the fort.

At night, they slept across the fire from each other, but

sometimes Blossom didn't sleep. She lay there watching War Cry and wishing she were curled up in his embrace. She had felt so safe and secure in his arms. No, she must stop thinking about him. She rolled over, listening to the soft chirping of the crickets in the summer night. In a few days, she would be twenty-two years old. It had been both the happiest and the saddest year of her life. So much had happened in the few weeks she had been here. Had it really been weeks? Maybe in reality, it was only days or hours, even a heartbeat in the time frame of Eternity.

They saw few people. Sometimes they went hungry, but more often than not, the Pawnee brave snared rabbits with a rawhide loop and caught fish with a knife tied to the end of a long stick. If there was food, he saw to it that she got the major portion, even though she protested. He had said he would take care of her and he did. However, from that night, he did not touch her. She knew it was just as well, even though she longed for his embrace.

The atmosphere stayed strained as they crossed Nebraska, and to Blossom, it seemed like forever before they finally rode into the fort late one hot afternoon.

Curious heads turned as they rode in, but they didn't stop to talk to anyone.

"Kid, I suppose you'll want to go to Doc's and tell him about the president; I'll take care of the horses."

"All right." She dismounted at Doc's office, staring after the warrior with a resigned sigh as he rode away, then went inside. "Hello, Doc."

He looked up from behind his desk. "Why, Miss Blossom, we had gotten awfully worried about you."

She shrugged as she sat down. "There's not much to tell; the President thought I was insane and they locked me up."

His bushy white eyebrows raised. "I was afraid of that! You've got to admit that in your time period, too, if someone got in to see the president and told him they had traveled back in time, they'd probably do the same thing."

"No, they'd call in a psychiatrist and then the tabloids and television crews. I feel so helpless, Doc." She brushed a wisp of curl from her eyes. "I—I wanted to warn them, and no one would listen."

He leaned back in his chair and eyed her thoughtfully. "Some things don't change much; maybe we're fools to think we might make a difference."

"War Cry got me out of the hospital and we've had a heck of a time getting back."

He peered at her over the tops of his steel-rimmed spectacles. "So now what are you going to do?"

"I don't know." She put her face in her hands a long moment. "I don't think I can take War Cry with me if I return to 1995; he wouldn't fit into my civilization anyway."

"If you do go back," Doc said, "you'd better not tell them you've traveled in time, they'll treat you just like President Grant did; put you in an asylum."

"Or in drug rehab," Blossom said. "I'll be twenty-two in a couple of days, but I feel like an old lady."

"You'll feel better after you've had some rest," Doc smiled. "When is your birthday?"

"August 5th."

"That soon? I'll bet Hazel will want to give you a birthday party." He got up from his chair.

Blossom stood up, too. "I don't know if I want you to invite War Cry—"

"Oh, Terry might not even be here." Doc stroked his mustache. "The Pawnee left a few days ago on their big summer hunt. Buffalo have been spotted south of here, and I imagine he'll be riding out to join them."

Good. It would be so much easier not to have to see him every day, knowing this was a love that could never be. Blossom paused with her hand on the doorknob. "I'll go over to the house and clean up. It's almost dusk; are you quitting for the night?"

"No," the old man shook his head, "I've got a few more

things to do; then I'll be along. Tell Hazel to keep my supper warm."

She nodded, smiled, and went out. At almost supper time, the streets were deserted. She looked around, wondering where War Cry was, angry with herself that she cared. Maybe if she just happened to pass by the stable, she'd see him, and anyway the stable wasn't out of her way.

Blossom walked through the coming twilight. Down an alley, she saw that pitiful little servant girl, Myrtle, hurrying toward the barn. Now what was she up to?

War Cry had fed and groomed the weary pair of horses in the stable and was saddling up his big paint stallion when he heard a noise and looked up. "Who's there?"

"It—it's me." Myrtle came toward him slowly. "I saw you ride in a while ago."

"Yes, it's too long a story to tell, but I got Miss Blossom back okay. I'm getting ready to join the other braves on the big hunt that I hear's already started. You doing all right?"

The girl hesitated, began to cry.

"Myrtle, what's the matter?" War Cry took her by the shoulders, stared down at her.

"Oh, I got trouble, and I don't know what to do!" She looked up at him, tears streaking her homely face. "You and Miss Rusty be the ones that been nice to me, and she's gone away."

"Gone where?" He had known that someday the mysterious red-haired beauty would go; he could only wonder if she had gone looking for her lost love, or was closing the book on that and attempting to make a fresh start some place where no one knew her.

"Just gone." She wiped her eyes. "Now I got no friend."

His heart went out to Myrtle; she was so pitiful and forlorn. "I'm your friend, Myrtle. Tell me what's troubling you; maybe I can help."

"Can't nobody help," she wept. "I—I got relatives down near the Injun Territory, maybe I can go there."

"What's happened?" He was mystified by her plight.

"I—I think I'm gonna have a baby." She sobbed uncontrollably. "I'm disgraced; that's what I am!"

"A baby?" He couldn't imagine this pitiful, half-witted creature with a sweetheart.

"It ain't what you think; I'm a good girl; I am. He forced me," she sobbed.

"Forced you? You mean, he—?"

"You know, he—he was drunk, dragged me into the barn one night after Miss Rusty run him out of her place."

War Cry swore under his breath. "Who was the bastard, Myrtle?"

"If I tell, I might get into trouble."

"It looks like you're already in trouble," War Cry said.

"It—it was the captain."

He felt a chill go through him. "Captain Radley?"

She began to cry again as she nodded. "I don't know what to do."

He was as angry as he was sorry for Myrtle. He pulled the pitiful girl up against him, stroking her hair. "It'll be all right. We'll figure out what to do."

She held onto him as if she was drowning in her misery. "I—I can't have no baby; my mama told me I should never marry; we got bad blood in our family that gets passed on."

"Shh! Stop crying; it'll be all right," he murmured and stroked her hair, "I'll try to think what to do."

Blossom had followed Myrtle out of curiosity and now crouched behind the barn door, watching and listening. She saw Myrtle in War Cry's arms as he stroked her hair. She had to strain to hear, but she caught a few words. ". . . Stop crying; it'll be all right. I'll try to think what to do."

And the half-witted girl saying, "I—I can't have no baby;

my mama told me I should never marry; we got bad blood in our family that gets passed on."

Stunned, Blossom only barely heard the rest of it. War Cry stroked the girl's hair, assuring her everything would be all right; he would figure something out if she would leave everything to him.

Blossom couldn't bear to see or hear anymore. Shaken with disbelief, she backed away from the door, fled down the street in the twilight. Could he have been so rotten as to take advantage of that poor girl? Blossom didn't have much worldly experience, but she thought men might do a lot of things when they were drunk or hot with desire. She wanted to go back and confront him, have him assure her that there was some mistake, yet Blossom had seen the scout with his arms around the girl, heard their words with her own ears.

Almost blinded by tears, Blossom hurried to Doc's house. How could he have been unprincipled enough to take advantage of some pitiful cleaning girl?

It was difficult to maintain her composure when she knocked and the old lady opened the door.

"Why, Blossom, dear, I'm so glad to see you!"

Blossom managed to stay controlled as she answered the usual questions about her trip, who she had seen, how the weather was up north? "I—I'm awfully tired; so many things have happened. Do you suppose I could rest awhile before dinner? Doc says he'll be a little late."

"Of course, my dear, your old room is ready."

Blossom thanked her, fled to her room, closed the door. Somehow, Blossom had thought the scout would be different than most men. She considered going to see Myrtle, decided against it. She wasn't good at confrontations. Well, this certainly made Blossom's decision easier.

Slowly, Blossom opened the old trunk, wondering again about Blossom May Westfield. She took out the one silver hoop earring, stared at it, put it back. The old volume of poems seemed to mock her. She picked it up, opened it.

How do I love thee? Let me count the ways . . .

The faded dried blue prairie blossom marked the page. When she closed her eyes, she could recall the way War Cry had made love to her that very first night he had taken her so completely. She picked it up, sniffed the faint, sweet scent, and remembered all over again the warmth of his big body, the taste of his mouth, the way he had made her his own. A memory was something no one could ever take away from you. She still loved him and nothing, not even this betrayal, could change that.

War Cry brushed past Private Wilson, strode through the open door, and leaned on Captain Radley's desk with both big fists. "We need to talk," he said through clenched teeth.

The officer took his feet off his desk, brought his chair down on all fours with a bang. "What happened to 'sir' or 'Captain Radley'? You are the most arrogant—! I ought to throw you in the guardhouse!"

War Cry lowered his voice to a whisper. "You can't, you slimy little bastard! You fired me, remember? You might want to hear what I've got to say, before I go over your head to the major."

The officer's pale face turned mottled red with anger. "Are you threatening me, you savage—"

"I just got through talking to Myrtle; you know the little maid that worked for Rusty."

The captain stood up slowly. "I—I can't see how we'd have anything to discuss, Injun."

He must not lose his temper and be goaded into striking the man with Private Wilson just outside the open door. "Think about it, Captain, and think about kissing your career goodbye. Then if you want to talk about it, I'll be in the root cellar out behind the barracks in five minutes."

Sweat began to bead in great drops on the pale, handsome

face. The officer ran a nervous finger around his blue uniform collar as if it were choking him. "All—all right."

War Cry turned and strode out without another word. It was supper time and most of the streets were deserted in the summer heat. Soon it would be dark. He didn't want to take a chance on being seen with the captain. What was he going to do?

He thought about it as he headed for the dark root cellar behind the barracks. He couldn't force the captain to marry the pitiful girl, but he might scare him into giving her some money to help her through this difficult time. Pulling back the heavy, creaking door, War Cry went down the steps and into the low-ceilinged gloom of the small, underground chamber where potatoes, carrots, onions, and other foods were kept in storage. The place smelled like a damp cave—or a burial vault.

Within minutes, War Cry heard footsteps above and the captain called down the steps. "Terry, are you in there?"

"Yes, come on down."

"Ye gods! Down there?" There was a long moment of hesitation. "I—I don't like closed-in places."

"Being locked up in an army prison cell for years would be even more scary, Captain." War Cry smiled without mirth. He knew the captain's fear, and he intended to put it to good use.

Cursing drifted down the steps. "I'm not coming in there; you come out here!"

War Cry pushed his jaunty cap back and sat down on an overturned tub. "I don't know that you want even one word of this overheard by anyone passing by."

"God damn you! You know how I feel about closed-in places! Come out of there!"

War Cry smiled to himself. "Captain, either you come down, or I'll go right to the major's quarters."

"Okay, okay." He came down the steps very slowly, looking about, his eyes wide with fear, great beads of sweat gleaming on his handsome face. "Let's talk fast."

"Relax!" War Cry stood up and gestured the nervous officer to a seat on the tub. "It isn't a grave."

Lex Radley let out an oath. "You did have to say that, didn't you?" He sank down on the tub. "Tell me what you've got to say quick, so I can get out of here!"

War Cry moved to where he was standing between the sweating officer and the steps. "I ought to beat your brains out for what you did to that girl!"

"What? Why, you low-class Injun scum, how dare you!" He jumped to his feet, but War Cry struck him hard in the chin.

"Sit down, you uppity little whelp, before I lose my temper and finish the job!"

Radley sat down on the tub, blood trickling from his cut lip. "You'll get the firing squad for hitting an officer!"

"Why, Captain Radley, sir," he emphasized the sir with cold sarcasm as he folded his arms across his brawny chest, "you must be mistaken! I believe you tripped and fell!"

"You don't think I'm going to let you get away with that, do you?" Lex wiped the blood from his lip. "The Brewsters and the Radleys are blue-blooded old families, and no red-skinned Injun—"

"I wonder what your aristocratic mother would say if she knew she was soon to be a grandmother from the rape of a dull-witted servant girl?"

Sweat mixed with the blood on the handsome pale face. "You—you can't prove that."

"Myrtle is pretty convincing; I'm sure the major would be interested in hearing her story."

"She's lying! Why, it's not mine and besides, she let me—"

"Yes?"

"It's not as if she was anyone important; she's just a white trash wench. I was drunk!"

It took all the control War Cry could muster to keep from

jerking the fine young gentleman up off the tub and shaking him until his teeth rattled. "She's a human being and you treated her worse than most of us would treat a dog!"

The captain blinked, looking past War Cry toward the stairs. Clearly, he was eager to get out of this small, closed-in cave. "So what do you propose to do?"

"You ought to marry her, give your child a name."

"Marry her?" The man threw back his head and laughed. "You must be joking! Why, Mother would be appalled at giving our illustrious name to some half-witted, low-class bastard—"

War Cry grabbed him by the collar, lifted him off the ground. "On second thought, you aren't good enough for Myrtle." He dropped the man back on the tub and stepped to the foot of the stairs. "I think the answer is to give her a sum of money, let her go live with her family and do the best she can."

"And suppose I won't?"

"Then I'm going to bring the major into this. You might find yourself with a dishonorable discharge and in prison. What would Mother think of that?"

"By god, you're bluffing; I won't do it!"

War Cry turned slightly and looked up the stairs behind him. "You know, a man left down here with that big heavy door shut could probably yell for hours before anyone came to help him. It would be just like being buried alive!"

Before the captain could move, the scout turned and ran up the stairs. With the officer yelling protests, War Cry closed the big cellar door, sat down on it. Below him, he could hear the captain's muffled screams in the darkness, his hands beating and clawing in vain at the wood.

War Cry yawned and watched the sun set slowly in the west, ignoring the frantic pounding and shrieks from below. Now the captain was begging and pleading. Then silence.

After a long moment, War Cry opened the door. The captain lay balled up at the foot of the stairs, his hands over his face, his natty uniform drenched with sweat. War Cry took a deep breath and frowned. In his terror, the officer had soiled himself, too. "All right, Captain Radley, will you give the girl the money?"

The man half-rose on his elbows, shaking visibly. "I might say I will and then not do it."

"In that case, sometime when you least expect it, I'll grab you from behind in the darkness, haul you over, and throw you in again."

The man staggered to his feet. "I'll tell the major what you've done!"

"And then, I'll tell him what *you've* done," War Cry countered. "Besides, if you told him a Pawnee scout was following you around, threatening to throw you in a root cellar, he'd think you'd gone insane; it sounds too ridiculous."

"Damn you. I'll get you for this!"

War Cry shrugged. "I'll worry about that when the time comes. Are you going to give that girl some money?"

Lines of defeat etched the handsome face as he nodded and reached for his wallet, counted some bills out. "You give it to her; I don't want to ever see the stupid bitch again."

"That's not nearly enough," War Cry said.

The captain paused, cursing under his breath, then he finished emptying the contents of the wallet into War Cry's outstretched hand. "I hope you rot in hell!"

War Cry shrugged as he turned to go up the stairs. "Every man makes his own hell, I guess. I'll bet yours is being buried alive forever. Happy nightmares, Captain!" War Cry went up the steps and into the night, relieved that this duty was over. He had done what he must to help Myrtle in the only way he knew how. From now on, he'd have to watch his back. Before, the captain had only disliked him, now he was a bitter enemy. Well, it didn't matter; War Cry had been planning to leave the fort anyway. He couldn't bear to keep seeing Blossom and not have her.

He went to get his things. He'd saddle up to join his tribe

on the buffalo hunt, and before he left, he'd give the money to Myrtle. The local train didn't go to Indian Territory, but there was a stage due late that night. Myrtle would have enough money now to be on it; go back to her relatives.

He thought of Blossom and shook his head. She was right; this thing between them could never work. Maybe she belonged with some white man like the captain. Whether it was because she came from another time or not, it was obvious that she and War Cry could never make a go of it, no matter how much he loved her. Blossom had said she had a birthday coming up. He was glad he wouldn't be here for it. She could invite Captain Radley. Maybe that pair deserved each other!

Twenty-two

Blossom paced her room, puzzled over the exchange she had seen in the barn. Something didn't make any sense. She just couldn't believe War Cry would do such a thing. In a few minutes, she heard Doc come into the house, his wife greeting him cheerily.

"Dearie, you just sit down and enjoy your paper. I'll get your dinner warmed up."

Blossom steeled herself and went into the parlor. In the kitchen, she could hear Hazel humming as the old lady rattled pans. "Hello, Doc."

He looked up from his *Tattletale*. "Oh, hello, my dear. Are you doing well?"

She managed to keep her face expressionless as she nodded. "Have you seen Terry?"

Doc put his paper down. "The Pawnee have already left on their summer buffalo hunt, and he's ridden out to join them."

"Oh." Abruptly, Blossom remembered what War Cry had said about the danger from enemy war parties. "Did the army send any troops with them?"

Doc shook his head. "I mentioned it to the major, but he said Captain Radley had recommended against it. The cavalry doesn't think the Sioux would venture that far south, almost to the Kansas border, and within range of the fort."

An uneasy feeling ran up Blossom's back and she hugged herself, went to stare out the window. What was that strange premonition like a memory or an old nightmare that she couldn't quite recall? The rumbling thunder came to her mind; that old dream that had always brought her out of bed screaming.

"My dear, is there something wrong?"

Blossom shook her head. *Thunder.* She could not rid herself of the thought. "I'm just a worry-wart, I guess. You think we're due for any rain?"

Doc peered at her over his spectacles, looking perplexed. "In this heat? Why, with August here, we could use a little rain, everything's drying up. There's only one good thing about that; the buffalo herd will have to find creeks to drink from and that limits where they can roam."

"But the Sioux would know where those places are, too, wouldn't they?"

"There's only so many creeks and streams in southern Nebraska, my dear. You worry too much."

She clasped her arms around herself. "You're right, I'm being silly, but considering the danger, I don't know why the Pawnee didn't call off this hunt."

"Well, for one thing, it's hard to break old customs, but mostly, they need the meat. They can hardly live on what they grow in their gardens and skimpy government handouts. My guess is this may be their last big hunt, poor devils! At this rate, the white hunters will have decimated the herds in another year or two."

Blossom remembered her Western history. "You're right about that." *Buffalo hunt. Something else floated around the shadowy edges of her memory; what was it?*

"Don't worry, my dear, everything will be all right." He returned to his paper.

Blossom watched him reading, wishing she could get up the nerve to question him. No, she might not want to face the hard truth. She considered confronting Myrtle, decided there was no polite way to ask the girl such personal questions. Captain Radley was the officer in charge of the scouts.

She didn't want to approach him, either. She had to do something. Maybe if she went for a walk, she'd think of some solution or at least ease her emotional turmoil.

"I've got to go out; I—I have an errand." She took a shawl off the hook by the door.

"In the dark?" Doc looked up again. "Not safe for women to be out alone after dark, don't know what the world is coming to."

Some things don't change very much after all, Blossom thought wryly. "I'm just going for a walk; that's all."

She fled out the door before the kindly old man could ask more questions.

What to do? Blossom had always dodged tough realities, but this was something she had to face. She walked aimlessly, certain in her heart that War Cry couldn't have done something so unscrupulous, yet there didn't seem to be any other rational explanation. She was passing Captain Radley's office now. The light was on and the window was open. She tried to sneak past.

"Miss Blossom, is that you?"

Oh fudge! She didn't want to talk to him, but he'd seen her. "I—I was just on my way back to the Maynards' after getting a breath of fresh air—"

"At night and all alone?" He came to the window and gestured, "Do come in while I finish putting away this paperwork, then I'll walk you home."

She'd seem churlish if she refused. Reluctantly, she went inside. The captain must have just had a bath, she thought, he appeared to be wearing a fresh uniform and his black hair was damp.

"Sit down." He gestured to her and she noted for the first time that there were bruises on his face and his trembling hands looked swollen and discolored.

"Captain, are you all right?" He'd been drinking, too, she thought; there was a half-empty bottle on the desk.

"I—I'm just fine," he said, "a—a door fell on the old root cellar and hit me."

"Oh. I hope you're not hurt." She started to ask what he was doing in the cellar, decided it really wasn't any of her business. She looked around his office. As usual, the windows and the door were wide open, but in the heat of the first week of August, the breeze was most welcome.

"I'm fine; it's not important." He made a dismissing gesture and took another gulp of whiskey. "Mrs. Maynard said she was thinking of having a birthday party for you. I assume you've come to extend a personal invitation?"

She tried to return his smile, but she felt too miserable. She looked over her shoulder at the open door, lowered her voice. "Can we talk privately?"

"Certainly." He played with the glass, his fingers nervous and never still.

His hands looked bruised, too, which further mystified Blossom. Maybe when he had fallen, his hands had taken the brunt of it.

"My dear Miss Blossom, I'm so glad you survived that terrible trip to Washington, I hope that scout didn't—"

"Captain, I—I want to talk to you about Myrtle."

His handsome face paled even more. "Now, look, I—"

"I know whose child she's carrying," Blossom hastened to say, blinking back tears.

"You do?" His tense fingers dropped the glass and it shattered unnoticed on the floor.

Blossom nodded. "I—I walked into the barn unexpectedly, saw her in War Cry's embrace, heard them talking." She couldn't keep tears from clouding her eyes. "I've been such a fool!"

He let out his breath audibly as if he'd been holding it. "Oh, Miss Blossom, you're upset! Allow me to get you a glass of sherry." He went to the sideboard and got out the decanter, looked back over his shoulder at her. "Have—have you talked with anyone else about this?"

She shook her head, accepted the liquor gratefully.

He sat down slowly on the edge of his desk and studied her. "I am so sorry you had to find out that he's not as nice a person as you thought. I must try to help that poor girl!"

Blossom took a gulp of the sherry, feeling the bracing spirits all the way down. She couldn't believe War Cry was capable of such low behavior, but everything was pointing in that direction. Had he fled from her out on that hunt, afraid she would ask questions? "I suppose I've turned out to be a poor judge of character, Captain. Not every man is as noble as you are."

Captain Radley took the glass from her hands, clasped both her hands in his, gave her a sympathetic look. His hands were as cold and clammy as a dead man's, Blossom thought, but she willed herself not to pull out of his grasp. It didn't seem very polite.

He said, "Maybe things can still be set right. As I recall, you're a fortune-teller; do you see any future for us at all if I can get this sad mess straightened out?"

So he still didn't believe she was from the future, either. What difference did it make? "My tea leaves don't give me all the details, Captain," she answered, pulling her hands from his. "I recall a very large portrait of you in a museum. You'll reach the status of colonel, have many descendants who become giants of business and industry, and live to be ninety-seven."

He laughed. "Well, now, that's reassuring! I guess I can stop worrying about being buried alive."

"What?"

"Never mind." He made a dismissing gesture. "Who's the matriarch of all these future descendants?"

She shook her head. "I've told you all I know."

He took a deep breath, grinned broadly, went to close the window. "I feel invincible now. You'll never know how comforting your prediction is."

She thought of all those Pawnee women and children out

on that buffalo hunt. They would be skinning and cutting up meat while their warriors ranged some distance away killing more of the great herd. A disturbing memory pulled at her mind. "Captain, Doc is worried that the Pawnee are out on that hunt with no army escort."

He looked annoyed and shrugged. "They've got most of their best warriors with them."

"But they're vastly outnumbered should a big war party of Sioux or Cheyenne decide to attack."

"Don't you worry your pretty little head, Miss Blossom. That's south of here; the Sioux don't usually range almost to the Kansas line."

"But they might, and most of the Pawnee women and children are on that hunt," Blossom reminded him. "If anything goes wrong, it would look bad on your record."

The captain seemed to consider a long moment. Clasping his hands behind his back, he gave her a knowing nod. "You're worried I might not get promoted. I misjudged you, Miss Blossom, you're as shrewd as my own mother."

Was that supposed to be a compliment? "I knew that once you thought of that, you'd reconsider."

"I'll see the major about it; insist that we need to protect those women and children." He smiled warmly at her. "I do hope Mrs. Maynard will delay the birthday party until I return. Maybe we can make a fresh start on this relationship."

"Perhaps." She wouldn't believe all this about Myrtle unless War Cry told her it was true. In the meantime, she would live in mental pain until he returned from the hunt. "Well, goodbye, Captain, I'll see you when you get back . . . if I'm still here." Blossom thought of the old shaman and his prediction.

"What?"

"Never mind, I mustn't detain you from your tasks."

He came over and took both her hands in his again. "Miss Blossom, I'm so glad we had this talk. I'll convince the major I should countermand my own advice. It'll take a little time getting the troop equipped and mounted, but I'm looking forward to your birthday party on my return."

"Right." She didn't feel like celebrating; she felt like crying her eyes out. She extracted her hands from his cold ones, turned, and fled from his office.

Lex watched her go and rubbed his hands together with satisfaction. So things were not a disaster after all! He had dreaded Mother finding out about the slow-witted barmaid and her bastard. The Brewsters were old line aristocracy and had never let the wealthier but more humble Radleys forget it. "Blossom, you are going to be Mrs. Lexington B. Radley," he stared at the window at her departing back, "and Mother need never know about my little escapade." He couldn't remember when he'd felt such relief and happiness. The idea of being in crowded, small spaces no longer bothered him. Contrary to his nightmares, he was going to live to be ninety-seven years old!

Blossom. He leaned against the window, watching Blossom's hips sway as she crossed the street in the darkness. She would give him smart, good-looking heirs, and with her uncanny ability to read the future, she could tell him what to buy and sell. Hadn't she predicted he would be rich and prominent?

What to do about that damned Pawnee scout? Lex rubbed his swollen jaw. Things would never run smoothly until he got Terry out of his way so he couldn't tell Blossom who had sired that trashy wench's child.

Lex hummed to himself as he reached for his pistol and extra cartridges. He'd lead that patrol all right. Besides the fact that it would make him appear noble in Blossom's eyes, Lex had something else in mind. He didn't expect to run into any hostile war parties, however, everyone knew buffalo hunts were dangerous. Men were sometimes trampled by the stampeding herd or killed by stray shots.

Lex checked his weapon and buckled on his holster before heading toward the major's house. He would never feel secure as long as that damned Injun scout lived. On this hunt, Terry was going to meet with some terrible accident; Lex was already planning it!

Spotted Tail sat before his tipi, staring into the horizon and remembering the ancient days when the buffalo were like a great brown sea moving across the prairie and the Lakota were a powerful people of many horses. He looked down at his wrinkled brown hands, knowing the buffalo and the horses were fewer now and an old warrior had to content himself with memories of brave deeds. When he thought about the future, he felt the winds of change coming. Soon the whites would swarm over everything like the pale white termites he found when he turned over a rotten log.

Already there was almost no game left to hunt and the Long Knives punished those who killed enemies. They said it was wrong, yet only a few winter counts ago, the whites in the blue coats had been killing their brothers in the gray coats. Their thinking was strange indeed, but who understood the minds of termites?

He heard the sound of moccasins, turned to see Scarlet Arrow's handsome young son running toward him. "Fire Arrow, you bring news?"

The boy, who was no more than eight or ten winter counts old, stopped in sudden confusion as if he had suddenly remembered he should be learning the dignity of a warrior. "Yes, my chief. Buffalo, a great herd of them to the south!"

Spotted Tail stood up and patted Fire Arrow on the shoulder. The boy's father, though a brave warrior, had not always been kind to this only son when the father drank the white man's firewater. "It is good. We will link up with our friends led by Two Strikes and Little Wound. Soon we will eat fat hump and roasted tongue. Around the fire, we will tell of the old days that were and are no more."

"I will be allowed to ride in the hunt; kill my own bull?"

Spotted Tail considered. He should say no. The actual hunt was dangerous work for skilled warriors. This sturdy boy was too young to take part in anything but the skinning and cutting up of meat.

"I would be much pleased to take part," the boy pleaded, his dark eyes wide with eagerness. "With the white men slaughtering the great herds, there will not be many more such hunts."

"What you say is sad but true," the chief nodded. "Because your dead father was a brave warrior and a good friend, I will allow this."

Being still only a boy, Fire Arrow seemed to forget himself for a moment and crowed in delight, then remembered his dignity. "Great chief, there is still more. Our scouts even now bring word that our ancient enemies are also following this herd."

"Pawnee! White men's slaves!" Spotted Tail sneered. "We will deal with them, too."

"The bluecoats will be angry if we break their rules," young Fire Arrow reminded him.

"Your father who was my friend, lies even now on a burial platform because of a Pawnee scout. I care not for what the white men think!" Spotted Tail spat on the ground in contempt. "Go! Have the camp crier spread the word. Not only will we kill buffalo, many Pawnee scalps will hang in Lakota lodges before this hunt is finished!"

Blossom went back to Doc's house, lost in thought. When Mrs. Maynard tried to engage her in conversation, she pleaded a headache and went to her room. War Cry. No, he could not, would not have done something as low as to bed that pitiful cleaning girl. For comfort, Blossom opened the trunk, reached for the book of poetry. In its pages lay the dried blue flower. It was bittersweet to remember those moments in the big scout's arms, and yet, she could never forget, no, not in a hundred years.

How do I love thee? Let me count the ways . . .

She returned her precious book to the trunk next to the one silver earring. Would Myrtle tell her the truth? Did she really want to know?

Blossom blew out her lamp as if retiring for the night and went through her back window. She hurried down the streets toward the bordello, paused as she neared it. Now what should she do? In this time period, a girl couldn't just walk into a place like this; it would create a scandal. She wondered with a smile what people of this settlement would think if they could see a women's single bar with the girls putting dollar bills down the jockstrap of some dancing hunk? Not that she had ever done it, in fact, she'd only been in a place like that once for a bachelorette party for a girl at work. Blossom had felt as uneasy as a Victorian lady and could hardly wait until she could flee the sleazy atmosphere.

Loud music and laughter drifted from the saloon's open windows in the August heat. While she paused in the shadows, Blossom saw someone come out the back door carrying garbage. "Myrtle?"

The girl turned at the sound of her name. "I know you. You're that teacher the Doc took in. What you doin' out at night?"

"I—I wanted to talk to you, Myrtle."

"About what?" The girl's homely face mirrored suspicion and fear. "I ain't done nothin' wrong."

"I didn't say you had." Without thinking, Blossom put a comforting hand on the girl's shoulder. "I'd like to help you, Myrtle."

The girl began to cry. "How did you find out? Ain't nobody ever been kind to me but Miss Rusty and Terry. Miss Dolly ain't good to me."

This pitiful creature! It angered Blossom to even think War Cry might have taken advantage of her. "Isn't the scout going to help you?"

The girl sobbed and nodded. "He said he would, but I don't know what he can do. I tole the captain, but he called me terrible names, said it wasn't his'n and he'd make me out a liar if I told."

"Captain?" Blossom asked, puzzled. "You mean Captain Radley?"

"Uh huh," Myrtle sobbed. "I tole him no, I wasn't that kind of a girl, but he'd been drinkin' and dragged me into the barn. When I scream, he slap me and tell me hush up!"

Blossom took a deep breath and didn't know if the emotion she felt was relief or anger. "Are you telling me, Myrtle, the captain is the father of your child?"

The girl sobbed and wiped her nose on her dirty apron. "I never told nobody but Terry, I thought maybe he could help me, bein's as how Miss Rusty is gone away."

Lex. It was Lex's baby and he'd raped this pitiful wretch. For a moment, Blossom thought she was going to be sick. "It'll be all right, Myrtle," she said softly. "I don't know what to do to help, but it will be all right."

The girl wiped her face on her apron again. "I'm leavin' soon, goin' down to Indian Territory. I got kin near there I kin stay with."

Blossom tried to think what would be considered a good solution in this day and time. "Maybe the captain could be persuaded to at least give this child his name."

"He just laughed at me! 'Course, he can't keep me from givin' it his name if I've a mind to, can he, Miss Blossom?"

"I—I really don't know; I don't think so."

Myrtle grinned through her tears. "That's what I'll do then. He's such a high-and-mighty 'un, thinks he's so fine! I'll give his name to my baby and tell him to pass it on down. Captain'd hate that, wouldn't he?"

Blossom nodded. "I expect so."

If this weren't all so tragic, it would be ironic. And to think that coldhearted villain had been wooing her only this evening.

Myrtle blew her nose. "I got me some money; Terry brought me some he said the captain give him for me. It be enough for a stage ticket and to live a while. I can make it on my own if I have to."

Blossom hugged her. "Oh, Myrtle, I wish I knew what to do. When the men get back from the hunt, maybe—"

From inside the saloon, a woman's voice called, "Myrtle, you out there? There's dishes to wash!"

"Comin', Miss Dolly!" She turned her homely face toward Blossom. "I thank you for your carin', Miss, but I'll figure it out somehow. Now I got to go!"

She grabbed up her garbage pail and turned to run inside, leaving Blossom staring after her.

Now what? Weary and heartsick for the unfortunate girl, Blossom started toward the Maynards' house. War Cry was innocent. How could she have ever thought otherwise? On the other hand, Captain Radley deserved to be horsewhipped. What a rotten villain! Such a shame that his future was so long and bright!

She reached Doc's house, crawled in the way she went out. The lights were still on in the parlor, and Blossom couldn't sleep. She needed to talk to someone. Putting on a robe, she went into the parlor where Doc sat reading his paper. Hazel must have gone to bed.

"Doc, can we talk?"

He sighed, put down the paper. "Is something wrong, my dear?"

She didn't know what to say to him. Blossom fiddled absently with a piece of bric-a-brac on the mantel. "How long have you known War Cry?"

"*Ter-ra-re-cox?* Quite a while. Why?"

She didn't answer. Doc couldn't help her with her problems; for once, Blossom was going to have to make tough choices all by herself.

Abruptly, the sound of a running horse drifted through the open front window and Blossom ran to look out. An Indian messenger galloped through the fort's gates. "Oh, my! Something must be up!"

Doc was already out of his chair and hurrying out the front door to hail the man. "Hey, what's going on?"

"Must report in!" the Pawnee yelled. "Others bring warning, Lakota on the move!"

Doc yelled, "Lakota? Where?"

The young brave gestured, "Big band of Brules and Oglalas riding toward buffalo herd!"

The messenger raced on toward the fort. Doc turned and came back in the house. Blossom faced him, her heart pounding with apprehension. "Doc, the captain says the cavalry is getting ready to go out there."

He shook his head and she saw the concern etched in his weathered old face. "That'll take a while to get organized. They can't get there fast enough. The Sioux are the bigger tribe and they'll be hunting more than buffalo!"

"Doc, in that case, it's up to us. We've got to warn the Pawnee!"

Twenty-three

Doc looked at her. "Young lady, this is too dangerous; a woman can't go!"

The girl of 1995 would have agreed, but War Cry's safety was all she could think of now. "Doc, they'll need a doctor and all the help they can get! If you don't take me, I'll steal a horse and follow you."

Doc muttered something under his breath that might have been an oath. "Headstrong, feisty filly! All right, let's get moving then."

Blossom was already running to her room. "Get your medical bag and canteens," she yelled over her shoulder. "I'll get dressed and meet you at the stable!"

She dug to the bottom of the old trunk, came up with a simple, blue-flowered calico dress, held it up in the lamplight. Strange, why did it seem so familiar?

"What difference does it make?" she said to herself and jerked it on, grabbing her shoes as she went out the door.

She ran all the way to the stable. "Here I am, let's go!"

Doc frowned. "Dag nab it! This is foolishness! I don't have a sidesaddle for you."

"That's okay, I'll manage." Blossom smiled in spite of herself as she swung up on the horse. "It's a good thing I learned to ride on the Murdock farm."

The two of them rode away from the fort at a gallop, heading south in the moonlight.

Doc yelled, "It may be quite a ways and I'm not as young as I used to be."

"We'll make it!" she called back with more certainty than she felt, crouching low over her horse's neck. "I just hope we get there in time." If I do, I'm about to change history, she thought with a prickle of apprehension. What kind of terrible events might I be unleashing for the future? On the other hand, suppose I don't get there in time and nothing is changed? They rode through the night, stopping to rest the horses now and then.

A full moon. There had been a full moon the night she had been flung back into this time. Circles, she thought. Is this a sign? She glanced behind her toward the east and wondered how long until dawn. A realization hit her. This is my birthday, August 5th.

Doc looked over at her as they rode. "You all right?"

She nodded, not at all certain. Could this be the day the old Pawnee shaman, Beaver Robe, had hinted at? She didn't even want to think about it.

They rode a while, walked and cooled the horses, then mounted up and took off again. It will be light soon, Blossom thought. Happy birthday, Blossom Ann, she thought, you're twenty-two years old today. Funny, she remembered the diploma in the big trunk, Blossom May Westfield had been twenty-two years old.

Doc gestured toward the horizon, bringing her out of her thoughts. "I swear I saw a line of mounted warriors silhouetted against the light on that distant rise."

They reined in and looked. There was nothing along that rim of the dark world but a moon that looked like a twenty-dollar gold piece shining on an empty expanse of prairie. The wind picked up a little, moving the dry grass along that ridge.

"Well," Doc said, pulling at his mustache, evidently perplexed, "maybe it was just the movement of the grass I saw, although I would have sworn it was a Sioux war party."

A chill went up Blossom's back. "We—we could be killed and scalped out here if you're right."

"I told you that, young lady, but you were so headstrong and determined to come." Doc's tone was as grim as his face, but there was a hint of admiration in it, too.

Headstrong? No, not me. I'm a timid mouse.

"Let's hope Captain Radley and his troopers are not far behind us," Doc said.

They nudged their horses into a lope and took off again at a ground-eating gallop.

In a few hours, the sun would be coming up, throwing golden shafts of light across the prairie. The horses were lathered and blowing. Doc looked pretty tuckered-out himself, Blossom thought. "Doc, we'll have to cool these horses out, or we'll never make it."

"You aren't fooling me," he grumbled, "you think this old codger is getting tired."

"Oh, fudge, don't be so prickly!" She dismounted and began to lead her horse, too concerned about War Cry to think about anything else. "This wasn't the way I'd planned to spend my birthday."

He dismounted, too, puffing as he walked along. "When we get back to the fort, we'll all have a big party and celebrate. It'll be a grand, happy time; you'll see."

She took a quick gulp of water from her canteen. "How much farther do you think it is?"

Doc shook his head. "No way of telling; but there's always dust rising from a running herd; we'll see it from a long way off. If I remember right, there's a canyon off over there somewhere." He made a vague gesture. "Good water and grass; herds like to graze there."

A canyon. Funny, now she seemed to recognize this landscape. Why, that's Massacre Canyon, Blossom thought with sudden horror, she remembered it from her childhood; it wasn't far to the Murdock's future farm from here. Funny, she had never questioned how it got its name. She hoped she wasn't about to find out. "You ready to go again, Doc? If we don't find the Pawnee in time to warn them . . ."

"I know." He swung back up on his horse. "Let's go!"

In the first gray light of dawn, War Cry smiled with satisfaction as he reined his horse in and watched the women and children beginning to stir around the camp, while the men tested their bows and bridled their favorite horses. Cricket attempted to catch his eye, but he ignored her, his thoughts on Blossom and their conflict.

While he had arrived only days ago, the Pawnee had been enjoying a successful hunt for the past several weeks. About four hundred of his people had gone up the Platte Valley to Plum Creek then turned south again to Turkey Creek and on into the valley of the Republican River. All in all it had been one of their most successful hunts; several hundred buffalo killed as the tribe followed the herd. The beasts were so stupid, they wouldn't move until the noise of the rifles finally panicked them into a stampede.

With the first pink light on the eastern horizon, Sun Chief rode up next to him, leaning on his pony's neck and watching the women cutting up meat, the children laughing and playing in the nearby creek. "It has been a good hunt; my heart is happy you could join us."

War Cry shrugged. "It may be our very last big hunt; I could not do otherwise."

"True." The chief's brown face saddened. "Only a few days ago, we met white buffalo hunters out slaughtering the herds."

"What did they want?" War Cry frowned, remembering the hunters he had rescued Blossom from.

"These told us Sioux were in the area, but we did not believe them," Sun Chief scoffed. "We think they were merely trying to scare us away so we would leave the herd to them."

"Who knows when white men speak with forked tongues?" War Cry said. "But the two who ride with us seem to be all right." The young white men, John Williamson and L.B. Platte, had come along to make sure no trigger happy settlers mistook the friendly Pawnee for hostiles.

"No matter, we almost have enough meat," the other said. "After this morning's hunt, we can return to the safety of our village."

War Cry grunted agreement. With four hundred people strung out down the ravine—most of them women and children—the Pawnee were in a vulnerable position should they be attacked. They were now north of the Republican River and to the west of Frenchman's Fork in this place called Nebraska. He stared down at the giant herd of buffalo from his place on a ridge. The beasts had been grazing peacefully but now they were sniffing the air suspiciously and moving like a great brown sea. Even from here, he could smell the scent of their rank bodies and crushed grass, hear the low bellow of the bulls. The dawn's first rays seemed to touch the brown fur with pink and gold light; shimmer on the dewdrops of the wildflowers.

Buffalo were stupid animals; they would only run a few miles, then they would stop to graze again. War Cry checked his rifle, watching the signal warrior up on a nearby rise with his lance raised. Yes, this might be the very last Pawnee hunt. The old ways were dying fast, and all the tribes were going to have to learn to live in the future.

The future. War Cry frowned as he thought about Blossom. Though he loved her, he knew she was lost to him; she would never be his again. All he had of her was the memory of the hours she had spent in his arms. It would have to be enough. The dawn breeze changed direction and now the slight scent of the little blue prairie flower came to his nostrils. He smiled gently, remembering the one he had picked and given to Blossom that night he had made love to her. For only a moment, he wondered what the white girl had

done with that flower? Probably tossed it away, he thought
with a sigh.

The braves were saddled up and ready, gathering to ride
after the herd. For a breathless moment, time seemed to stop
as everyone waited. Now the signal lance came down. War
Cry's hand tightened on his rifle as he urged his paint stallion
forward. Around him, shrill cries rang out as the warriors
galloped toward the giant herd. The restless buffalo raised
their heads, seemed to see the men and began to run, dust
rising up around them as thousands of hooves hit the ground.
He could almost feel the ground shake beneath him.

Like the other hunters, War Cry had stripped to his breech-
cloth and now the dawn breeze caressed his almost naked,
muscular body. Shouting with triumph, he galloped toward
the running herd. He was an excellent shot and when he
took aim from his swift horse, he brought down his prey,
one after another, the fat animals turning end over end in
the August morn as his bullet found a vital organ.

He raised his voice in a shrill yell of triumph as he
charged after the herd, thinking as he did so that the thousands of hooves drumming the ground sounded just like rolling thunder on this clear, hot morning.

Doc gestured toward the horizon. "I see something!"

All she could see was a dark cloud rising from the land.
"Storm?" Blossom shouted. "I hear the thunder!"

Doc shook his head and shouted back, "Dust from the
buffalo! Thousands of them!"

Blossom scanned the horizon as they rode. The herd was
still a long way off. She couldn't see anything but the rising
dust along the ridge, yet the thousands of running hooves
created a drumming that seemed to vibrate through the
ground she rode on. Almost like an earthquake, the earth
trembled under the hooves of her horse and the rumble grew
louder as she and Doc rode toward the rising cloud of dust

in the distance. It certainly sounds like a storm, Blossom thought, but the sun was shining and there were no other clouds. The hot August wind blew across her face and it carried no scent of rain. Thunder, it sounded like thunder, and she had always been so afraid of that noise. Why?

Oh please, God, she prayed as she and Doc galloped, we've got to get there in time to warn the Pawnee!

The old Lakota chief, Spotted Tail, reined in his war pony and studied the cloud of dust rising from the distant ravine that snaked between the hills for many miles. Then he heard the shots echoing and the shouting drifting along the canyon. His lip curled with hatred and disdain as he looked back over his shoulder at the hundreds of Brule and Oglalas warriors who rode with him. "The Pawnee wolves dare to venture into the area of our hunting grounds."

Young Fire Arrow sat his pony next to him. "Today I take my revenge on the bluecoats' pets."

"You are only a whelp yourself," the old man cautioned him. "Leave the vengeance to men!"

Many Wounds rode up, his face painted for war with crimson and ochre streaks. "The enemy have their women and children with them; that gives us the advantage."

"Pawnee!" The old man spat on the ground. "The soldiers tell their pets they have the right to hunt our buffalo, but *we* do not give them permission."

Around him, he heard the low murmur of agreement. He looked over at the handsome young boy. "Today, Fire Arrow, you will not only see our warriors count coup on many Pawnee, you will watch us kill fat buffalo for the feasting!"

"Honored elder," the boy said with respect, "please, may I ride along?"

Spotted Tail shook his gray braids. "No, you might get caught in the stampede and trampled, or an enemy might take your scalp. Maybe next year."

"There may not be a next year," the child said solemnly, "and I at least want to witness the vengeance against my father's enemies."

The gathered Lakota murmured agreement.

Two Strikes edged his horse closer and spoke now. "The boy speaks true, let him ride with us."

"All right then," Spotted Tail admitted defeat. "You may ride along the edges of the hunt and watch us run down the Pawnee coyotes and take the meat and hides they steal without our permission. Perhaps you can kill a small calf that has fallen behind. That way, you will bring a little meat to the feast tonight and so make your dead father proud."

The old chief paused and listened to the sounds of rifle fire, shouts, and running hooves from the canyon. Shots echoed faintly in the distance. "We will make this ravine run red with the blood of their women and children before we ride after the warriors and kill them as they hunt."

"What is this place called, oh, Great One?"

Spotted Tail looked toward the other Lakota chiefs now riding up to join him, even as he nudged his horse forward to the chase. "I don't know what the whites call it," he said, "but when we finish today it will ever after be known as Massacre Canyon!"

Captain Lexington B. Radley threw up his arm to signal a halt to the Third Cavalry that rode in the column behind him. He took off his hat, wiped the sweat from his face. Even though the dawn was just now streaking the sky pink, he knew it was going to be a hot day. In the distance, he heard the faint sound of thunder and the ground shook ever so slightly. From the ravine ahead of his patrol, a dark, faint cloud rose up, but he knew it wasn't a rain cloud, it was dust from the great herd of buffalo.

A sergeant galloped up to him, saluted.

Lex saluted carelessly. "Report."

"Sir, there's Lakota in the area, all right, hundreds of them! If we'd hurry to warn the Pawnee, we might save—"

"Did I ask for your opinion, Sergeant?" Lex eyed him coldly.

"Well, no sir, I was only thinking about all those women and children. You know they're probably out there scattered along that canyon skinning and cutting up meat while the warriors continue the hunt, and I thought—"

"You aren't paid to think," Lex snapped, "that's for officers."

"Yes, sir," the man saluted again, his eyes cold in a ruddy, hostile face.

He didn't want his men to think he was a coward, Lex realized, it might hinder his advancement. "What I meant to say," he added, "was that it is my first duty to protect my patrol and bring them back alive."

"Yes sir."

All the men were watching Lex; he could feel their hostile gazes on him. "Besides, if there's hundreds of Sioux warriors out there, this column is liable to get wiped out trying to stop them."

"We ought to try, sir," said the young lieutenant next to him.

"Damn it, I intend to!" Lex lost his cool demeanor. "I'm just cautious; that's all. The Pawnee have fifty or a hundred warriors, they can put up a pretty good fight!"

The lieutenant cleared his throat respectfully. "Not if they don't know the Sioux are coming, sir, and they're badly outnumbered."

"We'll do our duty, Lieutenant," Lex snapped, "and I don't need you to remind me of what that is. Looks like to me to be several miles over there to the hunt, but maybe we'll get there in time to stop the massacre. Actually, when the Lakota see us, they'll probably call off the attack and clear out, not wanting to be seen breaking their treaty. Let's move, Lieutenant."

"Yes sir."

Lex led off, trying not to smile as they rode. His collar was choking him again. He reached up and unbuttoned it, glad to be out on the wide prairie. Last night, he had had that dream again about being buried alive. People were walking past, looking at him. He had screamed and screamed, but no one seemed to hear him or responded. Lex had awakened with a start and sat up suddenly in bed, cold sweat running down his face. No, that wasn't going to happen to him; everyone knew history was set in stone and couldn't be changed. He was going to live to be ninety-seven years old and marry Miss Blossom May Westfield.

Smiling, he put spurs to his chestnut gelding, loping toward the distant rising cloud, his mind intent on his plan.

Blossom. He wanted that girl as his wife, but first, he was going to make sure that damned Pawnee scout, Terry, didn't return from this hunt to interfere. If the Sioux didn't get that arrogant Injun, Lex would shoot him himself. In all the excitement, who would notice where the shot came from?

Next he'd have to do something about that half-witted girl, Myrtle. It wouldn't be too difficult to have her meet with an accident, either.

Lex grinned as he galloped toward the buffalo hunt. Yes, a little planning, a little work clearing out those who stood in the way of his ambitions, and he'd be on his way to money and prominence. He licked his lips at the thought of Miss Blossom Westfield as his bride. Besides the pleasure her nubile body would give him, he intended to have her pregnant with his son as soon as possible. All Lex had to do was get that damned Pawnee scout out of the way!

Blossom knew they were too late even as she and Doc galloped into the canyon. The early dawn light reflected off fallen lances, burning tipis. Everywhere, Pawnee women and children lay dead, the camp in flames.

She reined in, staring in stunned disbelief, hearing Doc mutter, but she didn't know if it was a prayer or a curse on his lips. As they paused, looking around at the horror of scattered bodies, the destroyed racks of meat, she spotted Cricket lying dead near her wrecked tipi. "Oh, Doc!"

He shook his head, "It's too late for her, her throat's been cut, but I think I see one woman still alive." He reached for his medical bag as he dismounted.

"Doc, do you need help?" Blossom called.

"Go on and warn the others!" he shouted back. "There's nothing you can do here!"

Blossom took off at a gallop, her heart beating with fear and apprehension, but not for herself. Her thoughts were on her beloved War Cry. She was putting herself in danger, but that didn't matter. All that mattered to her now was warning the Pawnee, saving her love and the others. Where was Captain Radley? Wasn't he supposed to be coming to help?

Somewhere in the distance, she thought she heard a cavalry bugle drifting on the wind. Too far and too late, she thought as she rode up on a little rise. The dust swirling in the August dawn rose like a dark cloud, obscured almost everything. The sounds of stampeding buffalo and the way the ground shook left nothing to the imagination. She could smell the rank scent of the big running beasts and the heat seemed to radiate off their furry bodies. Faintly, she heard shouts and the sound of bullets echoing over the thunder.

Thunder. In her mind, she was suddenly back in the museum, listening to the thunder and wondering why it sounded so familiar? Then the dust cleared just an instant and Blossom gasped as she recognized the scene: it was the exact moment of the buffalo hunt that hung on the stairwell above the museum stairs. She was reliving that moment frozen in time!

War Cry struggled to keep his horse on its feet as he was caught in the surge of running buffalo. When he glanced around for help, he saw the soldiers coming over the hill, but they weren't coming fast enough, and there weren't enough of them. Around him, the Sioux were swarming like wasps moving in for the kill, mingling their horses among the shouting outnumbered Pawnee, picking them off even as War Cry's people attempted to leave the hunt to cover the retreat of the surviving women and children fleeing up the canyon.

There was blood and dust everywhere, the cool wind reeked of it and when he tried to breathe, he couldn't keep from coughing. Grit coated his tongue when he gasped for air and dust plastered his almost naked body. War Cry would sell his life dearly; the remaining women and children must be saved! He reined in, hanging on to his rifle, falling back to cover the retreat. Around him, gunshots and shouts echoed; the drumming hooves became a roar.

War Cry. Had someone called his name, or did he only hear it in his mind? Frantically, he looked around, seeing nothing but dust as his horse was swept along in the stampede. He aimed, took a Lakota from his horse, heard the man scream as he hit the dirt, only to be ground to a faceless mass under the thousands of running hooves.

War Cry. He searched the horizon and in the swirling dust, he thought he saw his beloved Blossom's face as the rider hesitated on a little rise. Was she here and her mind calling out to his?

The rider was so far away, he couldn't hear her; maybe she was only a mirage, a dream after all. He was being swept along by the confused mass of fighting Indians and running buffalo. If his stallion went down in this crush, there wouldn't be enough left of him to identify, but he galloped along, only trying to keep his horse on its feet, as the attacking Sioux warriors slaughtered brave Pawnee women and children. He shot another enemy warrior from his horse and then realized his rifle was empty and he had no more cartridges. He would use it as a club, he vowed. War Cry was not afraid to die fighting his old enemies! Somewhere nearby as the herd rushed on, he heard a shout of challenge, looked up.

A young Sioux boy charging toward him with a lance and fury in his dark eyes. Then the inexperienced youth was caught in the crush of the stampeding buffalo, his small paint pony fighting to stay on its feet. The boy dropped his lance and hung on for dear life, as the furry brown sea swept him and the faltering pony toward their deaths.

War Cry hesitated, then his gaze met and locked onto the boy's frightened eyes. Fire Arrow. He recognized the boy from that time in the Lakota camp—his enemy's little son. Any moment now, that faltering pony was going down and be trampled under thousands of hooves. The boy was attempting to be brave, but his dark eyes were large with terror as he looked toward the Pawnee warrior.

He was an enemy boy who would spend his life trying to kill War Cry. Let him die as Pawnee children were dying even now.

War Cry saw an opening in the flow of the herd. He could rein his horse toward that and in seconds be outside the running stampede, safe from horrible death. Let the Sioux boy die.

Even as War Cry reined his horse out of the herd to save himself, he heard the enemy boy cry out in terror, knew that any moment now the child would be swept under the pounding hooves. In the distance, he saw the sunlight reflecting off the shiny brass buttons of the coming soldiers, but they would be too late for Fire Arrow.

Why should he try to save an enemy boy? He could be riding to his death in the attempt and might not save the child, either, but there was only one thing a man could do. He threw away his rifle so he would have his hands free, reined his powerful stallion sharply, fighting the brown torrent of running buffalo as he tried to reach the boy and his exhausted pony.

"War Cry!" Blossom watched him from the little rise,

houting at him to save himself. Off to her right, the captain
nd his patrol were galloping into the foray and she sighed
vith relief, thinking Lex might help the embattled Pawnee
ave whatever was left of their tribe.

Good! War Cry was reining his horse toward that lull in
he running herd; in a few seconds, he would be safely out
of the stampede.

Abruptly, even as she watched, she saw him toss away his
ifle and wheel his horse back toward the midst of the run-
ing animals. She stared in disbelief; what was it he had
een?

Only by straining her eyes did she see the frantic boy on
is little pony, struggling to keep from going down. Why, it
vas young Fire Arrow, the Lakota child she had seen that
lay in the enemy camp!

And in that split second, she remembered the history book
n the museum: . . . *during the Massacre Canyon battle with
he Sioux that August, a warrior named Ter-ra-re-cox was
cilled in a vain attempt to rescue an enemy boy* . . .

Ter-ra-re-cox. Terry. She made the connection in a heart-
eat, even as she screamed, "No!"

Even as she shrieked her denial of her lover's death, she
ooked down at her dress and recognized the fabric a new-
orn baby had been wrapped in. Why, she *was* Blossom May
Westfield, who had fled into the future to be reincarnated on
his very prairie rather than face her lover's death!

Now she saw Captain Radley galloping closer to War Cry
as the Pawnee fought his way toward the trapped boy. The
warrior was too busy to even see the officer; the officer had
nis pistol drawn. She saw the fiendish delight on Lex's pale
face as he reined his chestnut gelding into the stampede, saw
nim aim. He was going to kill War Cry without giving him
a chance!

The Pawnee and the boy were scheduled to die; it had
been written in history and history is written in stone; even
cowardly Blossom May Westfield had realized that.

"No!" she screamed again, and this time it was in courageous defiance as she urged her horse forward into the running herd. It was suicide, she knew; what could one person do to change history?

"By god, I'm not a timid mouse and I can try!" She slapped her horse with the reins, fighting her way into the running herd. She might be trampled, but it didn't matter. All that mattered was saving her beloved's life.

War Cry didn't appear to see Lex, he was too busy keeping his paint stallion on its feet as he reached out and grabbed the boy even as the small pony went down. Now he was fighting to rein his horse through the running herd, not even seeing the captain taking aim at his broad back.

How do I love thee? Let me count the ways . . .

Without another thought for her own life, Blossom raced her horse into the galloping stampede. Lex brought his pistol up, grinning in triumph as he focused on War Cry's back.

"No!" she screamed again. "I love him more than life!" She rode recklessly into the line of fire, felt the bullet hit her shoulder, but the sound was muted by the roar of the running herd. Her shoulder seemed to be on fire and she wasn't sure she could stay in the saddle. She was fighting to stay on her horse and she didn't think she could, but it didn't matter.

She glanced back and saw Lex's surprised face.

"Blossom!" he shouted and his horse hesitated. With his attention on her, Lex was thrown forward as the chestnut horse stumbled. She caught one glimpse of his pale, terrified face as he flew from the saddle, and she heard him scream as he fell toward the ground.

She was about to slide from her horse, too, but it didn't matter. She had saved her lover, and God help her, she had changed history! No, maybe she was putting history back as it should have been. Her love would live and the sacrifice was worth her life; she loved him so!

Weakly, Blossom struggled to stay on her horse as the

stampede surged around her. She wasn't going to make it, she realized, she was going to fall and be trampled to death.

Through the swirling dust as her vision blurred, she saw the little Lakota boy safely up on a rock where her beloved had left him, and then the Pawnee warrior's face as he fought to ride his great stallion through the running animals toward her. "Hang on, kid, I'm coming for you!"

The sun came out from behind a cloud, glowing in a golden circle. In that moment, she knew the Window of Time was opening, only a heartbeat away, and the choice was hers, but only once. Almost in a dream, she saw her beloved's face as he reined his way through the running buffalo. Only a heartbeat separates Life from Death, she thought. To live, will yourself back to the stairs of the Pawnee Bill museum and leave him behind forever, or stay and die as he tries to reach you.

She was afraid to die! Her horse stumbled with exhaustion and around her the roar of the thundering hooves grew louder. Her vision was blurring, and she was in so much pain. Such a temptation to slip back through time to 1995 forever.

"Hang on, Blossom! I'm coming!"

He was so close now, and yet so far—too far. She was reeling in the saddle, knowing she wasn't going to make it, but he was coming toward her in the swirling dust, his devotion in his dark eyes for her to see, reaching for her, reaching even as she fell.

"Blossom, if you trust me, reach out!"

Bet on the sure thing or take a chance on his love? In that heartbeat, she made her choice, reaching out to him with both hands, even as she had that night in the museum. *How do I love thee?* Enough to put all my faith and trust in you with my life in the balance!

As her horse stumbled and fell, he grabbed both her hands, completing the circle, and she knew at that instant that the eternal magic was love, pure unselfish love.

His strong hands lifted her from her horse, pulled her into his embrace, holding and shielding her against his wide chest. He urged his big horse on as they fought their way out of the stampede to safety. "I was afraid you wouldn't be brave enough—"

"Brave? Why, there's no woman feistier than I am!" She threw back her head and laughed with sheer relief despite the pain of her shoulder.

"And no woman more loved," he promised as he held her close and kissed her. "Let's get Doc to look at that wound."

She clung to him as they rode to meet the smiling Lakota boy and the rescuing army. "Oh, War Cry, I think I've just changed history."

"Or set it right, kid."

She returned his kiss, knowing she had found a love that would last for all eternity.

Epilogue

Sunday morning, June, 1995

Squinting against the early morning sun, Dr. Terri Murdock stopped the car in the parking lot of the Pawnee Bill Museum and got out. An elderly beagle lay asleep on the path, and a big yellow cat watched the goldfish in the small lily pond.

In a ditch in front of the native rock house, a homely, dirty man labored.

"Hello," Terri smiled, "is anyone about?"

He paused, looked at her vacantly. His eyes were too close together and he had buck teeth, but beautiful black, wavy hair and a pale complexion. "I donno, lady, all I do is sweep up, clean the septic tank, and such."

Terri regarded him a long moment. None too bright she thought, and looked at the employee name sewn on his shirt: LEX. "You from around here?"

The dull-witted ditchdigger nodded. "Long time. Great-great-granddaddy was a officer in the cavalry."

"Oh, really?" It didn't seem likely, but she was basically kind and polite. "My great-great-granddaddy was a Pawnee scout for the cavalry. I wonder if they knew each other?"

"Injuns!" The vacant-eyed man sneered and returned to his shoveling.

Oh well. She was too self-confident to let racial prejudice bother her. She had a plane to catch to Washington, D.C., Terri thought, and a passenger to pick up here. She reached to finger the one silver hoop earring she wore as she went up the steps and into the old ranch house.

A pleasant-looking man in Western clothes came out of the parlor, accompanied by a mixed Chow dog. "We're not really open early on Sundays, Miss. I'm just checking things out. We think we might have had a break-in last night."

"Oh, really?" Terri bent to pat the dog.

"Doesn't seem to be anything missing. It was probably stray lightning that caused the security to short out, set off the alarm. I'm Mac, the director. Dog seems to have taken a real liking to you."

Terri shook hands, brushed back her long straight black hair. "I'm Dr. Terri Murdock. I was born in the area, but I've been in L.A. for years."

"Oh, yes, I know your family," he said, nodding with approval. "Murdocks are one of the biggest and best known families in these parts."

Terri laughed. "Not many have eight children anymore! Dad and my brothers are still farming and Mom's working at the big Rusty Thompson Charity Hospital. Who was Rusty Thompson, anyway?"

"It was a woman, a mysterious red-haired beauty, they say. Legend has it that her husband was a real hard-case, but he loved her enough to change, become a respectable rancher. Then they struck oil. Most of the inheritance supports charities like battered women's shelters and hospitals. Speaking of which, I heard about the excitement at the hospital—that drug addict with AIDS."

"Yes, good thing that doctor was on the scene; he grabbed the guy while Mom was fighting to subdue him. If that doctor hadn't been there, she might have gotten that needle in her hand."

"Close call!" The director whistled. "Isn't it a wonder though, how some little thing can change history?"

Terri nodded. "We just never know the extent of it, do we?"

He doffed his cowboy hat, ran his hand through his hair in confusion. "Oh, yes, now I remember. You're the Murdock girl who won that medical research scholarship, aren't you?"

Terri smiled. "Yes. My folks' farm is doing well, but if it hadn't been for that Maynard scholarship, I couldn't have done it. I've wondered who *he* was."

"Just some old country doctor trying to do a little good, I reckon, like that Lamarto fella; they say he's a prince of a man; unselfish, lots of good deeds with his millions."

"That's what I hear. I haven't met him, but he's really a crusader for morality, and he's offered to provide further funding for my research." She looked around the old ranch. "I understand you have a book with a picture of my great-great-grandparents' grave in it?"

"Sure. More than that, there's a big portrait of them hanging in a grouping in the parlor; friends of Pawnee Bill, they say." He stared at her a long moment. "Ma'am, do you know you're only wearing one earring?"

Terri laughed and reached up to touch it self-consciously. "I know; I wear it for luck; found it in my great-great-grandmother's old trunk when I opened it; no telling what ever happened to its mate." She thought a minute about the other item she had found there.

The director led her into the parlor. "Here's that book you were probably talking about." He gestured toward the table. "Your ancestor was pretty well known, she and her Pawnee husband. Quite a story there probably, if the truth were told."

"No doubt." Terri flipped through the pages and found a photo of the gravestone. Yes, that was her great-great-grandmother, all right. Blossom May Westfield and her Pawnee love, *Ter-ra-re-cox*. Terri had been named for him. At the base of the monument was the inscription: *With Gratitude From Fire Arrow*. Probably some old friend of theirs.

"There's the big portrait," the director gestured toward the wall, "handsome-looking couple; he lived to be ninety-seven

years old, they died on the same day. You look a little like
both of them, ma'am."

Terri studied the strong faces in the picture, satisfied and
proud. The handsome Pawnee looked at the woman in the
portrait as if she were his very life. The woman had brown
hair and large blue eyes and she held both his hands in hers,
looking up at him with an unmistakable gaze of devotion.
Terri thought then of a poem she had found in that old
book: . . . *And if God choose, I shall but love thee better
after death.*

Yes, this was a couple who must have loved each other
very much; their expressions mirrored that devotion.

"I haven't got much time," Terri said, "I also wanted to
see that ghost painting I keep hearing about. I'm due in
Washington, D.C. for a special announcement."

Mac turned, leading her toward the stairs. "I heard about
that; in fact, I read it in that paper, *Tattletale.*"

"*Tattletale* is the real crusading conscience of this country," Terri added. "It deserved the Pulitzer and the other hon-
ors it's won."

"*Tattletale* says you've discovered some cure for AIDS and
cancer?"

"Well, it's not a cure, but an exciting breakthrough," Terri
said. "I was looking through my microscope late at night,
thinking how aspirin—the big medical discovery of the last
century—was originally found in an old Native American
cure, willow bark, and then, this past spring, researchers had
decided that birch bark might be the answer to melanoma,
the deadly skin cancer."

The man looked back over his shoulder as they walked
toward the stairs. "You mean, it's something simple like
that?"

"Sort of. I wondered if there wasn't some ordinary native
plant that we were overlooking in our search." Terri paused,
remembering. That was when she had stopped for coffee late
at night and opened her great-great-grandmother's old trunk,

found the earring and the faded poetry book, *Sonnets from the Portuguese.* The dried blue blossom she found there had seemed like a sign, and she could only wonder why her ancestor had saved it. "Would you believe the new breakthrough may be in that little wild blue prairie flower that grows all over the plains?"

"Stranger things have happened." The man paused on the stairs. "Here's the picture. It's got glass over it because all the tourists want to touch it."

Terri walked up next to him and stared at the painting of Indians and a buffalo stampede. The artist had done a good job; the buffalo looked so real, it was as if they were frozen in time. She could almost smell their hot breath, hear the thunder of hooves and their bellowing, feel the rising dust.

The director's face furrowed. "Odd, here's an earring laying by the picture frame."

"Just one?"

He nodded, picked it up, held it out to her. "Hey, Dr. Murdock, this seems to be the mate to the one you're wearing. Why don't you keep it?"

Terri took it, staring in confusion. "You're right. Funny, mine's been in a family trunk for well over a hundred years. I always thought this was supposed to be unusual. Obviously it isn't that rare if there's another lying about where some tourist dropped it. I couldn't take it, it isn't mine."

"Aw, go ahead," Mac gestured in dismissal. "It doesn't look valuable, and I doubt some tourist is going to drive all the way back to reclaim it."

"Well, if you say so. . . ." Terri put it on. "You know, Native Americans say a circle is a symbol of Eternity and spirit magic because it has no beginning and no end."

"I've heard that." Mac wiped his weathered face.

Terri stared at the big painting. "So where's the ghost?"

"Oh, you have to go up to the top of the landing to see it," he said, leading the way. "It looks so lifelike, you'd swear it was a real person trapped in there. Folks come from all over to gape at it."

Terri went up and stood beside him, staring at the painting of confused action and galloping buffalo. "I don't see—oh, my god!" She gasped in amazement.

"I told you."

In the midst of the stampede, a handsome cavalry captain was falling from his running chestnut horse toward the ground. The young man did look real, almost as if he were frozen forever in time behind that protective glass. He had wavy black hair and pale skin, but his mouth was open in a horrid, silent shriek.

Terri sighed. "What a great painting! That poor soldier looks familiar, somehow, and almost real, like in a horror movie or maybe an Edgar Allan Poe story."

"I don't tell many folks this," Mac lowered his voice, "but this isn't a place I like to be at night all alone. That painting's been hanging here ever since the ranch was built, and I reckon will hang there forever. Late at night, that captain seems so real, I swear you can hear him screaming, wanting out!"

"How scary!" Terri shuddered, then glanced at her watch. "I've loved talking with you, but I've got to go." She started down the steps. "Thanks for the tour. I'm meeting someone here and we're flying on to Washington together; he's also been doing interesting medical research." There was a more compelling reason Terri wanted to meet him.

She said goodbye to the director, patted the ugly mixed Chow dog, and went out into the parking lot. The elderly beagle had moved into the shade and the yellow cat stared down at her from a tree limb. The early morning sun beat down on the Indian-hating dullard laboring in the ditch as a pickup stopped out front, let a man out.

The newcomer, carrying his luggage, looked toward her and she noted he was a tall, handsome Native American. "Dr. Murdock?"

"Yes," her pulse speeded up as she went forward, offering her hand. "I presume you're Dr. Steve Arrow?"

He nodded and shook hands. "I'm honored to meet you," he said. "I know your whole family. You've been doing marvelous work out in L.A in the research lab."

"Tattletale has been providing most of the funding," Terri said, "due to their great humanitarian publisher, Vic Lamarto. I've been wanting to meet you and thank you for saving my mother."

He shrugged broad shoulders. "Ann's a good nurse. I'm just glad I was there the night that crazed addict ended up in the emergency room. I shudder to think what might have happened if I hadn't been."

"She might have gotten AIDS if that needle had gone through her rubber glove," Terri said.

"No big deal." He looked embarrassed at the praise. "Ann talks about you all the time, but she didn't tell me you were so pretty." He smiled with white, even teeth. "The Murdocks have a Pawnee ancestor?"

She nodded. "Our two tribes were once enemies."

"I know, funny how things turn out, isn't it? There's always been a legend in my family that my great-great-grandfather's life was saved by a Pawnee scout at that Massacre Canyon thing. Wouldn't it be an interesting twist of fate if it were *your* ancestor who saved him so that four generations later, I could be there to save your mother?"

She smiled, thinking he was the most handsome man she had ever met. "That's too big a coincidence," she said.

"I don't know; lots of history turns on some tiny thing. You know what the old saying is: For want of a nail a shoe was lost, for want of a shoe, a horse was lost, for want of a horse, a battle was lost."

"You have a point there!" She laughed as she took his arm, thinking that for a doctor, he had all the muscle and the virility of an ancient warrior. "I'm sure if both our ancestors were at Massacre Canyon, they'd be amused to look forward a century and a quarter and see us meeting this way."

He smiled at her. "Interesting pair of earrings. Look antique."

"Well, one of them is. I just found the other right here in the museum this morning."

"Is there a story attached to that?"

She shrugged. "Who knows?"

They walked across the grass toward her car.

He said, "I think I'm going to enjoy this trip to Washington, Doctor."

"Call me Terri."

"All right, Terri." He leaned over and picked a little blue prairie flower growing by the curb, handed it to her. "This is just the color of your eyes. I hope this is going to be the beginning of a very long relationship."

She took a deep breath of the scent of the flower and wondered again about how a similar blossom had ended up so carefully preserved in an old book of poetry in her great-great-grandmother's trunk. "Since we're both interested in medical research, and both have Native American backgrounds, we should surely work well together."

He put his hand over hers as they paused by the car and smiled at her. "I was thinking about a different kind of relationship."

Terri's heart skipped a beat. This was the man she had been waiting for all these many years, the one saved just for her. Call it Fate, call it woman's intuition, somehow, she knew it. She held up the keys. "You drive? I just did that road from Tulsa."

"Freeways. I wonder what my ancestors would have thought of them? I keep thinking that someday I'd like to get back to the land." He opened her car door.

"I must take you up to see my folks' farm," Terri said as she got in, "we've got horses; if you ride."

"Do I ride? Better than a Pawnee girl, I bet!"

"First chance we get, you can put your money where your mouth is," Terri said with spirit. "We'd better get a move on, we've got a plane to catch."

"And feisty and spunky, too; I like that. I hope you're ready for all the hoopla and publicity, Dr. Murdock. Your discovery will probably change history."

"Change history? That can't be done." She smiled, studying his strong, dark features, liking what she saw as he got in and started the car.

"Then maybe we'll make a little history of our own."

"I'm game if you are." She felt the electricity crackle between them. Yes, this was going to be a great trip. Terri smiled and settled in for the ride as they drove out of the parking lot, headed away from the Pawnee Bill Museum toward Tulsa.

TO MY READERS

Yes, there actually is a painting with a ghost in it at the Pawnee Bill Ranch museum west of the town of Pawnee, Oklahoma. However, it is not a painting of buffalo and Indians, but of two hunters in a boat with the mysterious specter in the background that can only be seen when standing at a certain place at the top of the stairs.

Several of the docents told me the tales of hearing footsteps descending the stairs when there was no one else in the house, and of smoke coming out of the chimney when the house was empty and no fire in the fireplace. Yes, there is a secret door upstairs that leads out on the roof; ask about it. I created fictional employees, except for the old beagle, the yellow cat, and the mixed-breed chow. Those pets belong to the director. I would like to thank the real employees and volunteers at the ranch for their help in research.

If you are interested in Pawnee Bill and his time, I suggest reading *Pawnee Bill,* published by the University of Nebraska Press, and written by a noted historical expert and friend of mine, Glenn Shirley.

The little town of Pawnee is about fifty miles west of Tulsa, Oklahoma. The ranch and museum are open every day of the week from 10 to 5 weekdays and 1 to 4 Sundays and Mondays. There are several nice bed and breakfast inns in town and camping facilities on the local lake. Certain times during the summer, the Original Pawnee Bill Wild West show is recreated. Contact the Pawnee Chamber of Commerce for more information.

Some of you may be surprised to find out Native Americans were often at war with each other. The Pawnee and the Lakota were traditional enemies. For those of you who want more information, I suggest a book called *Counting Coup and Cutting Horses, Inter-tribal Warfare on the Northern Plains 1738-1889,* by Anthony McGinnis, Cordillera Press, Evergreen, CO.

All that is left of historic Fort McPherson, near North Platt, Nebraska, is its national cemetery. If you're in the area, you might be interested in visiting Buffalo Bill Cody's ranch which is a popular tourist attraction.

There's a monument at Massacre Canyon commemorating the August 5, 1873 slaughter of several hundred Pawnee by a Lakota raiding party near the present town of Trenton in Hitchcock County near the Nebraska-Kansas border. I would like to thank the friendly people of Trenton who were so helpful while I was in their area doing research. There is still much controversy over which tribe had the right to be hunting in that area and how many Pawnee were killed. Understandably, those who were buried were interred with haste, and some bodies were left lying on the prairie. Several years ago, the Pawnee gathered up their dead from scattered points in Massacre Canyon and reburied them in one location under tons of concrete so they would never again be disturbed. The press was not invited to this sacred ceremony and the grave is unmarked; only a few people know its location.

This massacre was the last great battle between enemy tribes and led to the Pawnee being moved to Oklahoma to put more distance between them and their old enemies. A good research book on their sad life during and after removal is: *Pawnee Passage, 1870-1875,* by M. R. Blaine, University of Oklahoma Press.

The so-called devil's cattle traps or witches bogs actually

xist in certain isolated areas of western Nebraska near the Vyoming-Nebraska state line. While they may not be as leadly as described, they are still a nuisance to local farmers. ometimes cattle and horses do stray into the alkaline bogs nd become trapped in them. I first learned of this unusual latural phenomena while reading a book called: *Tales of the Vestern Heartland*, by Harry E. Chrisman, Swallow Press,)hio University Press.

Sadly, there is no real breakthrough in cancer and AIDS esearch yet, but it is bound to come. The little blue flower s fictitious. As I said in my story, the once deadly killer, mallpox, is now confined to a few laboratory test tubes. Iowever, you may be surprised to know that Bubonic Plague, he ancient Black Death that wiped out millions of people n the Middle Ages, is still around. The plague made its ap-earance in America from rats aboard ships arriving in Cali-ornia at the turn of this century. Since then, the plague has lowly been working its way east, the infection now carried by fleas on related rodents such as prairie dogs and ground quirrels. In 1983, there were forty cases with six deaths in America. It responds well to treatment, but I wouldn't handle any prairie dogs.

Only one infectious disease is still on America's top ten causes of death—flu. Some of you may be surprised to learn hat in World War I, our country had ten times more deaths from influenza than soldiers killed in battle. A fascinating book on epidemics is: *Man and Microbes, Disease and Plagues in History and Modern Times*, by Arno Karlen, Put-nam & Sons Publishers.

As difficult as it may be to believe, there actually was a soldier named Thompson who won our country's highest award, the Medal of Honor, for bravery in the Indian wars and then deserted. He is lost forever in the pages of history without a trace. I've always wondered why he deserted and what became of him? Let us hope he really found an eternal love.

The 1873 train robbery near Adair, Iowa, is reputed to b Jesse James's first train robbery. However, it is not America very first train robbery, as some people believe. That dubiou honor goes to the Reno brothers, who robbed a train nea Seymour, Indiana, in 1866.

While *Timeless Warrior* may be the first of my novels yo have read, it is the fourteenth book, (plus one anthology) my continuing Panorama of the Old West series from Ze bra/Kensington Publishing. These do not need to be read order as some of them are written out of sequence. All th stories connect loosely in a long historical saga. Some them are still in print; ask your bookstore.

I am always pleased to hear from readers. If you will sen your letter and a stamped, self-addressed #10 envelope, I wi send you a newsletter and an autographed bookmark. Ac dress: Georgina Gentry, P.O. Box 162, Edmond, OK 73083 0162.

So what story will I tell next? I have gotten many request that I pick up the story of two children, Keso and Wanni mentioned in earlier stories, *Quicksilver Passion,* and *Chey enne Splendor.* In the spring of 1997, here comes that ro mance played out against the 1879 Ute Indian War in th rugged, wild mountains of Colorado.

Keso, (Fox) the street-smart Cheyenne urchin, was foun in Denver and reared by Cherokee Evans and his wife, Silve the former dance hall beauty. The couple has also raised th beautiful half Arapaho girl, Wannie, whose Indian nam means Singing Wind. Keso has loved Wannie all his life, bu Wannie thinks of him as her big brother.

Wannie goes off to a back East finishing school and fall in love with a rich, elegant rake who makes Keso seem lik a rough clod by comparison. When she brings her fiancé home to Colorado, they will be caught up in the middle o the bloody Ute war and only Keso, with his survival an hunting skills, may be able to save them. As for beautifu Wannie, she will become a Ute captive to be fought ove and given to the savage winner of a life-and-death battle. Our innocent, spoiled beauty is scheduled to be a warrior's prize . . .

Wishing You an Eternal Circle of Love,
Georgina Gentry

SURRENDER TO THE SPLENDOR
OF THE ROMANCES
OF ROSANNE BITTNER!

UNFORGETTABLE   (4423, $5.50/$6.50)

FULL CIRCLE   (4711, $5.99/$6.99)

CARESS   (3791, $5.99/$6.99)

COMANCHE SUNSET   (3568, $4.99/$5.99)

SHAMELESS   (4056, $5.99/$6.99)

TODAY'S HOTTEST READS
ARE TOMORROW'S SUPERSTARS

VICTORY'S WOMAN (4484, $4.50)
by Gretchen Genet

Andrew—the carefree soldier who sought glory on the battlefield, and returned a shattered man . . . Niall—the legandary frontiersman and a former Shawnee captive, tormented by his past . . . Roger—the troubled youth, who would rise up to claim a shocking legacy . . . and Clarice—the passionate beauty bound by one man, and hopelessly in love with another. Set against the backdrop of the American revolution, three men fight for their heritage—and one woman is destined to change all their lives forever!

FORBIDDEN (4488, $4.99)
by Jo Beverley

While fleeing from her brothers, who are attempting to sell her into a loveless marriage, Serena Riverton accepts a carriage ride from a stranger—who is the handsomest man she has ever seen. Lord Middlethorpe, himself, is actually contemplating marriage to a dull daughter of the aristocracy, when he encounters the breathtaking Serena. She arouses him as no woman ever has. And after a night of thrilling intimacy—a forbidden liaison—Serena must choose between a lady's place and a woman's passion!

WINDS OF DESTINY (4489, $4.99)
by Victoria Thompson

Becky Tate is a half-breed outcast—branded by her Comanche heritage. Then she meets a rugged stranger who awakens her heart to the magic and mystery of passion. Hiding a desperate past, Texas Ranger Clint Masterson has ridden into cattle country to bring peace to a divided land. But a greater battle rages inside him when he dares to desire the beautiful Becky!

WILDEST HEART (4456, $4.99)
by Virginia Brown

Maggie Malone had come to cattle country to forge her future as a healer. Now she was faced by Devon Conrad, an outlaw wounded body and soul by his shadowy past . . . whose eyes blazed with fury even as his burning caress sent her spiraling with desire. They came together in a Texas town about to explode in sin and scandal. Danger was their destiny—and there was nothing they wouldn't dare for love!

Available wherever paperbacks are sold, or order direct from the Publisher. Send cover price plus 50¢ per copy for mailing and handling to Penguin USA, P.O. Box 999, c/o Dept. 17109, Bergenfield, NJ 07621. Residents of New York and Tennessee must include sales tax. DO NOT SEND CASH.

FABULOUS
CONSUMER SWEEPSTAKES!

One Grand Prize winner will receive
A ONE-OF-A-KIND PAIR
OF SILVER HOOP EARRINGS
that reflect the beautiful details
of those featured in the story.

OFFICIAL ENTRY FORM

Please enter me in the "TIMELESS WARRIOR" Sweepstakes.

Name_____

Address_____

City_____ State_____ Zip_____

Store Name_____

City_____ State_____ Zip_____

Mail to: "TIMELESS WARRIOR" SWEEPSTAKES
c/o Zebra Books
850 Third Avenue, NYC 10022-6222

Sweepstakes ends 6/30/96

OFFICIAL RULES

1. To enter, complete the official entry form. No purchase is necessary. You may enter by hand printing on a 3X5 piece of paper, your name, address and the words "Timeless Warrior".
Mail to: "Timeless Warrior" Sweepstakes, c/o Zebra Books, 850 Third Avenue, NYC 10022-6222.

2. Enter as often as you like, but each entry must be mailed separately. Mechanically reproduced entries not accepted. Entries must be received by June 30, 1996.

3. Winners selected in a random drawing on or about July 31, 1996 from among all eligible entries received. Winners may be required to sign an affidavit and and release which must be returned within 14 days or alternate winner will be selected. Winners permit the use of his/her name/photograph for publicity/advertising purposes without further compensation. No transfer of prizes permitted. Taxes are the sole responsibility of the prize winners. Only one prize per family or household.

4. Winners agree that the sponsor, its affiliates and their agencies and employees shall not be liable for injury, loss or damage of any kind resulting from participation in this promotion or from the acceptance or use of the prize awarded.

5. Sweepstakes are open to residents of the U.S. except employees of Kensington Publishing Corp., their affiliates, advertising or promotion agencies. Void where taxed, prohibited or restricted by law. All Federal, state and local laws and regulations apply. Odds of winning depend upon the total number of eligible entries received. All prizes will be awarded. Not responsible for lost, misdirected mail or printing errors.

6. For the name of the prize winners, send a self-addressed, stamped envelope to: "Timeless Warrior" Sweepstakes Winner, c/o Zebra Books, 850 Third Ave., NYC 10022-6222.